Playing Dirty

With the High Springs Ladies Bridge Group

KELLIE KELLEY

Also by Kellie Kelley

Sunday Dinners

ISBN: 10 1719214204

ISBN-13: 978-1719214-209

Acknowledgements

Thanks to all the readers who encouraged the writing of a sequel to *Sunday Dinners*. I especially appreciate the great assistance from my Spanish teacher, Eldie Morris. A big shout out to my editors, Tina Pendarvis, Sharla Elliott and Gloria Lindsay. A special thanks to Chief James Fansler, Lake Placid, Florida, for answering police related questions. Finally, to my family who runs to help me when I yell and forgives the liberties I take with their character traits. Love and adoration to my niece, Dee Dee. (She's luminous.)

Chapter 1

J.W. Collins needs Maebelle Merriwether's endorsement to win the upcoming sheriff's election. He is going to canvas her neighborhood and see if the old windbag will give him a few minutes to discuss his platform. He is the first to announce his candidacy. An early participant can have an edge to winning, but some of his business deals might surface as unfavorable. He needs a true conservative to back his campaign. Ms. Merriwether can send his ticket to the top if she approves and will announce it to the community.

J.W. or Jack, as some of his friends call him, makes a point to see Maebelle every Sunday, even though he sits a few pews back at the First Presbyterian Church in High Springs, FL. He puts his best foot forward on Sundays, coupled with his big wide smile. He has the dental bill receipt to prove it; ten thousand dollars' worth of porcelain crown work.

He rings the bell. No one is in a hurry to answer it. He presses it again.

Miss Flo opens the big heavy door. "Rang twice, you must be selling something."

"Hello, little lady. Is Ms. Meriwether here?"

"Who is you calling little lady?"

"Begging your pardon, ma'am."

"Miss Maebelle is in the kitchen busy making dessert. Is she expecting you?"

"No, ma'am. If she isn't available, I would like permission to come by here again or set up a future time I might call her."

"Miss Maebelle sets her own calendar. I am not her secretary or servant, but her friend and housekeeper. You must reach her yourself. She is a busy lady in the community."

"Yes ma'am, you are so helpful. I'll do just that. You have a glorious day now."

I'll call the church office and have Jackie give me her number. Of all the uppity people, the nerve.

"You have a blessed day too."

Flo surveys the front stoop as she is closing the door and adjusts the front door wreath. It is September, and almost time for the fall wreath to come out. Everything looks swept and orderly.

Flo walks to the kitchen and tells Maebelle that Mr. Collins was at the door. "He is going to call for an appointment. He is looking for face time Mae. I can spy a politician as well as I can spy a bad preacher."

"I know who he is. He is very cunning. I make a concerted effort to avoid him and his not so veiled efforts to attract my attention in church of all places." Maebelle pauses. "I think the bread pudding is going to be delightful."

Chapter 2

Ruby Lee Robinson is wearing a cranberry twin set sweater outfit today to Maebelle's home. It is part of her capsule wardrobe that contains all shades of red from cranberry to carmine. Indeed, she is invested, literally, in her signature colors, having been to two separate color specialists that have told her what to wear daily. She does not think it extreme to carry out the crimson theme whenever she can. One professional mentioned that in consideration of her porcelain skin, it was unimaginable that Miss Ruby would deviate from the shades of red color palettes that both colorists gave her. Her make-up drawer contains rows and rows of red lipsticks. Her bedroom carpeting is sangria. Upon occasion, she feels the other bridge ladies are somewhat jealous of her achieved look. Red portrays her confidence and passion in life, and she is passionate about a lot of things. She eyes her "currant" pumps. Yes, they coordinate perfectly. Ruby surveys her vast jewelry armoire of exceptional costume pieces and selects a sparkling red Swarovski crystal necklace with matching earrings. She is going to be daring today in her black leather skirt and wear a red lace trimmed half-slip. The girls will turn green with envy. Green, certainly, is *not* her color. Ruby does not live far from the Merriwether's. Maebelle's home was the first home built in the prestigious Oak Manor Estates in High Springs. Ruby feels like they have a sort of camaraderie between them, an understanding of class in society.

Maebelle has no such mutual understanding whatsoever with Ruby Lee Robinson. Maebelle tolerates her at the weekly bridge table because she is dependable, punctual, and probably because she lives nearby. It is questionable however, why Ruby drives her obnoxiously red car that looks like a fire truck and overcrowds the driveway to Maebelle's house, when she only lives four houses down the street. It is unnecessary to say the least.

The weekly bridge club gathers at 12:30 sharp. The ladies will enjoy a dessert of the hostess' choice and coffee or tea. The rotation for the hostess occurs every eight weeks, ample time to get your home ready to receive the High Springs Ladies Bridge Club.

"Ms. Merriwether want that I should make peach tea or *raspppberry* for today's game?"

"The word is razz berry Flo, the 'p' is silent."

"Yes um."

"Dear Flo, you mustn't say want that, simply say, should I." Maebelle's tone is a little different.

"Yes um."

"And I have pleaded with you many times, not to say 'yes um'. You are not using correct language skills, and you are not a servant in this house."

"That's exactly what I just tells Mr. Collins, I'm not your servant."

Flo has the ironing board out and is starching the tablecloth that Maebelle purchased on her last trip to England. The Merriwethers were aristocrats, old Saxons, dating back to 850. Thomas Merriwether made his money in textiles, and Ms. Maebelle, as the community knows her, enjoys a comfortable life in High Springs. Of course, their home is overbuilt for the area. It has taken awhile for the other half of society to catch up on fashionable homes. Her gardener, Mr. Henry, keeps their gardens, lawn and driveway impeccably groomed.

Maebelle and Flo traversed the grounds only yesterday to pluck the finest specimens from her gardens. The silver chalet bowls are excellent vessels for Maebelle's flowers and always a topic of conversation while the ladies are visiting.

Today's dessert is a white chocolate blueberry bread pudding with a vanilla sauce. Naturally, there are other snacks in bridge bowls for the rest of the afternoon. But the bread pudding is most certainly a family recipe and closely guarded.

Mr. Thomas Merriwether passed several years ago and Ms. Maebelle entertains any time she can. Maebelle is the pronounced Grand Dame of the county, hosting bridal teas, book clubs, and the occasional political meeting. Ms. Maebelle is unswervingly Republican in her thinking and is never too rattled to discuss opposing views on any subject. This is an election year and discussions are becoming heated. Maebelle is undecided which candidate she will be endorsing. She artfully dodges questions about whom she supports but an announcement *will* be imminent.

Flo finishes the ironing and places the floral centerpiece on the table and begins setting the silver and the water glasses on the table. Maebelle is gathering the bridge tallies and score booklets and newer cards for playing. She feels amenities and protocol must always be present with the ladies, or anyone for that matter. Rules must be strictly enforced and reinforced.

Elsa Jane Monroe agrees with Ms. Maebelle. Both are conservative and traditionalists. Elsa truly believes the South is going to rise again. Her thinking scares some of the other club participants and frightens Flo. Behind closed doors, Flo shares with some of her friends that she doesn't think Elsa Jane Monroe has moved into the twentieth century. There has never been a whisper of prejudice but the idea of black folks moving back in the world is terrifying to Flo.

Elsa Jane's dress is always the same; white long sleeve blouses with stand-up collars and her signature double strand of pearls. She always carries a sweater with tiny pearl buttons, but rarely does anyone see her actually wear it. Her hair is upswept in a French twist and she often wears small cameo earrings. Elsa is an excellent bridge player; focused, polite, diplomatic and often wins the afternoon prize of three dollars. Some of the ladies sheepishly go along with the fifty-cent donation. They don't really believe that the afternoon's activities are truly gambling. The remaining quarters go to the person with the lowest score and a small token is reserved for *traveling prize.*

Two of the ladies always arrive together. Maxine and Adeline have been best friends since high school. Their husbands work with each other, and the four of them take annual vacations. Sadly, they play bridge alike. If one is attentive, a player will be cognizant that they similarly lead the same cards and adhere to identical bridge thinking like leading from kings. Notably, Maxine and Adeline usually arrive a bit late which clearly irritate some of the ladies. Ms. Maebelle has a sunny personality and she is not particularly bothered by a couple of minute's tardiness. Her position is simple; everyone will start without them.

It is fifteen past twelve and everyone has arrived except Betty Bowers. Tommie volunteers that she saw Betty in Walgreens and that Betty has been under the weather earlier in the week.

"I did not receive a phone call that anyone would be absent today," Maebelle seems a bit annoyed.

Suddenly, the doorbell chimes and Betty arrives. She is short of breath carrying her usual thermal glass of refreshment.

"The flowers are so gorgeous," Tommie is the first to comment. I always appreciate the beautiful seasonal arrangements. It reminds me of my grandmother's cottage I used to visit in Savannah."

"Please, Tommie, don't age me anymore than I am already," Maebelle says almost pleading.

Maebelle is starting to cut the dessert and plate the individual pieces. "I'm going to pass the vanilla sauce ladies, so that you can serve yourselves."

Harriet speaks up and asks if she could just have a teeny tiny bite. "I feel like I am needing to cut back on my caloric intake."

All the ladies' heads turn and stare at Harriet. If she weighs 100 pounds soaking wet, it would be a surprise.

Maebelle abruptly answers. "No, I did not go to the trouble of making this elegant dessert, iron your napkin, and invite you to my home to serve teeny, tiny bites. Please cut your calories at your own house, or anywhere else. Our club must remain free of guilt from over indulging when we are gathered together. Ladies, please enjoy. Harriet? Coffee with cream?"

"Please, with sugar, Maebelle. Thank you."

"Absolutely, dear."

Betty is starting to fidget and looks for her tumbler. Maebelle has a keen eye, aware that Betty has a drinking problem of sorts.

"Oh Betty, sweetie, Flo has refreshed your beverage and washed your tumbler. It is with your purse on the divan." Her new glass holds raspberry tea, and Betty gives a weak smile, barely whispering a thank you.

It would be impertinent to say anything to Betty bringing a foreign glass or tumbler to the table Maebelle thinks, but 'gracious me alive', presentation is everything in the South and Maebelle Merriwether's lovely table simply, cannot have any eyesore. That tumbler is a big eyesore to Maebelle.

"The dessert is lovely," Maxine states, and Adeline nods her head in agreement.

"I've noticed the blueberries and all the berries are so big this year," Adeline begins to speak by herself.

"Yes, and expensive," Elsa Jane responds. "I remember when our staff would pick them for days in the hot afternoons, and then they'd take them to the canning house, and put them in jars. Of course, we all had domestic help back then."

"Indeed," Mae gives a wink to Flo as she passes by.

Ruby asks if everyone is aware that Jack Collins is running for sheriff. "You know he had a political rally at the Ford dealership over the weekend."

Ruby and her husband Ron own the car dealership in town and have a big parking lot out front to attract lots of folks.

"Ron has talked to a lot of people and he thinks Jack will win the election."

Maebelle Merriwether thinks that method is an undignified way to attract voters. Balloons and hot dogs have no place in the political arena. She gasps, silently.

"I'm surprised J.W. isn't seeking your endorsement Ms. Maebelle, or is he?"

"I believe Flo mentioned he dropped by rather unexpectedly. I regret I cannot take time out of my day's activities to see everyone that knocks on the door. Unless, of course, they are wearing a Girl Scout uniform, and selling thin mints."

All the ladies laugh. Everyone understands protocol.

Maebelle continues, "Naturally, I will be inclined to review his platform."

Ruby adds, "He used the concrete platform at the top of the stairs in front of the two large glass doors."

The ladies glance around at each other in disbelief. The thought occurs to some that the red colorant on Ruby's hair might be seeping into her brain cells.

Elsa Jane looks around for Flo, "Could you be a dear, and bring me some more tea?"

Flo looks at Mae and picks up the pitcher and walks over to Elsa Jane's seat. She does not display the usual elegance in handling the crystal pitcher but rather plops it abruptly down on the right side of Elsa Jane's plate. "There you go Miss Elsa." She bristles by and looks again to her friend Ms. Maebelle.

Ordinarily, Ms. Merriwether does not require accolades about her desserts but to clear the stuffy air, she asks if everyone is enjoying the bread pudding. Mae glances over at Harriet's plate and it is devoid of any crumbs. She guesses Harriet will be eating a rice cake at home for dinner this evening.

"It's time ladies, please bring your beverages to the card tables." Maebelle is already standing.

Betty takes her glass, grabs up her purse, and makes haste to the bathroom. In a few minutes she emerges, and her complexion is once again rosy.

Miss Flo comes up to her. "I'll take your old glass from you."

Before Betty can say anything or protest, her glass is snatched from her hand. Their eyes meet, and Flo says, "Your new glass is at the table." Betty saunters to her seat, defeated.

The tag team effort Flo and Mae discussed is working so far.

"Does everyone have their money in the bowl?" Mae looks around the table.

Julia Anne Button, the newest member of the club, gazes at Mae. "I totally spaced about the quarters. I have my lucky button in my pocket though." Mae is not apathetic.

"Julia Anne, I don't like scolding you, but this makes several times now that you have failed to bring your quarters. A button can be remembered, but two quarters cannot?"

And Miss Maebelle is not finished. She is talking one on one with Julia Anne Button. "It is unfortunate, that you do not think enough of us to remember the small rules of our club.

I know it is such a silly thing, Julia Anne, to be talking about, but it is about consideration, mutual respect and manners that we all abide by the rules. Now, please try harder, as we all have buttons to spare. Can you dear? Be a better member? Tie a string around your finger, write a note, something to aid in your forgetfulness, because I have noticed that when you win the pot, you always take the silver home, and not your lucky button piece. Bless your heart now, please try."

"Yes, Ms. Merriwether."

Chapter 3

The cards are shuffled and dealt. Ruby starts the bidding at two hearts. Her partner, Maxine, is still counting her points, sort of twitching, and looks at Ruby bewildered.

"Pass."

Harriet passes, and Adeline passes. Three passes. Ruby is near to passing out herself.

"I swear, I mean, begging your pardon Maxine, but two hearts is a demand bid. May I ask you why you did not see or feel the need to keep the bidding alive?"

"You may not ask, dearest Ruby. Everyone has a bid and mine is pass."

Ruby is silenced by the look Mae gives her from the other table.

The game gets underway and Ruby is once again in trouble with her bid. When Maxine lays her hand down, she has no trump support and her hand contains a worthless singleton Jack.

Maxine offers no comments on the failed contract but mentions she likes Ruby's sweater ensemble, especially the necklace.

At first, Ruby is unresponsive, but cannot help herself commenting, "That is playing dirty, not responding to my bid."

The other table has a lively first round bidding and Mae and Julia win the contract. Mae lays her hand down, playing the bridge 'dummy' and begins spooning out peanuts from the bowl beside her.

Julia makes her bid, and Mae smiles.

Betty and Tommie capture the next bid at Mae's table. Betty uses her handkerchief to wipe her brow. "Is anyone else moist today?"

Everyone comments they are fine, and the bidding resumes.

Ruby once again, has high cards and bids. She looks imploringly at Maxine.

Elsa Jane passes, and Maxine jumps and changes suit. *Eureka, finally. Ruby is excited.*

Harriet passes. Ruby asks for aces by bidding, and Ruby realizes they have one problem. There is a king out and Ruby will have to finesse. *Darn it!*

Harriet blurts out that she doesn't have anything to stop them and Ruby says a prayer of thanksgiving. It is a lay down after that comment.

Eventually, the ladies change partners and the playing continues.

Tommie says she heard from a reliable source that the youth pastor who doubled as the music director is not returning next year at the First Baptist Church. Some in the church feel that he is too overweight to be a positive influence on the young people that attend.

"Are you serious Tommie?" Adeline, who carries a few extra pounds sounds appalled.

"Well, I would not want it repeated, but yes, that is the consensus of the majority."

"Well, I suwannee, sounds unchristian if you ask me."

"Well," Tommie continues, "They did ask many members, and it was reiterated that young people are active, and need examples about becoming temples of God, something like that."

Maxine echoes, "I suwannee."

"I believe he's been offered employment in Alabama."

Maebelle has counted her cards three times. She clears her throat. "Our club does not resort to tales being carried and wagging our fingers at others. May we continue with the game? It is your bid, Betty."

"One Canadian club."

"Excuse me Betty, was that one club?" Maxine seems puzzled and leans in with her good ear.

"Yes."

Maxine bids three clubs.

Everyone passes, but not without a huge sigh from Maebelle.

The afternoon goes by quickly, and Maebelle announces the final hand. Julia already at the other table now, says she is glad they are ending early today. She needs to pick up her girls from their violin lessons.

She doesn't know how much more screeching in their house she can take. It appears the twins might have to follow a different path from music. Taking violin lessons was her mother-in-law's idea. Julia would have been happy with the girls' choice of cheerleading, but violin lessons have commenced. It was her husband, Terrance who insisted on the violin. Terrance is High Springs' leading attorney and wants his girls to experience refined music. There is absolutely nothing refined about the twins' musical talents.

Julia Button was a home economics major in college and making cheerleading accessories for her girls would be a lot more fun for her or so she thinks. She is a gifted seamstress and crafts beautifully. Cheerleading would be right up her alley, but it will be next May when tryouts occur again.

Maebelle reminds everyone they will be playing next week at Tommie's home. "It is a little further out of the city limits, so please plan accordingly so everyone can start on time. Now, let's see who *is high today.*" Maebelle sifts through the tallies.

Julia, very sheepishly, whispers, "I believe I am high today, Maebelle."

"Of course, you are dear, it doesn't surprise me in the least." Maebelle gathers the silver from the bowl, and places in Julia's palm.

"Oh, here dear, how careless of me to forget the button," and firmly plants the button last deeply in her palm and presses down. Maebelle pauses and smiles.

"Thank you, all dear friends, I hope you all enjoyed yourselves today." Maebelle's eyes circle the room, and everyone is smiling and gathering up their belongings. Everyone except Betty, that is. Flo indicates by a nod to Maebelle that Betty might be visiting the lavatory.

The ladies are at the bottom of the outside steps when Betty emerges from the bathroom with her purse and tumbler.

"Thank you Maebelle for hosting such a lovely game." Seemingly, her spirits have lifted. Mae and Flo both think so in more ways than one.

Maebelle and Flo clear the table of dessert plates and silver. They move on to the card tables and put everything away.

Flo states she will check the bathroom. Maebelle understands completely.

Chapter 4

Ruby is in her red SUV and plans on stopping by the dealership. The bridge club ladies are not the only ones who can benefit from her sexy, hot look she thinks she portrays today. She is confident Ron appreciates her stopping by unannounced and letting the guys who work for him say hello. She imagines some of them thinking they can get away with flirting with her when she leans in the doorway of their cubicles.

Ron's secretary, Debbie announces Ruby's entrance and Ron immediately comes out of his office.

"Have fun today sweetheart?" Ron asks as he takes her hand and walks in his office. Once inside, Ron assumes his position in his overstuffed chair.

"Well?"

"I broached the subject about Jack, but Maebelle instinctively cut me short. No one else picked up the torch so I couldn't go there twice."

"You should have waited a few minutes then brought up Jack's candidacy again." Ron never looks at her when he is speaking. *Never send a woman to do a man's job.* "Go on home, we're eating there tonight. I would not want to take you anywhere in that black *pleather* skirt, and if it's real leather, it looks cheap."

Ruby bites her lip, straightens the creases down on her skirt, and adjusts her necklace. *He is so cruel, why would she want to do anything for him?* She exits past Debbie, and in a barely audible voice, "So nice seeing you Hon," and quickly departs the building. Ruby starts to tear up but pulls out of the parking lot and goes a few blocks into the parking lot of the Hideaway Lounge. She will have one cocktail to soothe her injured ego.

She ambles to the back and sees Betty immediately. Betty has a couple of empty glasses on the table, and motions for Ruby to sit down.

"Hello, friend, I've never seen you here. First time?" Betty is confident it is but asks anyway.

"Yes. I need to unwind before going home. Ron is so anxious about the election, but when I stopped by, he was curt to me. I figured I could have a pity party here."

"Men. Go figure," Betty's responds.

"Exactly."

"Marriage is a great institution, if you want to be institutionalized." Betty continues to give her opinion.

The server appears with another drink for Betty.

"What will it be honey?" The server directs her question at Ruby.

"Oh, a glass of Riesling."

"No, hon. We have Chard, Cab, and Merle."

"Okay, I'll have Chardonnay," and Ruby continues to bite at her lip.

Betty Bowers is divorced and that's about all anyone knows about her personal life. All the bridge ladies agree Betty is an excellent player, but very few see her socially outside of the club. On occasion, Betty talks about her German Shepherd dog Rex, and her rural country home.

The server appears with the glass of Chardonnay and sets it down on the table.

Ruby salutes Betty with her glass in the air, "Cheers."

"Yes, ma'am. Cheers."

Betty asks Ruby about Jack Collins and his election bid. "Your husband seems to be fairly active in getting him elected."

"Yes, they have been friends for a long time. I wish Ron would stay out of it."

"The other candidate is young but very well educated I understand. I met his wife and mother at the Woman's Club Summer Tea, both lovely ladies. Well, you know what they say, behind every good man is a good woman."

"Oh my, I've never heard of that." Ruby seems perplexed.

"I'll be leaving with this last drink. It's cheaper to drink at home, and Rex is probably eager to run around for a few minutes. Rex is my dog, you know."

"Me too, this hasn't been my best day, and I'm ready to call it over." Ruby takes her last sip and reaches for her wallet to retrieve a dollar to leave as a tip on the table.

Ron does not make it home before nine and does not bother to call Ruby and tell her he'll be late. Ruby doesn't bother to prepare supper either. She has wiled her time away watching Wheel of Fortune and snacking on cheese and crackers. There is little to no conversation between them before they both retire to bed.

Chapter 5

Maebelle Meriwether enjoys a proper English breakfast and Earl Grey tea every morning. She thoroughly reads the daily news from front to back. The High Springs Herald is a small paper but has lots of contributing writers that tell about the events within the county. Ms. Maebelle will initial the top of the page whenever she finishes it, to let Flo know the paper can be disposed of in the trash.

One article captures Maebelle's immediate attention. It is off to the side, but quite visible on the front page.

Collins Endorsed by Lady Merriwether

A reliable source confirmed that the High Springs Ladies Bridge Group discussed the endorsement of Jack Collins for sheriff campaign yesterday at the palatial estate of Maebelle Merriwether. Mr. Collins was canvassing that sector of town a day earlier and was seen at the door of Republican socialite Merriwether. An unnamed source who answered the phone number the Herald was given, substantiated that Maebelle was backing Collins. When Jack Collins was reached by the Herald, he was elated and said he looked forward to having Maebelle on the winning team.

"This is complete rubbish! I cannot believe my eyes. There is no such endorsement, and who is this source that the Herald proclaims they spoke to in this household?"

Something drops off the table and breaks. Miss Merriwether looks around, still holding the paper in her hands and eyes the floor. One of her favorite English bone China coffee cups is in a hundred pieces.

Flo is rushing from the kitchen. “I heard it,” and Flo stops dead in her tracks and looks down.

“Oh my, Mae, this was one of your mother’s.”

Maebelle shakes her head in disbelief that she can be so careless. She straightens the paper and folds it into a square.

“Flo, we’ll be going into town if you are up for a drive. Frankly, I think I'm a tad shaky, but I shall gather my wits about me, and get to the bottom of this preposterous lie.” Maebelle stands up from the table, looks at the shattered cup and asks Flo if she can pick up all the pieces and place them in a small bag or box for safekeeping.

Mae enters her bedroom and walks inside her closet. She selects a blue suit and lays it on the side of the bed. She steps into the bathroom and examines her hair in the mirror. It looks presentable; not much damage since her beauty shop set two days ago. She attaches a few bobby pins and sprays a bit of hair spray. She brushes her teeth over the sink, although she is absolutely positive there will be no smile on her face where she is going this morning. Mae applies some powder and rouge on her cheeks and adds her favorite lipstick. Reaching in her jewelry box, she obtains her long strand of pearls inherited from her grandmother and lays them on the bed beside her suit.

Her undergarments are stored in the chest of drawers, and she pulls one out of the drawer with ease. Assuredly, Ms. Maebelle does not go to town without the proper foundations or hosiery. It may be 2018, but a lady must always present herself without flaw.

"I'll be about forty-five minutes and then I shall be ready. Mr. Henry can bring the motorcar around for us if you will be so kind to ask him for me."

She finishes dressing and returns to the lavatory and removes her hairpins. A quick combing, a dab of perfume, and she is down the hallway to look for Flo.

Flo removes her apron. A quick glance at the table reveals Flo has picked up the breakfast tray, and broken china. Maebelle snatches the folded paper off the table, clutches it tightly, and opens the closet door to obtain her handbag.

Flo anticipates her every move and understands her mood. Flo opens the door leading outside and greets Mr. Henry.

"Good morning, Ms. Merriwether. I am going to replace the wave petunias today in the east garden."

"Yes, Mr. Henry," is all Mae responds.

Flo looks over at Mr. Henry and nods her head sideways as if to convey to Mr. Henry, the petunias are not important today and takes the keys from his hand while opening the driver's door. Mae is already seated on the passenger side fidgeting in her purse trying to find her gloves.

The driveway seems a shorter distance today as there is no conversation about the plantings, or fragrance of the lilies all abloom as the two head out the driveway.

Mae clears her throat. "Please, Mrs. Williams, drive me to the High Springs Herald. You will need to park, then come in, because I do not know how long I will be there."

"I declare Mae, you ain't, uh, referred to me as Mrs. Williams in such a long time. Is, I mean, are you feeling alright? The sun is mighty hot this time of year, and you have all those…layers on underneath. I am concerned."

"There is no cause for alarm Florence, as I am in my complete faculties and I am on a mission of principle and justice."

"Yes um." Flo understands not to anger Ms. Merriwether. Her anger might rattle the car windows, nothing Flo cares to witness.

Chapter 6

The High Springs Herald is located at the roundabout on Central and Park Avenues. Street traffic is light, but the sidewalk coffee houses seem to have an abundance of morning patrons, as Flo passes and turns into the parking lot. Flo usually enjoys Maebelle's Chrysler but today there is a noticeable difference in being behind the wheel. She feels like she is delivering a tiger to get his lunch.

The car hardly stops against the concrete bumper on the asphalt when Maebelle emerges from the car straightening her pearls and laying her skirt down flat. Flo hurries to Maebelle's side to see if she requires any help. Locking the doors with her key fob, she offers Maebelle her arm.

"I am quite capable Florence, quite capable I tell you," unaware she has repeated herself.

Flo walks beside her on the sidewalk, ever so often looking back to check for the tiger's tail. Flo proffers the door, and Maebelle moves with tunnel vision to the reception counter.

"There is no time for delay," as Mae acknowledges the receptionist. "I am Maebelle Merriwether, needing to see Mr. Farnsworth in his office. It is urgent."

"Is Mr. Farnsworth expecting you? I will ring his secretary." Before the receptionist can look up from her directory, Mae is headed down the corridor to the back-corner office.

Patricia Whitney has been Mr. Farnsworth's secretary for twenty-five years. She tried to retire many times, but she is irreplaceable as Mr. Farnsworth has told her on many an occasion. She sees Mae immediately through the glass partitions and stands up to greet High Springs' leading citizen.

"Ms. Maebelle, so good to see you, what brings you downtown to our neck of the woods?'

"Patricia, thank you. Will you please advise Mr. Farnsworth I am here to see him immediately?"

"Of course, it is our pleasure to receive you. May I offer you some coffee, I mean hot tea, Ms. Maebelle?"

"Thank you, I will take it in Mr. Farnsworth's office."

Maebelle is still standing as Flo slowly enters the office.

"I declare Maebelle, your short legs have running shoes on today," Flo says in a panicked voice. Maebelle has her handkerchief out and is wiping the sweat off her brow. Flo takes a seat as Patricia rings Farnsworth's inner office. The office door opens.

Alan Farnsworth is a busy man and everything he does requires scheduling. He has a commanding voice and full dark brows that furrow when he becomes irritated. The brows are upward as he glances over and speaks to Ms. Merriwether.

"I always have a few minutes for the community's grand dame. Come in, Maebelle, you're looking well."

Maebelle walks in and sits down in one of the office chairs across from Mr. Farnsworth.

"I will come right to the point. There is no need for useless debate, and idle conversation Mr. Farnsworth. In this morning's paper, you have an article saying that I have endorsed J.W. Collins for the sheriff candidacy. NO such endorsement has been made. I repeat, I have not endorsed any candidate, publicly or privately. NO one from the Herald telephoned me or my staff and this article is complete rubbish, false, and misleading to the citizens. I am hereby demanding a retraction, and an apology. You should have a swift rap on the knuckles my man. It is careless and revolting to read such untruths and I shall hold you personally responsible for placing my good name under a cloud I tell you."

"Ms. Merriwether…"

"Don't you Ms. Merriwether me. I will seek legal representation and bring a hornet's nest around your ears for this reprehensible and sloppy journalistic blunder. Where in God's name did you get this source you are quoting? I demand to know this instant."

"I had my reporter call a number we were given to verify Ms. Mae." Alan Farnsworth is indignant.

"My friends call me Ms. Mae, Mr. Farnsworth, and you certainly are not a friend of mine. Kindly call me Mrs. Merriwether as I sit here in this office. I am incensed beyond what my blood pressure can take." Mae takes her purse and raps it on the front edge of his desk.

"I'm waiting, Mr. Farnsworth, for the name of your source? I am not feeling especially patient this morning."

Mr. Farnsworth loosens his tie and reaches his intercom to buzz Patricia.

His buzz is futile as Patricia and Flo are both at the door with their faces firmly pressed against it, listening closely to Mae's tortuous charges. Flo is shaking her hand and whispers, "She has done released the Kracken." She has witnessed one other time in her employment, working for the Merriwethers, when Mae had been this mad and Flo has not forgotten it. Flo walks backward to her seat, and Patricia steps forward to answer Farnsworth's ring, feeling weak in the knees.

"Yes, Mr. Farnsworth?"

Please call the reporter for the Merriwether endorsement article so that Ms. Merriwether might calm herself down.

"I will not make one ounce of allowance for you, Mr. Farnsworth. You simply cannot feather your own nest without recourse to me and my tarnished reputation. I expect full disclosure and vindication in the next issue of the paper." Mae stands up and gathers up her handbag from the desk.

"I presume we have a mutual understanding, Mr. Farnsworth. Further discussion will be with my legal representative. Good day."

Mae turns to leave, and Mr. Farnsworth's mouth is agape. He does not have any breath to utter any word and looks exasperated.

One could hear a pin drop as Maebelle and Flo make their way back down the corridor of the Herald offices. As they pass by the different cubicles, employees pretend not to notice the source that has stilled the ordinarily manic morning sounds.

Flo opens the door going to the outside and they begin their walk back to the car. Mae's head is tossing back and forth like a tiger advancing on his prey, panting a bit, yet controlled.

"Why don't you stay here in the shade while I walk down to the get the car? I can drive around and pick you up."

"Nonsense, Florence, I am perfectly capable of walking back the same way I walked in here."

"Yes um." *I've been called Ms. Williams and Florence twice now. This is going to be a red-letter date.*

Chapter 7

"Next, we will attempt to go downtown on Walnut, to Banks, Baum, and Button," Maebelle continues tersely. "I believe it is the two-story brick commercial building on the far right. Terrance Button is married to Julia Anne, and I will need to obtain his legal counsel. I need a lawyer with teeth, and according to Julia Anne, he has all thirty-six of his."

"Yes um." Flo understands the directive.

Flo starts the car and sets her blinker for a right-hand turn. It is a short distance to the Three B Building. The historic building of Banks, Baum and Button is one of the High Springs' landmarks. Century old London-town bricks were used in the construction and are all handmade. When coupled with unique bull nose bricks, it creates a distinctive pattern often photographed by tourists. There is ample parking in the spacious lot adjoining the building, and Flo navigates the big Chrysler under a maple tree and parks.

"Florence, you know how I feel about ambulance chasers, don't you?"

"Yes um," Flo responds. "Folks should weather their own problems unless there is severe neg-la-gents." *I do hopes I pronounced that correctly.*

"Absolutely, correct, but these are personal injury attorneys and I mean to have satisfaction. I believe I have been personally injured Flo."

"Yes um," Flo is noticing how Miss Maebelle seems changed.

The car door opens and Maebelle, still wearing her gloves and clutching her handbag steps out onto the pavement. Flo follows suit.

"There is a hint of fall in the air Flo," as Mae looks up at the old maple tree and sees patches of color.

Entering the building, there is a large desk with a secretary seated who has a headphone on top of her head and an extraordinarily large telephone apparatus beside her. She smiles.

"How may I be of service to you?" the secretary asks.

"My name is Maebelle Merriwether and I would like to speak to Terrance Button."

"Yes, ma'am." The young girl steps around her desk. "If you will follow me please, Ms. Merriwether," smiling, "I am sure you don't remember me but I am Sarah. I used to sell you Girl Scout cookies several years ago."

Mae takes a second look. "My word yes. I do recall. You have grown up." Maebelle turns to Flo.

"Please wait here for me, as I do not know how long I will be."

Sarah interjects, "There is room for both of you in Mr. Button's office. You both can follow me."

Down the hall they walk, passing by a beautiful sitting area lavishly appointed. Mae eyes a gorgeous Henredon desk. Sarah points out, "This area is Mr. Bank's office."

Another corridor appears, and Sarah stops at the desk and addresses another receptionist.

"Darlene, Ms. Merriwether would like to see Mr. Button. She doesn't have an appointment per se, but she and Mr. Button are old friends." Sarah winks at Maebelle and asks if she would like some tea.

"Thank you, but no dear, I'm fine." Mae finds a chair and sits down. She reaches in her purse, retrieves her handkerchief, and dabs under her eyes.

Darlene is on the phone and glances over at Maebelle. She whispers, "Yes, sir."

Darlene hangs up and looks over again. "Mr. Button will be out momentarily."

Terrance Button is indeed an old friend of Maebelle and Thomas Merriwether. Terry played with their daughter Penelope in the Merriwether home while their parents played bridge in the evenings. Secretly, Mae is fond of Terry, and hoped that he and Penny would have a courtship one day. But Penny was a wanderer, dabbled in the arts and was an environmental activist. After high school, the children drifted apart taking different forks in the road, but Maebelle regards him affectionately.

The inner door of Terrance Button's office opens, and he walks out with a wide smile showing his delight in seeing his old friend.

"What did I do to deserve a visit from one of my favorite people? You honor me Maebelle." He walks closer and gives her a big hug, and Maebelle blushes with appreciation.

"Come in, and let's have a visit." He gestures where she can sit, and then he turns to Darlene.

"Please hold my calls and bring Ms. Merriwether some hot tea with lemon."

The door closes behind them, and Terrance takes a chair next to Maebelle, gazing at her.

"You are looking well. I assume you are still stacking the decks. How else can you explain always winning at the bridge table?" He laughs, and she laughs softly too.

"It's skill I tell you, and devotion to my craft."

"Truer words never spoken. How is Penny? Is she in the rain forest saving some rare beetle?" he says lightheartedly.

"She is residing in an orphanage home in Guatemala working with children. I only hear from her about every two weeks, but she is well." Maebelle sighs. "I guess I am never going to have any grandchildren, Terry."

"What is troubling you that you are here in my office? Or is Julia not performing that well at the bridge club? You know Julia does not have that competitive spirit that abounds in you Maebelle."

"No, Julia is doing fine with bridge. It's a grave personal matter Terrance that brings me to you this morning. Seeking publicity is not the norm for me, but I have always considered our community of High Springs as my family. When Thomas and I settled here, there was little to offer for commerce, and very few residents."

"While tourists loved the river for camping and such, the visitors were not investors in our town. Thomas was an investor, saw the potential, and we both thought this area was a great place to raise a family with goals and morals. But corruption is seeping in Terry. I believe the greed and selfish ambitions of some of our business leaders and government officials is taking hold in High Springs. They are masquerading as public servants. I am coming to my point, Terry."

"Yes ma'am," as he listens intently.

"This morning, an article appeared in the Herald that stated that I have endorsed J.W. Collins for sheriff. The newspaper, without verification from me, printed that and I believe has libeled me. It is fair to say that in the minds of most readers, that broadcast is true, when in fact it is not. In the last hour, I visited Mr. Farnsworth at the Herald, and demanded to know his source. I insisted upon a full retraction and apology. I informed him I would seek legal representation to ensure my good name and reputation don't go down in the gutter with Mr. Collins' campaign. I am emotionally distressed about this. I need my attorney with some teeth in him to bite the head of the serpent."

"Lucky for me, I've had recent dental work, my dear Mae. Are you seeking financial retribution as well, or will you be satisfied with a printed retraction?"

"I am conflicted. The article states that it was discussed at the bridge game held at my house. I am concerned that a friend that I have trusted, and I have welcomed into my home has perpetuated this myth."

"I simply do not have the facts and getting a paper to name sources can be difficult. It is a false statement that they negligently and intentionally published, and I contend it is harmful. If seeking money will stop future negligence, then I am willing to spend money for satisfaction. If the suit is favorable to me, I will donate the monies to a charity."

"I will need a statement from each member in attendance, under oath, stipulating that an endorsement of Mr. Collins candidacy was not given. Was the subject brought up Maebelle?"

"Yes, Ruby Robinson did ask if I would be endorsing him, but I do not discuss my political opinions at the bridge table. I know her husband is a big supporter of J.W.'s but when she mentioned it, I believe I stated the weekly card game was not the place to inject ourselves in local politics."

"Mae, I know Alan Farnsworth to be an honest man. Perhaps, this is an honest mistake. I will phone him *and* write a letter of concern, with some muscle, I mean teeth in it, and see where it leads. You do not need to worry. I want to see that rosy smile of yours again that I know you possess. Mae, while you are sipping tea, I could give Alan a call and see if he can release that information."

"Yes, that will be fine. If there is no need to sue, then I can be reasonable so long as I also see a printed retraction."

The secretary knocks before entering with a tray of tea and cups. She pours for each of them.

Terrance asks his secretary to place a call to Mr. Farnsworth at the Herald.

"Certainly, I will buzz you whenever he is on the line, Mr. Button," and smiles as she passes by Maebelle on her way out. Immediately, the intercom sounds, and Terry picks up the telephone.

"Good Morning Alan. Terrance here. This is a professional call on behalf of my client, Maebelle Merriwether. She has retained my services to clear up this misunderstanding."

"Terrance, I am perplexed. Just now, I reviewed everything with my reporter. She told me she called the number that was given to her by an unnamed person. She said a woman with a British accent answered. However, we have done some checking and the phone number she called is not Ms. Meriwether's."

"The number is no longer working, and the phone company replied to our inquiry and said that it is a number related to disposable, prepaid telephone minutes and is unable to be traced. It appears we have been tricked into thinking Ms. Maebelle was giving the endorsement, and someone has gone to a lot of trouble to ensure that J.W. Collins is the recipient of Maebelle Merriweather's favor. I don't know what to say. It's the newspaper business. We act on a lot of anonymous tips. I guess the British accent was all the confirmation my reporter needed. I am sorry this happened. Um…it is never our intention to report false information. I will print a retraction in the next issue, Terrance. If that does not appease Ms. Merriwether, then she can pursue her lawsuit. I am insured Terry, but understand my hope is that she will be satisfied with a retraction."

"I will discuss your explanation with my client. Thank you."

Terry sets the phone down and turns to Maebelle, "That corruption you mentioned earlier, I'm afraid, is within our community for sure." Terry relates what Alan has told him to Maebelle, and she takes it all in.

"Someone wants your endorsement enough to go to elaborate efforts. The reporter said a woman with a British accent answered the phone and naturally, she thought it to be you."

Mae is slightly scowling and thinking. "And the retraction?"

"Alan will attend to it with the next edition."

"My advice is if the new article does not meet your expectations, then we will take legal action. Maebelle, it is a big pill for the Herald to swallow. Are you willing to pause and see if his apology goes far enough?"

"Yes, I want to believe he is innocent in all this tangled web." Mae puts her cup back on the tray. "I'm appreciative Terry, very thankful for what you've done. Now, I will not waste anymore of your time today."

"It was good to see you also. I'll start on a preliminary investigation and I'll look forward to what the paper will print next. I will be in touch with more information as it develops. Now, let's enjoy some tea for a few minutes." They chat about old times and Terry's parents, now deceased.

Mae stands up, reaches for her handbag and gloves, and makes her way to the door to leave.

"Again, thank you," exiting out the door, immediately seeing Flo, waiting in the adjoining room.

"The color has returned to your face, Mae," Flo feels the need to say something.

"Flo, until the retraction is made, I do not feel like dallying around in town, only to have more people ask me or assume I am endorsing Jack Collins."

"Yes um."

Maebelle's mood seems to be better on their way home. When they pull in the driveway, Mae remarks on the beautiful lilies and how wonderful they smell.

Flo silently smiles to herself

Chapter 8

After lunch, Mae mentions to Flo that she thinks she needs to lay down, as she feels troubled and exhausted. Perhaps Mae senses a dark and slippery road ahead of her, perhaps, it is just her intuition. Flo is troubled too, as she understands her friend isn't her old self.

Over the next two days, Mae questions in earnest if one of the ladies of her revered bridge club could have betrayed her. She rests a lot and reads her latest book from Amazon.com entitled *"Sunday Dinners,"* authored by Kellie Kelley. She tries not to think about the division of opinions between the residents of their small community. She believes that there is visible opposition between a deputy within the department and a newcomer in the political arena with a different vision that's becoming a large problem.

The local Republican Party is backing Daniel Black. His father is a major in the Florida State Highway Patrol and well respected in the local area and surrounding counties. Although churches aren't specifically endorsing Daniel, many members of the local church congregations are donating to his campaign and holding pot luck dinners to introduce Daniel to the right people. His background is business and finance and Black's campaign manager is focusing on a slogan that emphasizes that the sheriff's budget needs to be "in the black."

There are numerous attacks hurled at Daniel about his inexperience in law enforcement, but he maintains that a good leader devoid of corruption can get the department out of debt and keep deputies doing their jobs. A lot of folks are insisting on cleaning house within the department and ridding the county of the good ole boys club and cronyism. Daniel Black is a solid citizen with pronounced credentials.

Saturday is Flo's day off from the Merriwether household. Flo entertains her own card club on Saturday nights. She enjoys her three friends spending a couple of hours at her own house playing poker. They prefer the five-card stud game. It is fun to gamble and occasionally win a pot of loot from friends she's known for twenty years. The loot consists of paper slips that are actual favors a friend can redeem when needed. Someone is always needing an extra hand or chore done. It is friends supporting friends. Of course, Flo is asked about the endorsement article printed in the paper, and she tells her friends there must be a rotten apple in the barrel.
"We need to keep our eyes and ears open sisters and learn what's going on. Either someone in Ms. Maebelle's club has betrayed her or there is something else in the election that is crooked. Either one is bad."

The current sheriff who is retiring says he will not be endorsing Collins, or anyone else for that matter.

He wants the good citizens of High Springs to come to their own conclusions as to the better candidate. He is however, retiring under a bit of a cloud because of budget overruns.

Jack Collins is a seasoned deputy for Alachua County, although he has not received any promotions in his seven years of employment. Last year, he was transferred to the patrol car maintenance yard. He sits at a desk, shuffling lots of paperwork regarding necessary repairs that need to be made on patrol cars to ensure deputy safety and keep the cars on the road. Once he announced his candidacy for sheriff, it appears no one else in the department was interested in submitting their application.

Jack and his wife of twenty years live on the south end of town in a large newly built home. Jack throws it out there regularly for anyone to hear, that his wife has inherited some assets from a family member. They enjoy more than their share of new vehicles and toys, surprisingly for a deputies' salary. Jack brags regularly 'that you never see an armored car at a funeral' to his friends.

Chapter 9

Detective Boyd Price is on assignment in Alachua County for the next three days. He is on loan from Volusia County in direct contact with the state prosecutor's office. He and another detective are to be undercover, gathering facts into one consolidated report. Boyd and his new assistant Eddie, assume the identity of road and property surveyors, and are staying in a rented house. Boyd hopes they will not be more than two days away from his home in Pierson, FL. He does not like being away from his wife, as they are newlyweds, so he stays focused on his mission to get his job done quickly and efficiently. At the south end of town, Boyd and Eddie haul out their tripods and leveling rods like they know what they are doing on the side of the road. Each one is wearing a brimmed hat and a glow in the dark vest, on loan from Landpointe Surveyors. They have everything they need to look and act the part of civil engineers, including a truck with side panels that read "Landpointe," in large black font. They park their truck off the hard road, onto the grass, and proceed to gather their implements. It is a particularly hot day as they ease up the driveway to J.W. Collins' ranch style home, moving their equipment as they walk. Eddie follows Boyd's lead, sometimes doing a couple of hand signals in the air like it actually means something. Boyd is making notations in a notebook and adjusting knobs on his leveling rod when J.W. Collins pulls his King Ranch truck onto the long gravel drive.

"Do you copy Eddie?" Boyd quietly says in his radio.

"Tag number copied and photographed, sir."

J.W. slows his vehicle and presses the button to the automatic window. Looking directly at Boyd, J.W. yells out, "You boys hot?" and then he laughs.

Boyd acts like he doesn't hear him at first, then signals to Eddie, and drops an orange flag to the ground. Boyd wipes his brow with his bandana and keeps his sunglasses on.

"Sir?"

"You boys working on state business or private?"

"Sir, plats, Landpointe, GPS Mapping." *The answer is a bunch of bull.*

"Okay," and J.W. waves goodbye, and drives on down to the end.

Eddie is walking toward Boyd, and he picks up the tripod and turns it toward J.W.'s four door garage.

"Eddie, there's a boat I see. Can you make it?"

"I'll get the tape out and lay it on the road, to get closer," Eddie responds on his radio.

Suddenly, a garage door opens, and a new Ford Expedition Platinum emerges and backs out.

"Eddie, you copy?"

"Yes sir, and a six-passenger golf cart parked in there, He also has a very nice pool. These high-power prisms let you see it all. Copy all, sir."

Boyd speaks into the radio, "I'll move the truck, and we'll get some water and load up the equipment."

"Water sounds good sir."

Inside the truck, Boyd is writing down information in his book. Eddie is still drinking water, then begins to speak.

"I think before we leave, we need to put a stake in the ground with orange tape, maybe paint some orange letters or symbols in the grass. Okay with you, Boss?"

"I suppose that would look official." They both laugh. When Eddie finishes, Boyd turns the truck around. They load up their materials and head back toward town. Boyd's phone rings, and he answers.

"Detective Price speaking. That's affirmative. Probably at six, sir, when we I put the information into the computer, then sir." Boyd promptly hangs up.

Eddie says he hopes they are calling it a day.

"Not quite. We'll take a break to rest at the house. Then, we have a little nighttime surveillance that will probably take a few hours."

"When do we eat?"

"We can eat after our rest at one of the local restaurants."

Boyd puts the address of the rental house in the GPS and heads the truck that way. Eddie mentions he can use a shower.

"We both can, and a cold beer. I'll stop at the Shell station up the road."

The guys walk in and head to the restrooms. Boyd waits in the hall and allows Eddie to use the lavatory first. Boyd hears some conversation about the sheriff race at the counter and casually edges toward the men talking.

"Yeah, J.W. has a big fund raiser at the Rocking H Ranch. The street talk is that Collins thinks checking on all the immigrant labor at the Hernandez Farm is a waste of deputy time. If he's elected, there will be undocumented workers everywhere."

The guys look over at Boyd. "You for Collins or Black?"

"Yeah, I'm just renting for now, just visiting."

Eddie bumps him from the side, and tells Boyd, "I'll get the beer."

Boyd steps to the bathroom and makes a mental note about what he has just heard.

Eddie purchases a six pack of beer and some teriyaki jerky and is standing by the truck.

"Hey, that King Ranch Ford just drove by. I recognize it."

"We're going to swing by the sheriff's department first." Boyd drives by slowly and notices the truck is parked.

Eddie sheepishly asks, "Are we investigating a deputy sir? Holyeeee crap!"

There is no response from Boyd.

"You need money for the beer? Let's keep that beer consumption to one, until we get through tonight Eddie."

Boyd did not know who owns the house where he and Eddie are staying. He believes the investigation he is conducting is at the request of the state's attorney's office. He retrieves his overnight bag and gun holster from the company truck and sits on the porch with Eddie. Boyd removes his shirt and his safety vest. His tee shirt is soiled from perspiration and he discards it as well.

Eddie follows suit. Now they can relax with a beer and Eddie hands him the bag of jerky.

"Sir, are you allowed to talk about the case?"

Boyd looks directly at him. "This is in the preliminary stage of an investigation. As I mentioned as we drove here, we are gathering facts on certain individuals. Tonight, we are going to a Ford dealership to check out work being done on patrol cars in the service department. Apparently, the service department services the police cars during the evenings when they aren't in use."

The guy driving the King Ranch is a ten-year deputy, currently in charge of vehicle maintenance. There have been cost overruns which send up a red flag. A local car dealer seems to enjoy all the county maintenance work. The deputy and the car dealer have an agreement or relationship we need to know more about. Additionally, we need to know the facts about how and where the deputy lives in the community.

"Yeah, his house and property look expensive, and he has several new and expensive personal vehicles." Eddie is thinking out loud.

"Also, there have been some troubling campaign missteps because this guy is running for sheriff. Let's get a shower, rest a bit, then we'll grab a bite to eat."

Chapter 10

Boyd attempts to call his wife Dolly after his shower. She doesn't pick up, and he leaves a voice mail. Out of town assignments are worrisome to his wife and she is extra emotional these days since they are expecting a baby. Heck, he realizes he is emotional too, and he hates being away from her. His phone rings, and he picks it up automatically, without looking to see who is calling.

"Hey son, I'm at the hospital with Dolly and she's being checked out. She is spotting some and is experiencing a few cramps. A doctor is going to do a sonogram as a precaution. Dolly said ya'll were scheduled for one Thursday." Boyd's mother pauses to be sure he has heard her.

"Are you there with her now?"

"I just stepped out of the room. Her sister Rita came, and is in there with her."

"I just phoned her, and she didn't pick up, and I understand why now. Has she seen the doctor yet?" Boyd waits for an answer. "Okay, can you take her your phone and let me talk to her?"

"Of course, son."

There is a couple of seconds that go by, and Boyd hears, "Hey honey."

"Baby, are you okay? My heart just skipped a beat."

"I'm fine, really, I got a little concerned, but you know everybody panics whenever I hurt. Really, I'm good. I just want us to have this second sonogram together."

"They took some blood a few minutes ago. I'll probably go home in a couple of hours. Rita is here but she is leaving for Tallahassee soon. I miss you."

"I miss you too. Don't worry now. When did you start feeling bad?"

"I was just walking to water the plants outside and felt something. It's so hot here today. They're going to take some pictures. You and I can look at them together when you get home."

"Dolly, I love you and I'm going to be home as soon as I can. Can I speak to mother again?"

"Yes Boyd?" Janet Price will do anything for her son.

"Mother, please do not leave her side until I get home. Can you watch over her please?"

"Yes, son, I will."

"Thank you, Mother," and there is a heavy sigh. "She is my life, and I know you will take my place."

Boyd hangs up the phone and becomes still for a few minutes. Finally, He looks at his watch, 5:00. *Thank you, Lord, for hearing my prayer.*

Eddie comes out the door and suddenly halts. He senses something is wrong.

Boyd looks his way, "My wife is expecting, and she's been taken to the hospital. I think she is fine. She sounds okay. My mother is there with her."

In complete surprise, Eddie puts his hand on Boyd's shoulder and presses it.

"Lord, my partner and I ask for divine healing and we pray you will hear our needs and be with Mrs. Price. Amen."

Boyd nods his head and leans into Eddie and gives him a man hug. "Thanks Eddie, I don't like being away from her. I will remain positive. That is the best thing I can do. If you're ready to go, we'll dress, go eat, and gather some more information."

They are ready to go in a few minutes and Boyd is driving back to the main part of town to look for a suitable restaurant.

"Eddie, do you have a favorite food you like to eat?"

"I'm a southern boy, by way of Puerto Rico, I like everything."

"I think there is a good place up the road. I noticed it when we came in on north Main Street. It's called *The Great Outdoors.*"

Their mealtime is relatively quiet. Boyd says he would like to leave as soon as possible. "There is someone I need to interview tomorrow morning, but if we can go there after dinner, and take care of that meeting, then we'll be set for the surveillance at dark. It will mean a lot to me if I can get home tonight Eddie."

"Of course. I understand sir."

Boyd leaves half of his meal.

Eddie remarks, "You didn't eat much sir. Everything will be okay, sir."

"I think so, I'm just spoiled by my wife's cooking, and I'm thinking about her. If you're ready, we'll go now."

Chapter 11

They settle in the truck, and Boyd gets out his notebook and the computer. He takes out his phone and dials.

"It's ringing, I hope we can connect."

"Hello," and a British accent is heard.

“Hello, this is Detective Boyd Price, with the Alachua County Sheriff Department.”

“You have reached Maebelle Merriwether. Your caller ID does not indicate the sheriff department.”

“No ma’am, my partner and I are undercover for Alachua County. I assure you we have the proper credentials. To remove any doubt ma'am, I need to tell you we have been sent to interview you because of a direct request from the states attorney’s office indirectly connected to a Terrance Button, attorney. May we drop by your home, Ms. Merriwether? As I mentioned, we are undercover acting as civil engineers and we are dressed as such. I have a number you can call to verify our identities before we arrive so that you will be at complete ease. I will give you our badge numbers, and when you make this call, you may ask the person answering the phone for our badge numbers. It is due to the fact we are not traveling in a patrol car, Ms. Merriwether. This is the reason I am asking for your cooperation.”

“I'll have those badge numbers and your names now Detective. How much time before you arrive?’

“About twenty minutes, ma'am.”

“That will be fine. Let me have that number please.”

“Ms. Merriwether, please do not call your local sheriff department, as that is what our investigation is about.”

“Oh, I can promise you I will not be a part of any trickery.”

“Yes ma'am.”

Immediately, Maebelle calls Mr. Henry and asks him to come to the main house. "Be prepared to stay a few hours." She calls Terry and Julia Ann answers the phone.

"Julia, its Maebelle. I need to speak to Terrance. It's very important."

Terrance assures her that he has started this big ball rolling, but for her to press forward and call the number she has been provided.

Mae says goodbye to Terry and dials the number Detective Price has given her.

"Special Operations," Officer Lansing speaking.

"This is a party calling from High Springs, Florida. I have two officers on their way over whose identities I need to verify." She gives Officer Lansing the badge numbers.

Office Lansing politely asks her to hold.

Quickly, Officer Lansing is back. "Is this Maebelle Merriwether I am speaking with?"

Caught off guard, Mae sheepishly admits. "This is she."

"Ma'am, your officers are Detective Price and Martin, Volusia County Sheriff's Department. The badge numbers are correct."

"Please ask to see their photo identification and badges when they arrive."

"Most assuredly, good day." Maebelle is satisfied.

The Landpointe truck makes it way to the driveway of Maebelle Merriwether's residence.

Eddie remarks on the grounds. "It is pretty, isn't it?"

"My wife would love it."

They arrive at the front door; park, get out, and go up the steps and ring the bell.

The front door opens, and an older man appears.

"Mr. Merriwether? Immediately Boyd produces his badge. I am Detective Price, and this is Detective Eddie…"

"I will take these to Ms. Maebelle. I will be right back," and shuts the door.

Shortly, Maebelle appears at the door.

"Come in, please."

She has their badges in hand and offers them back. "May I see a photo ID, please? Very well."

"Please have a seat in the living room."

Boyd clips his badge on his belt and Eddie does the same.

"May I offer you some coffee or tea?"

"No thank you, ma'am,"

"Very well then."

Mr. Henry leaves the room.

Boyd speaks up, "It is probably a good idea for Mr. Merriwether to be present."

Mae smiles, "Mr. Henry is my gardener. Thomas Merriwether died several years ago."

"I am very sorry," Boyd responds, and Eddie shakes his head in unison.

"Ms. Merriwether, as I mentioned, we are undercover working for the state attorney's office. Please tell us in your own words, the details of your complaint and reasons for calling the state's attorney."

"I did not call personally. I understand my attorney has filed paperwork regarding this matter. A week ago, I received a visit from one of the sheriff candidates at my door, unannounced I might add, seeking my endorsement. I did not receive him. Understand, I weigh carefully placing my name behind a candidate these days. The following day I was entertaining my bridge ladies, and the subject was mentioned, and the question was asked if I was going to endorse J.W. Collins. I discourage political chatter during our ladies' card game and dismissed the inquiry. Lo and behold, the Herald printed a story the next day saying that I had. I was shocked, and immediately set out to see the publisher, and my attorney Terrance Button. Mrs. Julia Ann Button was here that day and told her husband, Terrance, the very same story. However, the editor and owner of the paper is maintaining their reporter called a number and a person with a British accent verified the information. You can imagine how violated I feel. Someone is purposely trying to influence this sheriff race and I must wonder why."

"Terrance did a little detective work on his own and he has advised me that the phone number that was researched is a throw away cellular phone, with no known owner.

Someone has gone to a lot of trouble to snag this election by crooked and unethical means. Begging your pardons detectives, Thomas Merriwether always said, if one ferrets deep enough, they will generally bring up some dung. Wouldn't you agree?"

Boyd and Eddie don't really know how to respond.

"Detective, I have an uneasy feeling about all of this. J.W. Collins may think he is clever, but frankly, I have felt a bit stalked, and at church of all places. What is so important about this election that a deputy already in the department needs to go to these lengths? The Ford dealership is backing J.W. Collins, and I have an uneasiness about the whole matter in our community. Call it a gut feeling, if I am permitted to speak so crass."

"Ms. Merriwether, do you feel any one of your bridge ladies has a vested interest in seeing Mr. Collins win?"

"One of my bridge ladies is Ruby Robinson, actually a neighbor, four houses down. Her husband owns the Ford dealership. But a vested interest? It is unlikely to me that Ruby cares about anything other than herself, but she is a dear, mind you."

"Ms. Merriwether, have you always endorsed a candidate?"

"My husband, Thomas, invested in our community, deeply, and I suppose, it was he that was involved in the political circles. I admit; however, I feel the need to further his legacy."

"Do you give a monetary contribution as well?"

"Yes, indeed, I give 5,000.00 dollars to the political candidate I endorse."

Boyd makes continuous notes. He glances at Eddie and he too, is writing in a little black book.

"Detective, I pride myself on a sharp and educated mind. Playing bridge often keeps those brain cells working and memory intact."

"Yes ma'am, my mother plays a lot. She lives in Pierson."

Maebelle looks puzzled and does not speak for a few seconds. "Oh, I have played Tournament Bridge with several ladies from Pierson. Your last name is ...Price. Why of course, Jane Price."

"Janet, ma'am, Janet Price is my mother."

"Oh, it is such a small world, Detective. She is from Georgia, I recall. Oh my, who would think? She is a lovely attractive lady. I can see where you get your handsome looks. Please tell her I send my best wishes. I am so delighted to meet her son."

Boyd looks at Eddie and is at a loss of words again. "Yes ma'am."

"Detective, on the money front, I have recalled something the last few days. Mr. Collins enjoys telling our good folks around here that his wife has inherited some money from a deceased relative. I have reflected, and I know her parents who live in Branford, and most of her relatives are there also. I do not believe there is any significant money there to be inherited. I believe finding the truth about this might be interesting."

"One other thing, my dear friend and housekeeper, Flo, phoned me today. She has her friends keeping their eyes and ears open. She told me that her nephew works at the Ford dealership as a mechanic. Darius has worked there several years, and he told his Aunt Flo they are hiring night mechanics. He said they bring county patrol cars into the service department after hours. He said the manager explained that the deputies need the cars during the day, and that is why they are serviced at night. I find it unusual new patrol cars would need much work at all. Our current sheriff has received a lot of criticism that he is running over his budget without much explanation.

"Mrs. Merriwether, have you ever thought about becoming a detective?" Boyd says smiling.

She laughs, "I have read a lot of Nancy Drew mystery books, mind you."

"Is there any other information you can think of?"

"Not at the moment, but I would like to have your phone number."

"Mrs. Merriwether, the number I provided to you to verify our badge numbers will be the number you can call and leave a message. I urge you not to discuss this case, however troubled you become. For your safety, the investigation must take its own course. Please refrain from discussing we were even here. This is the foundation of a grand jury probe and I must personally ask you for your assurance that you will not discuss our visit this evening with anyone. It is critical."

"You have my word, detectives."

"Thank you, we will be on our way."

"Give my best to your mother. I feel like we're family," and she leans into him to hug him, and Maebelle hugs Eddie too.

Mae walks them to the door. "Good night."

Boyd starts the truck up, "Eddie, this is starting to smell bad. What do you think?"

"Like the dung Maebelle mentioned. Sir, it is troubling. I will tell you I would not want to be on Ms. Merriwether's bad side. It sounds like Jack of Spades has met Queen of Hearts. What's next sir?"

Chapter 12

"After our stake out, do you want to try and head home tonight?"

"Thanks Eddie, I admit I am concerned about my wife. I'll call at this service station. I'd like to get some coffee."

"Sounds good."

"Can you go in and get it while I place a phone call?"

"Yes, sir."

Boyd pulls in and parks, and Eddie jumps out and disappears in the store.

Boyd dials his mother's phone.

"Hey son, she's sleeping."

"Is everything okay? What did the sonogram reveal?"

"The doctor told her to take it easy and to stay off her feet for a few days, drink more water, less tea and coffee. She won't like me telling you this. I feel guilty."

"How is her spirit?"

"She's up, excited, wants to talk to you about the sonogram, said she wishes you were here to get the news with her. The doctor put the gender identity in an envelope so when you get home, ya'll can open it together. She won't have it any other way."

"If she stirs, will you tell her I phoned? Do you think she'll be going home tonight?"

"Doubtful, but she may insist. The doctor is being cautious, I am sure."

"I'm coming home tonight but it will be late. Mother, thank you for staying with her. Please do not leave her. I know it's a lot to ask of you, but I don't want you to leave her at all. Please, and tell her I love her when she opens her eyes. Will you?"

"Yes, son, I will."

"And I love you too Mother."

"I know son, but it is always so nice to hear."

Chapter 13

Eddie is back with hot coffee for the two of them. Boyd hangs up the phone and reaches for the java.

"I feel better."

"Good sir. Glad to hear it."

Boyd pulls out onto the highway.

"It's just down here. I noticed a lounge, 'Something Hideaway.' Let's see if we can park there, settle in and take notice." Boyd backs in a parking spot and retrieves some binoculars from under the seat. Eddie readies a camera that had a big scope on the end of it. Boyd looks at his watch and makes a notation in his file. You can hear each of them swallowing their remaining coffees as they wait.

Boyd whispers. "We need pictures of tag numbers as well as driver pictures. We can both take notice of time and check each other's remarks later. I will turn on a recorder that will pick up any conversation that we have from one-time frame to the last notation. This recording will document our activities and might serve us well."

The big pole lights of the Robinson Ford dealership lot act as beacons on the asphalt. A neon lit service department sign illuminates vehicles as they pass in and out. Overhead lights shining in various car stalls indicate service work is being done.

The detectives do not wait long. A patrol car turns into the gate, and there is a horn beeping, three singular beeps.

Boyd makes note. *Strange announcement, perhaps a signal?*

The patrol car enters a stall and parks. The driver exits.

The clicking of a camera is the only noise you can hear in the cab of the Landpointe truck.

A man dressed in a blue mechanic uniform steps out of an adjoining stall and looks toward the highway. Another second patrol car whizzes by Boyd and Eddie and enters the fenced car lot. The mechanic motions for the driver to park in a specific stall. Before the driver exits, there is conversation at the driver's window between the mechanic and the driver. A third patrol car enters, followed by a black King Ranch Ford. It is definitively a parade without any festooning. Eddie continues to snap pictures and captures all the drivers' photos as well as a nice head shot of J.W. Collins waiting in his truck. All three drivers, seemingly of Spanish descent climb into the King Ranch and the Ford truck begins to back out and make a turn around to leave the yard and enter the highway.

Both Boyd and Eddie lean down as if picking items off the floor board as the Ford truck motors by them.

Eddie is the first to speak. "I have used plenty of film, and believe I have all tag numbers, and car units, including driver photos. What do you make of this sir?"

"It's troubling; unusual that three cars might need servicing at once for a mid-sized town like this. Service is usually done on a rotation. The state attorney's office will have to pull service records to see what work is being done. If there are kickbacks being made from the dealership to the deputy in charge of the maintenance pool, then I suspect this is a case of police corruption and will be handled by the prosecutors. Our job of gathering all evidence will be evaluated.

A disheveled man taps on Boyd's window and Boyd lowers the power window some. "Hey man, can you spare a few dollars for a beer?"

"Sorry, I haven't been paid this week, but I've got a bottle of water if you have a powerful thirst."

"Alright."

Boyd lowers the window more and hands him the Dasani water.

The man takes the water from Boyd and remarks, "I can probably get two dollars for it. That'll help," and he walks away with plastic bottle in hand.

Boyd looks over to Eddie who is clearly trying not to snicker. Boyd grins and says, "We're in the wrong business." Boyd tells Eddie he needs to make a few notes on his report but that it shouldn't take too long. He turns off the recorder and opens his file folder and his computer. Eddie jots down something in his black book.

A few minutes have passed. Boyd eyes his watch, makes a last mark in his file, and looks over to Eddie.

"Do you mind if we head home? I know you are tired, but since we knocked out the interview with Ms. Merriwether, I believe we are finished here. Do you agree?"

"I'm good to go. I'm sure you want to see your wife in the hospital."

"Thanks, my mother is there with her, but I need to be there also. We're supposed to find out the gender of the baby soon. We're going to be older parents and I am concerned she is having a tough time."

"Congratulations man. Yeah, let's motor."

"Eddie, can you drive awhile, while I put this information in the computer. My boss is expecting the details of our investigation as soon as possible."

"Sure thing."

The truck pulls over, and the men trade positions. Eddie takes the driver seat and heads northeast on the highway.

"I didn't ask you Eddie; do you have a wife?"

"No sir, I haven't found the right one."

"Well, you'll know when you meet her," Boyd adds.

"Yeah, well, the last girl I dated cussed like a trucker, hated her brothers, dressed like a nightclub server…"

"Well, surely, there was something good about her."

"Like what sir?"

"Well, she had a pretty smile, nice hair or nails, sweet personality…."

"Keep going sir……"

Boyd laughs, "Oh Eddie, I'll be on the lookout for you."

Eddie tells Boyd he thinks they'll be home about two in the morning.

Ms. Merriwether has a sense of calm about the whole ordeal after talking with the detectives. Terrance demonstrated he took her complaint seriously and was aggressive. She admired commitment in any form. Maebelle is determined not to let anything break her or deter her from complete satisfaction. It is important to her that her friends not think she has clouded judgement. The paper will come out again tomorrow. She expects to be vindicated. Mae continues to think that this erroneous article is the work of something more sinister and not any betrayal from one of her beloved friends. In a few days, they will play bridge at Tommie Lou Maloney's house, and Mae hopes her doubts will diminish. She does not want to verbalize her internal conflict among the bridge group.

Chapter 14

Tommie Lou Maloney has a unique residence on the Ichetucknee River. The property once belonged to her grandparents. The house was originally a small cabin built up high to protect it from the occasional river swelling. Through renovation and lots of tender loving care, the house is larger and is becoming a sanctuary to all who visit. It is hard to imagine that the pristine six-mile river with crystal clear water could overflow beyond its usual twenty-foot width, but it happened. Tommie knows that nature plots its own course and it is that nature and memories of her grandmother and their playing bridge together that keeps her living there. It is September now, and hints of the fall season are starting to appear. In the shaded thickets and shadowy hammocks, there is a change in the foliage that is alluring and captivating. There is plenty for the naturalist to appreciate. There is a vantage point on the porch where one can take in wildlife, exotic flowers, and hear a choir of birds singing in a canopy of cypress tree tops. Tommie Lou loves the no maintenance and invasiveness of the ferns that surround the house. From time to time she throws out wildflower seeds hoping some will take root and adds new metal bird houses. All are simple joys she does for herself. Tommie Lou has a knack for decorating and making guests feel comfortable. However, making dessert for the bridge ladies is sufferable for her.

She will not pretend she is anything akin to Maebelle Merriwether's Southern, by way of Britain, cooking skills.

Tommie does not bake anything, but prepares a disguised crockpot of simmering spices, sure to make the ladies think they are about to experience the best coffee cake in the land.

She is an expert in decorating the table, an expert in being a food stylist and is an expert in leading the ladies to think she is the ultimate homemaker. All the elements are visible: the large glass flour canisters, the wooden dough box, a red gingham apron, and a crock of assorted kitchen tools, none of which Tommie knows how to use. What she does know, is how to use her head and her imagination and make an outing to her house pleasurable.

Yesterday, Tommie ordered a Cream Cheese Pound Cake from a friend and neighbor. She carried one of her grandmother's cake plates over to the neighbor to place the cake on after it was baked. She is planning on serving fresh strawberries to accompany the slices of cake and she will add a dollop of crème fresh. Attending to the simplest of details reveals how important the bridge group ladies are to her. She keeps the recipe close at hand, in case any one of the ladies per chance will inquire.

Of course, the closest she will come to an iron will be the QVC shopping channel on television, so a linen tablecloth is out of the question. It will be perfectly fine to use her best placemats that showcase her bold wood table. She knows an old gentleman who crafts handmade unique birds out of twigs, cones, pods, fibers and the sort that are exquisite. It will be her table favor to the seven ladies that visit her river home.

The natural theme will be carried out in the centerpiece with dried hydrangeas, and interesting little collections she has gathered on her trail walks, like mosses, and lichened pods. She is *almost* ready to receive the High Springs Ladies bridge group.

Tomorrow the bridge group will meet at Tommie's house, and Mae does not want the Collins endorsement to be a topic of conversation while they are playing cards.

Chapter 15

Maebelle is aware she is fidgeting a lot. She feels her stomach tightening and hardening. At times, she can feel her knees are giving way too. Perhaps, her lack of productivity will improve soon. She will have a light supper of cottage cheese and fruit and finish the good book she started. Her telephone rings, and she answers it quickly.

"It's me, Maebelle, Flo," as soon as she hears her voice. "I wanted to know if you need anything. I can bring it to you, because I know you don't feel like going out. Have you been alone all day?"

"No." and immediately she is reminded. *Please don't discuss with anyone we were here Miss Maebelle, the detectives told her.*

"Well, Mr. Henry has been here, as usual, Flo."

"Yes um. I will go now. You know how to reach me."

"Thank you, my dear friend."

Mae enters her kitchen and prepares her supper. She places a small scoop of cottage cheese on top of the salad greens and adds some cantaloupe. She hears a familiar knock and Mr. Henry pops his head in to say goodnight.

"Alright, Mr. Henry. Goodnight, and I think the mums are lovely. Have a pleasant evening."

"Thank you."

Miss Merriwether sleeps better and wakes up early. She is in her robe and she is having her first cup of tea and a scone when Mr. Henry knocks, then steps in the door with the Sunday paper.

She quickly scans it and there it is; bottom right hand corner, third page.

We Apologize

It has been called to our attention that Lady Maebelle Merriwether has not formally announced an endorsement for any sheriff candidate. The Herald strives to report facts, and we regret our article was not completely factual.

"Three lines. Three lines and that represents an apology?" Miss Maebelle reads it out loud once again. She has an almost bitter smile on her face. Her lips part, and she licks them and moves her tea cup in front of her. Her mood is only slightly lifted. *The real culprit is still at large, and I will continue to fight.*

J.W. Collins is also reading the paper. He clenches his hand, pounds the table and his coffee spills. He reaches across the table for his cell phone and dials.

"Hello."

"I thought we had this all sewed up. Instead of wind, that old bag should be filled with lead. I was sure we had a mutual understanding."

"You need to chill. So, she got to the editor and made him retract it. No one can trace it back to me."

"There is no 'me'. It's us. If I am investigated, you're going down with me. You're making big money bleeding the county. You better have my back."

"Relax, we're both making some big bucks."

The call ends abruptly.

Jack starts breathing through his nose and his face tightens. He glances at the clock on the wall. It is time to pick up his amigos and get the squad cars back to the motor pool. They'll be finished in a few minutes and then they all can go to the Rocking H Ranch for his fundraiser. He puts three twenty-dollar bills and three five-dollar bills in his pocket. It is quick money for the guys who have helped him move the cars.

Chapter 16

The fundraiser is sponsored in part by Robinson Ford. They are giving away fifty free car washes and oil changes for folks who give a hundred-dollar contribution. The menu is roasted pig cooked in the ground with all the expected Spanish food fare. Rocking H Ranch employs a lot of Hispanic men, many whom live on the property with their families. It appears that J.W. Collins has a feeling of connection to the Spanish community and openly supports undocumented workers in the town of High Springs.

Ruby Robinson loves parties. Tonight, she is going to wear a white off the shoulder peasant top with red tiny pompon ball trim around the neckline. She has a long layered red cotton skirt and red cowgirl boots. She thinks her silver Concho belt will provide the perfect accessory. Admittedly, Ruby is frustrated at Ron's lack of attention lately, and finds herself spending more than her clothing budget allows. Ron can be irrational at times about her spending. He does not understand she is dressing for success, so she can be a source of pride to him. Ruby finds some large silver hoops in her jewelry box and puts them in her ear lobes and smiles in the mirror as she walks by.

"It's about time we get rolling," and Ron takes one look at his wife.

"God, Ruby, we're not going square dancing, just to dinner. Maybe I need to approve your dress attire before we go out together again." He isn't pleased.

His words sting, and she wants to lunge at him. She crumples and fights back angry tears. No more words are exchanged between them in the car on the way to the ranch. When they arrive, Ron opens his door and walks off leaving her in the seat alone. He meanders through the crowd and is talking politics. She plans on keeping her distance from him for the rest of the evening. *So much for being a source of pride.*

"Hey Ruby," her friends speak in unison. Maxine and Adeline are attending also.

Ruby looks surprised to see them. Maxine offers that their husbands have done a lot of work for the ranch owner, Mr. Hernandez.

"Oh, of course. Ron insists I accompany him to these events, but he always has so many friends to acknowledge."

"You look very pretty tonight, festive," Adeline remarks, looking down at her own denim jeans and tennis shoes.

"Thank you, Ron likes for me to dress up when I go out with him. I should probably go find him."

Maxine says, "He's over there talking to his secretary."

"Okay, he probably has my drink now for me. See you gals tomorrow."

Ruby moves slowly and deliberately toward Ron and Debbie who seem to be enjoying one another's company. The closer she gets, the more uncertain her steps are. Someone grabs her arm, and she turns back to look.

"Señora, a dance maybe?"

Ruby does not know his name but recognizes him as someone who works for Ron. She thinks he is young and foolish, and she does not want to hurt his feelings, so she accepts. He bows slightly and softly says, "After you," and shows her every courtesy and respect on the dance floor.

The song ends, and the boy says "Gracias, senora."

She nods and smiles and turns her head to see if Ron notices she's been dancing. He has moved to the food line, still chumming it up with Debbie. She decides to find a cocktail with her name on it and find the liquid courage within the glass. It goes down smooth and she looks at the bartender.

"If you please," and sets the empty glass down in exchange for a fresh one. She still has a tingle in her throat, so she tries sipping the new drink as she walks away. She smiles to everyone as she makes her way to the buffet line. She glances around, and Ron is oblivious to her whereabouts. She doesn't know why she has bothered to come at all. *From now on, Ron can do his own dirty work.*

Ruby is eating by herself. Other party goers walk by and greet her as she is dining and say hello.

Finally, Ron comes and stands behind her. "I've met a lot of new people, maybe sold a few cars tonight."

"Funny, I haven't met anyone." She knows she sounds snarly and she means to sound that way.

Ron doesn't acknowledge her attitude. "I'm ready to go."

"Of course, you are. You sure you and Debbie don't have anything further to discuss?"

"Let's go," and he grabs her arm to expedite their departure.

They find their car and Ruby gets back in the same way she got out; by herself.

They are pulling out to the highway, and Ron starts dictating that tomorrow he expects her to get some information at the bridge club outing.

"For instance?"

"Like who Maebelle is endorsing. She's holding out for some reason."

"Why don't you leave it alone, Ron? Why do you care who the next sheriff is?"

"I've spent a lot of money investing in Jack. If you know what's good for you, you'll try and convince the old snob." Ruby does not bother to respond to him. She wants to go home and take her boots off.

Ruby is laying down in her bed when she thinks about the next day's bridge outing. She will invite Maebelle to carpool with her tomorrow to Tommie's house on the river.

Chapter 17

Mae dresses early and is having a poached egg on an English muffin when Flo brings her the phone. Flo hands it to her and whispers that Ruby is calling.

"Good morning, Ruby."

"Hey, and good morning to you. I thought we could ride together to Tommie's house if you'd like to go with me."

"Oh, well, that is thoughtful for you to include me. I suppose it is a good idea. Mr. Henry can wash and wax the car while I am gone. I do like to be prompt though."

"Yes, Mae, I'll pick you up at your front door about eleven thirty in the morning."

"Very well, I'll see you then."

Maebelle finishes her breakfast and is sipping tea when Flo comes to retrieve the portable phone.

Flo raises a brow, "Should be interesting at the card table today, don't you think?"

Maebelle blinks, "I hope so, my dear. I'll go get myself ready. Could you alert Mr. Henry that I will be leaving the motor car for him to detail today?"

"Yes, um, shall I look for you something red to wear?" Flo says unable to control her own laughter and leans against the table for fear of falling.

"Florence Williams," Maebelle exclaims. Her mouth twitches and she is laughing also.

Maebelle looks in her closet, and chooses a light, loose blouse. Tommie's house is a bit warmer in temperature than most of the other ladies' houses. She dresses quickly and gathers herself a freshly pressed handkerchief from the bureau drawer. She laughs silently again when she thinks about wearing something red to accompany Ruby.

Mae walks in the kitchen and pours herself some orange juice from the refrigerator. It is cold and refreshing, and she holds the glass alongside her neck. *I am starting to feel the seventy-four years of my life, and I don't think it's a good feeling.*

She places her glass in the sink, walks back to the living room, and begins to read the paper.

An hour passes when Flo comes from one of the bedrooms to find Maebelle.

"Your fire truck has arrived to pick you up," and Flo laughs out loud. "I am a little bit jealous Mae of this new-found friendship developing," laughing out loud a second time.

"Flo, I have found over the years that jealousy is never a pretty thing," and Mae turns her head, so Flo can't see her laughing too.

"Hopefully, Miss Ruby has the good sense to ring the bell and not use her siren," Flo continues to snicker.

The doorbell rings. Flo is all smiles as she pulls the door open. "Good day, Miss Ruby."

"It is a good day, isn't it?" Immediately she sees Maebelle and asks if she is ready.

"Yes, indeed," and Mae winks at Flo and exits the front door.

Ruby has made up her mind that she is not going to discuss the sheriff's election at all today. Secretly, she's thinking she might even vote for the other candidate. Her husband Ron may think she is stupid, but she is quite capable of making up her own mind, and grateful that voting is completely private.

"The weather is delightful, don't you think Maebelle?"

"Yes, quite."

"I imagine it's a bit cooler down at the river where we are going."

"Aye, I suspect" Mae answers.

"Oh, I meant to tell you how beautiful the mums are on your grounds. I don't know how much joy they give you, but I know the entire neighborhood receives joy from driving by your home, Maebelle. It's always lovely.

"It is kind of you to say, Ruby." *And it is, very kind.*

"I believe this is the turn, and Ruby turns into a winding narrow road. One can hear the crunch of the abundant fall leaves under the tires as Ruby drives over them. She slows even more and cannot help noticing the large red maples with all their beauty. The maples are the stars of the road as they approach Tommie's riverside home.

Ruby stops and speaks softly to Maebelle. "I'll go around to open your door. Be careful, those leaves might be slippery."

"Thank you, Ruby." *Can it be I have misjudged her? Time will tell.*

Chapter 18

Some of the other ladies are already seated and talking when Mae and Ruby enter. Tommie greets them both, and states, "We're just waiting on Harriet."

Tommie tells the ladies that just a few moments ago, before everyone arrived, she saw two white tailed deer around by the cypress trees. "At first, I thought it was a white squirrel on one of those big buttressed trunks but then I realized it was the back side of a deer, and then I saw another."

"I suwannee," Maxine and Adeline say in unison.

Tommie continues, "Yes, this is my favorite time of the year. It seems you can see all kinds of wildlife: turkeys, river otters, and wood ducks."

Tommie is interrupted by a hard knock on the door. "It's probably Harriet," and Tommie goes to answer.

Harriet carries in a large farmer's basket of fresh vegetables, brimming with color. She takes off her hat, and gently pats her hair down in case it is out of place.

"Sorry to be late, I just picked these for ya'll. My garden is just starting to produce. It's all organic, and so good for you. Help yourselves."

Everyone is surprised. No one had any idea that she was growing anything, or that she had an appreciation of natural foods.

A light bulb went off in Mae's head about the comment she previously made about cutting the dessert she served in a large portion the week before. However, she quickly remembers Harriet devouring it all up. *Organic? There is a story here.*

Harriet places the basket on the other table and sits beside Betty. Harriet detects a faint smell sitting down, but hopes it is not her perspiration and deodorant that permeates the air with alcohol.

"Welcome, my friends to the river." Tommie smiles. "I always like to give a part of the river to my guests, so ladies, these birds on the table are made especially for you. Each one is handmade by a local artisan and unique like I know you all to be. Don't forget to take one home and nurture it. Let it nest in your home."

Tommie takes the glass cover off her prized pound cake and slices it and plates the pieces for all the ladies to pass around.

"Please pass the strawberries and crème fresh around. Would everyone like coffee, or tea?"

Betty asked if she can just have water and stands up and goes to the kitchen. She returns with a glass of ice and what appears to be water.

Tommie looks over at Julia and asks her to say a prayer of blessing and afterward, the ladies begin to enjoy their desserts.

"Oh my, Tommie, the texture of the cake is outstanding. Did you use cake flour?" Maebelle is inquiring.

Tommie swallows hard and is off guard just a split second. "I'd love to share my recipe with you. I'll go get it, I left it in the drawer."

Adeline comments most of the time that she tends to overcook her pound cakes and sometimes they are dry.

"Well," Tommie says, "all ovens cook differently." *If they only knew whose oven actually cooked it. No worries.*

"My compliments to you Tommie," Ruby joins in the conversation.

"Thank you all," Tommie is elated.

Betty seems a bit nervous and lets everyone know she saw the article of apology in the paper. "The Herald rarely apologizes Maebelle. How did they get that information so wrong? None of us even discussed it last week."

"I'm afraid I have no idea." Maebelle acts and looks perplexed.

Maxine speaks up. "Adeline and I attended J.W.'s fundraiser last evening but I don't think either one of us are voting for him. We were obliged to go to the function with our husbands because they do business with Mr. Hernandez, but I think I can make up my own mind who I think is the better man for sheriff."

"You are so right, Maxine," and their heads nod in the same direction.

Everyone looks at Ruby between bites.

"Right now, I am ready to divorce my husband over this election. Maybe I am just now cognizant of it, but Ron is a complete arse."

No one can believe what they are hearing. Julia Anne starts clapping her hands. "Good for you, Ruby. Stand up for what you believe in."

Betty applauds her too, "That always works for me."

Maebelle Merriwether clears her throat and cannot believe that these timid ladies have suddenly become raucous. Completely unplanned and spontaneously, Maebelle spews, "The British are coming…too…"

The High Springs ladies bridge group is alive and well.

In a few minutes, Tommie removes the bowl of berries and crème from the dining room and puts them back into the refrigerator. She replaces the glass dome on the cake. "Did anyone collect the quarters?"

"I did," Julia Anne answers, "and I believe everyone has participated." Maebelle winks at Julia Anne.

The ladies look at their tallies and find their seats at the card tables. It is all about cards for the next couple of hours. There is a big breeze that comes up through the trees, and a pot of red geraniums falls over on the porch.

Harriet asks Tommie if she ever gets frightened living alone.

"About animals or weather?"

"Oh, I am referring to intruders."

"Well, I keep hoping."

Maebelle gasps. Ruby drops her fork. Harriet chokes. Maxine and Adeline's mouths are both open and Elsa Jane exclaims, "Well, I never, ever heard such."

Tommie realizing that she has blundered big time, offers that she is joking of course. "I am so sorry, truly, I am kidding, of course, I wouldn't wish that on anyone.

Seriously, I know that it is not a laughing matter, I hope you know I'm not serious."

Julia Anne picks up her bird and turns it over to see how it is made. "These are exquisite. Thank you, Tommie."

"You're welcome," feeling relieved she's been rescued from her tasteless joke.

Chapter 19

Elsa Jane speaks up. I have been fairly silent on this sheriff's race but now that I know ya'll are supporting **my** candidate, would anyone be interested as a group to campaign for Daniel Black? We desperately need volunteers in the campaign. Daniel started the campaign late and is behind in our preliminary poll."

"What sort of volunteers?" the ladies inquire.

"We need people to make telephone calls, canvass neighborhoods, and host small gatherings so Daniel can explain his positions of various issues. There is a meeting tomorrow night at the Woman's Club Building. Daniel Black and his family will be there. It is going to be a town forum meeting with people from the audience asking questions. Whoever can show up to help will be appreciated. At the same time, you can get to know the candidate better."

The group is nodding their heads and listening.

"Count me in," Julia Anne exclaims.

"And us too," Maxine speaks for herself and Adeline.

"This will really make my husband mad, but I am ready to join forces and pray Ron doesn't kill me."

Tommie looks at Betty inquisitively and Betty tells the group, "I don't know how much help I can be, but I'll join you."

Tommie adds, "This is a heck of a club meeting." All the ladies turn their eyes on Maebelle and wait.

Maebelle draws in a deep breath and sticks her nose up slightly in the air. "I smell victory for High Springs."

Fresh energy fills the room. It arrives too late to help the card game, but the ladies are united and have purpose.

The quarters are given to the winners and Tommie leaves the ladies to get some plastic bags so they can divide the veggies that Harriet brought. Harriet beams with pride as the gal's remark on the freshness and beauty of the vegetables. Everyone is leaving and they all thank Tommie for her hospitality.

"You're quite welcome. I guess I will see ya'll tomorrow."

Ruby opens the door for Maebelle and places their bags in the back seat. Ruby starts up the car and turns on the air conditioner. "God, give me courage and strength," she blurts out. "I may be getting a divorce soon."

Maebelle turns her head to acknowledge. "My dear, you seem worried and fearful."

"Of course, Ron has told me more times than not that this election is very important to him." Ruby is staring out the window and her voice becomes elevated. "But, I am important also Maebelle, and he treats me like a piece of old dirty candy on a sidewalk."

"You poor dear, your self-respect is worth everything, don't you realize?"

"I'm beginning to, Mae," and Ruby catches herself fighting a sniffle or two.

"I am willing to help you any way I can, Ruby."

Theirs is the last car to pull out of the driveway on their way home.

The silence is finally broken as they pass by the dealership. “Ron never makes it home before nine or ten,” Ruby offers. “Our marriage is not one of togetherness,” she continues.

“Oh dear, I dare say, I don't like to see you full of doom and gloom. Perhaps, some counseling?”

“Maybe,” and Ruby is quiet and focused.

Maebelle waves goodbye to Ruby from her front door entry and ponders on all the events that happened today. Mae rings the bell to her own front door because it is locked.

Flo opens the door, “Thank God you is home Mae.”

“Has something happened? Your face is stained with red.”

“The mailbox, that's what's happened.”

“Did someone hit our mail box, oh dear.”

“No, it's what I found in the mailbox after you left this morning.”

“Whatever are you saying?”

Flo reaches across the foyer table and hands Ms. Mae an envelope. Maebelle continues to walk to the table and sets down her bag. Mae opens the envelope and pulls out a piece of paper with words glued on it, apparently all clipped from a magazine and glued on the paper in some cryptic note. She reads it to herself.

Back Jack or Fall Dead

“You sees what I mean, Mae. Now, someone is threatening you. You has never had an enemy until now.”

“Yes, well, someone is trying to intimidate and scare me, but it will take a little more than this.”

“Well, I am scared. Fall dead, Maebelle? That scares me.”

"The person that sent this is a coward, or they wouldn't resort to such tactics. This is a lot of bully and bark. Whoever it is, this person has a stake in the sheriff's election or they would not be so determined."

"I think you should call the police, Ms. Mae, and right way. I'll go get the phone."

"No, Flo," and Maebelle is looking directly into Flo's eyes. "Flo, we must not share this with anybody. I suspect there is corruption in the sheriff department and calling them will send a message that I am on to their scheming. Other people, investigators, are at work on this problem. I must trust these other folks and let them handle this. I beg you, I must have your word Florence, that you will not speak of this to any of your friends. Are you in this with me all the way?"

"I reckon so, don't see that I have much choice."

"Did you share this with Mr. Henry?"

"He left early to go to the garden store."

"Very well, you may leave also. Flo, remember you mustn't speak about this. I believe the rat will be caught when the trap is laid."

Flo gathers her things and departs. Maebelle sits on her couch and reflects on how she should handle this. She looks at the paper again. It is a piece of stationary, she thinks, with the top letterhead removed. She retrieves her bag from the table, reaches in and finds her cell phone. Two rings and Julia Button answers.

"Hello Julia Anne, I would like to speak to Terry."

"Sorry, he's not home yet from the office."

"Thank you dear, I'll try the office number."

Maebelle dials the offices of Banks, Baum and Button.

A voice answers, "Terrance Button, Esquire. How may I assist you?"

"Hello, this is Maebelle Merriwether calling for Terry, I mean Terrance Button."

"Please hold."

"Hello Maebelle, you just caught me."

"It is my good luck, Terry. I came home from bridge today to find a mysterious note in my mailbox."

"Mysterious how?"

"It is a cryptic note. Words cut out of magazines that spell out *'Back Jack or Fall Dead'*. Of course, Flo panicked and wanted me to call the police, but the detective that visited me made me promise not to contact the local authority."

"You must be ruffling some feathers Mae, by not endorsing J.W. I will attend to this and pick up the note in the morning. Will that be alright?"

"Of course."

"Good, and try not to worry. I'll see you tomorrow around eight after breakfast."

"Very well, thank you Terry. We can have tea. Goodbye."

Chapter 21

Maebelle is alone in her house, and deep in thought. *I am more determined than ever to endorse Daniel Black, and tomorrow night he shall have my endorsement publicly.*

Maebelle wakes early and her breakfast is interrupted by a pounding knock on the back door. Mr. Henry could not wait for Maebelle to answer because he has startling news. He pokes his head in, clearly anxious, and is very animated. He begins a jibber jabber of words, and motions for Ms. Merriwether to come with him.

"Mr. Henry, can't this wait? I am just now having my morning tea."

"No, Maebelle, it cannot wait. His face is beet red; he is perspiring, and he pulls off his sun hat and shoos it quickly. See for yourself."

"Very well," She steps out the back door and walks alongside Mr. Henry, and then abruptly stops. "Mr. Henry. What is it?"

Mr. Henry has trouble speaking. "The mums, look at the mums, and the lilies, they're all dead. Everything is gone, destroyed, down the road in ruin."

Maebelle is squinting in the early morning sun. She adjusts herself and looks upon her normally beautiful gardens. It is a sea of brown, wilted and spent flower blooms everywhere. The beautiful blossoms of yesterday have waned and collapsed. Deterioration is everywhere. The beauty has perished.

Mr. Henry appears lifeless too and looks imploringly at Ms. Merriwether. He is breathless, his eyes are bulging and blinking in rapid succession, and he begins to stutter.

"Who …… would do this?"

Maebelle is trying to comprehend. This is no mistake of Mr. Henry's. Her stance is unmoving as she surveys her once beautiful gardens. Unsmiling, she shakes her head and reaches for Mr. Henry's hand.

"Let us go inside, Mr. Henry and have something cold to drink." their steps are hesitant and heavy as they prop up one another and walk back to the kitchen back door.

"Here, Mr. Henry," and he sits down. "I'll get us some orange juice."

Maebelle pours two glasses of orange juice and joins him at the table. "Drink some Mr. Henry. Won't you join me, everything is okay. It is nothing we cannot replace." She places her trembling hand on his shoulder. His head is bowed, and his skin is still flushed.

In a bit louder tone, Maebelle begs Mr. Henry, "Please drink this now." She finally gets his attention, and he swallows the juice in louder gulps.

"There now," Maebelle softly speaks to him, "everything is all right."

Slowly. Mr. Henry starts to respond, and in a stupefied gaze, utters, "The devil is at work here."

"You may be right Mr. Henry, but we will get our knickers on and fight and stand our ground against whatever force of evil presents itself."

The back door flings open, and Flo arrives, rushing in.

"Is anybody alive in here? Are we having a nuclear disaster? Everything is dead outside. Lordy, we have been dusted. I feel like our front door should have a cross painted on it. Has ya'll called the police now? This is a lot more than bark and bullies. Ms. Mae, this is Star Wars happening to us."

"Flo, please calm yourself and sit down. Some tea will be nice. I am expecting Terrance Button."

"I'd be hoping he brings his Tommie gun. I am scared to death that someone will be poisoning us next."

Maebelle, exasperated, "Flo, please, no more drama. Let's all have tea and let our nerves settle."

Mr. Henry remains quiet.

Mae quietly asks him if he would like to take the day off.

"Mae, I don't know what to do, I don't know where to start."

"You can start by taking off whatever time you need. Whatever help you need to take out the plants, you may certainly hire them. I don't want you to stress any, Mr. Henry. We will plant back."

"But who Miss Mae, who, could do this to you? What is their motive and why?" Someone that is trying to scare me, that's who. But I won't run like a fox with my tail between my legs."

"We will simply inform neighbors we are putting out new top soil, fighting cinch bugs. Mr. Henry, whatever you would like to explain will be fine and will suit me. We mustn't say anything about being threatened or call the police, I beg of you."

Ms. Merriwether is interrupted by the doorbell. Flo rushes to the door and opens it.

"Hi Flo, I believe Maebelle is expecting me." It is Terrance Button.

Maebelle hears his voice and turns to say, "Well, we might as well gather around the table, everyone is involved in this now."

Mae turns to Terry and tells him she will go get the note for him to read.

"Okay, but what has happened to your flowers? Did Mr. Henry kill them with fertilizer?"

Mr. Henry raises his head. "No, this is not fertilizer. Someone deliberately killed the plants with a chemical, probably Roundup or something like it. It will take me two or three weeks to replace the plants."

"This is heinous," and Terry is clearly shocked.

Mae returns with the envelope, pulls the cryptic note out, and hands it to him.

Terrance Button examines the note and puts it back in the envelope. "Tell me what happened outside, Mr. Henry. When did the plants start dying? In your estimation, when was the chemical applied to the grounds?"

Mr. Henry puts his hand up to his head and runs his fingers through his hair. "I would say three or four days ago. If not, the perpetrator used a mighty strong solution. I could take a few specimens up to the county extension office for analysis, but it might create more rumors for Ms. Merriwether."

"I'm sure there will be talk as soon as a few people notice the destruction. I think that getting the dead plants out immediately will deter a lot of gossip. Go about your normal day as if it were planned. I will tell you that a vigorous investigation is underway, and we don't want to tip our hand that it is happening. Eventually, whoever is responsible will slip up and fail to cover their tracks. Please keep our conversations close to your vest for everyone's safety. I will take some pictures of the outside when I leave." Terrance Button slips the note inside his suit jacket and stands up from the table. He puts out his hand to shake with Mr. Henry. "This is none of your doing Mr. Henry. Please try to put this hateful wrongdoing out of your mind." Terrance looks over at Flo.

"There ain't no use in trying to sugarcoat anything with me, Mr. Terry. This is pure evil, the devil's work, destroying beautiful gardens like this. Ms. Maebelle ain't never done any harm to nobody, and she helped everyday folks all the time. I don't know what is going on, but I know this is a job for the FBI, you know, the federal government, that's what I'm thinking."

"Alright, Flo, I hear you. Please keep your ears open and we all need to keep our mouths shut. I insist. It is very important."

Everyone is listening intently. Terrance gives Maebelle and Flo a hug and goes to the door to leave.

Outside, Terrance takes his phone and snaps some instant pictures. He gets in his Jeep and drives away.

Flo is picking up the breakfast dishes as Mr. Henry and Maebelle discuss the new plantings.

Mr. Henry has calmed himself and tells Maebelle he will be leaving for the garden center and will start immediately on the cleanup.

"Very well. Mae calls to Flo and walks toward her into the kitchen. I brought home some fresh eggplant from the bridge game yesterday and I look forward to a little casserole for lunch. Late this afternoon, I will be going to the town forum meeting for Mr. Daniel Black at the Woman's Club Building. The bridge group has unanimously decided to begin working in his behalf to get him elected."

"The whole bridge club? Including Ruby, don't take your love to town? That same one? How in the world did that happen? Did she find out Mr. Black's favorite color is red? Oh boy, I think her husband will be angry when he knows she is supporting the other candidate with *his* money. Lordy, this is too much excitement for ole Flo. Sure nuff is. I say, Ms. Mae, you *is* spitting at danger."

"Florence Williams, I say, you do go on a bit much."

Chapter 22

Since the forum is an evening affair, Maebelle decides to dress in a suit. Mr. Black is completely unaware of her intention to endorse him but that is exactly what Maebelle has in mind. Her husband Thomas taught her to fight fire with fire and she fully intends to set the forum ablaze. It will be exciting.

Before Flo leaves for the day, she brings the Chrysler around to the side door for Maebelle's convenience.

"I will be happy to drive you to the meeting, Ms. Mae."

"Thank you, Flo, but I want to appear unafraid and forthright. I will try to be calm and straight forward. And no offense, but I can't be that when you are by my side with your eyes darting all over the room. But, thank you for offering my dear friend."

"Yes, um."

Maebelle is heading out the driveway slowly, almost tearful surveying all the damage of her destroyed flowers. No doubt, the gardens will make a comeback, and it will happen sooner than some people might think.

The parking lot is about half full, and Mae turns in and parks with resolve and determination. Getting out, she waves to Elsa Jane. Immediately, Elsa Jane hurries to catch-up so they can enter the forum together. The crowd is larger than Maebelle expects. Nonetheless, she patiently waits her turn to be introduced to Daniel Black.

He has a firm handshake and engages Maebelle with his eyes. She likes that he listens to her question intently and does not rattle some rehearsed talking points. Daniel Black's wife is conservatively dressed, displaying grace and natural beauty. Maebelle finds the pair to be unpretentious and genuine.

A worker in the campaign asks that everyone be seated, so that Candidate Black may address the audience and answer some questions. He steps up to the microphone and rests his hands on the top of the podium.

"Thank you for coming to our forum. I'd like to thank the host couples for planning the forum and for setting everything up and providing the lovely refreshments. I appreciate it very much. I am a conservative running for the office of sheriff and I am a registered Republican. I have not lived here all my life like most of you good folks, but my heart is here, and I want to make a difference in the way our sheriff's department is run. As a firm believer that everyone must pay their own way, I want to see savings for the taxpayers, and some real cost cuts. We can do this by bidding out a lot of our repairs and maintenance for the building as well as our county vehicles. My education is in business, and I…

There is a stir at the back of the room, and murmurs echo from the crowd. J.W. Collins has walked into the meeting and is looking for a seat.

Someone yells from the back. "What are you doing here? We came to hear Daniel Black."

Jack turns his head, and in a boisterous, arrogant laugh says, "Well, I did too. I came to hear how he proposes to run our sheriff's department when he has no experience. He has never been in law enforcement. He pushes a pencil for a living. This is a public forum, isn't it?"

Folks are getting irritated, mumbling under their breath, and control of the group is slipping away.

Daniel leans into the podium and chuckles. "Yes, this is a public forum for invited guests that are contemplating supporting my candidacy, J.W. We did not invite you nor want your input. Daniel glowers and points his finger at J.W. Your arrant behavior in coming here tonight is indicative of a candidate that divides our community and frankly your presence is most objectionable. Please leave now and try to conduct yourself more professionally." The small crowd stands up and applauds.

J.W. appears embarrassed for a few seconds, but quickly gains composure, squaring his shoulders. In a strong voice, he says "I will be out in the parking lot for anyone who wishes to hear my viewpoint on real issues."

It takes a few seconds for people to settle down. Mr. Black, wearing a half smile utters, "This has to be a first. If I may continue, Mr. Collins mentioned I was a pencil pusher. It's more like an adding machine operator. I've had a career in business, and proven track record of managing large budgets, and I think this is what High Springs needs in its sheriff department. I invite you to submit pertinent questions to my inbox at *danielblackforsheriff.com.*

I will answer all inquiries and look forward to hearing from you, the people. Thank you."

A photographer from the Herald is snapping a few pictures, and Maebelle decides she will give the Herald another headline. She walks up to the podium and clears her throat.

"Hello friends, I prefer to be a bit less conspicuous, but I am stirred by the solid candidacy I am witnessing and Mr. Black's ability to be straightforward in his approach. Therefore, I would like to pledge my support tonight for Daniel. Tonight, I will be writing a check to his campaign and urge my friends who care about our local government to do the same."

The applause is overwhelming.

"Thank you so much, Ms. Merriwether. I won't let our community down." Daniel is smiling and seems very appreciative.

"You're welcome. It is my pleasure."

The photographer swings around and captures a nice picture of candidate Black and Merriwether together.

The folks are getting out of their seats. Most of the ladies' bridge group is in attendance, and they make their way over to Ms. Maebelle's side and give her kudos. Maebelle appears jubilant especially after her harrowing day and meanders through the meeting room to greet old acquaintances.

Chapter 23

It is time for Maebelle to be leaving and she tells Elsa Jane she is happy to be participating. She steps outside to her car and gets in it to drive home. Maebelle travels down the road for about two miles when she realizes she negated to give the campaign chairman her personal check. She puts her blinker on and turns in to a driveway, and then backs out to the road and head backs east on the highway. Everyone will still be there. It won't take but a few minutes, she says to herself.

She has trouble seeing and realizes the car approaching is flashing their bright lights on her and is crossing the center line. They are getting closer and closer and she makes the decision to go farther on her side. She underestimates the loose gravel on the shoulder and control of her vehicle is lost. The car flips on its side and slides down alongside an embankment. Small trees and bushes finally cause her Chrysler to slow, then rest in a pile of dirt.

The traffic is cordoned off by the police as a helicopter lands on the highway and Maebelle is carried on a stretcher and is airlifted to Shands Hospital in Gainesville. She is in grave condition, with multiple injuries, by all accounts.

Ron Robinson tells the investigator he was driving home from work, at a speed much slower than he usually drives and met her vehicle. She veered off the main highway to the side of the road.

"Yes, I told her that an ambulance was enroute, and she just checked out. Officer, I called one of the wreckers at my dealership as a courtesy to Ms. Maebelle."

"I'll have her car towed to the yard where it will be safe until she decides what she wants to do with it. Anything I can do to help, I'll do. She's a grand lady, I hope she recovers."

Ron walks to his truck and gets in and starts the engine. He speaks to the passenger now crouched in the floorboard.

"Stay down there until I get clear of all the lights, and police."

"Is she going to live?"

"I don't know, they are transporting her to Shands. I'll drop you off at the house."

"I'm so tired of being the dirty little secret Ron, I feel like a criminal hiding like this."

"Oh, here we go again, can't you just be patient. Am I not taking care of you?"

"I think it is me that is taking care of you."

"Seriously? All you do all day long is watch your soaps and bag some marijuana. That's not asking too much of you when you live rent free, and have a car provided, is it? I thought you were enjoying our little arrangement."

She doesn't answer him and continues to sulk.

"By the way I will be getting another parcel in tomorrow."

Ron pulls up to a secluded overgrown driveway and drives down to a house. He turns off his engine and leans over and kisses her hard.

"Ouch Ron, you bit my lip."

"Well, I thought you liked it rough."

"I think you have forgotten what I like."

"Alright, be mad, I'll see you tomorrow. Go on, get inside." She slams the door behind her and doesn't look back as he is driving off.

Ron Robinson arrives home at ten o'clock. Ruby is asleep in the bedroom. *That talk he had with her this afternoon probably tired her.*

Ruby's cheek is still swollen, and she has a bruised lip in the morning when she gets up. She does not want to face the bastard today. She might kill him for the way he treated her yesterday. She knows she hit a trigger with him when she announced she was going to the Daniel Black forum. *Ron's demeanor is constantly changing. He'd better watch his step. She knows she is no match for his physical brute, but she will not be powerless. Their relationship, long in decline, is existing in a house sitting on sand, and she is not about to be pulled down in it. The pittance he doles out monthly to her is insufficient to say the least. She is intelligent. She will find a way.*

Chapter 24

A deputy arrives at Flo's residence at ten forty. It takes Flo several minutes to realize someone is ringing her front doorbell. With robe in tow, she yells through the door. "Who is it?"

"Ms. Williams, it's the Alachua County Sheriff's Department."

The door opens enough for the safety latch to catch.

"Step back, so I can see your uniform and badge."

"Yes, ma'am."

Flo surveys the officer and looks onto the street and sees his patrol car.

"I been right here, all night, watching my television, ain't seen nothing."

"Yes, ma'am." He pauses. "Ms. Williams, I need to tell you, Ms. Merriwether has been involved in an accident. We need to reach her next of kin."

The door opens wide, and she tells the man to come in. Flo is visibly shaken and sits down.

"I know where she keeps her 'in case of death papers.' I'll go get dressed."

"Ms. Williams, she hasn't died, she's badly injured. I believe she has been transferred to Shands in Gainesville."

"Thank the Lord for that one."

"Ma'am, I'm need a relative's name to contact."

"Her daughter is in Guatemala and the orphanage number she works in is at Ms. Merriwether house in her desk. I'll have to call you tomorrow with it."

"Ms. Williams, I will drive you to the house now or I can follow you to the Merriwether home and wait while you get the information."

"Oh, okay, of course. It has to be done now. I wasn't thinking. What happened?"

"She ran off the road on the way to town about nine fifteen in the evening."

"Ran off the road? That does not sound like Maebelle Merriwether. Let me get dressed."

"Yes ma'am, I'll wait outside for you."

"Yes, you will."

Flo dresses quickly, finds her purse and a sweater hanging up beside the door, and then steps outside. 'You can follow me. I may spend the night at the Merriwether estate."

Flo makes a mental list about who she should call when she arrives. First, she will call Terrance Button, then Mr. Henry.

Flo arrives at the estate in a few minutes, and the deputy pulls in behind her. She unlocks the door and turns on the lights. Flo lays her purse down on the table and continues walking to the library where all of Ms. Merriwether's important papers are stored. She sits at the desk and sifts through various papers.

"Here it is, Penelope's address and phone number." She hands the information to the deputy.

"I do not know what time it is in Guatemala, but whatever it is, it is important that we call now. May I use the phone?" the deputy asks.

"I reckon you can."

The deputy dials.

"St. Mary's Orphanage," is heard after the second ring.

"Hello. I am calling from the USA, Florida. Do you have a Penelope Merriwether there? Her mother has been involved in a car accident."

"Please hold the line."

The phone is answered again. "This is Penny Merriwether."

"Yes ma'am. Officer Brian with Alachua County Sheriff Department. I am with Florence Williams at your mother's residence. Your mother, Maebelle, has been involved in a car accident and has been transferred to Shands Hospital in Gainesville. We are notifying the next of kin.

There is no response at first. "Is she injured badly?"

"I do not have that answer. It happened almost two hours ago. It was a single car accident involving only Maebelle."

"I understand. I will plan to get the first flight out. Thank you, officer. May I speak to Florence please?"

Flo takes the phone, "Hello Penny."

"Flo, I will call you when I have a reservation. If I can't reach you, I will call Terry, but I should be there sometime tomorrow."

"Yes um, I am excited to hear you is, are, I mean, coming home."

"Okay, I'll see you soon."

"Yes um." Flo hangs up the phone.

The deputy turns to leave and asks Flo if she will be alright.

"Yes sir, I am going to call Ms. Merriwether's attorney, Terrance Button."

Flo searches the address book and flips through it to find Terrance's phone number. She finds Julia Button in the listing. This number will do. She dials the number.

Julia Button answers.

"Miss Julia, this is Florence calling. Ms. Merriwether was at the meeting tonight for Daniel Black." She catches her breath.

"Yes, it was exciting. She stood up and endorsed him and gave a financial contribution. The bridge club is supporting him, you know."

"Yes um, Ms. Merriwether was involved in a car accident tonight. The police came and told me. I need to speak to Mr. Terrance as soon as possible."

"Oh, no, I'll go take the phone to him."

Flo is nervously waiting on the phone for him to pick up.

"What has happened Flo? Tell me what has happened."

Flo explains that the police knocked on her door and told her about the accident. Ms. Maebelle was airlifted to Shands. I don't know what is injured, Mr. Terry, but I got the number for Miss Penny and the police called her. She says she was coming immediately."

"Can you give me her number, Flo? I will touch base with her and pick her up from the airport. I will drive to Shands tonight and find out the extent of her injuries."

"Here is the number. I will get the house ready to receive Miss Penny. Please tell Ms. Mae I am praying for her."

"Thanks, Flo, I know you will, and thank you for calling me."

Chapter 25

The triage unit of Shands was prepared to receive Ms. Merriwether. The flight crew advised the hospital that Ms. Merriwether was slipping in and out of consciousness. Her blood pressure was low, and she was being given fluids. They administered saline solution over a large wound on her lower thigh area. She appeared banged and bruised on one side of her head and her left shoulder. The medic did not have any statistics on medications, age of patient, or anything else that could be helpful. The Alachua Sheriff Department was on the scene and would be in contact with the hospital soon. Perhaps the information gathered would be beneficial in treating her.

The helicopter lands, and a team of hospital workers rush to attend to her. Immediately, they begin to ascertain her injuries. One of the nurses ask Ms. Merriwether if she can hear them and understand. With eyes wide, she weakly nods her head. She is grimacing in pain and all of the nurses are trying to be easy with her. The emergency room doctor in charge is shouting out orders to the various staffers in the room. A large gaping wound of severely damaged tissue seems to be the focus of concern. The doctor calls in a plastic surgeon for his opinion.

An aide from the desk area tells the doctor an attorney representing Ms. Merriwether is waiting for him in one of the family rooms.

In a waiting area, Terrance Button calls the Merriwether home and speaks to Flo again.

"I'm here at the hospital and it has occurred to me that you might know Maebelle's daily medications. Can you read off the prescription bottles to me? I don't know anything yet, Flo. I haven't spoken to any doctor." He pauses, "Yes, I'll wait for you to go get them."

Terrance writes down the information. "Incidentally, Flo, how old is Maebelle?"

Flo answers that she is going to be 75 this year.

Two officers appear in the waiting room, hearing that Ms. Maebelle's attorney is there waiting.

One officer extends his hand to Terrance's and introduces himself.

"Currently, all indicators are that she left the road off the right shoulder. She was headed east back to town. An approaching truck saw the whole thing happen. He is a local resident who owns the Ford dealership in High Springs."

"Say what? Do you mean Ron Robinson?"

"Yes, that's him. Very helpful man had her vehicle towed there to the maintenance yard. Apparently, he knows her."

"Lots of people know Maebelle Merriwether." Terry looks over as a doctor enters the room. He walks over to Terrance and begins speaking.

"I'm the emergency room physician. Our patient is suffering from many injuries. She has a broken foot, a dislocated shoulder, and a thigh that we really don't know how to close the wound."

"We have called in a plastic surgeon to advise us, and we are getting her ready for surgery. That will probably take a few hours. I understand you are her attorney. Do you have power of attorney, to sign the necessary papers?"

"Yes, I can do that. Her daughter will be arriving back in the United States sometime tomorrow."

"Well, we will know something soon when the plastic surgeon has had a chance to thoroughly examine the wound."

"I don't understand. Why can't the wound be closed?"

"Something hit the leg with such force that it broke the skin and damaged a lot of soft tissue. There is no skin to replace. The wound is subject to immediate infection. Grafting it at this time without debridement will be ill advised given the amount of sand and debris we have tried to clean out of the wound. In surgery, the foot will be set, they will look at that shoulder, suture a couple of cuts above her eye, and figure out what they are going to do about the leg. It is likely the plastic surgeon will take over her long-term care. She is probably facing several surgeries, but most likely it will be another doctor's call."

One of the officers jump into the conversation and offer that Ms. Merriwether was trapped in her car upside down and it might have been the steering column that hit her leg.

The doctor does not comment and tells Terrance that he will be sending the surgeon in to speak to him if he is going to be staying there in the waiting area.

"I'll be here. I am a friend of hers, as well as her personal attorney. Thank you, Doctor."

Terrance turns toward the officer. "Am I to understand, that Mr. Robinson was driving the vehicle that was meeting her on the highway, driving toward Ms. Merriwether?"

"Yes. He said he saw her veer off and he stopped and called the ambulance."

Terrance listens intently and thinks it a strange coincidence that Ron was meeting Maebelle head on, and wondered why she was heading back into town, away from her house. He glances at his watch and decides the phone call he has in mind making can wait till tomorrow. He calls his wife Julia instead.

"Hey honey, I am here in the waiting area. A doctor just came in and said she has multiple injuries. She will be going into surgery soon. Listen honey, did anything happen at the meeting tonight?"

"Happen? Maebelle gave Daniel her support right after J.W. Collins made an ass of himself showing up at another candidates' forum. That takes a lot of gonads."

"Julia! Your language."

"I am just being truthful. Maebelle said she was supporting him and giving him a check to help with the campaign."

"And did she present a check?"

"Not that I can remember. Have you seen Maebelle yet?"

"Oh, no, she is in the emergency room, going into surgery soon. I will be here tonight waiting in the surgery waiting room. At least until she is in her own room and I can lay eyes on her. Goodnight Julia."

Terrance fixes himself some coffee and reflects on all that has happened in the last few days. *The note, the plants and flowers, now this. Tomorrow he will call the states attorney and see how they are doing on the investigation.* He grabs a couple of magazines off one of the tables in the sitting room. A few hours pass and the phone right next to him rings.

"Hello,"

"Is there family waiting to hear about Maebelle Merriwether?"

"Yes, I am."

"This is the recovery nurse; the doctor will be right in to speak to you."

"Oh, thanks."

In thirty minutes, in unhurried fashion, a doctor walks in the room, still in scrubs, and looks at Terry. "Merriwether?"

"Yes."

"Please step over here." He is holding a couple of pictures and inserts them in the lighted box.

"Here are the injuries." He points to the first film. "She has a broken foot in several places. Often, we find in car accidents, that drivers tend to press hard on the floorboard, it is a reflex action trying to brake anywhere you can. I inserted three pins," and shows Terry where they are located.

"We sutured two cuts above her eye and one on her forehead and took out some pieces of glass. Her shoulder also needed a pin and I repaired a tear on the rotator cuff up here," and he points. "The plastic surgeon is coming in to talk to you."

The door opens again, and another doctor and a nurse walk over and shake Terrance's hand.

He extends his hand, "Jeff Hays, head of the plastic surgery department and this is my surgical assistant."

"I hope we have a strong female in Merriwether. This is a difficult injury to mend." He opens a file folder he is carrying and shows a picture to Terry.

"Wow," Terry exclaims.

"Wow is correct, as we cannot close the wound now. We have packed it and hope we do not get any infection. The leg is wrapped in gauze and tomorrow we will monitor her white and red blood counts and play the waiting game. She will need a skin graft; how large I do not know. If infection gets in, we will take her back to surgery for additional debridement.

"What is that, Doctor?" Terry has no idea.

"Basically, it is high powered jets of water that remove dead or decaying skin or tissue. She may lose tissue every day, she may even lose her leg. It will be touch and go for a few days. She will be in a room shortly. I imagine she will be asleep, but you can be in there with her."

With grave expression on his face, Terry thanks the doctor. The nurse speaks up and lets Terry know that Ms. Merriwether will be going to room 1500.

"Okay, thanks again," Terry tells them both as they are leaving. Terry decides to go by her room regardless if she is asleep. Afterwards, he'll drive home to get whatever sleep he can.

Tomorrow, Penelope will be arriving, and he will need to pick her up at the airport. Perhaps she will let him know something soon about her travel plans.

Terry passes by the nurse's station and enters Maebelle's room. She is being attended by a team of nurses taking vitals. He hears Maebelle moan and asks the nurse if she is in pain.

"I am getting her injection ready now. She is going to be out of it for the night."

"It is pitiful to see her like this." *She looks utterly pallid and helpless.*

Terry turns to one of the aides. "I'd like to leave a note on the table for her."

It's now four a.m. in the morning my dear Mae. I will be back tomorrow. Hang tough! Love you, Terry.

Flo and Mr. Henry are having coffee at the side table in the kitchen.

Flo looks at Mr. Henry, "Miss Penny is coming home to a real mess."

"That's for sure. I wish the grounds looked better. I was only able to plant back a little block yesterday. It will take several weeks to get it back looking like it was."

Chapter 26

The front door bell rings and both Flo and Mr. Henry jump in their seats. Simultaneously, they go to the window.

"Ms. Maebelle would scold us for looking at the window first, like peeping Toms," Flo says, "but these days, surprises have not been good ones." She peers out from the curtain, "and today don't look like an exception. It's Ruby Red Grapefruit if you know what I mean" … and points to her brain and makes circles with her pointer finger.

Flo opens the door. Immediately, Flo notices Ruby's bruised cheek and a sore on her bottom lip. "Good Morning Miss Ruby. Did you have a wreck too?"

"It was carelessness, that's all. Mr. Henry, did you over fertilize? Everything was so beautiful, and now it's all dead."

"Kind of you to notice."

"We are having coffee in the kitchen. You are welcome to join us."

"Okay, is Maebelle sleeping in? I couldn't go to the meeting last night. I stopped by to ask her how everything went."

"Oh, Ruby, Ms. Maebelle was in an accident last night. She is at Shands. We are waiting now to hear something from Mr. Terrance. Miss Penelope is on her way here from Guatemala. I already got her room ready. I spent the night here."

"What? In her car? Oh, dear God. I have not heard. Do the ladies of the bridge club know?"

Flo looks at Mr. Henry. "We have no idea."

Flo leaves to go answer the phone. "Good Morning to you too. Yes sir."

She listens while the caller talks for a few minutes, and then she answers, "She is a strong woman, Mr. Terrance, I got to believe she will pull through this. Mr. Henry is with me now. Ms. Robinson has just come over and is here too."

She is listening to Terrance intently, "Yes. Mr. Terrance, we remembered. Well, let me write this down, because I know the bridge ladies will want to know the facts. Hold on, a second, please."

Flo grabs up the nearest pen and note pad she can find and begins writing. There is silence from Flo as she writes. Her face is pained, and small tears form at the corners of her eyes. "Yes, sir. I know you do too. Goodbye."

Looking at Flo, Ruby gives way to her emotion and gives Flo a big hug. Ruby tells them she is going to call the church and get a prayer chain going.

Flo nods her head, and says "The Almighty is the Great Physician, that's for sure."

Ruby states that she is on her way to the hair dresser and she will stop by the florist and order Ms. Maebelle some beautiful flowers.

"Yes um, that will be nice."

"Goodbye, Mr. Henry. Flo, I'll see myself out."

Flo immediately turns to Mr. Henry and relays the information about Mae's condition. "Mr. Terrance also reminded me we aren't to speak to anyone about what has been happening around here."

Mr. Henry says he is going to start on another block of plantings, and he walks outside, putting on his big straw hat.

Chapter 27

Ruby's appointment isn't until eleven o'clock. She has plenty of time to stop by the dealership and get her monthly check. Seeing Ron will put a damper on her day. Ignoring him will be her best recourse. She pulls in, parks, and walks through the showroom to her husband's office.

Debbie, Ron's secretary for over two years, is typing away on her computer, and is startled by Ruby's hovering.

"I stopped to get my check." Instantly, she is irritated because she sees a planter on Debbie's desk. Ruby recognizes it as one of the plants Ron sends on a regular basis to clients and friends.

"May I?" as she plucks the card from the dish garden.

Thanks, sweetie, for all you do for me, The "Big" Boss.

Ruby holds the card in her hand and stares at Debbie.

Debbie feels the intimidation and offers to tell Ruby that she had picked up a package for him from J.W. Collins at the sheriff's department.

"Oh, how thoughtful of you."

"Uh, Ron is in a meeting with the sales guys."

"Would that be 'Big' Ron?"

"It's a diet joke between us," and Debbie is embarrassed having to explain once again. "Here is your envelope," Smiling, Debbie hands it over.

Ruby feels demeaned thinking Ron's secretary is privy to their financial agreement and openly demonstrates her resentment.

Ruby comments, "Remember the grass always looks greener on the other side, but rarely is." Ruby briskly walks out to the parking lot and drives off. On the way to the beauty shop, she uses her cell phone and starts dialing the florist. She is on the phone walking in to the salon telling the flower lady that she wants a one-hundred-dollar Victorian arrangement delivered to Maebelle Merriwether in Gainesville.

The florist tells Ruby she just took an order earlier from the dealership for a planter.

"This is a different order but bill it to my husband, Ruby explains. Please sign the card, with love from your neighbors, The Robinsons. Thank You. I guess you know where to send them." Ruby hangs up. She loves letting people know she lives next to Maebelle. *Sort of...*

Glancing over, she sees Elsa Jane under the dryer. Ruby sits down beside her and pulls the hair dryer up so she can talk to Elsa Jane.

Elsa Jane asks if her face is bruised or was that eye shadow?

"Oh, just some carelessness. Did you go to the forum last night?"

"Oh, heavens yes. Daniel Black gave an outstanding talk, even stood up to J.W. Collins after he so rudely showed up. Maebelle endorsed Daniel, and gave him a financial contribution, although she forgot to give the check to me."

"I was just there at Maebelle's house. Flo said she had a car accident last night and is in the hospital now. She told me Penelope is on her way home."

"Oh no, we'll have to go and see her, although I can't go for a couple of days. The campaign has me stuffing campaign literature into mailers. The committees are ramping everything up, striving to get momentum. Last night, I felt the energy from the crowd. I haven't felt this good about a cause since I did the welcome wagon basket for new people moving in to High Springs. That was a long time ago."

Ruby answers, "That *was* a long time ago." *Anybody that thinks the south is going to rise again would most certainly remember welcome wagon. Not amazing.*

The exchange between them ends as Ruby is called by the colorist and Ruby follows her to the back of the shop. Ruby thumbs through some magazines while the color sets on her hair. She notices a Spanish model on the front cover, and Ruby thinks of Penelope living in that foreign country, wondering how much Penelope has changed.

Chapter 28

Terrance is almost at the regional airport in Gainesville. Penelope used her brains and purchased a puddle jumper ticket to get from Miami to Gainesville.

The memories of his relationship with Penelope floods his mind. He wonders if he will even recognize her. He parks the car, and heads for baggage claim. Someone about Penelope's height dressed in a colorful striped tunic and a large hat, wearing a pair of huaraches captures his attention. He can only see the back of her, but he walks right up and says, "Welcome Home." A weathered stranger turns around with almost no teeth and smiles at him.

"So, sorry, I thought you were someone I know."

"Looking for me?" Penelope pulls at his jacket. "You are as lost as ever. Same ole Terry," she exclaims, and reaches up to give him a hearty hug.

"Penny, you are home at last, and you are a sight for sore eyes." He means it. Her hair is auburn, long, beautifully streaked by the sun rays, he is sure. She is a woman that has taken care of herself. She is fit, and her skin looks supple and conditioned. He hugs her again.

"You haven't changed much Terry, just a little more distinguished."

"I'm hearing handsome."

"I'm saying notably unmatched. You're still full of it, I see."

"It's part of my continuous charm. Do you have luggage?"

"One large, coming around now," and she points to it.

It has custom tags all pasted on it. Terry laughs when he sees it. "Still smuggling contraband, I see. Bringing in Mayan artifacts from museums?"

"You know me well."

"Madame, if you will follow me. Do you want to get right to the hospital?"

"Yes of course."

Penny slings her Boho handbag over her shoulder and walks beside Terry.

He finds his car, opens her door for her and they buckle up and begin the short trek to the hospital.

"Good flight?"

"Not really, I am worrying about Mum. What are her injuries?"

"I haven't checked in since I left at four this morning. I'm not going to distort the facts, so brace yourself."

"Spoken like a lawyer."

Terry sighs, "She has a long road to recovery. It is her leg. Today, when we arrive, the prognosis might be better. I'm hoping that infection won't set in, but she has an open wound the doctors cannot close yet. But the old gal is an iron gate, if anybody can rally, she can and will. And there are other problems, Penny. I have about twenty minutes to give you some information." Terrance shares all the ongoing investigation, and his speculation, her visit to his office and concerns he has.

"This is a lot to absorb Terry. Mentally, my mother is an unmeasurable benchmark, but physical injury might weaken her more than we expect. We'll see how it goes. Does she know I'm coming?"

"I haven't told her. After surgery she was admitted into her own room. I went home, showered, and came to pick you up."

"I'm forever in your debt old friend."

"She's very special to me too, Penny."

For several miles more, there is silence in the car.

"We have arrived," Terry announces. "I'm going to let the valet park us, so we can get right up there to the room."

"Thanks, Terry."

Terrance hands his keys to the boy hustling over to his car as he's getting out and grabs the ticket the boy hands him. He takes Penny's hand and shows her the nearest elevator.

Entering the room, neither are prepared for what they see. Once vibrant, Maebelle looks like she has aged fifteen years. Penny sits down beside her mother she lovingly calls Mum, leans in and kisses her bruised hand. Maebelle stirs and cracks her eyes. Buoyed with emotion, Penny begins speaking in a soft voice. "Hey Mumsy, it's me, just like a bad penny, I always show up." She reaches up to kiss Maebelle's forehead and then her cheek. A tear drops from the corner of her mother's eye.

"Mumsy, I'm here to take care of you. I need you to be strong and get better. Squeeze my hand if you know I'm here."

Maebelle squeezes, yet her eyes are still closed.

The nurse comes in and tells Terrance that Ms. Merriwether experienced a rough night.

"We have kept her sedated, so she won't move her foot or leg."

"I understand," Terry replies.

Penny becomes emotional. "Has a doctor been in today?"

The nurse tells her no, neither of them, but they are expected. Terry motions for Penny to step out of the room with him.

In the hallway, Terry says someone needs to be there to ensure one of them will hear what the doctor will say when he arrives. He suggests he go down to the cafeteria and get them a sandwich or a nice salad.

"That is very thoughtful. Yes, anything will be good. I don't want to be gone and miss any information."

Terry leaves and Penny returns to the room and sits beside her mother.

She reaches in her handbag and pulls out a comb and a couple of hair clips. She stands up and combs her mother's hair and adds a couple of the clips "Now Mumsy, you look freshened." She eyes some lotion on the table and squeezes some into her hand and gently rubs it on her mother's arms and hands. Maebelle squeezes Penney's hand. Penny knows for sure she is aware that she is here. "Mumsy, I'm home. It won't be long now till we go home and see Flo and Mr. Henry."

The nurse returns and tells Penny it's almost time for pain medication.

"Can't we hold off a bit and see if she can wake up?"

"Of course, please call me if she becomes uncomfortable."

"Nurse, can she have liquids and food?"

"Yes, water, I'm not sure about food. Nothing till the doctor comes in and checks the reports from the mornings blood work. His assistant did call the floor nurse and said the doctor will be making the rounds within the hour."

Terry breezes in with a sack of goods. "She already looks better."

"I think so, I combed her hair. Mum would not want to be a mess," and Penny smiles.

Terry opens the bag and brings out a couple of sandwiches, and two small salads.

"If you want to split a sandwich with me, that'll be great, and I'll eat one of the salads," Penny suggests.

"That is fine with me."

They are eating their late lunch and do not notice the doctor has arrived and is reviewing Maebelle's charts outside the door.

He enters the room as Penny hurriedly swallows and wipes her mouth. She extends her hand. "I am Penny Merriwether, Doctor. Tell me how my mother is doing."

"For her injuries, remarkably well. The sedatives are starting to wear off, and we will see how much pain she will be able to tolerate. Everything will heal in time."

"Her leg injury is extensive, and the damage may expand some more. She has lost a lot of soft tissue, and that tissue has been exposed to bacteria. Right now, the blood report is good. If we can keep infection out, she will be able to get the skin graft, and then that area will begin to heal too. It is touch and go for a few days."

"I understand and thank you for explaining it to me. Are you giving mother antibiotics now?"

"Yes, all we can, without damaging the liver and other organs," the doctor explains.

"How about food? I'm worried she will go down without some nourishment."

"I will put on the orders she may eat, but I doubt she will want much for a few days. We will see what she can tolerate. Alright, I'll talk to you later."

"Thank you, Doctor."

Terry shakes his hand and the doctor leaves quickly.

Maebelle stirs and slowly opens her eyes. She looks at Terry and smiles.

"There it is, what I've been waiting for."

She looks over to Penelope unable to contain her biggest smile. She moves her hands and waves her fingers in a motion for her daughter to come closer. Penny kisses both of Maebelle's shining cheeks. They both have happy tears dripping from the corners of their eyes.

"Mumsy, are you thirsty?" Maebelle nods her head yes. Terry grabs the Styrofoam cup of water with a straw in it and places it up to her mouth.

Surprisingly, Maebelle raises her hand and holds it steady. She drinks it slowly and nearly finishes it all.

"Thank you, my mouth is dry. Penny, sweet girl of mine. I thought I heard your voice. I thought I was dreaming. It is you," and Maebelle is beaming with love, and her face brightens. She looks down at her foot and then her leg. "Oh, dear me. This is quite a bandage. Am I going to be okay?"

Penny stands back, takes Maebelle's hand and sits down beside her.

"Mumsy, I sure hope so. You have a broken foot, and your leg has a big gash in it. The doctors are worried about infection setting in, you'll need a skin graft to close the open wound."

"I will? Oh dear, doesn't sound like we're going home any time soon."

"We need to be patient, Mumsy. You took quite a spill."

Mae has a distant gaze on her face. Clearly, she is thinking back in time.

Terry speaks softly, "Do you know what happened?"

Mae continues to drift in thought. "I was heading back to town to give Daniel Black my check. I forgot to give him my five-thousand-dollar pledge. I was heading back to the forum, when a truck forced me off the road."

"Did you say forced?"

"Yes, he forced me. He was coming at me, fast, over the center line and then on my side, I had no choice but to go off the road. The side of the road was bumpy, and I guess I lost control."

"I was trying to stop. Did they find my check? How 'bout my Chrysler? Is it drivable?"

"Everything will be fine, Mumsy, we'll find the check, and see about getting you another car. Had you made out the check yet?"

"No, it was blank, but the amount was filled in, and I had signed it." Suddenly, Maebelle looks worried.

"Oh," and Penny glances around and looks at Terry.

"I'm on it." and Terry steps out to the hallway.

He places a call to the local banks and explains that he is the attorney for the Merriwether estate and if anyone tries to cash the check, please call the authorities, and please stop payment on it.

When Terry returns, Penny is asking Maebelle if she feels like she can eat some broth or light soup. “We need to keep your strength up.”

Maebelle shakes her head in complete understanding, “soup sounds good.”

Penny gets up from Maebelle’s bedside and leaves the room in search of a nurse, who can call an order of soup to be brought in as soon as possible.

Terry sits down in Penney’s seat and picks up Maebelle’s hand.

“Miss Mae, you've given me quite some shock these last few days. There is never a dull moment with you, is there? I may not be here tomorrow as I am going to push forward in this investigation and demand some answers. I spoke to Penny and made her aware of what has been happening, so you do not need to hide anything from her. Is there anything else you can remember about the accident? Just think.”

Mae is hanging on to his every word. She looks down at her bed.

“I remember being frightened. I was sure I heard several footsteps immediately after the car finally stopped. There was perfume, heavy perfume, but I never heard a woman's voice. The voice I heard was one I have heard before. The man said he had called an ambulance. That's all I can remember.”

"Okay, I'm going to get Penny a rental car, so she can have transportation back and forth from High Springs to here. And, Miss Flo wants me to tell you she loves you."

Mae closes her eyes and smiles. She whispers, "Me too."

Penny returns with soup on a tray. "Has she fallen asleep?"

"No, I'm not asleep."

"Good, because I have soup, and I think the nurse is coming for another blood draw and meds."

"Are you leaving, Terry?" Penny asks.

"Yes, I need to get back and make some calls. I'll get you a rental car and have it brought to the valet area. Please check there whenever you go to High Springs tonight. I'll obtain a cell phone for you and I will bring that over to you later tonight.

"Good bye, Mae, now eat that soup," and he gives her a kiss on her forehead.

"Thanks, from both of us," and Penny hugs him bye.

Terry nearly collides with a hospital volunteer who is bringing a vase of flowers in and a small planter. She places them on the window sill where Maebelle can view them. Penelope reads the cards aloud to her mother, and she smiles.

Chapter 29

Driving back to High Springs, Terry reaches his secretary on his cellular. "Please make a list as I give it to you: Call the police department and get a fax sent over, Ask about items found in the car before it was towed to Robinson's, Call Robinson's and see if they inventoried the car when it was delivered to them. Reach the state attorney's office and ask them to call me back. The person I spoke to is in the Merriwether file. Call the phone company and get a cell for Maebelle's daughter, Penelope. Call Julia, never mind, I'll call Julia. Call the rental company and get a car for Penelope Merriwether delivered to the valet at the hospital. Call the valet and let them know a car is coming for her. Call Flo at the Merriwether residence and tell her I'll be stopping by tonight, and that Penny will be spending the night there tonight. Did you get all of this?" Terry waits for the answer. "Good, thank you, I'll be there in about twenty to thirty minutes."

Terry reflects about what Maebelle remembers. In all the years he has known her, Maebelle is not your average bear. She is keen and sharp. He would trust her instincts on any given matter. Terry knew this with certainty.

Terry was pulling into the 3B parking lot when his cell phone rings. "Hello, Terrance Button." He does not sound patient.

"Hey Terry, Ron Robinson, Robinson Ford. Your secretary phoned us and wanted an inventory for the Merriwether car we towed in. That's considered private, and we would need a court order or official document to release anything we found in the car."

"With all due respect, Mr. Robinson, you are not the police department. You don't get to discern who gets that information. In fact, I don't recall anyone from the Merriwether family or their personal representative asking you to tow that car into your yard."

"Are you their personal representative?"

"Another assumption on your part, Mr. Robinson, is that I need to discuss with you my relationship with the Merriwethers."

"Look here, I was merely trying to help in a time of crisis."

"Then help by providing me with a list of items you removed from the car and stop wasting my time. Just go ahead and delay in answering my request and I will enjoy reducing you to the pile of crap you are." The call abruptly ends.

Ron buzzes Debbie into his office. "Where's that package you picked up for me?"

Debbie is dumbfounded. "It's right here on your couch, and she points to the package wrapped in brown paper. Something for Miss Ruby? She came in earlier."

"Hell no, she has enough things. I'm leaving the office now for a little while."

Ron grabs the parcel and stomps on out.

Debbie sees him drive away in his truck, and wonders who called that made him jump to extreme anger. This wasn't the first sudden explosion she has witnessed. She really despises working for the pig. He can straighten his own desk. She wants to leave early to meet her sister for dinner. She has a great lead on a new job her sister might be interested in. Despite Debbie's best efforts to help her sister, Dana.

Her sister often makes poor choices and always wants to make a quick buck. Dana lives on the outskirts of town in a house Debbie thinks she can't afford.

Ron comes down the driveway shifting gravel under his big tires because his driving is so erratic. Busting through the door, he says he needs a shower to cool down.

Dana takes this opportunity to open Ron's wallet and take a couple of bills. She sees a blank check signed by Maebelle Merriwether. Slowly, she tugs at it and it comes into light. Five thousand dollars is a lot of greenbacks; way more money she receives from working on her back and pretending Ron is making her happy. Taking it from the billfold, she quickly hides the check in a tampon box. She returns to the kitchen table, opens the package Ron brings in and begins to weigh and bag the marijuana.

Ron finishes his shower and calls her into the bedroom. He is sitting on the edge of the bed. When she comes closer, he pushes her onto the bed and pulls her hair. She simmers with anger and holds back a scream.

"Why are you acting like an animal?" she demands to know.

"You don't question how I act, just do what you're told, and I won't tell your sister about our arrangement. You're beginning to bore me."

"The feeling is mutual"…. Dana quickly responds, and then Ron's hand slaps her hard across her face and knocks an earring from her ear.

"Never mind. I was going to take you somewhere special, but you don't deserve anything."

He starts to dress and doesn't bother to see she is fueled with rage. She goes to the bathroom and shuts the door. In a minute, she hears his truck drive off. She looks in the mirror. His handprint is emblazoned on the side of her entire cheek. She dresses, packs her overnighter, adds the tampon box, a few bags of weed and grabs her purse.

Debbie is calling on her phone. "Hey, are we still meeting for dinner?"

"Oh, yeah, I was just going to call you. I'll meet you there at your office."

"Okay, I'm finishing up. Ron left a little while ago, and I am glad. He is a raging bull this afternoon."

Dana does not comment. "See you in a few."

Debbie looks at the clock. It's five and she sees Ron's truck pulling back in. She turns off the office light and goes into her bathroom. She fears another confrontation and wants to leave now.

She hears his heavy footsteps entering his office and listens as she the door shuts. Quietly, Debbie emerges from the bathroom and eases out the door in time to see that Dana has arrived. Debbie meets her head on and asks where her car is.

"Oh, I left it at the Hideaway. Do you mind if I use your bathroom?"

"Go ahead but be quiet. Mr. Robinson just came back into his office.

"Sure, quiet as a mouse," and Debbie tells her where the bathroom is. Dana is wearing her shades, her ball cap and still has her back pack on.

Ron is yelling on the phone and does not hear anything or anyone.

In a few minutes, Dana exits the building and joins Debbie waiting in the car.

Debbie tells her she's been looking forward all day to their outing, so she can tell her about the job she heard about that Dana might be interested in.

"Sounds good, where are we eating?"

"How does the *Great Outdoors* sound?"

"Great, I'm really hungry."

"I'm heading that way."

They enter the restaurant and the evening edition of the Herald has hit the new stands around town. It appears everyone in the restaurant is conversing about Maebelle Merriwether's car accident. Folks are confused because it did not make sense she was traveling back into town after leaving the Woman's Club Building. A lengthy article indicated that Maebelle's entire bridge group attended the Daniel Black forum except for Ruby Robinson. People are gossiping that Ruby is holding out because Ruby's husband Ron is spearheading a vigorous campaign for the other sheriff candidate, J.W. Collins. The Herald goes on to read that Maebelle was transferred to Shands Hospital with extensive injuries. The hospital public relations person will not comment on the current condition of one of High Springs' most revered citizens.

J.W. Collins is traveling home after work when he catches the Merriwether story on his radio. He has been brewing all day about last night's forum and his lack of support from the conservatives that were attending. Perhaps he and Ron underestimated Daniel Black's appeal. He picks up the phone to call Ron. The call goes to voice mail. "*This is Ron, come on down and let's make a deal on a new Ford, Americas' number one truck for four years in a row. I can't call you back unless you leave your number.*"

"Buddy, you got my number, we need to come up with another plan now that Maebelle is out of commission. I'm getting worried. This is not the deal we made. The election is less than six weeks away. Call me. I am not patient."

Debbie's big idea of a job idea went flat on Dana. Dana didn't care for nursing home jobs. Housekeeping departments were mundane and physically draining. Dana said she needed to be around people, like bartending.

"Cash tips are always good, and I can sleep in most mornings. Have you heard of them needing people at the Hideaway?"

"No," Debbie is agitated.

"Well, don't get sore about it. I just need something a bit more independent. Bars are good places to meet people. Besides, I might move back to Lake City."

"Isn't Lake City where your last boyfriend used you, and he's still in rehab?"

"Yep, I'm done with men using me, finished."

"Hey, your face looks all red. When I first saw you, I thought you had just got up from sleeping, but now you look as if an iron hit you."

"Oh, there's our food, and I am hungry." *It was a good escape from more prying questions.*

They finish their meals and Debbie offers to pay. "I know money is tight now for you. You need to give up renting that house."

"Done. I moved out today. I've got a friend I can stay with for a few days."

"Do you still have a phone?"

"No. I gave it up. It's not like I know many people here in High Springs to call."

"It's pushing past eight, I need to do a little laundry tonight. Are you going over to your friends?"

"Yeah, I guess."

"Get in, I'll drop you by your car."

"Great."

They arrive at The Hideaway. Debbie glances over to Robinson Ford. "Ron must be working late."

Dana doesn't respond. She gets out of the car, and says goodbye, and thanks Debbie for supper.

"You're welcome."

Chapter 30

Dana watches Debbie drive off and starts walking to the front door of The Hideaway. She meanders down the aisle and sits on a bar stool next to a lady. The woman says hello.

Dana answers her back, "Hi."

A bartender comes to take her order. Dana ask her how much for rum and Coke.

"Well drinks are three fifty. Brand booze is four fifty."

The woman on the bar stool speaks up, "Put that on my tab." She's looking at Dana. "Hi, I'm Betty."

"Gee, thanks, Betty. I'm Dana. Do you come here often?"

"Is every day often?"

Dana smiles, "I was wondering if they are hiring."

"I'll ask, I know the owner."

Pretty soon, Betty exits the bar stool and goes to the back. In a minute or so, she returns and smiles. "He'll be out in a minute. He's a sucker for pretty ladies."

"Is he a nice man?" Dana is sure Betty will know.

"Yes, and very happily married."

"That's awesome."

"Lived here long?" Betty's beverages are making her friendly.

"Not really."

"You remind me of my daughter. She would've been thirty-five today had she not passed away."

"I'm so sorry, how did she die?"

"Her boyfriend was violent. It just started out a few smacks at a time, and then his behavior escalated. She was beautiful, like you."

"Oh," Dana responds, but is starting to feel uncomfortable.

An athletic guy with a shaved head comes from the back. He stops at the bar stools where Betty and Dana are sitting. Looking at Dana, "You need a job?"

"Yes."

"Do you have transportation?"

"Yes."

"Do you have kids?'

"No."

"Do you have a drinking problem?"

"No."

"Don't give out a ton of information, do you, I like that in a person. Okay, I'll try you out. I'm Sid, you can start tomorrow. Be here at six. My wife will be here then, and if she says you won't work, then you have to leave."

"Thank you, I'm a people person. I'll work hard. My name is Dana. See you tomorrow."

"Gosh, thanks again Betty. Maybe I can serve you tomorrow," Dana seems happy.

The TV monitors all around the bar suddenly have a news story of Maebelle Merriwether. The hospital spokesman says they are upgrading her condition to fair. Police are still investigating the single car accident close to the city limits of High Springs. Mrs. Merriwether has publicly endorsed Daniel Black for sheriff in the November election.

Dana was glued to the television as is Betty.

"Do you know her?" Dana asks Betty.

"Yes, very well. I play bridge with her once a week and have been to her home many times. She's a grand lady and respected by all. I haven't heard if we're playing this week because she is still in the hospital."

"Another drink Betty?" The bartender asked politely.

Betty looks at her new bar bestie, "One more? For new found friendships?"

"Sure, to celebrate my new job." Dana laughs.

Chapter 31

Penelope catches the news reel about her mom too, as she is exiting the hospital. It has been a long day, and she still needs to pick up the car from valet and drive home. Her mother is only slightly improved. The doctor tells Penelope that Maebelle is not showing any signs of infection yet. Penelope exits the building and finds the valet captain. The car Terry rented for her arrives and she is all set to go. It will be good to get a shower, prop her feet up, and see Flo. Penny has not been home in two years. Bless her mother's heart. Not once has she made Penny feel guilty about moving away and traveling. Seeing Terry always makes her smile. Truthfully, she had thought of him often and *the what if* of their relationship. She starts the car and pulls out on the highway listening to the radio.

Terry showers and shaves and tells Julia he is going to Maebelle's. He invites Julia to come along too. "Penny would love to meet you."

"Thank you no, you guys will probably discuss business all night. That's not for me."

Terry leans over and kisses her forehead. "Thanks for understanding Julia."

Leaving his house, Terry checks his phone to see if the state attorney's office has returned his call. He listens to his messages.

Terry, thanks for your call. We have cleared the current sheriff from any involvement in the case. We expect his full cooperation in our current investigation. I will be in touch with you by the end of the day tomorrow. Thank you. Finally, we are getting traction and this investigation is moving.

Terry pulls into the driveway of Maebelle's residence. Terry looks around and notices that Mr. Henry is making headway on the grounds. There are headlights approaching, so he waits on the steps. It's Penelope in her rented car. He goes toward her car door to open it for her.

"Hey, any trouble finding the old place?"

"None."

"How was Mae when you left the hospital?"

"Some flowers arrived, and it seemed to lift her spirits, but she was getting sleepy. The doctor is still concerned about infection."

"I just remembered I still have your luggage in my car. I'll retrieve it for you now."

"Thanks." Penny stops in front of the door and rings the bell.

Flo opens the door and she is so excited. She gathers up Penny, almost lifting her from the brick steps.

"Oh, Miss Penny, so happy you have come home. Come on in, just keep coming, and sit yourself down and get comfortable. Oh, Mr. Terry, you too. I've got fresh apple pie, not too long out of the oven." Penny and Terry are already inside the house.

Flo hesitates and is still looking around the outside. Clearly, the events of the last few weeks still have her spooked. Flo closes the door.

"Tell me how Ms. Mae is feeling. I desperately need to go see her, maybe make her some homemade soup."

"She is slow but sure, Flo. She's a trooper, but this has been a hard kick to her. She needs more time to recuperate. I believe she will get there. Are you and Mr. Henry doing alright?"

"Yes, we are fine. Of course, Mr. Henry has been busy replanting from all the damage, but like Ms. Mae reminded us both, everything can be replaced." She looks down, and sadness comes across her face, "but we cannot replace Ms. Maebelle." Her eyes become glassy, and she reaches for her handkerchief tucked inside her right pocket.

"Bless you Miss Penny, you still look bright and young, you still looking mighty fine, I do declare. Was leaving and going to Guatemala a good thing?"

"Well, it was a change."

"Yes, but an earache is a good change from a toothache. Both hurt." Flo is matter of fact. Penny looks at Flo and laughs. "Now, how 'bout that pie I mentioned. Mr. Terry? Coffee too? Or do ya'll prefer some decaffeinated coffee?"

"I never turn down pie or coffee. Thank you, Flo." Terry's eyes light up.

"Anything Flo, will be appreciated."

Flo heads for the kitchen.

Penny is looking all around the house and memories flood her brain. “Some things will never change.”

Terry doesn't want to comment. “Penny, I have been exercising my power of attorney to keep the ball rolling here…but you might need to get signed up on her banking account, if you aren't already.”

“Before I left, I was on the accounts, but I'll check first thing in the morning. Flo might need more monies transferred into her household account since Mumsy isn't here to transfer funds every week. Did you find out anything about the car? Was the check found in the car? It worries me that it is signed and is blank.”

“If it is cashed, it is the banks responsibility now, as they have been notified. What do you want me to do with the car? I can sell it for salvage. Towing it into Gainesville to the Chrysler dealership will be costly, if you want to trade it there. They will probably give us salvage price anyway. I know you don't have time to wheel and deal on a car now. Let me find out about the insurance policy and find out how long the rental car will be covered. Come to think about it, the insurance company may take care of getting rid of the damaged car for us, that is, if it is totaled. I do not have a good rapport with Ron Robinson, so I'd like to ignore him altogether. I can take care of the payroll. I'll ask Flo…”

“Ask Flo what?” and she enters the drawing room with a serving tray.

"Flo, this looks fantastic. I need to ask you, are you paid every week, or every two weeks?"

"Two weeks, Mr. Terry. And just so you know, Mr. Henry hired a couple of Mexican men, I mean Spanish, to help him replant. He will be back first thing in the morning."

"Flo, I'll leave my phone number for him to call me. I will bring the money here for him to pay the extra workers."

"Mr. Terry, folks are calling here. I have been vague in my answers. Some of the bridge ladies…."

"Has anyone strange or out of the ordinary called?"

"No one has called or visited. Every time I open the door, I look around and pay attention."

Penny looks at Flo, "This pie is so good Flo, and a hot cup of coffee is so welcoming. Thank you for staying here and making my homecoming special. I confess, I need a bath soon, and I think that will refresh me."

"Penny, one more thing," Terry asks, "the states attorney's office will be getting back to me tomorrow about their ongoing investigation. What time will you be going back to the hospital?"

"I should be there before eleven, or at least I hope so."

Terry puts the last fork full in his mouth and wipes his lips with his napkin. "I will go now, so you can get to that bath." He stands up. "Sleep well, I'll see myself out."

Inside the house, Penelope grabs her suitcase and heads down the hall. She stops by her mother's room and walks in and sits on the edge of the bed. Mumsy did like her comforts, she observes. She wonders what her mother would say about how Penny lived in Guatemala.

No one in the country she just flew from could possibly understand how people in America can waste so much and demand more. Penny's friends deem material possessions as insignificant and unimportant. She sleeps on a cot every night in the orphanage, and her paltry possessions can fit on a small table. Privacy is a luxury. All this, as she looks around, was what she left to go find herself. Now, she finds herself liking home.

Home is where Terry is headed. He asks himself how everything could have taken such a wrong course. The acts against Maebelle are unconscionable. He feels like the attacks are against his own family. Silently, he promises himself he will set a course to destroy the people responsible for this unpardonable wrongdoing.

Julia is waiting for him as he enters the door. Terry hugs her tight. "Thank you for waiting up for me, but you shouldn't have."

"Truthfully, I wanted to check for lipstick on your collar, gonna tell on you kinda of thing. You already know what I'm going to say."

"Yes, I do, but I'll always enjoy you making your case." Terry grins and gathers her up and kisses her passionately. "Jules, I love it when you get a little jealous. It keeps me on my toes."

"You never call me Jules, unless you want to be romantic."

"I'm that transparent? You're right, I am. I need to hold my wife close to me and let her know I do not take her for granted."

"You've said all the right words, and that's all I need to hear." She takes his jacket and hangs it up in the closet.

"Now let's go to bed. You need to sleep."

Penny is used to getting up early because little children are always knocking on her door begging her to open it. She misses their little faces longing for attention.

She dresses quickly, clips her long hair up and ties a beautiful Ombre turquoise scarf in it. She is not used to the Florida humidity. Walking out into the living room, Flo greets her. "Good Morning, were you able to rest?"

"The bed was heaven."

"Ready for breakfast, Miss Penelope? I asked Mr. Henry to join us. He is so excited to see you again."

"That will be wonderful."

"Will eggs be good for you?"

"Yes, I'll eat them any way you'd like to prepare them."

"Coming right up."

Mr. Henry knocks at the back door, then enters with the paper. He takes off his hat and holds it in his hand.

Hearing the back door, Penny walks towards Mr. Henry. He places his hat over his heart, and smiles. "Miss Penelope, it's been a long time."

She hugs him and kisses him on the cheek. "Mr. Henry, too long, I agree. Come sit with me at the table." Flo brings them both coffee. "Or would you rather have tea?"

"No tea, just coffee, please, and thank you, Flo."

"Yes, um," and Flo returns to the kitchen to poach some eggs. Immediately, Flo's cell phone rings.

She thinks it is strange that her nephew Darius, is calling her. *It must be an emergency.*

"Good morning Darius, you alright?"

"Aunt Flo, I'm already at work, you won't believe what's happened at the dealership. The police are here."

"Are you in trouble?"

"No. Auntie, Mr. Ron, Mr. Robb..in..son. He's dead. They found him in his office this morning from a gunshot. They say he's been dead all night."

"What boy, you saying Mr. Robinson got killed?"

"Yes, um. I got to go. We might close today. Someone is 'gonna come talk to all us mechanics and workers soon. I got to go."

"Okay, you be good now, and keep your own nose clean."

Flo scurries back into the dining room and relays the news about Ron Robinson.

"This big old pot of stew we are in is getting thicker, Lordy, what's going to happen next?"

Unmoving in her stance, Penelope's eyes look piercing and serious. She has questions but is unable to speak. W*ho? What? Why?*

All this time, she and Terrance are thinking everything is a plot that Ron Robinson orchestrated. Now *he* is dead.

Mr. Henry looks stunned.

Flo realizes she still has eggs to cook and goes back to the kitchen to finish.

Chapter 32

Four houses down from the Merriwether estate the police arrive at the Robinson residence. The doorbell rings several times, and Ruby starts to wake. *What is going on? Has she forgotten this is the day for the pest control people?*

She grabs her robe and heads downstairs to the front door. Cinching her belt to close her robe, she opens the door.

"Isn't it a little early for the Policeman's Benevolent Benefit Drive?"

"Mrs. Robinson, may we come in?"

"Come in? Now?"

"Yes, ma'am. There has been an accident at your husband's office."

"Oh, I'll go get him." She turns, and starts calling, "Ron, the front door is for you. I'll go get him. Coffee, Officers?"

"Uh, no ma'am. We'd like to talk to you, perhaps in your living room, you might be more comfortable."

"Okay, in here, and she leads them in the room. "But let's wait on Ron. I'll call him again."

"Mrs. Robinson, your husband Ron has died. He was found in his office this morning."

"What? From a heart attack?" Ruby looks all around to room. She is stunned. "He must have left early this morning, and I didn't realize. I can't believe it." Her eyes fill with tears, and she begins crying.

"We are so sorry to bring you this news. Ma'am is there someone we can call to come over?"

"No, we don't have any children, I only have my bridge club ladies. They are my friends, and my neighbor, Mrs. Merriwether is in the hospital."

"Perhaps, your clergyman?"

The policemen barely understand her. One of the officers suggest they call dispatch for a female policeman to come to the house to comfort Mrs. Robinson. The information is sinking in, and Ruby is starting to ask questions.

"Was he taken to the hospital?" Ruby struggles to remain composed.

"Mrs. Robinson, perhaps you need to call a manager to take the reins of the dealership while you sort out what you need to do. We can have someone bring him here to talk to you."

A female officer arrives and knocks on the door. She immediately enters as if she is expected.

"Hello, my name is Samantha. She sits beside Ruby, holds her hand, and gives her a hug. She offers to go make a pot of coffee, perhaps get her a couple of aspirin. Ruby nods her head yes. Ruby asks one of the officers to call Rusty at the dealership, so she can speak to him. In a couple of seconds, Rusty is on the phone, and Ruby asks him to do whatever he thinks is necessary. Ruby thanks him and tells him she will be at home, and he is welcome to stop by.

Ruby takes a cup of coffee and starts to sip. She is sitting in silence, trying to keep composed. Both male officers depart and leave Samantha to be with Ruby.

"Samantha, do you know any details?"

"I'm afraid I don't, Mrs. Robinson. The other officers mentioned you have a bridge club. Perhaps, I can call one of your friends to come be with you."

"Yes, thank you," as she fights back sniffles. Ruby reaches in her desk and pulls out her address book. "Could you please call Betty for me? I'm going back upstairs to shower. Can you wait till I get back down here before you leave?"

"Yes, I'll be here, and I'll call Betty now."

Betty answers the phone. Samantha gives her the tragic details and Betty tells her she will be right over to assist.

News is spreading quickly about the death of Ron Robinson. Terrance Button hears it on his radio driving to go to his office. *No surprise to me.* He calls Penelope on his cellular.

"Just heard the news on Ron Robinson on my car radio."

"It's hard to grasp. I was rendered speechless when Flo heard from her nephew that he was killed."

"The radio didn't mention how he died. Did Darius say?"

"Gunshot."

There is silence on Terry's end. Finally, he responds. "This web of deceit just continues to expand and dilate."

"Penny, I will be at the office today. Call me as soon as you see the doctor and have a report on Mae's condition. Do you need anything?"

"I'm good, rested and almost ready to leave."

"Have a good visit. Please break the news gently to her about Ron."

"Oh, good idea. Bye for now," and Penelope hangs up the phone.

Chapter 33

On the way to the 3B building, Terry passes by the Ford dealership. Traffic slows as drivers notice the ambulance and police cars parked all around. There is a special crime lab truck parked close to the front door. Terry drives even slower. Employees in groups of three are chatting among themselves. Terry notices there is a rope barring the entrance. He nearly misses the entrance to his parking lot because his mind is elsewhere.

Entering the building, Terry's gait is fast. "Good morning," he says it quickly to his secretary. "May I see you in my office immediately?"

"Yes, Mr. Button." Darlene closes the door behind her. With notepad in hand, she is ready to listen to her boss.

"If the police come today, for any reason, I am not available. I will not be here in the office today. Any search warrant they have for this office, must be handled by me. Please keep the door locked."

"You mean, after you leave?"

"I'm not going anywhere. I will be here. If you need to reach me, call me on my cell. Do not buzz me on the intercom."

Darlene responds. "Yes, sir. I do not know where you are." She looks puzzled, and curious. She repeats, "I do not know where you are."

"Thank you, that will be all."

"Yes, sir."

Darlene locks the door and pulls it with her to close it.

Terry dials the states attorney's office and reaches his contact.

"Thank God, you answered. Things are dicey here in High Springs. Have you heard the news about Ron?"

Terry clicks on his television and of course, the news about Ron Robinson's death is splashed all over the network.

On speaker phone, the deep voice of a man is clear to understand. "The sheriff called us first thing. The secretary found him. She is hysterical beyond words. The sheriff is concerned that talk within the office will be rampant. We have filed necessary warrants. Our crime lab is there now photographing, removing recorders, phones, some files. We have already put a call to the other investigators we used before. We won't know until this afternoon if the two men we used before, already familiar with the case will be available to us. This case just keeps getting bigger. Terrance, I am concerned for you, because you had an ax to grind with Robinson. Any information you want to give up, before it is uncovered?"

Sheepishly, Terry answers. "Yes, I believe Ron is the one responsible for Maebelle's accident. I have no proof, just my gut feeling and the voice of someone I know to have immeasurable intuition and wisdom. I did phone Ron yesterday and I'm afraid I wasn't very pleasant."

"Did you threaten him in any way? Can you verify your whereabouts all during the day?"

"I was driving, alone… when I spoke with him."

"And afterwards, the phone conversation, where were you?"

"I drove to the Merriwether estate and had a meeting with Maebelle's daughter and staff at the home."

"And when you left?"

"I drove home to my own house."

"They will be pulling phone records soon. I'm glad you told me. Anything else?"

"Only that Ms. Maebelle believes it was Ron that ran her off the road that night she had an accident."

"Well, that gives you motive. I don't know how much I will be communicating with you going forward. I know you understand. I am asking you not to phone me again. I am only interested in finding the truth Terrance."

"That's what I want too, and justice for my client and friend."

"Do you think you might be too personally involved?"

"Yes, that's the kind of lawyer I am, up close and personal. I'll say goodbye now."

Terry realizes he will be out of the loop for further information. He will rely on his steadfast belief that justice will prevail and the detectives that are summoned will be unrelenting in seeking the truth.

Chapter 34

Detectives Price and Martin have not spoken since their last trip together. Eddie calls Boyd.

"Sir, its Eddie. State's just phoned me, I guess you have already been called."

"No, I'm enjoying Sunday dinner with Dolly's family."

"Is she feeling better? I bet you guys are excited."

"It's an unbelievable high I am on. When I returned, the doctor put the gender identity in an envelope, so we could find out together. A crazy thing happened. We closed our eyes, and both reach in the envelope and pull out a slip of paper. She thought she had the answer, and I thought I had it. It was in front of her family, and when we opened our eyes, she had a blue slip, and I had a pink one."

"Twins? You have got to be kidding."

"Yes, we are blessed beyond what we could ever hope for."

"And she's doing well?"

"Yes, just that scare at first, because she is carrying two. She looks beautiful. Big and beautiful."

"You better not say that too loud sir."

"Yeah, I know, I stepped out of the room, so I won't get anything thrown at me. She is pretty emotional these days."

"Gotta go, this must be the call coming in."

"Captain, sir, yes sir. I can be ready in the morning. I need to make arrangements for my mother to move in with my wife."

"We're expecting twins, and I need to discuss my absence with her." Boyd pauses. "Yes, sir."

Boyd retrieves Eddie's phone number from his stored numbers. Eddie answers on the first ring. After a brief few words, Eddie answers. "I'll be there. Copy sir, uniforms."

Boyd has a weighted sigh. He calls his mother and gives her the news. "I won't worry if I know you are there. I can't thank you enough… Grandma." and Boyd chuckles. "I know. I'll put my big foot down and tell her it must be this way. I have some influence. It will not be easy leaving Dolly for a few days." Boyd hangs up the phone. *She will not be happy, but she is a trooper. He knows that for sure. She has proven it time after time. She has strength and resilience.*

Boyd joins the family and catches Dolly's eye. He smiles, and she mouths, "What's up?"

He gets closer to her and kisses her neck.

"Do we have to leave? I knew it, the neck kiss always tells me something is up."

"You are too smart for your own good."

"Are we leaving now?"

"I'm afraid so. I'll get your dishes and load up. Okay?"

She has a frown on her face as he goes out to the other room.

On the way home, Boyd speaks softly telling Dolly that he has a special investigation and he will be gone for three days, or maybe less. He continues talking and asks her to listen to his request and reminds her he doesn't make too many but this one is important.

Dolly is silent all the way home and doesn't wait for him to open her door. This is a first. She walks inside the house and sits in her chair.

"Oh, no. This won't work," Boyd tells her. He grabs her hand and pulls her hand and leads her to the couch. "Here, sit with me," and he doesn't let go of her hand. "Dolly listen to me, this isn't up for discussion. Mom will be here for me, and for you, and for our babies." He leans in and kisses her softly. Dolly is being stubborn.

"Is this really how you want to spend our last night together before I leave?" And he kisses her neck again. "And… I don't appreciate you not letting me open your door. I'm wounded." He kisses her on the neck again and moves up to her ear.

"I'm sorry. I'm emotional." With glassy eyes, she kisses him back. "We'll miss you."

Boyd places his hand on her belly and moves his hand back and forth over it. "You're a good listener and I love you for it. Will you help me pack my bag?" He pulls on her hand to get her up. "C'mon," and leads her down the hall.

Detectives Price and Martin leave at seven in the morning. Boyd asks if Eddie will make notes on the pad while he talks to him. He outlines the course of their investigation and all the angles, the sifting for information that is factual. He explains the quest for the truth must be absolute. A life has been lost, and Ms. Maebelle is injured and laying in a hospital in Gainesville. They need to turn over every rock and see what crawls out."

Eddie displays shock. "We will find the truth, sir."

Chapter 35

In a couple of hours, Boyd and Eddie arrive at the High Springs Sheriff's Department. They are relatively unnoticed as they enter the building. They knock on the door of the sheriff and enter. The sheriff leads them to a large conference room that will be their temporary office.

"Is there a key to this office, Sheriff?" Boyd asks.

"I'll go get it." The sheriff responds immediately.

"Please and any duplicates."

Boyd ask Eddie to call a locksmith immediately, so the existing lock can be altered. Eddie makes the call.

"Sheriff, if you will accompany me to J.W. Collins office." Boyd asks.

"Alright," but does not fully understand.

Boyd pulls a small book out of his case he brought in. The sheriff leads them to the east wing, and knocks before entering, followed closely by Boyd and Eddie. J.W. looks up from his paperwork and looks surprised. "Well, good morning men."

"Good morning," Boyd extends his hand and shakes J.W.'s hand. "I'm Lieutenant Boyd Price and this is Special Investigator Edward Martin. I apologize for the short notice, but you are hereby temporarily suspended from duty pending investigation of the entire department."

"Why? Just like that?" J.W. is disconcerted.

"Just like that. I'm sure you are familiar with how Special Investigations work. Here, I brought you a current manual in case you have need of it. I will have to ask for your badge and your departmental weapon now."

Startled, Jack releases his weapon, and removes his badge off his shirt.

"I guess I'll get my personal papers out of my desk." Jack seems blown away.

"No sir, the procedure is different in Special Investigations. I need to instruct you that your office key will no longer be effective. You can take a vacation of sorts, but you cannot leave the county without express permission from me. You are not permitted to call and or speak to acting deputies currently employed. Do we have a complete understanding?"

J.W. is stunned. He utters, "I guess."

"I'll repeat the question for you. Do we have a complete understanding?"

"Complete. How about my sheriff campaign?"

"Mr. Collins, your campaign is your business for now. Simply stated, you can't be involved in police business until you are cleared."

"Cleared of what exactly?"

"Exactly everything we need to know. If the findings render unfounded results, you will be exonerated. Thank you for your cooperation."

"Have I met you before?" J.W. is curious.

"We have never been introduced, Mr. Collins."

"I thought maybe you looked familiar."

"I wouldn't know about that. The sheriff will see you out."

"Are you being thrown out too?" J.W. asks the sheriff as they leave his office.

"This is a Special Investigation, and they are in charge."

The locksmith enters the building and waits in the outer reception room. Boyd walks down the hall, as Eddie remains.

"Oh, good, you're here, I'll show you the way. I need new locks on two offices." Boyd shows him the door. "Eddie, when he finishes, you can lead him back to our office. You can go ahead and start. Thanks for coming on such short notice."

"Okay, sir."

Boyd leaves again and stops by the secretary pool.

"Hello," and he is greeted by scared whispers of hello.

"I'm Lieutenant Price, Special Investigator. My partner Eddie Martin and I will be taking the conference office here for our mutual office. I will not be requiring any secretarial services from any of you. Nor will I need coffee or anything else. There will be no need to transfer any calls to me. Everyone that needs to reach me has my number already."

If you have any information that you feel we need to be aware of, please write or type on plain paper and place it in the box. You do not have to sign your name. Please type to remain anonymous. Any subject, even the name of a favorite restaurant will be appreciated." Boyd laughs a little.

"Thank you for your service and hard work."

Chapter 36

Boyd returns to the east wing and finds Eddie. He knocks once.

"Ready to ride?"

"Sure," Eddie responds, locks the door and follows Boyd out to their unmarked car.

"To lunch sir?"

"Okay, want to eat? What sounds good?"

"A sub or Mexican food?"

"I saw a Publix Supermarket. Let's go in and see what looks good."

"Sure." On the way to Publix, Eddie asks if they are staying in the same house as before.

"No, it's a bed and breakfast. Best not let anyone know we have ever been here in High Springs before."

The grocery store looks surprisingly new, and they head back to the delicatessen to survey their choices. Boyd selects a Moho pork and rice meal. He grabs a bowl of fruit and a case of Dasani water. He adds a half gallon jug of tea, and a box of Lance crackers with peanut butter. He turns to Eddie getting a foot-long submarine stacked with meats and vegetables. Boyd announces he's heading to the register.

Eddie pulls a couple of Powerade bottles off the shelf. "I'm right behind you."

Checking out, Boyd notices a couple of the ladies that are handling the registers, are commenting on Eddie's cute look.

"I think you have some fans."

"Oh yeah?"

"They're probably not your type."

"I don't have a type. Remember?"

"Oh, I think you do. You'll know when you see your type." They both grin, especially Eddie.

Walking out the door, Boyd says he going to find a little park to visit and eat on a picnic table.

A woman overhears him and tells them go on the road behind Publix and there's a big tree back there.

"Thanks so much, ma'am."

Under the tree, they eat their lunch. Boyd lets Eddie know they will probably be at the dealership all afternoon. "We need to exercise some diplomacy as we might be stepping on some local law enforcement toes and I'm sure they don't think they need any assistance."

"But we have seniority, right?"

"Yes, but you can get catch more flies with honey than you can with vinegar."

"Is that a Boydism?"

"No, my wife's southern family."

"Oh."

"Fruit?"

"Yeah, thanks.

Chapter 37

They finish up, pick up their trash, get in their patrol car and head west of town. The dealership is chaotic with police cars parked every which way. The crime lab is still there.

Boyd parks over where the service stalls are.

They get out and Boyd walks in and sees a couple of men at the parts desk where a car stereo bass is thumping.

"Manager here?" Boyd asks one of the guys.

"I think someone has already interviewed him," a service technician answers.

"I see, is the manager here?"

"I'll page him." The intercom is loud. "Rusty, to the service counter, Rusty to the service counter please."

A portly, freckled ginger haired man appears from the air-conditioned office.

"You paged?"

Boyd steps up and offers his handshake. "Good afternoon, Lieutenant Price, Special Investigations Bureau," Boyd notices his grimy fingernails.

Rusty answers, "It's good to meet you."

"May we go to your office and talk?"

"Follow me."

Inside the building, Rusty walks through a big tire display into his office and points to two chairs. Boyd looks at Eddie, and then asks Rusty if he minds that they record the interview.

Indignant, Rusty answers, "There is no reason I should mind."

"How long have you worked here?" Boyd is thirsty for information.

"Since high school. I was in the DCT, uh Diversified Cooperative Training program."

"Guess Ron was a small auto dealer back then."

"Yep, seen a lot of changes in the dealership and the way we mechanic cars."

"Tell me, do you repair any sheriff's department cars?"

"Yes, we service all of them I believe."

"I guess that's first thing in the morning, eh?"

"It's just the opposite. Ron came up with the idea over a year ago, to service them at night, when they weren't being used."

"Service them every couple of months?"

"Oh no, seems like there's always something going wrong. Figure it's the wear and tear on them, chasing down people and all that."

"Do you require a purchase order?"

"I don't see the billing. I'm not usually here when the cars come in for repair. Ron does the billing. I always figured he gave them a bigger cut than he gives us wrench monkeys, so he doesn't want us involved."

"How many hours are you working a week Rusty?"

"About 55."

"Getting compensated well?"

"Could always use more."

"Do you get the sense there are mechanics here who feel underpaid?"

"Well, men talk big but I think they are satisfied. There's no real uproar."

"Do you expect that you'll become the CEO here or do you anticipate Mrs. Robinson will take charge?"

"I will help her in whatever capacity she needs me. She called earlier and asked me to go over to the residence this afternoon."

"Do you own any personal handguns, Rusty?"

"Yes, I have a Smith and Wesson, 357 Magnum."

"Well, we won't delay you. Thank you for your candor and cooperation."

Boyd and Eddie stand and ask Rusty the shortcut through the showroom to Ron's office. Rusty points to the inner offices and the men move towards the door.

They are met by another policeman acting as a sentinel for the chaos they are about to face.

Boyd asks which officer is in charge. "Please point him out to me." Boyd walks inside the office and has a brief conversation. The crime lab is finishing, and Boyd is informed of the injuries suffered by Ron. No handgun has been found.

"Where is the secretary who found the body? Has anyone questioned her yet?" Boyd gets to the point quickly.

"No, Lieutenant, she is inaudible in her speech, and was allowed to leave."

"I understand."

"Has anyone taken anything from Ron's desk or handled anything in that area?"

"Nothing, we were told SIB investigators were coming, therefore we concentrated on removing the body, and removing blood stains."

"I appreciate that. We will take over here and begin recovering evidence where it is available."

Eddie puts on a pair of gloves and grabs a box from the outer office of the secretary. Boyd also dons a pair of gloves and pulls up a chair.

"Let's begin with his phone. I see some messages are on the telephone answering system. Eddie turns on his recorder and Boyd presses down the play button. They listen intently to the one from Merriwether's attorney. His wife calls and is obviously angry about him hitting her. Jack Collins doesn't think Ron is holding up his end of their bargain.

"Bingo," Boyd whispers. "Hostility is displayed from at least three." Boyd opens a drawer. He rifles through and finds personal checking accounts, receipts, and keys.

"I think we might better take everything." Boyd pulls out the bottom drawer. "Jack pot!" Boyd exclaims. There are weed packets everywhere, ready for resale. At the back of the drawer are some files marked 'personal.' "Let's take it all," Boyd directs Eddie.

Eddie responds, "Yes sir." He begins loading a box and taking it out the door, across the way to where their car is parked.

He places one box in the trunk and heads back for another. Eddie returns for the second box, and sees Boyd staring at the secretaries' desk. He reaches over to the planter sitting on the top and plucks the card from the card holder. The florist name is listed but the sentiment expressed from the sender has been torn off. He thinks about that. He looks down at the calendar and brings out his camera. Boyd takes a picture of the month of September and he flips back to the month of August and takes a snapshot of it as well.

With gloves still on, he tugs on the middle drawer and it is locked. *Strange, someone so upset about finding her boss dead has the presence of mind to lock down her drawer.* He pulls open her other file drawers and takes stock with keen eyes. He reaches underneath a stack of papers and grabs a little black book. He opens it and finds notations in what he supposes is Debbie's handwriting. There are dates and incidents where Ron Robinson had sexually harassed her including details of what was said between them during the encounters. The secretary has quite a stash of events, which obviously angered her. What she intended to do with her notes, is unknown.

"Look, Eddie, here is time, place and incident of a boss lording his position over a female employee."

Eddie looks over the pages. "Makes you wonder why there are so many entries. She has proof, yet he continues to get away with it."

"Did he?" Hearing the statement Eddie makes is profound.

Boyd takes additional pictures, and places the book back, exactly where he found it.

"We'll leave it here like we found it. Sometimes when you put your hook in the water and drag up a bit, you might get a bite."

"Eddie, we will need to pull all phone records for probably the last two months and see if there are some numbers that appear often. We can pull county records of vehicles and properties that Ron also owns. Boyd looks at his watch. It's almost six o' clock and the dealership is beginning to become deserted. Boyd locks the door, reaches in his box they brought with them and pulls out a roll of wide tape that is imprinted with the words 'Police, Do Not Remove', and seals the door across the frame. Eddie is already at the patrol car listing the inventory they are taking with them.

In the car, Boyd takes his cellular out, looks for a telephone number on his pad, and calls Mrs. Robinson.

"Hello," a faint voice answers.

"This is Lieutenant Price with the Special Investigations unit. May I speak with Mrs. Ruby Robinson please?"

"Speaking, this is Ruby."

"Ma'am, I know this has been a shocking day for you. My partner and I would like to visit with you tomorrow if you feel up to a few questions." Boyd waits for an answer.

Ruby clears her throat. "Yes, that will be fine. What time did you have in mind?"

"Whenever you feel you can, you might want a friend with you or your attorney to be present."

"Thank you. I will be ready at ten in the morning."

"Yes, ma'am. I am sorry for your loss, Mrs. Robinson."

"Eddie, will you obtain a search warrant for the Robinson estate for tomorrow? We will take it with us, when we go there tomorrow."

"It's been a full day, let's go get some supper. What do you say?"

"Want to go in uniform sir, or shower and change clothes so we can have a beer?"

Boyd grins, "A beer sounds good. We'll go to our quarters and freshen up."

They are driving toward the bed and breakfast and Eddie asks, "Earlier, you mentioned someone was injured in all this. Did you already know Ron was dead?"

"I was informed early this morning, but I was referring to the lady we met a few weeks ago, Maebelle Merriwether. She had an accident a couple of days ago. Her car veered off the highway and she is in the hospital. Her personal attorney told the state's attorney that she was deliberately scared off the road. She lost control of her car after going to a political forum for candidate Daniel Black. The attorney believes it was Ron Robinson because he was the first person on the scene.

"Wow, this can of worms just keeps getting bigger."

"Yeah, and we're in a kettle of fish, with lots of lines out, all entangled."

Maebelle Merriwether is showing improvement. Penelope sees her smiling and sipping tea when she walks into her room. Penny is surprised to see new visitors, greets them and gives her mother a kiss on her cheek. "Morning, you look rested."

Maebelle smiles, "I did rest better, although I would like to get up."

Penny faces the two ladies. "Mrs. Monroe, nice to see you again."

"Thank you, sweetheart. Have you met Julia Button?"

Penny reaches for the petite blond, and embraces her, giving her a long hug. "Finally, we meet. Terry has been our lifesaver."

"Yes, he has been very worried about his favorite High Springs lady. He loves your mother dearly."

"It is mutual, I assure you. She treats him like my brother."

"I see him more than I see you," Mae interrupts. "I asked them if they brought some cards."

"Not so fast, Mum."

"We did bring her a couple of books and magazines, and a hydrangea plant from the club."

"And it's beautiful. I think it's unusual, the pink with green edges, so pretty."

"Mrs. Monroe,"

"Please call me Elsa Jane."

"How is the campaign going?"

"Well, now that J.W. is on leave of absence from the sheriff's department, he is devoting his energy to getting out more in the community. It's a close race. We need more people and more funding to get the word out."

"Has my check been found?" Mae is looking at Penny.

"No, perhaps, I should issue another one, while the bank watches for the one that is lost. Elsa Jane, you can pick up a new check tomorrow morning," Penny smiles when she says it.

"That will be appreciated. Everyone in town is talking about Ron Robinson's death. We're going to Ruby's tomorrow to extend our sympathies. Poor dear. She really doesn't have any close friends except us, the bridge club. Betty has been with her since the police showed up to tell her Ron was killed."

"What did you say? Ron is dead? Whatever happened?" Mae is visibly upset.

A beeping sound is heard, and a nurse quickly rushes in and looks on the monitor. "Your blood pressure is elevated significantly Ms. Merriwether. Are you in pain?"

"No, I am fine, just received some bad news, thank you."

"Girls, please tell Ruby I am thinking about her." *I just can't believe it.*

Chapter 39

Ruby hangs up the phone with Lieutenant Price and continues her conversation with Rusty who arrived about thirty minutes earlier.

"I will appreciate you taking the helm of the dealership until I can sort out the finances and talk with my accountant."

"This is quite the shock for me. I would be lying if I said I wasn't afraid that whomever killed Ron may want me dead too. Rusty, tell me the truth. Do you know if Ron was involved in anything sinister and unlawful? I admit I was puzzled when Ron took such an interest in the sheriff campaign when he has never been political before."

"Truly, I concentrate on my work in the service department, Ms. Ruby. Ron watched our department closely, and often told me I needed to get my numbers up."

"What does that mean, your numbers up?"

"Ron wanted to see more service, and less mechanic labor on the payroll. I was constantly on the guys to work faster. It did not make me a popular guy."

"I see. Do you feel like someone else may be a better choice than you to be the manager?"

"Ma'am, I am a trustworthy and a loyal employee. I will give it considerable thought and get back to you on that."

"Rusty, I am planning on the funeral to be on Thursday morning. I think we should close the dealership on that day."

"Please reschedule everyone that is expecting service that day. I also will be changing the locks on everything, for safety reasons. I will get a new set of keys to you as soon as possible. Tomorrow, the police will come here, and I hope they have some information for me."

"Yes, ma'am. They visited me today at work."

"They did? What did they want to know?"

"If anyone was not happy at work. If I have a gun…"

"Oh."

"Ms. Ruby, I need to go. My wife expects me home for supper. I'm a family man, and I don't want to worry my wife."

"Of course. Thank you for stopping by."

Betty comes from the kitchen and offers Rusty something to drink just as he is standing to leave.

"No ma'am. I am leaving now."

Betty walks with him to the door. After he leaves, Betty turns her attention to Ruby. "Dinner is ready Ruby. I made a plate for you. I thought you might want to eat at the dinette."

"Yes, I need to eat something. I have been feeling a little nauseated. I'm sure it's just my nerves."

Betty gives her a hug. "You're going to get through this."

"You have been a big help to me, dear friend."

"I am glad to be here for you. Whatever you need, I will be here. I have an empty house except for Rex. I'm not worried about him because he has an automatic feeder and access to the back porch from the outside. He comes and goes."

"Well, thank you again. I am going to take a long bath after I eat a little something and try and get some sleep."

"Yes, you need to get some rest."

Chapter 40

At dinner, Boyd and Eddie talk about the case. They decide in the morning that they are going to lay out the conference table with possible suspects. They have a lot of information to sort through, and they decide they will get an early start. Breakfast is provided at the Bed and Breakfast when the sun comes up every day. Boyd says he'll meet Eddie in the dining room the next morning and says goodnight.

He wants to call Dolly and hear about her day. He found his soulmate when he married her and misses her terribly when he is away on assignment. Big changes have occurred since they were married. They are expecting twins, and he's received a promotion. Their new house is almost finished, and he wants them to move in before the babies arrive. He dials her number and waits for her to answer. Surprisingly, her voice answers with a message for him.

"Hi Bo, Mom and I went to the movies. She wants to see a particular show, and so I said okay. Really, I'm just going to put M & M's in my popcorn. I think it's a pregnancy craving. Sorry I missed you, but I love you."

He leaves a message. "Already feeding our babies junk food? I'm glad you are being entertained. Love you too. Sleep tight." Boyd laughs because he can envision her eating that concoction.

Chapter 41

Eddie is already seated when Boyd joins him at the breakfast table.

"I ordered some blueberry pancakes," Eddie says with a big grin.

"And you're eating eggs and grits too?"

"Yes, it's all good, sir. You work me too hard."

"I see," and Boyd seems amused at the number of calories the boy consumes.

"Good Morning," a tall girl with a blonde ponytail walks over and pours Boyd some coffee. "We have orange juice also, or grapefruit if you'd like some."

"I'll have orange, please," Boyd acknowledges her.

"Your friend is having pancakes; would you like some also?"

"Thank you, no." He looks over at Eddie and shakes his head in disbelief. *Where does all that food go?*

They finish up breakfast, and Boyd tells him he hopes all that food will last him awhile. Arriving at the police station, Boyd notices J.W. Collins' truck in the parking lot. Eddie comments, "Hey, isn't that" ...and before he can get the rest of it out, Boyd answers.

"Yes, it is, good observation."

"Something must be cooking ...we'll see."

Walking in, Boyd and Eddie immediately look around and J.W. is sitting on one of the desk tops talking to the secretaries.

"Good morning, boys." J.W. displays his usual flippant attitude.

Eddie does not respond. Boyd asks J.W. if he is there to see them.

"No, not especially, just came by to see the girls, and say hello."

"Mr. Collins, for the record, I'm Lieutenant Price, not your boy. Until such time that you are cleared, you have no business here visiting anyone. Even though, you are on your own time, the ladies in this office, are on the time clock, unless you ladies would like for me to clock you out."

"No sir, Lieutenant." The secretaries answer simultaneously. They give a dirty look to J.W.

J.W. eases on out of the office without saying goodbye.

Eddie unlocks the door and Boyd follows him in. They have a few hours to work before they are supposed to be at the Robinson home.

Eddie checks the fax. There are quite a few reports. All are warrants that he is expecting signed by a judge. Boyd refers to their conference room as the war room. On a wall, they have a piece of eight by ten paper with Ron Robinson's name at the top of the board. It branches out from there like a family tree.

Right now, they have three suspects, Ruby, Debbie and J.W. Collins, each having sufficient motive. Merriwether also has motive but unlikely she committed the crime. Eddie looks for patterns in the telephone calls. He matches cellular calls with calls they recognize.

One number cannot be verified but is listed on Ron's cellular bill as belonging to his network. The cell number for Terrance Button also appears. J.W. Collins' cell number comes up frequently, especially after hours. Clearly, they are personal friends and talk often.

Since the murder weapon has not been found, Boyd assumes the killer still has it in their possession. The medical report will reveal the caliber and type of gun. They will check and inquire if Ron owned any handguns himself.

The crime scene does not indicate any sort of struggle between the assailant and Ron. Boyd tells Eddie he thinks Ron was probably surprised by an intruder. After all, he was in his chair having a whiskey. There was only one glass.

Evidently, Ron was also dealing in marijuana sales. The weed packets they found are street packets, often purchased by habitual users. Boyd will send one of them for fingerprint analysis and see what turns up.

Boyd suggest to Eddie it is time to be going to the Robinson home to interview Mrs. Robinson.

"Right behind you, sir." Eddie closes his paperwork and locks the door behind him.

Chapter 42

Boyd remembers the neighborhood from when he visited the Merriwether's. He drives by slowly, coming to a stop.

"Look Eddie, remember these grounds were a showplace when we were here."

"I can't believe it. Look, there is the gardener. Let's ask what happened."

Boyd and Eddie greet Mr. Henry. He is startled to see someone walking up to him. He takes his hat off and rubs his head.

"Oh, yes, now I remember. You were here inside with Ms. Merriwether."

"What happened here, Mr. Henry?" Boyd sounds agitated.

"It's a mystery, pure evil. I wish I knew. One morning, I come out, it's all dead. Beautiful one day, lifeless the next. Maebelle says everything can be replaced, for me not to worry."

"How is she doing? Still in the hospital?"

"Yes, it might be awhile before she is discharged."

"We'll stop by and see her on our way out of town. You take care now," and Boyd leans in to give him a pat on his back.

Boyd and Eddie travel four houses down and find the right address. They get out of the patrol car. Boyd asks Eddie if he brought the warrant.

"Yes sir."

Boyd rings the doorbell.

The door opens. "Hello, Officers. Come in. Ruby is expecting you. She's in the living room."

Boyd extends his hand and offers his identification. Eddie gets his wallet out and does the same. "Ma'am, it's a pleasure to meet you."

Everyone is sitting, and Boyd begins. "Mrs. Robinson, I'd like to extend my sympathy to you for the loss of your husband. I realize our visit might be unsettling for you, given the circumstances."

Eddie quietly says, "My condolences also. I'd like to say a short prayer with you, if you'll allow."

Ruby is surprised, and softly responds, "That will be nice."

Eddie bows his head, "Lord we beseech you to wrap your love and shelter around Mrs. Robinson. Give her peace in her hours of need and grief. Amen."

"Thank you, deputy."

"Yes ma'am."

Boyd clears his throat. "Mrs. Robinson, can you recall the last time you spoke to your husband?"

"Unfortunately, I can. It was the night of the Daniel Black forum."

"Why do you say unfortunately?"

"Well, as a member of the High Springs ladies bridge group, we were all planning on supporting candidate Black."

"But... your husband..."

"Yes, I know, he was insisting that I vote for J.W. He told me over and over the election was important for him that J.W. be elected. I really don't know why. When he found out I was going to the forum, he became angry, and out of control. He hit me and cut my lip with his back hand. I had a bruised eye. Once again, I was being controlled. I stayed in the bedroom that night and didn't see him the next day when I went by the dealership. I saw that minx of a secretary that he has, who probably will lose her job very soon."

"Why do you call her a minx?"

"She enjoys making me feel unimportant. I believed she enjoyed handing over my monthly allowance, for lack of a better word. She purposely monopolized his time at public social events."

"Did you think, or believe they were having an affair?"

"I have no proof, but our marriage was deteriorating. I kept hoping for improvement. Honestly, I was always trying to impress him, but he was otherwise occupied and consumed with this election."

"Is there anyone that can collaborate your story about Ron hitting you?"

"I saw Flo the next day when I stopped by the Merriwether home. And I went to the beauty shop the next day and saw a bridge friend in there."

"Mrs. Robinson, do you own a hand gun or know if Ron keeps a gun here?"

"I have no idea. I was never allowed in his office."

"I understand. May we have a look in there? We did bring a search warrant, and we would like to look in the garage units also."

Ruby, somewhat taken aback, "Oh, I suppose…that it will be okay, anything to bring closure."

Eddie looks at Ruby and smiles.

"Bringing more evidence in will help bring closure to this tragedy, Mrs. Robinson." Eddie reassures her in a sympathetic tone.

"Alright then."

"We'll concentrate in the study first," and Boyd stands up and nods to Eddie.

Betty, listening in the study slowly gets up and walks in the room and sits beside Ruby.

Boyd takes out his camera and takes a picture of the desk with everything on it. Eddie and Boyd both put on gloves. Boyd pickups every file, and flips through various papers.

"Here is a folder marked 'Campaign'." Boyd opens it and studies it. It's a list of contributors and the amounts they have given. It includes many Hispanic names, showing the Rocking H Ranch as their employer. It appears the dealership has written several checks to the campaign. Boyd finds a pocket on the side of the folder. He reaches in it and lifts a small flat notebook with lots of entries. It lists names, with a purchase prices, and notations of bags.

"What does this mean?" Boyd recalls the small bags of weed tucked in Ron's desk. "Whoa, these are his customers. One name has bought many bags. Ron must be dealing. It looks as though Ron has given one guy a discount for quantity." Boyd takes pictures of every page.

Eddie concentrates on the middle drawer where pens and pencils are usually kept.

"Sir, didn't you mention a cryptic note? Look here. Here is a magazine with missing words. A pair of small scissors and a bottle of glue rested in a zip lock baggie. Boyd bags it up after a picture is taken on his phone camera and he puts all of the contents in an evidence bag. They will procure the full magazine and discover if the missing words are part of the Merriwether note left in her mailbox. Boyd remarks to Eddie, "It was just too easy to walk down four houses and put a note in that mailbox."

"Here's more, sir, pieces of stationary. Let's take several pieces and see which top of the letterhead is missing, if this is even a match."

"Who has that note sir?"

"I cannot recall, I have a picture of it in our briefcase."

They continue rummaging through insurance papers, life insurance policies and they find several keys. Apparently, extra keys to his truck, and Ruby's SUV. A cash box is sitting in the bottom drawer and it is locked.

"Look for a smaller key, Eddie, in that middle drawer. Eddie pulls his flashlight out of the briefcase and shines it into the drawer. A key is noticed at the very back, secured in the wood with a push pin stuck in the small key hole. Boyd takes his camera and gets a clear picture of how it is hidden. They try the lock and it snaps open. Lots of cash is stacked in no particular order. There is a car key fob in the bottom, obviously a Ford.

"It is strange that he would store a car key here unless he didn't want anyone to know about it."

"A secret vehicle perhaps? Or why wouldn't he just keep it on the lot for occasional use? If it's registered, we'll find it."

Separately, they both begin to count the cash. In a couple of minutes, Boyd writes down his total. Eddie comes up with the same amount. Eight thousand, seven hundred.

"Are you going to let Mrs. Robinson know about the money?"

"Right now."

Boyd opens the study door, and steps into the living room. Ruby and her friend Betty are planning the funeral details.

"Mrs. Robinson, may I see you in the study?"

"Yes," as she gets up from her chair, "did you find something interesting?"

"Yes, ma'am."

"After you ma'am," and Boyd follows her in and shuts the door. The cash is still on the desk top, and Ruby exclaims, "I never imagined!"

"Ma'am we found a key at the back of the drawer secured in the wood. We are going to leave it, as we have taken pictures."

"Is this mine?" Ruby sounds panicked, referring to the cash.

"Yes ma'am. We have no proof how it was earned, but we have suspicion that is was earned illegally, but it belongs to you, until we can prove otherwise."

"We are going outside now, ma'am. We will probably leave without saying goodbye."

"Again, I appreciate your cooperation and so sorry you are having to go through this."

Eddie picks up the briefcase and follows Boyd to the outside. The guys walk around to the back and open the three-garage doors. One unit appears to be a garden area. There are two classic cars in the other two units.

The garden area holds a variety of tools and there is a bench laden with sprayers.

Eddie counts six sprayers. "Why in the world would anyone need six sprayers?"

Boyd points to the gallon jugs marked glyphosate. "Six would be enough to cover the plants at the Merriwether yard and if you used it full strength, you could scare the dickens out of someone overnight."

"Oh, I see, sir, it you diluted it like you should, it would take several days to wither."

"It's a theory, Eddie. Let's get some pictures, and we'll take a sprayer and let the lab check whether the remaining liquid in it has been diluted or not."

"It appears that Ron was doing all the dirty work, but who wants him killed? Our strongest suspect is Jack Collins, but.... my gut tells me he's just a low-lying weasel. There's no proof yet of anything."

"Mrs. Robinson was pretty candid today, or I thought, sir."

"And somber. That was a nice prayer you said for her, Eddie."

"Everyone needs prayer sir. We are all flawed in some way and need to ask for God's guidance."

"Let's just walk around and see if there is anything interesting that pops out."

They walk full circle around the house with the sprayer and finally put the sprayer in the trunk.

They head back into town and pass by the Merriwether estate. Mr. Henry is still hard at work.

"What's next, sir?"

"I'd like to make time for Debbie the secretary. Or we can go back to the war room."

"Didn't hear lunch in that plan. Aren't you hungry?"

Boyd laughs and shakes his head. "I guess I am just too focused. You are a bottomless pit."

"Yes, sir."

"Why don't we get a sandwich and take back to the office, then I can call Debbie and schedule an interview."

"I will be happy with that. In fact, I can go to the store, drop you off and bring you back a sub or whatever. You can get started."

"There's a plan." Boyd pulls up in the parking lot of the department and gets out. Eddie gets in the driver's seat, looks at Boyd and tells him he'll surprise him with lunch. Eddie says he'll be back in a few and takes off for the store.

Boyd begins with a report showing properties owned by Ron Robinson.

The tax assessor's office lists the dealership jointly owned, their residence, a remote tract of land adjacent to the Rocking H ranch and a smaller old house on the west side of town. The small house and acreage and the tract of land was in Ron Robinson's name alone. Boyd writes down the address of the house and the land. He will have Eddie call for a search warrant on both.

Eddie returns with lunch and they begin eating. Eddie decides they will split a twelve-inch sub and brings in a big salad they can also half. Eddie begins eating while Boyd unwraps his sandwich.

"Well, what do I have here?" and Boyd has the biggest grin on his face.

"I ordered what I thought you would like, sir."

"It's this paper I am referring to, did you think I would like this? He reads off some words written on the paper. *Call me, my number is 386 738 4432, Pammy I get off at four this afternoon.*

"What? Must be the girl waiting on me, she was cute but way too young for me sir. She kept asking me to repeat what I wanted… I thought she was slow."

"I'm so sure," and shakes his head again. "Tagging along with you might be dangerous."

"Yeah, right."

Boyd explains the information he found and talks about getting the warrant.

"When we finish, I'll telephone Debbie."

The fax machine goes off, and a stack of papers come in all marked confidential. Boyd disposes of his sub sandwich papers and begins to read them out loud.

"Crime Lab report indicates the handgun used is a .38 Smith and Wesson Special. Close range. The estimated time of death is difficult to ascertain since the body was there all night. Their best estimate was around six o'clock. Blood samples reveal presence of Lisinopril, Viagra, and Marijuana."

"It appears our victim, Ron Robinson was a habitual weed smoker, which probably explains the cash stash and the weed packets."

Eddie tends to the fax machine as it begins printing scanned copies of the warrants they are expecting.

Boyd is using the departmental police phone and calls Debbie, Ron Robinson's secretary.

"Hello, this is Lieutenant Price from the Special Investigations Bureau. I know you have experienced a rough couple of days, but SIB is needing to advance our case and I'm calling to inquire if this afternoon would be good for you to be interviewed. You can come in here to the station or my partner and I can meet you at your home, whichever is more comfortable." Boyd waits while she is talking into the phone, then reassures her that the information she can give them is important and that she needs to get this traumatic ordeal behind her.

"Okay, I understand. Please meet us at the dealership at five. The office will remain private until we undo the police tapes, you can be sure." Boyd hangs up the phone.

Eddie is surprised. "She wants to meet you at the office?"

"Yes, she said she needs to give us something from her desk."

"Are we ready to ride?"

"I am ready," and both guys take an empty bottle of water for the road. Boyd locks the door behind him.

Chapter 43

The little house listed on the tax roll is west of town and Boyd finds it with ease. The driveway is small and narrow, purposely concealed from most of the traffic that passes by. Obviously, the owner likes it this way. They approach the house slowly and stop. Boyd knocks on the door, even though it appears no one is home. The door is unlocked. Boyd shouts, "Police, Police," and cautiously walks in. The house is furnished and appears someone is residing here. There is a strong odor of marijuana that permeates the air. The dining room table has an unbound brown wrapped package laying in the center of the table with its end open. Little baggies lay about, a weight scale is present, and a large spoon rest is there too.

Eddie walks in the bedroom, then the bathroom, and views some toiletries on the counter.

Clearly, the products are items a female would use. Eddie snaps several pictures. He turns to gaze at the crumpled bed linens and something sparkles in between the wrinkled coverlet. He pulls a pair of gloves from his pocket, puts the right-hand glove on and reaches in with the arm of his sunglasses and picks up an earring. He drops the earring in his left glove, and folds over the top.

Boyd is still in the dining room making a call to the crime lab. He gives them the address and looks up as Eddie shows him the glove.

"That's correct. I'll see you within the hour."

“What do you have there?” Boyd looks at the glove. Eddie tells him, “By the looks of the bathroom, and this earring, we have a female resident. The lab guys should be able to lift some prints off the shower doors and some of the products on the counter.”

“Could this be Ron’s love nest, where a girlfriend helped him market the weed? Or maybe she worked strictly on sales.”

“Ron did have Viagra in his system, and according to Ruby, their love life was devoid.”

Boyd looks at his watch. “Let’s get some pictures of both rooms Eddie. I’ll make a list for the crime boys and then we’ll let them do their job and leave.”

Boyd pulls out his black notebook from his jacket and writes a list of items where fingerprints might be present. Boyd hears the truck from the sheriff’s department drive up on the gravel. Boyd puts on his gloves and opens the refrigerator and takes a picture of the contents.

Two guys from the crime truck knock, then enter. Boyd greets them, and hands them the list. “Do me an extra thorough job, please.”

“Yes, Lieutenant. We’ll do our best.”

Eddie comes out from the back still holding the earring in his glove.

“Ready?”

“Yes, sir.”

Boyd and Eddie get in their car, and Boyd just sits there and thinks. Eddie searches his face, and realizes Boyd is trying to piece together this puzzle.

"I think it is possible there might be another player here, but how do we find her?"

Boyd starts the car and drives out the driveway, and glances at his watch again. "It is three thirty. I'm concerned if we go east to the property that we'll be delayed and late for our interview with Debbie."

"I think we should chance it, and then if we get behind, let's call the sheriff, and get him to go meet with her and stall for a few minutes."

"Good idea."

"Yes sir."

Boyd looks at his notes and travels west and comes to the Rocking H Ranch entrance.

"Looking at the plat, I think the road will fork around the curve, and it does." Boyd veers right. Approximately two miles down the road is a clearing with a concrete pad.

Boyd stops. They both get out of the car. They walk around the pad, and Boyd says, "I have no idea why this is here. Boyd and Eddie stare at the concrete. In unison, they both squat and look closer. Sprinkles of marijuana are all over.

Boyd asks, "Do we have an envelope in the brief case?"

"Yes," and Eddie goes to the car to get the case. Boyd gets close and gets a picture. It's faint, yet noticeable if you're looking intently.

Boyd uses the edge of the envelope to scoop up the residue and small pieces of grass. He gathers enough for a couple of tablespoons.

"Let's walk on the perimeter and check to see if there is anything, anything that sheds light." They separate and walk in opposite directions closely looking at the ground hoping for the proverbial needle in a haystack.

Eddie remarks "This grass has been pressed down by tires, someone driving over it."

Eddie leans down, and he picks up a piece of scrap of paper, brown in nature, like packaging material. Eddie meets Boyd and hands it to him.

"This and leaves, probably nothing," and tosses it down."

"Yeah but wait a second." Boyd bends over and picks it up again. He takes out his phone and punches up his gallery. He finds the picture of the dining room table. "Nothing to probably something," Boyd offers. Boyd compares the scrap of paper to the brown wrapping paper on the parcel laying on the table.

"This looks like a match. What do you think?"

"Could be, I'll get another baggie."

"I think we're done here."

They get in the car to leave with all the items they have collected. "We might make it back in time for the interview." Boyd writes down the odometer reading to pinpoint how far the land is from the highway.

"Got it," and he makes a notation in his notebook.

"It's too much of a coincidence," Eddie says, "that the Rocking H, is adjacent to Ron's parcel."

"It is perplexing, why here? Of all places."

Chapter 44

Driving up to the dealership, Boyd comments to Eddie, "It looks like a ghost town here, not like before, when we were taking pictures from our truck backed into the Hideaway."

Entering the outer office was like walking into an empty classroom; no voices and lifeless.

Eddie brings the briefcase in, following Boyd. Debbie has not arrived, and Boyd takes a seat across from Debbie's desk. Eddie sits in another side chair. Eddie asks Boyd if he thinks Debbie will open up or be a clam. Boyd does not have time to answer when the door swings open and Debbie walks in.

Boyd stands up, Eddie follows suit.

They are seated, and Boyd begins. "Thank you for your full cooperation. I am sure you are seeking some answers too. I hope you are feeling better." He is saying all the right words to get Debbie to relax. "Debbie, I need to tell you, we are recording this interview."

"I don't think I will ever be the same. If it had been a heart attack, I believe I could have handled myself better. But a gunshot is so violent, so brutal. I wonder how long he sat there bleeding or if he died instantly? I feel bad I hid in the bathroom when he came back.

"You hid? Why?"

"I was ready to leave at five. He was mad and angry today, a real live Jekyll and Hyde. I was tired of dealing with him."

"Did he demonstrate a lot of anger often?"

"Yes. One second he could strangle you, another minute he loved you."

"Did you say love?"

Debbie swallows hard and looks like she has let a cat out of the bag.

Boyd stares at Debbie intently. "And…did Ron Robinson love you?"

Debbie returns the stare. "The only person he loved was himself. The only thing he loved was the almighty dollar."

"You sound bitter."

"This job wasn't worth what I put up with from Mr. Big Shot."

"Why didn't you quit?"

"I was going to, believe me, but I wanted to be paid for all he crap that I endured. He harassed me, and he made sexual advances. I made notations and had every intention of filing a lawsuit. I know Mrs. Robinson hates me, and it is just a matter of time before I am fired."

"Why do you think she hates you?"

"She blames me for Ron treating her badly and ignoring her. Personally, I believe she hated him more than me."

"Did you ever witness them arguing?"

"He demeaned her every time he could. That's what bullies do, boost their own egos, in my opinion."

"We're investigating to learn who hated him the most, Debbie," Boyd looks at the secretary inquisitively.

"I imagine he had lots of enemies," Debbie quickly added.

"Did you ever see any drugs being used in his office?"

"I smelled marijuana often. He'd light a cigar to camouflage the marijuana smell....some smokescreen, don't you think?"

"How often did you see Deputy Collins in here?"

"Is he a suspect? I wouldn't doubt it. They had plenty of arguments on the phone. I could hear them when the door was left open. He didn't visit much, but sometimes Ron asked me to go pick up a package from J.W. He always said it was campaign material, but it was soft, like pillows, not like brochures. The packages were always wrapped in brown paper."

"Debbie, what about his personal vehicle?"

"I think they are all here." She looks confused.

Debbie's face looks sad, and she states that she doesn't know if she should go to the funeral tomorrow or not.

"I didn't wish him any harm, just wanted a better place to work for myself. Do you want to look at my little book that I kept about his behavior?" She gets a small key from her purse and unlocks her desk drawer.

"Uh, yes," Boyd answers, a bit surprised that Debbie would suggest it.

Boyd tells Debbie they appreciate her coming in, picks up the book from her desk and hands it to Eddie.

"Sure," her head hangs low now, and she mutters, that she will probably pay her respects, at least to Ruby Robinson.

"Uh, one more thing, the packages," and Boyd opens his phone and shows Debbie a picture of the brown paper from the table, does this look like it?

Debbie looks at the phone. 'Yes, it does. And they were always wrapped with twine."

"Thank you."

Debbie gets up and heads out. She turns back to lock her desk top.

Boyd notices her and asks, "Do you always lock it?"

"Yes, I think so. It's a habit. That way I know it won't be pilfered."

Chapter 45

"It's time for a shower, Eddie, and some plain clothes. I'd like to go have a beer."

Eddie has a huge grin on his face. "Sir, now I am back in your fan club," and he laughs.

The guys decide on visiting the Hideaway Lounge. The Bed and Breakfast they are staying in recommended that the Hideaway is noted for good burgers and steaks. Boyd is finally relaxing, and they sit at a table near the big curved bar.

A familiar face recognizes them and steps over to say hello.

Both men react and begin to stand up to acknowledge her presence.

"Oh, don't get up. Remember, I'm Betty. I was at Ruby's home when you came."

"Yes, ma'am. How is she doing?"

"Better. Some of the other bridge club girls are there visiting now. I needed to go home and check in on my dog."

"Is that the club Mrs. Merriwether plays in?"

"Oh, you know her? Yes, yes, it is."

"How is her recovery going?"

"The girls said she is improving every day. They closed the wound yesterday. Her daughter is here caring for her. Julia's husband too."

"Julia?"

"Julia Button, the wife of Maebelle's personal attorney."

"Yes, ma'am."

"I'll get the bar maid. She's new. Only started a few days ago. She'll get the hang of it. And she's pretty too," looking directly at Eddie.

Eddie smiles as Betty walks away. He mumbles, "Everyone wants to be a matchmaker."

They both look at the menu.

A bald man comes from the back and stops at the table.

"You guys hungry tonight? The steaks are good today. Fresh pole beans too. What do you need? Beer or drinks?"

Eddie answers, "Beer for me."

Boyd shakes his head, "Me too."

The guy yells over to the bar maid, "Two cold mugs here, Dana."

He looks at the guys, "She'll be right here."

In a few seconds, Dana comes from the back of the bar with two beers in her hand and puts them down on the table. "You guys already ordered food?"

"Yes."

"I'll get you some silverware. Everyone says the steaks are good tonight. I'll be right back."

"Thanks," Eddie is looking her way as she departs.

"Okay, here's one you are noticing," Boyd is amused.

Eddie smiles. "Wrong profession."

"And my partner wants smart too."

"I want it all. If I am going to commit to a lifetime I want it all. Brains and beauty."

Dana walks back with silverware and extra napkins in hand and looks only at Eddie.

"Hi, I'm Dana. Another beer?"

Eddie is staring at her too. It is awkward for Boyd as he is thinking Eddie is making a connection.

Eddie stutters, "Hey, you're missing an earring, and he is pointing to Dana's ear."

"Yeah, I haven't been able to find it. It'll probably turn up in my purse or car."

"I hope so." Eddie is still looking at her intently. "When do you think you lost it? It might be here around the bar."

"No, it was a couple of days ago."

Boyd straightens in his chair and his demeanor has changes significantly.

Dana walks off.

Boyd is still astounded. "Eddie, you are not just a pretty face. You have keen observation skills. Do you think this is the missing earring?"

"It's close sir. Don't tell me we're going to miss our steaks."

"No, we're going to need a warrant. We need to find out her last name and run her name in the data base."

Eddie responds with, "I'm thinking free dessert on you tonight, sir."

"You got it."

The steaks are brought to the table by the guy.

Boyd and Eddie begin to eat. "You're the man Eddie, you're the man. I think this is the break we needed."

Thirty minutes or so have passed. The bar is filling up with regulars, and Dana is clearly a bit overwhelmed by customers. Eddie takes his and Boyd's glass up to the counter.

"Sorry," Dana smiles, "I haven't had a chance to get back there."

"No problem," Eddie smiles, "I have all night, two more please."

Eddie waits for the beer and brings them back to the table. "She is too busy to ask her any information."

Boyd answers, "I tell you what, I'm going to step outside and call my wife in a few minutes. Maybe she'll see you alone and come over."

"You're not forgetting my dessert, are you?"

"Go ahead, and buy yourself a whole pie, Eddie, or whatever, you earned it."

Boyd walks out to their car, gets inside, and calls Dolly.

"It's about time I heard from my husband," she says as she answers.

"Honey, miss me?"

"Like a sore thumb. When are you coming home?"

"Probably, tomorrow. Is mom cooking for you or are you cooking for her?"

"Both, we're having girl time. We actually played bridge last night. She invited two ladies over."

Boyd is smiling. "And how are our babies? Are you staying off your feet some?"

"Yes, more and more. Julie set me up a short bench to make flowers in a chair that rolls around. It's comical. We need to decide on names. Everyone just keeps calling them pink and blue. Roan says he has names he wants to run by you when you get home."

"It's probably one of his old horses' names."

Dolly laughs, "Yeah."

"Okay, I'll call you on the way home tomorrow D. I love you."

"Me three."

"Three? Oh, I get it. Goodnight baby."

Boyd returns to the inside of the bar. Eddie is talking to Dana and is holding a slip of paper in his hand.

There's a check laying on the table, and Boyd picks it up and pulls out his credit card.

"No dessert?"

"I'll get it later." Boyd looks at him and smirks.

"Alright, Dana, it is nice meeting you. Perhaps we can talk some other time."

"You can pay me," and Dana reaches for the credit card and bill together."

Boyd follows Dana to the bar. While she is ringing his tab on the credit card terminal, Boyd is taking a hard look at her earring. She hands him back his card and smiles.

"Thank you, ma'am."

Boyd steps back to his and Eddie's table. Eddie has his wallet out, "the tip, sir?"

"Go ahead and leave one. I'll get the Dairy Queen bill."

Outside, Eddie looks at Boyd and stands beside the car door.

"Are you moonstruck?"

"Hardly, sir. I am thinking, that one of these cars must be Dana's car. Employees need wheels to go back and forth. Eddie turns, and looks up and down the various vehicles parked one by the other. Let's picture these Ford tags and see what comes up."

Boyd goes around and joins Eddie, "I'm guessing this is going to be a large Dairy Queen dessert."

"As you can see sir, I do so much better when I am well fed."

"I guess so."

Boyd and Eddie take pictures of the Ford cars.

"Here's a newer one, an affordable compact sporty model. I'll wager this is our missing car for the extra key fob."

"Let's hope one of them is."

Driving down the highway in search of the Dairy Queen, Boyd turns to Eddie, "Well, what is her last name?"

"It's Harrison."

"Did you have to ask for it?"

"Sir, you underestimate my charm and good looks. She dropped it at the table and told me what time she would be getting off tonight."

"Another one?"

Boyd, shaking his head in disbelief, gives the order through the drive-in speakers of the Dairy Queen.

"One small strawberry sundae and one large hot fudge turtle blizzard with a big cherry on top."

"Thanks sir, just what I needed."

Entering the police department, the next morning, they want to get an early start. They discussed the night before how they would divide the work, prepare the reports, and submit them to the state attorney's office for the grand jury. Boyd tells Eddie he believes there is a connection to the Rocking H ranch, and transportation and sale of marijuana between J.W. and Ron. He thinks J.W. Collins is involved with Ron, and he has a gut feeling his connection to Ron is all about making money.

Silently they work on opposite tables, sometimes receiving faxes at different times.

"I got it! Here it is, the lost car that Ron owns. This is probably the car Dana is driving. You are not going to believe this sir. Dana Harrison has the same last name as Debbie, the secretary."

"What?" Boyd ***is*** surprised. Immediately, he searches for the folder on Debbie and the information on Robinson Ford employee records.

"You're right," and Boyd begins reading the file. *Debbie states she was meeting her sister for dinner and did not want Ron Robinson to delay her plans. She hid in the bathroom while he entered his office.*

"Sir, the first time we were here in High Springs, we took pictures of three patrol cars with their Hispanic drivers."

"Can't we have those pictures blown up, and see if they work at the Rocking H? That might prove to be the connection between Jack and Ron doing business together. Coupled with the insane billing of mechanical work on patrol cars, I'm guessing it didn't need to be done at all. The crime boys can go over those cars and see if there is any residue of weed being transported there in the back of the cargo area. It's a long shot, but worth having the crime lab take a look."

"Good thinking. I need another pad. Let me see if the secretaries have an extra one." Boyd opens the door and walks out. There is only one secretary working.

"Are you the only one here?"

"Yes, sir, the other girls wanted to go to the funeral. Their relatives work for the dealership, and they asked off."

"Okay," Boyd asks for a legal pad, and looks at the suggestion box, and realizes he hasn't checked it. He picks it up, and announces that they will be leaving soon, that they will leave the keys on the desks for both offices. Boyd returns to the office and unlocks the suggestion box. There is a note in there.

Please check invoices from Robinson Ford for the two interceptor patrol cars on specific dates, and it lists them.

"Well, this is a little surprise. Sometimes, it pays to leave an offering plate and see what drops in."

Boyd categorizes all the folders and prepares his final report. He types for an hour and a half. Eddie types also.

Boyd gets up to get a bottle of water, and Eddie is staring at his paperwork. He looks up.

"Do you think Debbie was aware that Ron was seeing her sister?"

"I don't know. I believe the case will break wide open when the warrants are sealed, and everyone is called in. Dana is probably the missing link."

As the folders are being numbered and tagged, Boyd runs across a fax he has not seen. It must have been stacked up with some papers.

The information reveals that Ron has two guns registered to him. One was found in his personal vehicle and the other, a small handgun, is missing. The bullets that killed Ron are the same type of bullets that belong to the type of gun that is still missing. Ron might have been shot with a gun that belonged to him. There are only two guns like this that are registered in the entire county.

Eddie finishes with his computer work and inserts a jump drive in the computer to retrieve all the information. He unplugs his computer and begins stacking, labeling and numbering his evidence folders. He grabs a pack of crackers and bottled water. The crackling of plastic makes Boyd look up from his desk.

"Eating again? Have you ever been checked for pinworms? You know, they are prevalent in Florida!"

"I hope you are joking sir."

Boyd keeps his eyes on his desk.

"Sir? It's a joke, right?"

"Yes," and he chuckles to himself.

"Okay, I'm done here. The sheriff is gone to the funeral. I better write him a note and let him know that we are taking the files and have forwarded all information to the state attorney's office." Boyd also copies everything to a jump drive and deletes the files on the computer.

Eddie begins placing files in a large box and asks Boyd for the keys to the car. Boyd tosses them to him, and Eddie makes his way outside and puts one large box in the trunk.

Boyd loads another one when Eddie returns. "Ready to ship out?"

"Yes, sir." Eddie grabs the third box, the briefcase, and surveys the room and steps out to the hallway. He glances over to the secretary to say goodbye. "Thank you."

Boyd is already in the car with another bottled water and his sunglasses on. "Hopefully, you won't require any food before we make it to Shands. I want to see Ms. Merriwether before I go home."

"I just ate crackers. That will hold me for a few minutes, with emphasis on the minutes, sir."

Chapter 46

It's a short drive to the hospital. The parking lot has a couple of spaces designated for law enforcement and Boyd pulls in.

They take the elevator to Ms. Merriwether's room. Boyd tells Eddie he is going to the men's bathroom first and for him to go on.

"Yes, sir."

Eddie enters the room and sees a female doctor in a white lab coat attending to Maebelle. He catches the nurse coming and asks her who the pretty doctor is. He is speaking Spanish to her. The nurse looks puzzled. Eddie continues in Spanish, determined to find out from the nurse the doctor's identity, and start a conversation. Boyd enters the room and breezes by them both.

The lab coat comes off and Penelope hands it back to the nurse. Speaking in Spanish, Penelope thanks her, and tells the nurse that she is feeling warmer now. "Will you please tell the policeman that I speak perfect Spanish, and I am *not* the doctor? I am Mrs. Merriwether's daughter."

Penny looks at Eddie. "Donkey got your tongue?" Eddie turns three shades of red from embarrassment.

Boyd looks at Eddie. "If you are through embarrassing us both, we can introduce ourselves." Boyd shakes his head, "just as I thought you were going to make sergeant."

"All I can do is apologize and beg forgiveness."

Boyd, extending his hand, "I am Lieutenant Boyd Price from Volusia County SIB, Special Investigations Bureau."

"How is your mother doing? She is one special lady."

Maebelle hearing him, opens her eyes, and feels for his hand.

"You're still as handsome as ever. Did you tell your mother hello for me?" she asks in a weak voice.

"Yes, ma'am."

"I received her lovely card. She said you are expecting twins."

"Yes, ma'am."

"How exciting! A boy and a girl."

"Lieutenant now, I am not surprised." She looks at Penelope. "This is my daughter, Penelope Merriwether, and Detective Eddie, you must meet my daughter as well."

Eddie steps forward. "It will be my pleasure." He looks intently in Penelope's eyes. "Nice to make your acquaintance. Uh, that other man, who foolishly showed one of my multi personalities is my cousin, the side of the family with no manners." In Spanish, he tells Penelope she is very well spoken and that he is very sorry, that he was overcome with her beauty and poise."

She nods and giggles. "You are a mess."

"Yes, ma'am. I need training."

Maebelle is intrigued with the chemistry she is witnessing. "Penny, this young man came to see me a few weeks ago, I just love him. If I was younger…"

"I can see that these new visitors have brought you to life Mumsy."

Boyd squeezes Maebelle's hand. "Are you feeling better every day? Tell me how you are doing."

"Oh, I am healing, slow but sure. My daughter is here caring for me nonstop, along with Terry."

"Terrance is coming today," Maebelle continues. "He called me yesterday to tell me you men have been investigating Ron's death. I am so worried about my friend Ruby. This afternoon, I will call her. The service will be over. I did not want to bother her at all while she was handling everything. Poor dear, he was dreadful, but did not deserve to be killed in that manner. Are you finished with your investigation?"

"Somewhat, but you must not worry. You must get well and get back to your bridge game."

"And to my sheriff campaign. To be sure, I want the better candidate to win. Daniel Black has phoned me, and he is coming to visit me tomorrow. His wife is so lovely, and they are fine Christian people. We need more people with strong moral compasses."

The nurse brings in a food tray, sets it down and begins opening lids of food containers.

Boyd suggests Eddie take Penelope to lunch. "I will stay with Ms. Maebelle and visit with her while you dine elsewhere. I'm sure you can use a change of scenery Miss Penelope."

"I would love to take you to lunch and show you my better side," Eddie remarks.

"Okay, we'll start over, and I *can* use a change of scenery."

"Sir, we will be downstairs. May I bring you something back? A sandwich?"

"Yes, and a bowl of soup please." Boyd reaches for his wallet.

"I got this sir."

Eddie is all smiles as he and Penelope step into the elevator, heading to the hospital cafeteria.

Penelope is making herself a salad from the salad bar. She gets another bowl and helps herself to assorted cut fruits.

Eddie asks the server for the grilled fish entrée with rice and roasted red peppers. He decides he will take one of those dinners to Boyd also. *Boyd never finishes his sandwiches anyway. So far, his executive decisions have been spot on.*

Penelope waits back and then they both are at the register together. Eddie remembers drinks. "Can you grab a couple of waters? Please."

"Certainly," and that's when Eddie notices her beautiful teeth.

Eddie pays the girl at the cash register and thanks her. He finds a table and places his food tray down and turns to take Penelope's tray also. He removes all the food and takes the trays back to their bin. Returning to the table, he reaches for Penny's hand.

"I'll say grace, Penny." Eddie bows his head.

"Our Heavenly Father, I ask for continued healing for Ms. Merriwether and for angels to surround her and her loved ones. Guide and direct my partner and me through this investigation in truth and love, unity and peace. We ask that we be all things Godly. Amen."

Penny keeps her hand in Eddie's, and Eddie doesn't make a move either to release it. Eddie opens his eyes and sees Penny staring at him.

"That was a beautiful prayer."

"Religious upbringing," he offers. "Hasn't failed me yet."

Penny brings her hand back and takes her fork in her hand.

"Tell me about your family Eddie."

"I'm the youngest of four. I have three older sisters, and lots of nieces and nephews. My parents settled here from Puerto Rico in the sixties. I'm curious, I've been in your mother's home," he smiles. Lots of England, not so much Spanish. Where did you learn how to speak Spanish?"

"I have been living in Guatemala for two years. I love the people and the culture."

"What do you do there?"

"I work in an orphanage, St. Mary's. It's so rewarding, working with children."

"I imagine it is. Are you planning on returning there soon?"

"Mum will be coming home probably in a few days, and I will see how it goes. She will need my support, I know. Do you live in High Springs?"

"No ma'am, I live in Daytona. I am a Special Investigator with the sheriff's department. I work with Lieutenant Price on cases within the SIB, Special Investigations Bureau."

"This investigation involves my mother?"

"As much as I would like to talk to you about it, I'm not able to do so. Just know that Lieutenant Price is one of the best investigators in Florida. He is very thorough."

"It is obvious you guys work well together."

"Yes ma'am, he's going to be a dad soon, kinda late in life. He and his wife are expecting twins. I'm excited for him."

"Do you have any children?"

"No ma'am, never been married. Looking for the special one."

"And *are* you looking?"

Eddie looks like he is caught in a web. "Looking is probably not the right word, more like open. My sisters are always looking for me. I'm optimistic."

"And I probably shouldn't ask, but every woman wants to know a man's criteria for the special one as you would say."

"Inner beauty, it is imperative. A big sense of humor, strong family ties, and a good cook. Boyd laughs at me for wanting to eat all the time."

"So, the cliché is right, the way to a man's heart is through his stomach."

"Well, it's true for me. I'm available for any meal."

"I'll keep it in mind."

They are interrupted as Terrance Button recognizes Penny eating lunch. Terry walks up to the table.

"Penny, you really need to have council with you if you are going to be interviewed by police."

"Oh, I'm not being interviewed, we were just getting a bite to eat. This is Eddie, with the...."

Eddie stands up and extends his arm for a handshake, "Investigator Martin, SIB. Nice to meet you."

"Terrance Button, personal attorney for Maebelle Merriwether. I understand you guys have finished your investigation."

Eddie is surprised that he would be privy to that news already.

"You might as well know, I am the one who called the state attorney's office into this sheriff's election to investigate."

Terry asks Penny if Maebelle is improving.

"Yes, she has finally made the turn, and they are talking release in a few days. Maybe the nurses heard her planning a bridge game in her room. Did you attend the funeral today?"

"No," and he says it abruptly. "Julia attended with some of the other bridge club ladies to support Ruby."

"I wonder what will happen to the dealership, and if Mrs. Robinson will try and manage the dealership by herself."

Rather tersely, Terry states, "I don't know. Well, I'll go on up and see Maebelle."

"Oh, okay, we'll be up soon."

Penny continues to eat and asks Eddie if they are on their way home after they leave the hospital.

"Yes, we are. But I'd like to stay in touch with you after I leave."

"Yes, I'd like that too. Perhaps when Mumsy gets home, I can prepare that meal for you, the one you think you are always missing."

"I'm going to call for a reservation. Do you have a cooking specialty?"

"Specialty, you ask? I suppose I cook a variety of things, mostly Southern with a few authentic Spanish dishes I have learned while I have been living out of the country."

"I never complain about good food. Do you have a special someone waiting for you when you return to Guatemala?"

"As a matter of fact, I do. He's very special to me. We're very close. I knew his parents very well and our relationship blossomed after their untimely death."

Eddie's spirit is sinking, and his face shows it.

"Yes, he's my little man." She pauses.... "He's six."

Eddie swallows hard and it is audible. Immediately he looks at her and has the biggest grin. "Six, you say, six feet tall or six years old?"

"Yes, in fact he just turned six."

"Well, if he melted your heart, then he will melt mine too."

Penny is touched by his sentimental manner, and she smiles back at him. She glances at his plate, "I'm ready to go back to Mumsy's room whenever you are."

"Me too. I'll get this," and Eddie picks up all the table trash and takes it to the trash disposal. He grabs Boyd's lunch, joins Penny and they walk down the hall and take the elevator up to Maebelle's room.

Terrance and Boyd are talking outside the room and Terry reaches inside his coat pocket and pulls out an envelope and hands it to Boyd.

Penny enters her mother's room, and Eddie lags to catch up on the conversation with the men. When he has the opportunity, he tells Boyd, "I have your lunch here."

"Okay, I'll step inside the family waiting room and eat."

Terry goes back into Mrs. Merriwether's room, while Eddie and Boyd leave for the sitting room and find a small table.

Eddie looks very happy and Boyd comments that his face is glowing.

"I'm that transparent?"

"Remember I told you when you meet the one, you'll know it."

"You are right sir, I want to know her more."

Eddie continues, "I noticed Mr. Button gave you an envelope."

"It's the cryptic note that was placed in Ms. Merriwether's mailbox. We'll try and match up the magazine clippings to the original note. When we get back, we will probably meet again to compile all the reports. I am thinking we will have to take the young girl in for questioning."

"Still, I am perplexed by J.W. Collins' role, wondering if he was aware of Ron's girlfriend, or whatever she was. I recall Betty telling us she was new to the area. Perhaps that is something Dana just told her. We need to find out more about this girl." He repeats her name, *"Dana Harrison."*

Boyd disposes of his lunch plate. "I thought I was getting a sandwich, but this is really good. Thanks, partner."

"You are welcome."

Both walk back to the room to say their goodbyes.

"Ms. Merriwether," Boyd is almost whispering.

"I thought we were on a first name basis," and Maebelle has a slight giggle.

"Miss Maebelle, I hope you can leave soon and get back to playing cards."

"Me too. I have a sheriff candidate who needs me to start making phone calls for him to get him elected. Daniel Black phoned me a few moments ago while you stepped out of the room and wanted to know if he could still visit me tomorrow. He said Jack Collins was playing dirty with the campaign. J.W. needs to be exposed by a citizen other than Daniel Black."

"Well, you be careful out there. Don't try to be Scotland Yard all by yourself."

Everyone in the room laughs. They all know Maebelle's determination and mindset. Boyd leans over her bed and gives her a gentle kiss on the cheek.

"I'll talk to you sooner than you think. One day, I'll catch you by surprise."

Eddie is looking at Penelope and winks. Eddie reaches for Maebelle's hand and gives it a squeeze. "You take care."

Penny and Terrance walk them both to the outside corridor. Boyd shakes both of their hands.

Eddie steps up and shakes Terrance's hand and leans in and gives Penny a lengthy hug, and a soft kiss on the side of her hair. "I hope to talk to you soon."

He begins to speak to her in Spanish. "Yo voy a pensar en ti todos los dias hasta que nos encontremos de nuevo," *I will think about you every day, until we meet again.*

The sheriff campaign is heating up. During J.W.'s suspension from the sheriff's department, the community thinks he is just taking time off from work to solicit votes. Very few people are even aware he has been suspended. He is covering a lot of ground meeting and greeting in all the popular restaurants while Daniel Black is focusing on church congregations.

Mr. Black reminds voters he is not part of the old boys' club; he has fresh ideas he'd like to implement and save the taxpayers money. Both candidates express good talking points, but voters so far are reluctant to verbalize their commitment.

Daniel Black is grateful to Ms. Merriwether's bridge friends who have volunteered for various jobs. Tommie Lou met up with Maxine and Adeline at Ron Robinson's funeral, and agreed to meet at the campaign office and make phone calls. Their job will be writing down voter concerns on a pad of paper. Elsa Jane will make a report of concerns and itemize them for Daniel to look over. Harriet states she will be more active once she is done harvesting the first wave of vegetables coming in from her gardens. She shares with the other bridge ladies that she is concerned about Ruby, and that she took taken several dishes of food to the covered dish luncheon held after the funeral. Harriet tells the bridge ladies that Ruby looks pale and stressed. The ladies all agree it is understandable. Everything that has happened was so unexpected.

Chapter 47

Ruby insists Betty return to her own house.

"I'll be fine, I am a big girl, and even though Ron is gone now, I will be fine. You have been a big help and I truly appreciate it," she says as she hugs Betty goodbye.

Feeling sad, Betty drives off, remembering her own horrible day that she buried her daughter. Ruby's words, 'I will be fine' resonated in her mind. Betty was never *fine* after her beloved child was murdered. She knew she stayed depressed, and full of guilt that she might have done more to change the direction of her daughter's life. Betty drove to the Hideaway Lounge for some quiet time.

Dana is hustling at the bar side when Betty walks in. She gives Betty a wink and gets her a Canadian Club and ginger cocktail ready, sitting on the bar top when Betty climbs up on the stool. Betty looks around and sees there a few men talking to J.W. Collins about the election.

Jack is telling everybody he owes it to Ron to get elected, because Ron did so much for him. He's getting a little loose lipped and telling the guys that Daniel Black is a poor manager of money, nearly bankrupt himself. "How could he possibly run the sheriff's department?" J.W. asked his bar friends.

In return, some of the guys want to know from J.W. how he knows Daniel is bankrupt.

"Well, he doesn't have much money to even put in his own campaign. He's depending heavily on the Republican Party to spend all their money."

All the while, Dana would have to be blind not to notice J.W. Collins trying to get her attention. He keeps calling her *darlin'* and *honey.*

Finally, she acknowledges him, "Can I get something for ya?"

"Just call me Jack. All my friends do."

"Well, Jack, do you need another drink, or are you calling it a night?"

"Calling it a night? It's too early for a youngster like myself."

"Well, kids usually get to bed early," and turns her back to him without a second's hesitation.

Betty appreciates Dana's sarcastic comeback to J.W. Some of the guys listening in also chuckle which clearly irritates him. J.W. has in mind talking to Dana after work, about a business proposal he thinks might interest her. He'll be patient and wait till closing time.

Dana asks Betty why she has been a stranger lately. Betty explains that she was helping Ruby.

"However, Ruby just told me she is a big girl, and that I need to go home. How about you, are they giving you lots of hours?"

"Yeah, enough, I've been looking for a place to rent. It's hard to get on your feet when you start over. You know, rent, insurance, car payment. I need to turn this car I'm driving back in and get a good used one."

"Oh, you don't own that car you drive?"

"No, it is a loaner, and I need to buy something cheaper."

Betty ponders Dana's dilemma and offers that she has another vehicle she is not using. "Maybe, you can make payments to me. It's a 2010 Taurus, but it runs good, with plenty of cold air conditioning."

"How much? The new friend discounted price?"

"I'll take whatever the wholesale price is in the Kelly Blue Book. Does that sound fair?"

"It sounds like a deal," Dana is grinning from ear to ear.

"Okay, I can drive it in tomorrow and you can take it for a test drive."

"Gee, thanks, Betty. Another drink for you?"

Betty points to her empty glass. "Yes, I'm ready."

One by one, the bar buddies start to trickle out and leave for home. Betty tells Dana goodnight and passes by Jack texting someone on the phone.

"Goodnight Jack."

"Oh yeah, you too."

Dana approaches Jack and tells him it's last call.

"I'm done," Jack says. "Time to get some fresh air outside." He pulls out a twenty-dollar bill and lays it on the bar. "For you shugga, later"... and leaves his glass on the bar.

Chapter 48

Dana rushes to wipe down all of the bar top. Speedily, she cleans up the bar and goes through the closing procedure list. If she is late to the hostel house, they will lock the doors on her.

Stepping outside, Dana hurries to her car. She presses her key fob to unlock. Dana looks up to see Jack Collins pressing her side.

"I thought we could have a talk," Jack begins.

"About what exactly?"

"You always this unfriendly? Ron told me how sweet you were to him."

"Funny, he never talked about you at all."

"Well, Ron and I were in business together. I'm prepared to offer you the same deal. You can still be the distributor and get Ron's portion."

"How much will my cut be? Ron furnished me a place to stay and my customers met me there."

"The split will be fifty-fifty."

"Uh, I don't think so, Ron looked out for me. Now I will need to look out for myself. I am the one in danger of getting caught because I am the seller. I mean, look at what happened to Ron? He was killed by someone he was probably double-crossing. You have a badge you wear that keeps you camouflaged, and no one suspects you."

"But I am also the one that has to front the money now since Ron is departed."

"I really thought you'd be a bit more emotional about Ron's death."

"It was business, like it will be with you. Strictly business."

"Hey, I am a happily married man, sweetheart."

"Then, start acting like one. And here's another thing, I don't want to lose my job at the bar, so stop being personal with me like we are acquaintances."

"I'll need your number to text or call."

"I don't have a phone. Ron purchased one for me. You need to get me one, and if the split will be sixty-forty, we have a deal."

"When I am elected sheriff, it will be easier for me to bring in the goods. Just keep your nose clean so we can enjoy a mutual profit."

"Oh, and I'll need a gun."

"What? A gun! What for?"

"To protect myself."

"Do you know how to use a gun?"

"Of course,"

"Did you have a gun, where is that one?"

"I gave it back to Ron."

"I'm starting to think that you are one tough cookie. Remember we're not selling dope, we're just supplying some marijuana, some feel good you might say."

Dana grows impatient by the minute and asks Jack what time it is.

"Almost twelve."

"Damn, I'm out of here." She starts up her car and speeds off.

Chapter 49

It is Friday morning, and Debbie prepares for work realizing that this will probably be her last day. The dealership reopens today, and she is sure Ruby will be taking the helm and that she will most likely be fired. Debbie is emotional and just keeps repeating to herself that everything will work out, that change can be a good thing. She hasn't spoken to her sister lately because Dana doesn't have a phone. She sure could use an encouraging word right about now.

Entering the office, she brings in a box and places it under her desk anticipating loading it with personal items and then leaving.

Ruby Robinson arrives within a few minutes.

"Oh, great, fresh coffee brewing," she says as she approaches Deb's desk. "Could you bring me a cup, with cream and sugar in a couple of seconds and step into the office, please?"

"Yes, ma'am."

Debbie finds a pad, some of the mail, and her list she has prepared to aid Ruby in the transition period and walks into Ron's, now Ruby's office.

At the office door, she takes a deep breath and knocks. With hot coffee in hand, Debbie enters, finding Ruby staring where her husband normally sat.

Without looking at Debbie, Ruby asks where Ron's chair is.

Debbie hands Ruby the coffee. "I had it removed for you."

"I did not want you to be uncomfortable thinking about the chair your husband was…sitting in."

Ruby looks at Debbie with renewed interest. "Thank you, that was very thoughtful of you. I imagine this ordeal has been traumatic for you as well."

"Yes, ma'am."

"Please have a seat, Debbie."

"Yes, ma'am."

Ruby sips the coffee. "Yes, this is what I needed."

"Debbie, I need answers and I need help. This is my dilemma. I do not know if I can run this dealership. I suppose every person is capable with the right assistants in place, and I am questioning if you are one of the right assistants to guide me. Perhaps, I have misjudged you. Knowing Ron and the way he treated me, I am sure I am not the only one that despised his manner and bullying. I am ready to listen to your concerns. I tried to reflect in the last few days and erase my preconceived notions that you are my enemy." She stops talking and stares at Debbie now sitting across from her. "It is your turn to talk."

"Mrs. Robinson, thank you for allowing me to speak freely. Foremost, I want to do my job correctly and to contribute wherever I am needed. On many occasions, I feel Mr. Robinson, may God rest his soul, crossed the line and working here was difficult." Debbie takes another breath.

"Let me interrupt you here. When you say, crossed the line, what do you mean?"

"There were many times your husband made me uncomfortable, however, there was **no** time that I participated in anything that was unethical and personal with Mr. Ron."

Ruby stares at her and is letting what Debbie just said to her soak in.

"Then you are telling me that you can be trusted."

"Absolutely, Mrs. Robinson, I would love to keep my job and benefits, and help you get on your feet managing this place."

"Would a man be better suited for this job? How would you feel about two bosses, for instance Rusty, as a general manager of sorts?"

"I know that he is a loyal employee, and he was derided often by…the late Mr. Robinson." Debbie quickly adds, "I'm sorry."

"Listen Debbie, let's stop walking on eggshells. I believe in fresh starts. From now on, Mr. Robinson will be referred to as Ron. I do not want there to be awkwardness moving forward."

"Moving forward, this is the current mail and papers that need attention. I have prepared a report which might be valuable to you in these first days. The accounting department will also be a good source of information also to you."

"Okay, thank you. I'll look these over."

Debbie leaves and closes the door behind her. She sits at her desk and openly cries. For now, she still has a job. Her phone rings, interrupting her self-indulgence and she answers it.

"Administration, Debbie speaking."

"Hello, this is Maebelle Merriwether calling for Ruby. May I speak with her?"

"Certainly," and Debbie buzzes the inner office.

"Mrs. Robinson, Maebelle Merriwether is calling. Line one." Debbie hangs up and begins working again.

"Ruby, dear, I have been thinking of you so much, and I am terribly sorry for your loss."

"So much has happened Mae. It's so good to hear from you. How are you feeling, and when do you expect to come home?"

"They have closed the wound and I am hoping to be released tomorrow. Of course, I will continue my therapy for my shoulder, and in a couple more weeks, the cast will come off of my foot. Penelope is here every day at the hospital, and I hope she will stay a long time when I get home. Maybe her wandering days are over."

"Ron and I never had any children. You are blessed, Maebelle. The bridge ladies have all been to see me. It's just not the same without you, but soon, we will all be together again. Once the election is over, High Springs will be the quiet community again."

“And how is the election going?”

“With Ron’s passing, I will not be holding anymore political events here. I’m hoping J.W. Collins will not be visiting me under any circumstances. I want the election to be over!”

“I hear the campaign is getting ugly Ruby, and J.W., I fear, is playing dirty. The good folks of High Springs will decide.”

“I hope to see you in a couple of days Maebelle, and Penny too. I’ll call Flo and she can keep me informed.”

Chapter 50

Flo and Mr. Henry are accomplishing a lot, both in the home and outside on the grounds. The fall décor is all around, which Flo knows will bring a smile on Maebelle’s face. She already has the welcome home dinner planned.

Mr. Henry literally transformed the yard in a couple of weeks. The grounds are lush in fall mums and annuals. There are newly planted shrubs that add dimension.

Every day, Flo will add a few special decorations to areas here and there. She has taken some older floral pieces in to the florist and asked that the designer make a spectacular mantel piece for the fireplace. Flo did not have a clue how to transform old to new, but she described the look she was wanting to the designer. She thought an English garden look would be pleasing with lots of berries, pheasant feathers, vines and leaves. The finished floral was beautiful, and Penelope notices it immediately. Flo is busy restocking everything in the pantry she might need to cook in anticipation of visitors coming to visit Maebelle at home. She wants to be available for any care Maebelle might require and does not want to leave the house to go shop the grocery store for any reason.

Penelope stays later at the hospital than usual to be sure all the arrangements are in place, allowing her to bring her mother home. During some of her mother's naps, Penelope walks the halls and thanks the different nurses who have helped with Maebelle's recovery. When she gets home tonight, she plans on calling Tito, her little man in Guatemala.

She misses him and hearing the little guy giggle and laugh. She glances down at her watch. There is still time, because it is two hours earlier in the day in Guatemala. The phone rings startling Maebelle and Penny both.

"Hello," Penny almost sounds like a child trying to be quiet.

"Hello Beautiful, this is Eddie. How are you holding up?"

"Hello yourself, everyone is good. Mom is coming home tomorrow. I've made all the necessary arrangements with a medical transport company. She is so excited. We're all looking forward to further healing at home."

"This is really good news. I think being at home speeds up mending for sure. Do you need help? A police presence or escort?"

Penny giggles, "No, I don't think that will be necessary."

"I was trying to conjure an invitation to come see you. I don't want you to forget about me."

"How can any girl forget that flashy smile, that dark hair and those dark eye lashes that look like dust catchers?"

Eddie starts laughing. "Dust catchers? You're flirting with me Miss Merriwether. I like it. May I drive up and see if you need help tomorrow afternoon? And if I am in the way, I'll drive home, sulking of course, being completely miserable."

"Okay, if you insist. I have often heard that misery loves company. Apparently, you are the insistent type."

"Now, we're getting somewhere. I'll see you tomorrow with my flashy smile and dust catchers."

"Goodbye, Eddie." Penelope is feeling unnervingly giddy.

Of course, Maebelle is curious who is calling. She senses Penny is excited, yet apprehensive. "Penny for your thoughts?"

"Gosh, you haven't said that in so long."

"It's been a long time since I saw that look in your eyes."

"And what look is that Mumsy?"

"That star you have caught in your eyes that is twinkling."

"Well, we'll see, we'll just have to see if stars can hold their luster."

"It's time you get home Penny girl. Tomorrow is a big day. You don't need to come back in the morning. I will be alright in the transport. I will see you at home. Finally, home. I am so happy to go home. I hope I won't be a burden to anyone."

"Still so independent, you'll never change, Mum."

"I suppose not."

Penny leans over and gives her mother a ferocious hug and kisses her on the cheek. "See you tomorrow."

Penny grabs her sweater and goes to get the night nurse, telling her she is leaving. She blows her Mum a kiss but Maebelle's eyes are already closed.

In the parking lot, Penny thinks about Eddie's call. She longs to get to know him better, but she doesn't know yet how long she will be staying. She hasn't mentioned a thing about Tito to her mother. Penny begins the ride home, smiling about her little companion and all the joys they have shared.

Chapter 51

Dana decides on her ride home to the hostel that she will get up early and return the car Ron loaned her from the dealership. She will wipe it down removing any sign that she was driving it. Maybe no one is aware of her using a car and she and Ron's relationship can remain an arcane alliance. She doesn't want anyone questioning her about why she had the car in her possession. She'll leave it at the side area where the used cars are sold. It should be inconspicuous there, she hopes. Dana will walk a few yards to work and no one will be wiser.

Hopefully, the Taurus Betty mentioned will be a good dependable car for a while.

Dana drives up to park at the hostel and sees the lights are all out. This will be her second warning, and she is not looking forward to the lecture from the director. Dana rings the bell, and a short white-haired lady appears at the door in her house robe. Through the window, Dana can see her shaking her head and wagging her finger. Dana is ready with her excuse.

"I am so sorry, I stopped to help an elderly lady on the side of the road. She was walking her dog and the dog slipped out of her hand. I nearly ran over it but stopped in time. She was so upset, and me too, the thought of losing her pet like that made both of us cry.

"She offered me fifty dollars for helping her, of course, I couldn't take it. She was very frightened, but I walked her back to her house, reminded her to hold on to the leash tighter, even suggested she walk the dog earlier in the day."

"You probably know her. She was so sweet, just like you. Just needed some help."

"Oh, alright then, what was the neighbor's name?"

"Oh, I think she called the dog Tiffany. I told her I had to leave, or I'd be late."

"Well, you are a little late, but under the circumstances, it will be alright." She sighs.

"Yes, ma'am." Dana doesn't look back and goes down the hall to her bedroom, not wanting to press her luck.

Dana is restless as she tries to sleep. Without a phone, she doesn't have an alarm clock. It won't be long till she'll have a new phone and perhaps somewhere permanent to stay. She is saving tips as quickly as she can. The hostel house requires very little money from her, and she is close to saving enough to get an apartment. She knows her sister gets to work early and Dana wants to be at the lot before seven, so that she will not be noticed. She will take some Lysol wipes from the pantry to wipe down the car.

In the morning at the lot, she parks close to the used car area, and takes several minutes to wipe down door handles and the steering wheel. She wipes all knobs on the dashboard, just about everywhere she thinks her hands might have been.

She really has nothing to hide, but she wants to avoid suspicion about her relationship with Ron. She wonders about what her sister Debbie would think about her carrying on with a married man, especially Debbie's boss. Sometimes you do things to survive. Debbie wouldn't understand. She is always too emotional for her own good. Having relations with Ron was a means to an end. It was sustenance and sanctuary at one location.

She leaves the key on the seat after wiping it thoroughly, and shuts the door, pulling her hoody over her head and she walks slowly to the Hideaway Lounge.

"You're here a little early, aren't you?" Dana looks up and sees her boss standing over her.

"Oh, good morning. Yes, I'm meeting someone to sell me a car. It will be a cheaper ride, less insurance."

"Who is it?"

"Oh, Miss Betty, she comes in all the time."

"Well, c'mon in, and I'll fix some breakfast for us."

"Yum," and Dana follows him in.

Chapter 52

Eddie calls Boyd after he finishes his breakfast.

"Good morning sir. Need a favor."

"This early? What, there's no grocery store open to feed you in Daytona?"

"I've already eaten, sir."

"Of course, you have," and Boyd is laughing.

"Sir, I remembered your wife has a flower shop. I need some flowers. I thought I'd go see Ms. Merriwether with a beautiful bouquet. She's going home today to High Springs."

"You mean you're going to see Penelope with some flowers for her mother to impress her."

"Isn't that what I said sir?"

"I guess so, do you need to speak to Dolly, or do you want me to tell her for you."

"It's sort of a delicate situation sir, I might need her expertise."

"I'll get her, wait a second."

Dolly picks up the phone and says hello.

"I can tell by both of you laughing that Boyd has shared my dilemma."

"Only that you need a bouquet to pick up in a carry out box, full of beauty to convey she is special to you. It will be my pleasure to design something impressive. I look forward to meeting you Eddie. Do you know the address of my flower shop? I imagine you will be picking it up on your way."

"Do you know what time you will be here?"

"About two o'clock. I also have a gift I need wrapped expertly. Would you be willing to do that also?"

"Absolutely, it will be my pleasure. I'll have the flowers ready. Here's Boyd," and she hands the phone back to him.

"This will cost you buddy."

"It always does, to go first class that is. What are you doing on your days off?"

"I'm taking my wife out for her birthday. We're going over your way to her sister's condo in Daytona."

"Okay, maybe I'll catch up with you when I get back."

"Will I see you at the flower shop, sir?"

"Probably not, I've got to get to the new house, and tend to some other things like yards, etc."

"Okay, sir."

"Good luck Eddie, talk to you soon."

Chapter 53

Betty hopes Dana will be on time, so they can travel back to her house and she can pick her own car up. She is due at the Merriwether estate to welcome Maebelle home. It is going to be an impromptu soirée that Flo has organized just for the bridge ladies.

Betty parks the car, hitting the horn my mistake when she grabs her purse. That was all Dana needed to rush outside and meet her.

"Oh, good, you're here, because I need to rush back," Betty sounds anxious.

"Let me tell the boss that I'll be back to help him early because he just fixed breakfast for me."

Betty goes around to the passenger side and waits in the car with the air conditioning running.

Dana comes out again smiling when she sees that she is going to be the driver. With seat belt on, they pull out on the highway, Betty giving her directions all the way.

Betty explains she needs to be at the Merriwether home soon.

"Oh, how is she doing?"

"Good, she's coming home today."

"That was a bad accident. She shouldn't have been run off the road like that."

"Did you say run off? Where did you hear that?" Betty is surprised.

Dana stumbles. "I don't know, maybe I didn't hear it. I can't remember what I've heard. You know how bar people talk. They always have loose lips."

"That is shocking to me that people are saying such things." Betty is matter of fact. "I haven't heard anything of the sort."

"This car drives really nice, Betty. I appreciate you."

"You're welcome. I just wish someone could have reached out to my daughter when she needed help."

"Yeah, I understand."

"Here's my driveway," and points to it.

Driving up, Dana says, "Oh, your house is beautiful, and it looks really peaceful. I love all the trees."

"Thanks. Okay, kiddo, I'll show you around another day. Can you find your way out? I'll probably stop by the Hideaway this afternoon, and I'll see you then."

Dana starts to embrace Betty. "Let me give you a hug."

"Oh goodness," and Betty leans over and smiles. "See 'ya soon."

Dana pulls around and heads back to the Hideaway. Betty gets in her car and follows her out of the driveway headed for the Merriwether residence.

Chapter 54

Flo and Mr. Henry have done all the work for the little soirée party. Penelope is still sleeping in. The night before, she praised them both when she got home for all their efforts in getting the house ready. Mr. Henry has installed some new rails in Maebelle's bathroom. He fashioned a rolling chair that is padded to accommodate Maebelle's injured leg. Penelope shares with him that Maebelle needs to keep her leg elevated whenever possible. They assure Penny that Maebelle will have the best care. They will see to it.

Penny was up late the night before. She made several attempts to call the orphanage finally getting through on her fourth try.

She learns that Tito is asking for her but is doing well. Daily, Tito is saying prayers for Penny's mommy. Tonight, he is spending the night with a boy from his same village.

"Please tell him I called, and that I will mail him a letter, so he can read it to the class," Penelope tells her friend.

Penny wakes thinking she has already written Tito the letter. Her mind is playing tricks on her, probably because she is tired. A hot shower will be good for her, followed by a cup of coffee while she is waiting for her hair to dry.

Today is important, as Penny will be able to see if Maebelle has the drive to learn how to walk again. The big wound on her leg is grafted and her leg will be weak for sure. Penny knows all too well her mother's self-reliance.

One thing's for sure, Mae's spirits will be lifted now that she is returning home. Perhaps life will become normal again.

The bridge ladies are the only invitees for Mae's welcome home gathering. It is going to be a short brunch, so she can retire to her room for rest. Flo cautions the club to keep the conversation light. Everyone agrees. The group is delighted to be invited over and greet their beloved friend.

Penelope takes a long hard look in her mirror in the bedroom. Her hair is longer now, and she realizes she has become part of the Guatemalan landscape. She thinks she needs softening and wants to embrace her feminine side. Traveling back and forth to the hospital did not leave a lot of time for herself lately. She remembers seeing Julia Button at the hospital and thinking how cute she looked. Penny will ask her when she arrives to recommend a shop to pick up some newer clothes. She uses a flat iron on her hair, then twists a side portion off her face to showcase her great cheekbones. She brought a jade green halter top with her, and a matching jade print batik skirt. It will have to do until there is a day to shop.

She is finishing dressing when three of the ladies arrive. She wants her mumsy to notice that she has not forgotten her upbringing, what Maebelle taught her about looking her best.

She enters the living room and introduces herself to Maxine and Adeline. Tommie Lou tells her she is beautiful, just like a younger Maebelle.

Harriet and Elsa Jane are ringing the bell and Flo welcomes them. The telephone rings and it is Ruby. Quickly, she tells Flo she might be tardy.

"It's okay darlin, come when you can."

Julia sees herself in and gives Penny a big hug. "That color on you is stunning Penny."

"Oh my, I was going to ask **you** for a little fashion advice."

"My advice, is don't get around my husband." Immediately, the ladies laugh. They all know it is said in fun.

There is a little commotion outside and the girls realize that the transport van has arrived.

"Ms. Merriwether, we are here to help you. Please… you will need a safety harness in case you fall." The medical transporter is clearly annoyed.

"Rubbish," and points her cane directly in the male nurse's chest attempting to jab him with it.

"You might not see that," as she points to a rail, but I can use that for support. Where do they find you nursing students? At band practice? Well, toot, toot, I can do this myself." Frustrated, she is unusually snippant.

The young guy stands behind Maebelle, watching carefully to see that Ms. Maebelle picks up one foot, then the other, methodically concentrating, with a bit of grimace on her face.

It is all quiet in the house as everyone's attention is focused at Mae's efforts to negotiate a few steps.

"Flo, Penny, Mr. Henry, I'm home," she calls.

Flo cannot wait and opens the door wide. "Yes um, you sure 'nuff is, you is finally home, a sight for sore eyes." Flo goes to meet her with a wheel chair, and Maebelle looks around for the young male.

"Now, you there, don't be a dolt. Now is the time I need you to help me sit down."

"Yes, ma'am."

She is wheeled into her home amid claps and cheers from her gals, and she is grinning from ear to ear.

Flo pushes her to the living room, and Mae looks around, with eyes wide. "Flo, my home has never looked lovelier," with tears in her twinkling eyes, she softly says, "I thank you for taking care of it."

Penny walks over and hugs her mother. "Would you like tea now?"

"Lovely, dear. That will be delightful, and you look so lovely."

"Where is that young man now?" Mae is turning her head around as he is bringing in her personal satchel from the hospital.

Surprisingly, Betty enters from the back door with Mr. Henry who comes in for a beverage break. Betty approaches Maebelle and leans in to give her a hug.

"Oh, Betty, I'm happy to see you. Maebelle is expecting to smell a bit of alcohol but is taken aback by a weighty perfume.

"Betty, your perfume. I've smelled it before. What is the name of it?"

"Truly, Maebelle, I don't know because I didn't put any on. It must be my new friend who just hugged me, I guess," laughing as she is explaining.

Maebelle is perplexed. The memory of that perfume escapes her this very minute, but it will come to her, she feels sure.

Mae looks again for the man. "There, there you are, I thought you were lost. You probably need something to drink. Flo, please continue to be my hostess." Flo is beaming with pride, as she looks at the young man and says, "Follow me."

Mae's foot cast has been replaced with a softer version with a short wide heel built in the plaster. She has a compression hose on her right leg that zips down the back side. One by one, her friends surround her until Penny suggests that they wheel her into the dining room. They can all sit together at the table and converse.

"Flo, dear, may I trouble you for a handkerchief?"

"Right away, I'll be just a second," Flo answers.

Instantly, Mae is handed a linen hankie, and she wipes her brow. Her cheeks are rosy and she is taking everything in, smiling, often stretching out her hand to hold Penny's hand.

The doorbell rings again, and Flo answers it.

"Hello," Ruby dashes in wearing a red jacket with a cheetah collar and cheetah fabric piping on the pockets.

"Oh, Ruby, dear, how good of you to join us. Now we are all here."

Mr. Henry and the male nurse come from the back. He is holding a couple of bags with take away treats for him and the driver waiting outside.

"Good, you have refreshment. I can't thank you enough young man, you were such a big help. Have safe travels back to Shands."

"Yes, ma'am." *He is glad to be departing, for sure.*

The frivolity continues with idle chit chat about this and that around High Springs.

Maebelle clears her throat and drinks more tea. "How is the campaign doing? Any polls out yet telling us where the race is going, and which candidate is ahead?"

Elsa Jane, obviously in the know, tells everyone she thinks it is a dead heat. "J.W. Collins is playing the race card, and folks are thinking about not voting at all, because they are so turned off by all the commercials."

"Goodness, gracious, we simply can't have that. We must put our heads together and come up with a new idea."

The ladies shake their heads in unison.

"How 'bout next week, we come together and brainstorm again?"

Penny interjects, "Not on Tuesdays or Thursdays because those days are reserved for physical therapy."

There are hushed whispers of "Absolutely, of course, you can't miss that," by all the ladies.

Harriet is the first to approach Maebelle to say goodbye. "I brought you some fresh vegetables and left them with Mr. Henry. Get Flo to juice you some for energy."

"Harriet, love, there is nothing wrong with my teeth or jaw. I can eat!"

Everyone giggles. Maebelle thanks her. "You are so thoughtful."

"Glad you are home, you look wonderful," Harriet adds.

It seems everyone agrees it is time to leave the soirée much to Mae's pleading that it is too soon to break up the small party.

Penny wheels Maebelle to the front to bid the girls goodbye and shuts the door.

Maebelle is still smiling and looks at Flo and Mr. Henry. "My welcome home party was so special, and I loved it. I think however, it is time for a nap in my bed I have been missing. I may need some help."

Penny begins pushing her down the hall. Mr. Henry joins them and gets a walker in position for her to be stable. Penny shows her a bell to ring and give her a small lecture about safety and asking for help. Maebelle nods in understanding, and in a few minutes, Maebelle is comfortable and asleep.

Penny joins Flo in the dining room, clearing the dishes. "It was lovely, Flo. So beautiful and wonderful food. Thank you. Did you notice that Mum was so proud of you and the decorations? You and Mr. Henry went all out to make her welcome home reception so nice. We love you guys so much."

"I know that is true, and I loves you too," Flo answers and Mr. Henry nods his head in approval.

"Well, I think I'm going to my room and rest a bit too. I need to write a letter."

Penelope finds some note cards in her desk drawer and sits down to write. She will print it, so Tito can halfway make out the words with a little help from one of the nuns.

She tells Tito how much she misses him and his giggling, and that her mom is feeling much better. Maybe one day she can bring him to Florida to meet her. She writes "The weather is a lot like where you live now. I am going to bring you a present when I come back to see you and lots of candy for your friends, if you are good. I know you will be," Penny adds. "I love you Tito," and she signs it Opee. Penny remembers the day Tito started calling her by that name. He was barely speaking when he said it aloud. Little Tito did not communicate for weeks when his parents died. She addressed the envelope, and placed it on the bureau top, and laid down for a short siesta.

Chapter 55

Eddie is thinking about Penelope all the way to High Springs. She mentioned a boy at the orphanage, and his mind goes to him, wondering how different his life would have been without his own family to support him. Next week, he will be thirty-nine. His family tells him on a weekly basis that his father time is fleeting. He shrugs off their comments because he feels what is meant to be will present itself. On the other hand, Eddie realizes if he doesn't initiate something, someone else will, or the opportunity will be gone. He glances at the flowers Dolly made for him. They are beautiful; lime green, hot pink, and orange, artfully arranged. It is vibrant, colorful and a bit unusual. There are flowers there with big ruffled petals. He hopes Mrs. Merriwether thinks so too. *It was nice to meet Dolly, Boyd's wife.* She is the kind of person who pulls you into her world of flowers, and he understands the passion Boyd has when he talks about her. Dolly laughs a lot and Eddie can see that in Penelope too.

He is singing along to the song *Despacito* on the radio and wanting to eat tacos. He won't take a chance of giving in to his food cravings, or the chance he might spill food on his clothes. He is dressed to show Penny he has some life to him. Hopefully, she will notice he is not a dull policeman. She is special, and Eddie knows it. The fact that Ms. Merriwether is special also is icing on the cupcake. However, he *is* getting hungry.

The smell of something baking awakens Penny. Flo is removing a berry pie from the oven when Penny walks out barefooted into the kitchen.

"Gosh, I am going to gain weight staying here, Flo."

"You can stand a few pounds on you honey. You look healthy with some plump skin."

"I walk so much in Guatemala. I'm ashamed I've not walked at all since I have returned."

"Take a walk now, it's breezy, and the trees are so beautiful now with their colors, Miss Penny."

"You know what, I am. A walk will do me good. I'm going to get a hat and my shoes. I'll go out the front door and be back in under an hour."

Eddie heads up the drive to the Merriwether's and is feeling a little nervous. He notices the grounds are coming back to life. Mr. Henry has been working overtime to turn the place around here. *Here goes nothing, he thinks.* He gathers up his package and the bouquet and locks the door to his Jeep. With his elbow, he presses the doorbell.

I bet that is Penelope and she is locked out, Flo says to herself. She goes to the door, and opens it, all the while talking, "I know, I know, you forgot your key.....oh, it's you, uh, Mr. ..."

"Eddie, Eddie Martin," feeling the need to remind Flo.

"Come on in, won't you come in ...out of uniform too."

"Yes ma'am, I believe I'm expected."

"You is? I mean are?"

"I believe so. I spoke to Penny yesterday. I can see she has forgotten."

"I don't know about that, but she has been busy. She went for a walk. She's probably on her way back now, because she's been gone about forty minutes."

A bell rings from the back room.

"That is Ms. Maebelle calling." With a quickness, Flo rushes back there to check.

Eddie puts the flowers down and his package on the table and stands there. He keeps standing until he is sure an hour has passed, and he is ready for his next meal.

From the hallway, Flo and Ms. Merriwether emerge, Flo pushing her in a wheelchair with her leg up and out.

"I would have gotten up sooner had I known a good-looking policeman was waiting for me. Oh, my word, you are still in the foyer. I must have frightened Flo for her to come running before she offered you a seat in the parlor.

"Ms. Maebelle, it's truly good to see you," Eddie is grinning. He winks at her and she loves the attention.

"Come, sit down, Edward."

"Yes, ma'am, I brought you some flowers from Boyd's wife's flower shop in Pierson."

"My, oh, my, they are lovely. He was so thoughtful to send them by you. So exquisite, some of my favorites, peonies, viburnum and roses."

Eddie does not know what to say. *I didn't handle that very well.*

"Flo, please place them where I can see them, perhaps, on the coffee table. I thought I smelled baking, earlier."

"Yes um, you did. I was just bringing a pie out of the oven. First berries of the season Mae."

"Well, let's offer our guest some. Mr. Martin, I guarantee you won't find a flakier crust than what Flo makes. By the way, what is your real name, if you don't mind the inquisition?"

"Edward, ma'am, Eduardo Louis Martin. I like it when friends call me Eddie."

"Then, I shall call you Eddie too."

"Yes, ma'am."

"Eddie, did you scare my Penny off? Where is she?"

"That would be my biggest fear, Miss Maebelle. Flo mentioned she went for a walk."

"It's a beautiful time of the year for it."

Penny has come in the back door, and Flo whispers, "The detective is here, brought you some flowers and a package, right pretty too. He has taste, as your mumsy would say."

"Oh, geez, my hair, and I am moist from walking."

"Never you mind, I'll go get some reinforcements for you. Cut the pie, I'll be right back."

Flo skips past the room unnoticed, into Penny's room, grabs her lipstick, perfume, and comb, and a clip, her rouge too and slips them all in a hand towel and makes her way back to the kitchen.

"Here you go," and hands the towel to Penny.

"Thanks Flo," and she steps into the half bath and freshens up a bit.

"Okay, better? Flo?"

"The best, honey child, knock him dead."

"Hopefully not dead," Penny snickers.

Entering the living area, Penny lays down her hat in the chair, just like she had just come in from outdoors.

"Oh, Eddie, I forgot you were coming. I took a walk."

She leans over, and kisses her mother, "Nice rest, Mum?"

"Yes, and when I came out this handsome man was here to greet me. And, he brought us flowers!

“They’re beautiful, reminds me of Guatemala.”

“They’re from Boyd, Penny dear.”

“Boyd, or you?” as she flashes a big smile at Eddie.

“Actually, they’re from....both of us in a manner of speaking.”

Flo announces pie is served in the dining room. Eddie stands up and offers to assist getting Maebelle in getting to the table.

Maebelle promptly says she can roll herself, and she does.

They are all sitting at the table, and Penny eyes the package.

Eddie, not wanting Maebelle to think it was for her, quickly looks at Penny, “I brought you a small gift.”

“Me? Oh, how sweet.”

She undoes the ribbons and comments, “So colorful and pretty.” Inside is a bag of Guatemalan coffee from the Lake Atittan region.

“Thank you so much, however would you know that I’ve been craving this coffee, this particular brand is intense, and has a tangy sweet finish. It’s just like drinking a velvety liquid.”

“Well, it sounds like something we should be having now with our pie,” Maebelle exclaims.

‘You’ll love it, I’ll go make us a pot.” Penny smiles and leans over to give Eddie a kiss. She takes the coffee and offers, “It won’t take long to perk.”

Maebelle looks over at Eddie and surprises the heck out of him, by giving him a two thumbs sign, whispering, "I'm in your corner."

"I need all the help I can get to break down that guard she has."

"Eddie, have you ever been married?" Maebelle inquires.

"No ma'am. Currently I am interviewing candidates," and he heartily laughs. "I would like to have a wife who wants to be married, as a full-time job, not one who wants a career, but one who wants to have children, if that's possible."

Flo comes out of the kitchen with some cream and sugar, and coffee cups. "Smells really good," Maebelle remarks, and Penny is grinning ear to ear as she brings the pot out to the dining room.

So is Eddie, as he might be thinking he has made some points with Penelope.

"Everyone ready?" Penny asks as she begins pouring everyone some coffee and places the pot back on a hot pad.

Flo has already anticipated Maebelle wanting her tea and retreats to the kitchen to get the tea pot she has prepared.

"You're right, Ms. Maebelle, the pie is fetching, as we say in the South." Eddie is in his happy state.

"I'm not familiar with that term, Eddie."

"As in, fetch me some more."

"I see," and Maebelle smiles.

Eddie looks at this watch, and Penny notices. "It's about time I head back to Daytona. I enjoyed the pie Miss Flo. It is superb."

He leans down to take Maebelle's hand. "And you, you better take care of yourself, and take it easy, no foot races just yet, you hear? Or I may have to come back and arrest you."

"I'm thinking that might be delightful for an old Brit like me," Mae answers.

Penny stands up. "C'mon, I'll walk outside with you."

Eddie walks to the door, opens it for Penny and shuts it behind them. She turns back and grabs his hand. In a few steps, they are at the door to his Jeep. He doesn't let go of her hand, leans up against the door and puts his arm around her waist.

"You need to wear that color all the time. You might have noticed I cannot take my eyes off you. Seeing you and visiting with your mother today has made my day."

"Thank you, Eddie. The flowers are beautiful, and the coffee, the coffee was unbelievably thoughtful." It is a unique gesture that shows me you are one of a kind."

"Yes, ma'am, I'm a mitten without a match." He lifts his hand up to her eyes and pushes back her hair away from her face. "You are special to me. Will you have dinner with me tomorrow night? Would you like to come to the ocean for the day?"

"Do you live on the water?"

"On an inlet, a condominium. Will you come?"

She gazes into his eyes. "Yes, I believe I will. I can use a break and the ocean will be good for my soul. Give me your address."

Eddie releases her and reaches in his back pocket for his wallet and retrieves a card. "Let me get a pen," and he opens his car door and reaches in the console. He writes his address on the card.

Sounding excited, "I'll fix us a lunch, just bring yourself and no worries. I'll take you out to dinner and maybe some dancing. We'll have fun. He puts both of his arms around her and pulls her in close, and whispers in her ear. "Quiero besarte."

"I want you to kiss me too."

He leans in and kisses her, slow and careful, and Penny responds.

"Uh, huh, yeah, she be liking him, Miss Mae, ain't no doubt about it," as they close back the curtain and turn away from the window before they get caught eavesdropping. Maebelle and Miss Flo are partners in crime for sure.

Chapter 56

J.W. Collins makes the necessary arrangements for his new partner. He buys Dana a phone and will take it to her at the bar. He doesn't really have a plan on how to give it to her, but he is certain an idea will come to him. He walks into the Hideaway and greets most of the folks.

"Yeah, Daniel Black wants all the Hispanics rounded up and sent back." Jack is yelling so everyone in earshot can hear. "Who's going to pick the blueberries? They'll be no one to work at the lumber yard or the energy plant. Without jobs, their families will just file for more welfare, a big drain on our county. Think about it." He looks over at Dana, "Hey 'Shugga, I'll take a cold beer." He lays some money down, and the phone down on the counter, kinda close to the edge. Dana brings him a beer and puts it on a coaster. She takes the money. Someone taps him on the shoulder. Jack wheels around and greets the guy. When he reaches again for his beer, he notices the phone is gone. *She has keen instinct. He likes that.*

Betty walks in and saunters down to the end. Dana perks up when she sees her friend. "Hey Betty, want your regular?"

"Yes, just came from Merriwether's. Maebelle Merriwether came home today. All of us ladies in the bridge club were excited to see and visit with her. Despite her ordeal, she is a force to be reckoned with."

Dana smiles, "That's great news." She plops Betty's cocktail down on a napkin in front of her. "It's a little slow tonight. I was hoping to be busier. You know, tips. That's the bar business."

"Yeah it is," and Betty relaxes with her cocktail.

Eddie slows as he drives by the Hideaway. The car he believes to be Dana's is not parked. He is stopping for a burger for the drive home. He walks in. Jack sees him immediately, gets closer to him and looks straight at him. He pokes his finger in Eddie's chest.

"Didn't really appreciate the way I was treated the last time I saw you," in a bit of a slurred voice.

"Good to see you too," ignoring his comment, and finding a chair. Glancing up, he sees Dana and Betty talking to one another.

Dana tells Betty that she gave that guy her phone number, but he hasn't called her.

Surprised, Betty asks where she met him. "You know he's a cop investigating Ron Robinson's death."

"A cop?" Dana's jaw drops.

"Yes, a special investigator. He has a partner. I saw them at Ruby's house a few days ago."

"Are you kidding me?"

"No, not at all, what's the big deal?"

Realizing she was making a bigger deal than necessary, Dana said, "Oh, I just didn't know. Well, I guess I'll see what he wants."

She walks toward Eddie with a menu. "What can I get for you?"

"Hi," Eddie looks up. "It's ..Dana isn't it?"

"It is. I gave you my number. You never called."

"Well, I was working then, and then I traveled home."

"Working where?"

"On a case. I live in Daytona."

"What kind of case?"

Eddie perceives she is fishing for information and not flirting. *Something is up.* "I'm an investigator. I handle crime, fraud, insurance negotiations."

"Okay, do you know what you want?"

"Just a cheeseburger with slaw, please, and a beer."

"Be right back."

Eddie notices Dana is wearing a different pair of earrings, as Dana bristles by.

Collins has a flurry of testosterone and gets off his bar stool and ambles over for another snipe with Eddie.

"Guess you guys were looking for a needle in a haystack, huh?"

"Surely, I don't need to school you on how an investigation works, Deputy Collins. How's your campaign going?"

"Going good, just a couple weeks away now until you can call me sheriff."

"When and if that happens, I doubt we will have much interaction where that will come into play. Have a nice evening, Deputy."

J.W. does not appreciate the feedback and goes back to the bar.

Dana brings Eddie his beer and sets it down.

"You never told me your name."

"It's Louis."

Dana retreats to the bar, satisfied she has learned something about this guy she thinks is so cute.

Betty is curious watching Dana and J.W. both affront the guy while he is dining.

"What's up with the guy, Dana?"

"Nothing, what do you mean?"

"You know sometimes, a female has to be unavailable, so a male can pursue."

"You need another Betty?" Betty's message makes no impact.

"Yes, one more and then I'm headed home."

Eddie finishes his burger and decides while Dana goes to the back, he will make a quick exit. He leaves plenty for the bill and tip. He's heading home as quickly as he can. Eddie is excited about Penny coming to see him tomorrow. He will phone his sisters and enlist their help making his condo look and feel comfortable and welcoming.

J.W. steps outside and texts Dana.

Noticed you took your phone. I put my number in your data base under Weedeater. Your number is listed under FedEx. Tomorrow I'm getting a shipment. I'll call you and set up delivery time. Later.

Chapter 57

Penelope examines the card Eddie handed her with his number on it. She hopes she did not appear too anxious. Opening the door, she walks in the living room to talk to Maebelle.

"Are you hungry Penny?"

"No, not really, maybe I'll eat something light, like egg salad."

"Mumsy, Eddie invited me to the beach, and to dinner tomorrow."

"Oh, how lovely. He is certainly a fine man. Penny, so thoughtful, don't you think? You should go, let's go pack for you. Flo can help."

"What? Are you rushing me a bit?"

"Am I? I think you should go and have a rousing good time."

"Yeah.... Why not...should be fun. I like him, Mum."

"I can tell. You are made for each other, Penny."

"Well, we'll see."

Flo comes around the corner with a suitcase.

"Gosh, is everyone trying to get rid of me?"

"Yes," they say in unison, and then they laugh.

They are all in Penny's bedroom, selecting some outfits.

"Oh, gosh, a bathing suit, I didn't bring one, Penny remarks.

"I can't imagine why that wasn't the first thing you put in your luggage," Flo remarks.

"It might not be a problem yet, let's look at some of those clothes we put in the top of her closet, a long time ago, Flo. There might be a suit in that box," Maebelle sounds hopeful.

Flo reaches up and drags down the big box.

Penny opens it up. "Hey, I remember these, as she holds up some blouses. Uh, I think I'm a little old to be wearing tops showing my midriff."

"Well, you could wear that as a suit and I could hem the shorts in a boy leg bottom," Flo offers.

"I think I'll go early and stop by the mall. So, goodnight everybody," and Penny shews them away. "I'll finish packing."

Driving back to Daytona, Eddie realizes he has no food in his refrigerator, nothing to entertain a guest. Quickly, he needs reinforcements. He dials his sister, Edilia.

"It is lucky for you my brother that I am up late. Something must be important for you to call me. Needing pants hemmed? Oh, you must need a last-minute haircut from another one of my girlfriends that you never return their phone calls!" Edilia gets it all out in less than a minute.

"Hold on, hold on now. All my pants are hemmed, thank you. And phoning one of your girlfriends probably won't happen. However, I am expecting a guest tomorrow at my condo. I could use your expertise, sprucing it up, making it feel welcoming, you know, special."

"Also, the guest room needs a hospitality make over. My refrigerator is empty, por favor, dear sister, so I will be food shopping. The key will be under the mat. Oh, I almost forgot, I need a cute wicker basket, to pack us a lunch in to take to the beach."

There is a long silence. Finally, Eddie says, "Edilia, are you there?"

"This girl must be very pretty, very smart, very everything for my brother to invite anyone over to his man cave. Si?"

"Yes, I admit it."

"This will be free then, no charge my brother, anything to help you find your mate."

Eddie is grinning from ear to ear and thankful Edilia cannot see him.

"What time do you expect her to be over?"

"I really don't know, I invited her to a day at the ocean, so…it could be by ten or eleven in the morning."

"Alright, my too good looking for his own good brother, be gone to the grocery store when I get there. I'll be early."

Chapter 58

Early in the morning, Ruby receives a call from the states attorney's office. Debbie fields the call and is professional in her demeanor although she worries that their request will upset her new boss. Debbie presses the intercom to the inner office.

"Mrs. Robinson, are you available for me to come in and speak with you?"

Ruby is caught off guard. "If it's important to the welfare of this company, come now."

Debbie enters with her notepad and sits across from Ruby, who is wearing her red bi-focal glasses, already engrossed in tons of paperwork.

Ruby doesn't look up, "I'm listening, Debbie."

Debbie clears her throat a bit. "Just now I received a call from the state attorney's office. They called to inform us they are sending a deputy over with a subpoena wanting to pick up all paperwork from our service department for work done on the sheriff's department interceptors, and any other cruiser in the last year."

Ruby looks up, and her pencil tip breaks. "Have we done a lot of work for them? Is there a problem with the service?" Ruby punches her intercom to reach Rusty. She reaches him immediately. "If you are not with a customer, please come to my office now, thank you, Rusty."

"Seemingly, within seconds, Rusty knocks before entering and comes in.

"I'm sorry, I did not remember we had a scheduled meeting."

"We didn't, Rusty, please be seated. Debbie has taken a call from the state attorney wanting files for a year of work we have done for the sheriff department. Is there anything in that request that could embarrass the company?"

Rusty thinks a second. "Frankly, I don't know. All work done for the county was done after hours. Mr. Ron handled all of that privately."

"After hours, you say?"

"More to the point, after I would leave for the evening. I never saw any paperwork. Odd, you're the second person that has asked me about it."

Surprised, Ruby inquires, "Who else has asked?"

"The detective from Special Investigations."

Chapter 59

Of course, Edilia enlists the aid of the other two sisters, the twins; Carmen and Camila. The three of them will tackle all rooms together. Before long, the condo smells of Fabuloso and looks Fabuloso too. Nothing is left untouched. Nothing is off limits for the sisters to straighten, clean and organize.

Edilia brings a few of her garden roses that are fuchsia, and places them on a wicker tray on the guest bathroom counter top. She adds a new hairbrush, some hair clips, some special Maja soap, and a bottle of foaming bath beads. All the towels are pressed and misted with a light lavender scent. Edilia replaces shampoo and conditioner with new bottles.

In the guest room, Carmen and Camila make it sparkle, adding a reading book, a magazine on a tray, and bottled water on the night stand. A mini vase of roses sits on the dresser.

There is Latin music playing all throughout the day, and the sisters are giggling all the time they are working. They realize for Eddie to ask, that this girl is very important. They are happy to help their brother.

Eddie arrives back at the condo with four bags of groceries and unloads them quickly. He decides he will call Penny to be sure she is in route.

On the second ring, Penny answers. “Good morning.”

“Are you having any trouble finding my place?”

“I believe I am within ten minutes and I’ll see you soon.”

Eddie is excited and nervous. He has tried to think of everything, and remembers he needs some silverware and napkins in the basket.

The doorbell rings, and Eddie opens it wide. "Hello, my love, you're in that color again," he observes. Eddie pulls Penny to him and kisses her cheek. "I'm so happy you are here."

"Me too. I love the ocean. It's the best soul food around."

Penny looks around quickly. "Your home is cozy, and welcoming. Thank you for inviting me, Eddie. Is there a tour de force?"

"Absolutely, and Eddie takes her hand and walks her to the guest bathroom. "For Madame Merriwether," he points, and shows her the guest room. "You can change wherever. I want you to be comfortable."

"I am, Eddie," and Penny smiles.

"Come along," and he continues to lead her. "Here is the porch. It's a great view, don't you think?"

"The best."

"And here is my office and man cave where I online date, stalk women, and cyber bully."

"Quite the combination of vices, I'd say."

Continuing to walk, "This is my bedroom, and closet." Penny steps closer to the closet, "Any aliens lurking in here?" She amuses herself and opens the closet door.

Both are startled. All of Eddie's clothes have been arranged according to color, and all his shoes are lined up. *Edilia never fails me. Thank God, my sister loves me, he thinks.*

"Are you hungry or thirsty?"

"I'm ready for the surf and sand. I'll drink something when we set up at the beach. Right now, I'll go change into a swim suit."

While Penny changes, Eddie packs their lunch. She emerges in a peacock colored cover all and has her hobo bag with sunscreen in tow.

Eddie grabs the basket and they head out to his Jeep.

"It's a short distance," Eddie is telling her. "Here, put your bag with the towels and umbrella." Eddie opens the side door for Penny.

"How long have you lived by yourself?"

"I bought this two years ago. I looked a long time for the right spot. I'm happy here, even though my sisters are convinced I'm a confirmed bachelor. I tell them all the time that I'm taking applications for a permanent roommate, but they think I'm kidding."

"And are you? Taking applications?"

"Of course, I have a whole drawer of potential candidates, all alphabetized," and he starts laughing.

"I guess there is more to this story, and I'm sure I will hear it from you."

"Maybe, I will share, just maybe. We're here!" Eddie gets all the big stuff and ask Penny if she will carry the basket. Down on the beach, Eddie pushes the pole of the umbrella into the sand.

"Can we just go for a swim before we settle in to eat lunch?"

"Of course," Eddie takes off his shirt and Penny removes her cover up.

Eddie tugs at her hand. When they get to the water's edge, Eddie leans down like he is picking up a shell. He picks Penny up in his arms, and acts like he is getting ready to throw her in the water.

"You wouldn't dare," and her eyes appear enormous.

"I wouldn't dare?" He laughs, keeping her tight in his arms and walks further in the water and slowly sinks down in the water, holding her all the way. She lets out little screams, but they are silenced when Eddie kisses her neck. When he looks into her eyes, he laughs again, "Just so you know, I would dare." He releases her, and she is still holding onto him.

"I expect that you would dare, in anything, everything."

He pulls her to him once more, "Well, I don't want to short change you."

"No, of course not," and Eddie takes her face in his hands. "I could do this all day, but I don't want my hands spanked."

She smiles, "Let's go for a swim, Eddie."

Penny swims out a bit, and Eddie catches up.

"Watch the currents here. Do you know how to swim out of a current?"

"Yes, Officer Martin. I appreciate you being concerned for my safety."

"Absolutely, for your information, I passed chest compressions and mouth to mouth resuscitation with a superior grade."

Penny swallows some water and chokes because she is laughing.

"See there, you never know when those skills are needed. I wanted to ask, how's your mother today?"

"Feeling good. She and Flo practically forced me out of the house. Flo even offered to make me a bathing suit out of an old college outfit."

"You will look beautiful in anything, Miss Merriwether."

"Thank you, Mr. Martin. I guess with all those applicants, you are somewhat of an expert judge."

"You doubt my honesty, Miss Merriwether. I sense it in your tone. There **is** a drawer you know, where I store all of my potential applicant's names, addresses, and any pertinent observations I might have made." Eddie takes his hand and splays it on top of her head and dunks her under the water.

"Like a cork, she pops up, and shouts, "Eddie!"

He wags his finger at her, "Doubt me no more." He tugs at her once again. "Let's go eat, I'm hungry." He pulls her through the waves fast, enough so she is now standing up, and they're at the umbrella in a few seconds.

She towels off as Eddie spreads out a large cotton striped sheet. He pats the area indicating he wants her to sit.

He opens the basket, and he has ceviche for their lunch and a soft bread roll. He opens up a fruit bowl and offers her silverware and a napkin.

"These are your choices for beverage. Perrier, Sprite, wine, or cold beer. What does my damsel desire?"

"Sprite and wine mixed together. Wow, the ceviche bowl looks fantastic. Did you make it?"

"Uh, no, my friend, Pablo makes it. I think it is good. But you be the judge. I don't want to spoil your dinner appetite, so I opted for a lighter lunch."

"It's perfect Eddie, just perfect." Eddie reaches behind her neck and gathers her hair and straightens it up.

"I love your auburn hair. It's really stunning, Penny."

"Aww, you're too sweet, trying to make up for dunking me?"

Smirking, "Honestly, I don't know what came over me. Oh, I remember, you were doubting me."

"Understood, Officer Martin."

The next hour or so, they nibble, and share stories of their childhoods. They cover subjects like Eddie's modest upbringing, and he admits he was happy within a close-knit family. Penny admits she was spoiled, and enjoyed the finer things, but feels she lived with a lot of rules and structure. Penny asked Eddie if he always wanted to be in law enforcement.

“I believe it is my calling. Like Boyd, my partner, I enjoy what I do, and I believe in our system of justice. Soon I will have twenty years in. It doesn’t seem like that much time has passed.”

“Have you never met anyone special in your life?”

Eddie sighs, and then he smiles. “The word special to me is not used lightly. I am looking for that inner beauty, that unique woman with heart and soul, full of compassion and selflessness. Most of the ladies my sisters have introduced have been pretty, too pretty. Certainly, they are physically attractive, with an abundance of makeup and smart clothes for every occasion.

“Most are very nice too, but nice can be that woman that reaches out and helps a total stranger because she sees a need. Perhaps, she might not be dressed appropriately, but the lady that wins my heart will dig in, roll up her sleeves, no matter how she is dressed because she is thinking of others. My bride will embrace my family heritage, have a sense of what family unity means, and respect boundaries.” Realizing he is sounding like an interview committee of one, he stops.

“I apologize, all of the ladies are wonderful, and I want to have a connection. Pure and simple.”

Penny is quiet and looking into his soul. "You are giving a cogent argument justifying why a person should wait on the right one, the right connection. I want to be a teammate. I don't want to be told the plan, I would like to aid in the planning. Just like making love, it takes two for that act to be complete. I need a partnership and communication. That's my desire. That's my hope. That will bring me joy." Penny finishes speaking with a small smile, realizing it might appear she was making application.

Eddie reaches for her hand and lifts it to his lips and kisses it softly. "Want to take another swim?"

"Definitely, yes, let's do it," Penny's mood changes immediately.

They walk out hand in hand and sink into the water. Penny goes under to wet her hair thoroughly. She wonders if she should reapply some sunscreen. Several hours have passed since she applied it while changing in her bedroom. When she rises to the surface, she doesn't see Eddie.

She turns everywhere. He must be under the water. Glancing all around, Penny becomes aware that clusters of people are pointing her way. Easing closer to shore, she notices a few people running in the water and yelling. She hears the bull horn of several lifeguards. Is there a shark sighting? She is baffled and concerned, because Eddie is not in her sight. She hears some voices, "Look there, look over there." There is no understanding of what is happening. Suddenly, she sees Eddie at some distance from her, bobbing in the broken waves. He is swimming and kicking at an abnormal pace. Between the waves, he is on his back, towing something with him. The lifeguard is swimming toward Eddie and has almost reached him. *Dear God, it is a child.* Eddie and the lifeguard place the small body on the board, rushing to shore, and both wildly paddling. Penny moves as quickly as she can to reach the shore. She hears Eddie shout out, "Someone call an ambulance. Tell them Inlet 36."

Reaching shore, Penny rushes to grab their blanket, and races over to Eddie and the lifeguard. A lady is screaming, "Help him, help him before he dies."

The lanky young boy coughs up water. Eddie turns him on his side. Penny reaches through the small crowd and hands Eddie the blanket. The boy is still coughing up water. Quickly, there is improvement. The woman is still panicked and crying. Penny grabs her arm.

"Are you his mom?"

"Yes," crying as she says it.

Penny pulls her into a bear hug and holds her tight. "Shhhh.. now… shhhhh. Let the guys help your son. Shhh. Cry on my shoulder. Everything is going to be okay. Shhh, now." Penny can hear the ambulance siren coming in closer. Penny tells the mom, "Let's go get your identification so the medical people can help your son." The lady calms and seems to understand. Eddie asks the bystanders to step back. "We know you are all concerned, but let's give the EMS guys some room." The boy has opened his eyes, and the EMS team puts him on a stretcher. The mother and Penny reappear. The mother has her beach bag and is letting the guys know she is the boy's mother.

The lifeguard seeks out Eddie and shakes his hand. "Dude, you were under forever in that water. Where did you find him?"

Eddie is winded, trying to catch a breath and slow his adrenaline. "He was drifting along the bottom. I saw him when he went down and started looking for him. Thank God, I think he's going to be alright."

"Man, we need strong swimmers like you. Ever thought about being a life guard?"

"No, I have a profession, thanks."

"Probably should get your name, dude, for my report."

"Eddie Martin, Volusia County Sheriff Department. Alright, see you guys." Eddie starts to walk off, remembering his blanket. Everyone in the crowd starts clapping for him.

"Hey guys, thanks, but just say a prayer for the boy, that he is okay."

Eddie takes Penny by the hand and he heads back to his umbrella.

Penny says, I'll get you a sprite. You need to sit." Penny grabs a towel and pats him dry. "For a while, I thought you had abandoned me." She sounds perplexed.

Eddie moves her hair from around her face and kisses her cheek, "Never."

He falls back on the towel, completely on his back "Whew."

Penny leans in on her stomach and nuzzles beside him. "I'm very proud to know you, to be with you, Eddie."

Turning on his side, he reaches for her. "You have such a sweet spirit," and rubs his hand over the middle of her back for a few minutes. Realizing the time, he announces, "I'm ready to go get a shower, how about you?"

"Yes, I'm ready."

They gather up the belongings and head for his Jeep. He loads up and they depart. The ride back is relatively quiet. Eddie reaches for her hand. "Penny for your thoughts?"

Penny giggles, "Okay Maebelle, enough."

"Next time, I'll have to make it sound more original I guess. We have arrived."

Entering the condo, Eddie places the basket on the counter and unloads it.

"Please go ahead and get your shower. I'll see you when you get out. Our reservation is for six thirty. Is that alright?"

"Perfect," Penny replies.

Eddie steps in his own shower and reflects upon the events of the day. He looks up, "Thank you Lord, for using me today and for giving me strength."

Eddie is shaving when he hears Penny's shower turn off. *I'm sure she has everything she needs, thanks to Edilia.* Smirking, he remembers the shock of his too organized closet. Hopefully, he can find everything ***he*** needs. He splashes after shave tonic on his face. Still wrapped in his towel, he strolls to the kitchen and opens the refrigerator and grabs a beer. He makes Penny a wine spritzer and walks toward the guest bath.

"Penny," he calls, "I have some refreshment. Knock, knock."

She opens the door, with her robe on, "Gosh, thanks, I am needing it." She takes the drink from him and sets it on the vanity. Looking in the mirror, she talks to him, "Run along little doggie, so I can get beautiful."

"You are beautiful, I'm seeing just how much."

Eddie pulls the door to him and returns to the counter to get his beer. He takes it into his bedroom, and swallows half of it down. He reaches for his phone. He calls the hospital.

"This is Detective Ed Martin, checking on the boy that almost drowned today."

"Yes sir, please hold."

"Miriam speaking. The boy was released to his family, Officer."

"Good news, thank you, ma'am."

Eddie grabs a pair of jeans, and a green and blue pin stripe shirt. He rolls up the cuffs, puts his watch on, and adds some cologne. He combs his hair, all the while he looks for the right belt, finally putting his feet in a pair of loafers. Another beer calls his name, and he sits down in his chair and turns on the television.

Today, at Inlet 36, an off-duty Volusia County sheriff department deputy, apparently saved the life of an eleven-year-old boy. A strong current pulled the inexperienced swimmer visiting from Georgia to the bottom. Beachcombers told reporters the deputy was under water for an extended time looking for the boy and assisted the lifeguard in bringing him to the shoreline. Thank you, Officer Edward Martin, for acting quickly and saving the boy's life. We will have more on this story as the night progresses. Layton Moore, reporting, WSPS. Daytona.

The bathroom door opens, and Penny exclaims, "Wow, that hit the news wave quick. You're a celebrity!"

"Does it give me any extra points with you?"

"Of course, you've earned lots of stars today."

"Am I running behind?"

"You're good. I'm just winding down. Do you need help?"

"Just a little more time, be patient."

The hum of the hairdryer is enough that Eddie nods off in his chair.

Penny expects to make an entrance when she walks out of the bedroom, but Eddie's eyes are closed. She walks over to him and leans in and kisses his nose.

His eyes open, and he puts his arms around her and pulls her over in his chair with him.

"Wow, you are stunning." He strokes her hair. It's all straight, half pulled up, the rest down her back. She has a white peasant top on showing that beautiful sun kissed skin. He kisses her neck all the way up to her ear. "The smell of your skin is an aphrodisiac. It's a deadly potion."

"Thank you, you are quite the charmer." She stands up, and he gets out of the chair.

"We shall see about that one. Are you ready?"

"Yes."

Eddie turns off the lights except for a lamp and opens the door. He holds her hand walking to the Jeep, opens her door, and returns to his side of the vehicle.

Driving south, Eddie tells her he has a special place he is taking her and that hopes she will enjoy what he has planned for them. They arrive shortly at a restaurant called 'Blue Waters.'

Penny politely responds, "I'm sure it is lovely. I admit I am a little hungry and it smells divine."

Eddie puts his arm around her and she responds with a beautiful smile.

"You have treated me like a queen all day Eddie, and I have loved every minute of it," Penny smiles appreciatively.

"Of course, I believe you are my queen."

They enter the restaurant and Eddie tells the receptionist his name is Martin and he has a reservation, preferably on the water if possible. Eddie pulls out the seat for Penny and kisses the top of her head after helping her push her seat up to the table.

Penny asks, "Have you eaten here a lot?"

"A few times, mostly with family. It has good service and consistent quality food. What do you feel like eating tonight? I can recommend either steak or seafood. Or we can have some seared ahi for an appetizer and then a steak for dinner."

"Yes, that sounds good."

Travis, their waiter appears at the table and introduces himself.

"Excellent choice," Travis tells Eddie after he places the order for the ahi appetizer. Travis explains that their blue fin tuna is finished with a blueberry teriyaki.

The plate of ahi arrives, quite the presentation, in a white ceramic boat. The tuna is rolled in cracked black pepper, char grilled rare and placed over petite greens. There are two individual white shallow boxes of pickled ginger and wasabi. Sauce piped like a rope extends from the boxes, clever beyond words.

"This is beautiful, Travis," Penny declares.

Travis takes charge of the meal. "I believe you mentioned a steak. May I suggest the filet for two, accompanied by Hasselback potatoes, and green bean bundles with pignolia nuts? The lettuce wedge is served with an island twist, very popular sir."

"Thank you, Travis. That sounds good. I appreciate your suggestions."

"Absolutely. Enjoy the tuna." Travis pours the wine before he departs, and Eddie thanks him again.

Eddie is mesmerized by Penny. "The sun was good for you and you look beautiful tonight."

"Thank you, Eddie. The day was glorious, heart throbbing, and enlightening. You are a super guy, Eddie Martin."

Eddie smiles. "There was a bit of excitement. I called the hospital and the boy is okay. He has already checked out."

"The hospital gave you the information?"

"I might have mentioned I was with the sheriff department," and he flashes his awesome smile.

"Of course, you did. That is thoughtful of you to check on him."

Eddie begins eating along with Penny. "This is sooo good."

Penny nods her head in agreement. Travis appears periodically, moves plates in and out and refills their wine glasses. Eddie and Penny are consumed in one another, rarely noticing Travis at all. Two hours have passed, and the stage lights come on, and the dining room has darkened significantly.

"Do you like to dance Penny?"

"Yes, I don't know whether I am any good at it, but I love music of all kinds."

The music is soft, and diners are filling the dance floor. Eddie reaches for her hand and leads her out to the floor. He holds her tight. He has all the right moves, and Penny and Eddie are lost in each other. He kisses her neck and leads her back to their table. Travis has cleared their plates.

In the middle of the table, there is a plate containing two chocolate mice made from Hershey's kisses, cutely decorated.

Travis comes to the table. "Any interest in sipping cognac or brandy during the band segment?"

"I would love some Armagnac, please," Penny answers appreciatively.

Eddie responds to Travis, "For one please. I'm driving, and I'll taste hers."

"Of course."

In a few minutes, Travis returns with a snifter of the French brandy, warming it, tableside.

Eddie listens for another song he wants to dance to and once again, he and Penny exhibit great dance techniques. Penny follows his every lead and is enjoying herself dance after dance.

Eddie looks at his watch, and it is eleven as Penny excuses herself and goes to the ladies' room.

Travis drops by and picks up the check. Eddie tells him, no change needed. "Thank you for excellent service."

"You're welcome sir. It's a pleasure to see two people who love and respect each other." Eddie is surprised. Penny joins him, puts her arm around him, and whispers, "It's been a big day. Your date is losing steam."

"I'm ready," Eddie takes Penny's hand and they leave. Always polite, Eddie escorts her to her side of the vehicle and unlocks the door. Penny surprises Eddie, raising her arms around his neck and kisses him, "I've had the best date Eddie, the best night, and you're the best."

"You're most welcome. Now let's get you home, safe and sound." He sweetly kisses her cheek.

The drive home Penny is talkative. The brandy and the exciting night have put her in an amorous mood.

Arriving soon, Eddie escorts Penny to the door, with Penny leaning on him all the way.

Inside, Eddie asks Penny if she would like a glass of water. Penny smiles and tells him she wants to make application and see her competition.

Eddie heartily laughs, "You are doubting that there is a drawer, aren't you? Come with me," and he leads her to his night stand. He pulls open the drawer and it is full of papers, napkins, business cards. "I used to sort them alphabetically," and he is still grinning.

"Oh, my lord, you weren't kidding! Why? Why do you keep these? Are they all still being considered?" She is bewildered, and visibly shocked.

"There's only one being considered now," and Eddie scoops her up and kisses her passionately. Penny responds to his touch and returns his kisses with enthusiasm. Eddie stops kissing her and hugs her.

"Miss Merriwether, I think you have had a lot to drink tonight and I don't want to take advantage of you, because I value our relationship. I want it to grow more each day, each and every week."

"Oh, so my application is going to be stamped, ***pending.*** Is that what you want?"

"Penny, I want you, don't doubt that. But I want you for more than one night, or one weekend. I need a commitment. I want you to meet my family. I want your mother to know I have good intentions. And we need to talk about your return to Guatemala and how long you want to be gone. Penny, I am ready to find my mate, to find a partner in life."

"And how 'bout the drawer of potentials? Do you still want them?"

"We can dispose of them now, if it bothers you."

"Me bothered? Let's do it."

Eddie shakes his head sideways. "Just a second." He moves to the kitchen to get a plastic bag.

Returning, he grabs all the contents of the drawer and puts them in the bag. "Done," he says, "now the pressure is on. I hope you're up to the task."

Penny smiles and tells Eddie she is going to change and then she'll be out to say goodnight. She walks away heading to her room, feeling a bit guilty about her actions, and thinking about all the things he said. She realizes he is speaking from his heart and she is moved by his sincerity. *Guatemala, it seems so far away now, and there is Tito to consider. She will not give him up.*

Penny changes into her bed clothes, brushes her teeth and hair, and removes her makeup. The guilt of her being forward and her foolishness takes over her being, and she sits on the edge of her bed and stares. Eddie stares too, at her bedroom door, wondering what is keeping her. He made too much of all the women, mostly girls that have pursued him, wishing he'd never said anything.

Over months, the drawer had become a joke, a source of amusement. The truth is no one had touched his soul. Boyd told him that he would know when it happens, and he believes that statement holds true.

He walks toward her door, *heck she has probably gone to sleep*. He knocks softly, "Penny?"

She approaches the door and talks through it. "I'm sorry, I'm feeling really stupid now, cornering you like I did."

The door opens, and Eddie pulls her close. "Do not, I repeat do not regret anything." He puts each of his hands on the sides of her head and kisses her forehead. "We'll get this all straightened out. I want you in my life Penny. I want you to be sure of your feelings.' He picks up her chin and kisses her again. He strokes her hair, and whispers, "Your lips are so soft. You are so beautiful." He picks her up and lays her down on the bed.

He lays beside her, continuing to let her know how he desires her.

"I want to wait, Eddie," sounding a bit frightened.

"Okay….I understand," he whispers.

"Just lay here with me," as she is pulling the covers down for both of them.

Eddie puts his arm around the top of her shoulders, "Goodnight, love."

Eddie wakes several hours later. Penny is not in the bed, but the bathroom light is on and the door is closed. Eddie moves to his own bathroom for some privacy and to change, getting on his own bed clothes. He looks out the window and realizes Penny's car is gone from the parking lot. He goes back to her bathroom, and it is apparent she has left. Her bag is gone.

He can't believe this has happened._He picks up his phone to call her. Her leaving doesn't make any sense to him. *She isn't sure, that's it. Must be.* There isn't an answer. He looks at his watch. She must be back in High Springs by now. Eddie is worried. He goes back and forth in his mind. Does he drive to High Springs and get this sorted out? He will wait an hour or so and call her again.

Penny arrives home in a flurry of emotions. Finally, she falls asleep. Her arrival back home does not go unnoticed by the eagle eyes of Flo.

During morning tea and scones Flo mentions Penny is home sleeping.

"Do you think there is trouble in paradise?" Maebelle seems worried.

"Something must have happened. Maybe she came back to check on you," Flo offers.

"Doubtful, she has been traveling the world since college. Rarely, does she check on me, Flo." Maebelle sighs and continues talking.

"I'll just let this run its own course. Penny can be emotional. If there is a problem, it will surface, I am sure."

"Let's continue the plans for the big Daniel Black reception. When the bridge club is here on Wednesday, we shall pass our list of things yet to be done around for assignment and the best party in town will become a reality. All the girls are inviting guests. It should be a great crowd."

Maebelle and Flo are going over some recipes when Penny emerges from her bedroom in her robe.

"Oh, Ms. Penny, want that I should make you some of that special coffee."

Penny replies she doesn't want anyone to make a fuss about her. She sinks down in a chair at the dining room and stares.

Maebelle is consciously ignoring Penelope. She most certainly is patient enough to receive her information without prompting and continues to read the paper. Without warning, Maebelle exclaims, "Is this our Eddie?"

Penny and Flo both look over her shoulder as Maebelle reads aloud.

"Good lord, he does look good without his shirt on. Good lord, he done saved a drowning boy. Good lord, there he is, right there in the paper," Flo is animated looking at the paper.

"Flo, that's three good lords," Maebelle says. Maebelle looks over to Penny, who is tearing a scone into small pieces on a plate.

"Yes, I was there. Eddie and I were swimming and Eddie saw the boy go under."

"He saved him, and it was on the news last night."

"Did you go out to dinner?" Maebelle asks softly.

"Yes, it was a great day Mumsy. Eddie is a fantastic person."

"Yet, you are sitting here, with us, looking defeated."

"No, she acts like, more miserable, I think," Flo adds.

"Yes, I believe I will have some coffee Flo," Penny is getting irritated.

"Well, go on and fix yourself some, I offered while ago, now I wants to see the pictures of Eddie on the beach."

Penny gets up headed for the kitchen. Maebelle gives Flo the look.

"I knowed it was rude, Mae. I am just trying to teach her a 'lil lesson. She can't be messing around playing a game. He's too cute, very merchandisable," just saying.

Penny returns with orange juice. "The coffee is on."

Maebelle continues to read the article, with Flo reading over Maebelle's shoulder.

"Well, this is news."

"Is that the reason you is here? He is probably in New York being interviewed on Fox News, or maybe the Ellen De Generes show."

"That's it," Penny is getting mad.

"No, I'm here because I'm stupid, and a little ashamed. It was just easier to run away than deal with my mistake."

"Well, this ain't no runaway house, is it Maebelle? You better call him and invite him over to supper. Fried chicken makes everything better with menfolk. That and black-eyed peas."

"The way to a man's heart is through his stomach, ain't that right?"

"Flo, really, have you taken some sort of pills this morning? Now, I'll say it, Good Lord." Maebelle interjects.

It is all interrupted by the phone ringing. Maebelle looks at Flo who looks at Penny.

"Merriwether residence," Flo speaks politely. "Good morning, Detective Martin. Yes, sir, I am mighty fine. Yes, sir." Flo reaches over the table. Penny reaches for the phone, but Flo will have none of it. "It's for you Ms. Mae. Detective Eddie Martin calling." Flo gives Penny a wink, and hands the phone to Maebelle.

"Good morning, Edward. So good of you to phone." Maebelle listens intently and says, "Of course, yes. Thank you for calling. Bye now."

Maebelle flips the page of the paper while Flo and Penny nearly erupt.

Maebelle looks up from her glasses, "Oh, alright, he said something like you left early. He wanted to be sure you were safely here. He said he tried to call you, Penny. For what it is worth, a man like that won't try ten times."

Penny is silent. She'll give it serious thought. It is no secret that worry will steal joy. Penny's joy has almost vanished.

Eddie's phone rings. Without glancing, he answers, sure that it is Penny.

"Hey partner. It's Boyd. How did it go with Miss Merriwether? Where did you go for dinner?"

"I made reservations at Bluewater."

Boyd whistles between his teeth. "Well, then, you had a hefty tab, especially the way you like to eat. Nice, huh?"

Yes, everything was going great guns, and then she just checked out. I'm not sure why. She left early this morning, without saying a word. I was pretty worried, but spoke to Ms. Maebelle, a few moments ago and she arrived safely home."

"You called her mother?" Boyd is more than surprised.

"I wanted to be sure she arrived home safely before I tore out and began driving to find her."

"I hear disappointment in your voice. I don't know what to tell you. If it's meant to be, it will happen. I'm calling on official business. We're due in High Springs on Wednesday."

"We are? Will we be spending the night?"

"Not sure. Why?"

"My family has a birthday celebration planned for me on Thursday. Maybe I need to tell them to reschedule on Friday or Saturday."

"Sorry, that sounds like it might be a good idea. I'll buy you a cupcake if that helps your feelings."

"I'll take it. Call me and let me know when and where to meet."

"Okay. Oh, I almost forgot. Dolly read the paper about the near drowning, and the boy you saved. You have always been a hero to me, but glad you were there at the right time."

"Proud of you Eddie, honored to work with you too."

"Gosh, don't load it on with a pitchfork, because it pains me. But thank you, sir."

"Alright, talk to you later."

Somehow, Eddie does not feel like a hero this morning. He decides to wait, change gears, downshift to slow mode and practice patience where Penelope Merriwether is concerned.

Chapter 59

J.W. Collins has no patience with Dana, his new partner in crime. He expects his telephone call to her to be answered promptly. He has three shipments coming in. Two guys from the Rocking H are delivering bulls from Mexico by truck. The marijuana is hidden in a bed of hay. It is a smart plan as Customs agents usually don't want to climb in with two bulls in the trailer.

Since the police investigation, J.W. does not want to continue the use of police cruisers. J.W. is willing to pick up the parcels himself and get it to Dana.

Dana's phone rings again. Caller ID reveals the name *weedeater*. She is making good money now with tips, and J.W.'s proposal doesn't seem enticing to her. Reluctantly, she answers.

"Listen, the packages will be here today. Give me your address." J.W. is abrupt.

"Well, I don't think the manager of the hostel house will appreciate me bringing in marijuana that smells of high heaven. No pun intended."

"What? You live at the hostel?"

"Yep, been there since Ron died. Nowhere to go. Soon, I will have enough money saved to get an apartment, so this will be our one and only deal, J.W. I'll give you a list of my buyers and you can work your own deals."

"As sheriff? Are you kidding me?"

"Whatever. Bring them to me at the Hideaway. I'll leave my trunk unlocked and just put them in there."

"It's the white Taurus parked near the back. Deliver after ten. The owner has gone home by then. I need some sleep. I worked late last night." Dana hangs up.

J.W. makes plans to pick up the parcels. *It's just as well Dana is not going to sell anymore. She makes him nervous. When he is sworn in as sheriff, he won't need the money or the headache. He and his wife Sandy will have a prominent position in High Springs, and they'll be happy*. Jack phones his contact.

"Yeah, I know, I'll be there. You be sure you're on time, amigo."

Chapter 60

Several months have passed since the High Springs Ladies Bridge Group have actually played cards. Today's game is going to be short for several reasons. All the ladies are going to plan the big party for Daniel Black. It is the last opportunity for the folks in High Springs to come together before the election. Late supporters will have one last chance to ask more questions. The ladies expect a large crowd, and enthusiasm is abundant.

"So glad we are all on the same page here, and have the same goal; electing Daniel Black," Maebelle smiles. "Elsa Jane, please give us a report, and then we can discuss the menu. Afterwards, we can play six hands of cards."

"According to our survey," Elsa Jane begins, "We are finally ahead. There are some pockets in the Hispanic community still loyal to Jack Collins. Thankfully, with Ruby's support, some workers at the dealership are now speaking out to their families, cousins and the like. They are no longer intimidated, fearing loss of their jobs."

Ruby is quiet and nods her head in approval. Julia asks if we need some servers. Her twins can ask a few of their friends to help.

Elsa Jane outlines her plan of action. "Maxine, Flo and Harriet have teamed up, and have an abundance of fresh veggies. They are going to make several trays of crudités for some of the hors d'oeuvres," Elsa Jane continues.

Maebelle enlists some of the Presbyterian bakers and they are handling the cookies, assorted pastries, and pound cakes.

They are keeping it simple, so it can be easily handled. “Betty, can you handle a nice punch and some sodas for the group? I received a donation for Cokes and other sodas if you can stop and pick them up. What we don’t consume, we will return to the market. Tommie is getting the paperware together, with napkins, and such.

“Ruby, I know you are busy with your new duties. You have been more than generous, with advertising and providing mailers. I believe Daniel Black is so appreciative. He truly does care about the people.”

Maxine eyes a sweet potato pie sitting on the buffet. “Is that for us?”

Flo is smiling as she hears Maxine’s question. Flo answers enthusiastically, “Yes um, it is. I am going to cut it now, so everyone can taste Harriet’s organic sweet potatoes.” Harriet is smiling too.

Tommie inquires about Penny. “Has she returned to Guatemala already?”

“No, she is out doing a little shopping today and running some errands,” Maebelle smiles.

Four days have passed since Penny has seen or heard from Eddie. The thought of him being uninterested now preoccupies her mind. She deserves whatever treatment he wants to dish out to her. She is thinking about her future but wants to keep little Tito in her plans. It is time to tell her Mum all about this boy and her plan to adopt him.

The adoption papers were drawn before she abruptly left Guatemala. Surely, the orphanage explained her sudden departure to the board of directors. Hopefully, her absence will not be a factor or a deterrent in finalizing her goal of becoming his custodial parent. She prays Eddie is still interested in her after she shares her plan about Tito. It's going to be a package deal. *I love them both, she tells herself.*

Chapter 61

Driving to High Springs, Boyd outlines the plan to Eddie.

"There is a sealed indictment, contents still unknown to me, and we are to bring Dana Harrison in for questioning. It is unusual, but we will be taking her to the 3B building instead of using the sheriff's department. Depending on the outcome of her interview, she may or may not be arrested. It will be a sworn testimony."

"Are we going to go to her place of work?" Eddie asks.

"No, I have been advised that she is currently residing in a hostel house."

"Why the 3 B building?"

Boyd answers immediately. "The state attorney's office is concerned about Jack Collins being at the sheriff's department if we take her there. In an effort to keep our continued investigation secret, someone has already spoken to the owner and she is not scheduled to work this evening. Apparently, the investigation has taken another turn, and we will be privy to it very soon."

"Another turn? Are we going to the Merriwether estate today as well?" Eddie is trying to hold back his enthusiasm.

"Do you want to?"

"I don't know. I'm frustrated. I've just been laying low."

"I see," Boyd answers sympathetically.

Boyd makes a turn and the hostel house is in view. The car they think Dana drives is not in the parking lot. Eddie is looking for it intensively. They both get out and walk to the front door.

The manager answers the door promptly.

"Hello, I'm Detective Boyd Price and this is Detective Martin."

They both produce their badges simultaneously.

Boyd makes eye contact with the director of the hostel house. "We believe you have a guest here by the name of Dana Harrison. May we speak with her?"

"Is she in trouble? Because that's one of our rules, you can't be in trouble with the law. No dope, no overnight visitors, no animals."

"Ma'am, we are hoping she might help us with an investigation. Could you go get her? We'll wait."

"I guess you'll have to. I'll tell her to get dressed."

Boyd asks the director if there is a back door.

"Of course, but it stays locked, and I have the only key."

"Yes ma'am."

Boyd and Eddie wait an extended period. Finally, the manager appears and states, "She's a tough one to wake up; works late hours, but she's coming."

Dana is fully dressed when she appears, carrying her bag over her shoulder. "I've been expecting you."

Boyd looks puzzled. "Good morning, Ms. Harrison. We'd like your cooperation in an investigation we are conducting. Would you be willing to come with us for questioning?"

"Do I have a choice? You've already got me out of the bed."

"Yes ma'am, we all have choices. Some of them we make are good and some we make could have been made better. Please follow us, Ms. Harrison."

Eddie opens the back door of their unmarked car. Eddie tells her to put her seat belt on.

It is a short distance to the Biddle, Banks and Button building. Boyd parks the car at the rear of the building, and Eddie opens the door to assist Dana in getting out.

Boyd makes a call and the back door of the building opens. The three of them enter and go into a private conference room. A female officer is sitting in the room who greets Dana and offers her water or a cup of coffee.

"Coffee will be good, with cream and sugar, and thanks," Dana says.

"You're welcome. I'll bring a pot for you guys too," and she winks. "Good morning detectives."

Boyd tells the female officer, "Thank you."

Boyd suggests Dana be comfortable and explains that this will be a taped interview for the purposes of gathering information. "Eddie, if you will please read Ms. Harrison her rights."

When Eddie finishes, Boyd asks if she understands her rights.

"Yes, I do."

The female officer enters with coffee and everyone is served.

Boyd begins. "Ms. Harrison, our inquiries encompass several aspects of an investigation. First, we would like to know the nature of your relationship with the late Ron Robinson."

Dana is quiet and sips her coffee.

"I needed help and he offered. I was on the side of the road with car trouble. He came along and offered to tow my car in. The car wasn't worth saving but he gave me a job and let me pay him back."

"What kind of job did you do?"

Dana takes another sip of coffee and stares. "I watched his house for him, so nothing would be stolen."

"What is the address of this house?"

"It's outside of town, 1427 Woodland Trail. It's an old frame house. I think he used to play poker there with his friends."

Boyd clears his throat. "Is that all you did? Housesit?" He waits for an answer. "Did you have a romantic relationship with Mr. Robinson?"

"There was nothing romantic about Ron, Detective. He was a pig. He made a lot of promises he never intended on keeping. He took advantage of me because I was vulnerable. I didn't have a car, or any money, only what he doled out to me. I did a lot for him, and he just kept demanding more and more."

"Demanded what?"

Dana looks at the female officer, who is making notes on a computer.

"He practically raped me one night. Brought me gifts, in exchange for sexual things, uh, favors, I'd do for him."

"What kind of gifts?" Boyd is not giving much time for Dana to ponder.

"He bought me perfume, and a nice pair of gold earrings. We smoked weed a lot, that he provided for free."

"Did you have other 'things' you did for him?

"Like what?"

"Ms. Harrison, I'll be direct. Did you sell 'weed' for Ron Robinson."

"My life, my very existence, depended on doing what Ron Robinson told me to do."

"Did you buy the weed from someone local, or a cop?"

"I don't know any cops, only J.W. And I wish I had never met him either."

"When did you meet Mr. Collins?"

"Officially, about a week or ten days ago."

"Why do you say you wished you'd never met him?"

"Because he wanted the same thing, for me to sell weed to all of the customers Ron and I had."

Boyd continues to press for more information. "Do you know where Ron obtained the weed?"

Dana looks indifferent. "Really never thought about it."

"Did Deputy Collins want sexual favors also?"

"I let him know that is was a NO up front. I wasn't interested in that. He said he was a happily married man, but all men say that at one time or another."

"Have you ever been married?" Boyd asks.

"No. All of my boyfriends have disrespected me. Some hit me just like Ron."

"Ron hit you?"

"Yes. He had a vicious temper. He was a Jekyll one minute and Hyde the next."

"Was your sister aware you were seeing him?"

"No, never. She would hate me if she knew."

"Where did she think you lived? How did she call you?"

"I told her I had friends here. Ron gave me a phone to use. She would call me on that number. I haven't spoken with her in over two weeks. I gave Ron the phone back the last time I saw him, and I returned the vehicle."

"When?" Boyd is narrowing his questions to exact answers.

"A few days after Ron died, I left the vehicle in the used car lot."

"A friend of mine is letting me buy an old car of hers."

"What is her name?"

"Betty, "answering abruptly, offering no other information.

"Why would she do that?"

"I met her at the Hideaway. She helped me get the job. She says I remind her of her daughter that was killed. She is a sweet lady, drinks too much, but who wouldn't if your daughter died."

"When is the last time you saw Ron Robinson alive?"

"My sister and I had plans to go to dinner. Just before we were leaving, I used her bathroom. He was in his office, and I went in there and told him I was done with our arrangement. I screamed at him and told him that he had hit me for the very last time. I laid his gun down on his desk and walked out. He was drunk anyway, and mad."

"Did you say gun?"

Dana takes a large gulp of water. "Yeah, when I delivered the marijuana, I carried a gun. Some of these addicts try to scare you. With a gun, you can scare back."

"Did you keep the gun loaded?"

"That would be stupid to carry an unloaded gun."

"Have you ever fired the gun?"

"No, never even practiced with it. Look, I need to go to the bathroom please."

"Yes ma'am. I apologize for the lack of privacy, but Officer Pam will have to be with you."

"Whatever."

The ladies depart, and Boyd looks at Eddie who utters, “Unbelievable. Sir, I’m going to the lavatory myself.”

Eddie leaves for the inner offices in the 3 B building. Asking directions at the reception counter, Eddie turns to see Penny Merriwether entering the front door. Eddie gulps, as he never imagined running into her here.

Penny is equally shocked. She telephoned Terrance and made an appointment to discuss her plan to adopt Tito. They are face to face and both seem unable to speak.

Eddie leans over and kisses her cheek. “Penny, I’m …happy to see you… I’m on police business today.”

“I can see that, or I just assumed by the uniform. Eddie, I …owe you an apology. I was going to call you and explain my behavior. I do have an explanation. And I was rude, I’m sorry….and emotional… and embarrassed because I felt as though I had made a fool of myself.”

Eddie sees that she is getting emotional again. There are tears puddling and one drops down the corner of her eye down her cheek. He raises his hand and catches it. “I am not worth the tears I see on your beautiful face. Please don’t cry.”

She reaches to hug him. “I am sorry, Eddie.”

“Okay, all is forgiven, we can talk this out,” and he hugs her back.

“Listen, are you here to see ...”

“Terry, my old friend. I am enlisting his help, his legal expertise with a potential problem in Guatemala.”

"Oh, I see." Eddie does not see, nor he does understand and feels sort of left out of the communication loop.

"Okay, Eddie smiles, "we'll have that talk later." He hugs her again before disappearing into the men's bathroom.

In the bathroom, he is sure Boyd is wondering if he fell in the commode. He texts Boyd. *DELAYED!*

Boyd receives the text and looks bewildered that Eddie is giving him information on his toileting problems.

"More coffee, Miss Harrison?" Boyd looks at his watch. *Crap, it is eleven forty-five. I'll send out for food.*

"Since the lunch hour is approaching, we can send out for sandwiches. Officer Pam, would you please?"

"Of course. Miss Harrison, is ham and cheese okay?"

"Sure," Dana answers dryly.

Eddie returns. Immediately, he whispers in Boyd's ear, "Sorry, sir, I just ran into Penny in the foyer. She is on her way to see Terrance, that lawyer. It was awkward."

Boyd nods like he comprehends and announces he has sent out for sandwiches.

The sandwiches arrive, and it is not exactly old home week and family time. Boyd tries to make Dana comfortable, but the room is understandably silent. Lunch time is brief.

Officer Pam and Eddie pick up the trash, disposing of the lunch sacks quickly.

"If we can continue, please" ... Boyd resumes. "Ms. Harrison were you ever involved in the political campaign to get Deputy Collins elected?"

Dana is uneasy and starts to shift in her chair. Boyd reads her body language that she is holding back.

"Ms. Harrison, Dana, if you cooperate, I will make note in my report that you did so willingly to help us."

"In the beginning, when Mr. Collins first announced, Ron asked me to answer the phone when the newspaper called."

"The newspaper?"

"I used a British accent and pretended I was that Merriwether lady. I thought it was harmless at the time. Ron was trying to scare her, intimidate her, so she wouldn't support the guy running against Collins. I told you Ron was mean. I was scared sometimes myself. He frightened me that night he ran her off the road. He shoved me on the floorboard and told me he'd kill me if I uttered a word. At least he was kind enough to call the ambulance for her. I wanted out, but I didn't have anywhere to go."

"Why didn't you call your sister?"

"It seems like a good idea now, but I was ashamed. He threatened to tell Debbie himself a lot of times. Shame isolates and I know that now. I felt very isolated."

"Why do you think it was so important to Ron that Deputy Collins win the election?"

"I don't know what their deal was, but I think there was one. I believe Collins brought the marijuana in and passed it off to Ron. Sometimes, I think he used cop cars that went in for servicing to transport the weed. After all, who is 'gonna stop the police? The police? Doubtful. Everyone needs their cut."

"And what was your cut? For selling?"

"It was supposed to be forty percent, but Ron always took out for the car, rent, and gas. I had a few dollars thrown at me. It was never enough to get out from under him."

Dana's phone begins ringing, and she ignores it. It rings again. Boyd senses she is nervous about the phone.

"Would this be one of your buyers?"

Dana bites her fingernail and rakes through her hair with her fingers.

"Ms. Harrison, you have an opportunity to get out from this cloud of suspicion, like you say you want to do. Who do you need to protect?"

"Myself, haven't been listening?" she retorts in an elevated voice.

"Ron Robinson was killed by a gun that was registered to him. A gun you said you returned. You had plenty of motive and anger."

"I did not kill him. I wasn't in his office over five seconds. I finally got some money to get out. I left him that afternoon for good. I got money out of his wallet when he was in the shower."

"You took money? How much?"

Eddie notices that Dana is crossing her legs back and forth.

"I felt like I had an insurance policy, I didn't need to kill him. Killing him was never on my mind."

"What insurance policy are you referring to?"

"I took a check from Ron's wallet. A blank check. I figured I could cash it at any time and move somewhere else."

"Do you have the check in your bag?"

Dana bites her lip and reaches for a bottled water. Reluctantly, she says "Yes."

Eddie asks her to empty the contents of her bag on the table.

Reaching in her wallet, Dana pulls the check out, and lays it there for everyone to see. It is a five-thousand-dollar check signed by Maebelle Merriwether. The check recipient has been left blank.

Boyd stares at Dana. "Aren't you aware that by cashing this check would have you arrested in minutes?"

"Why? How?"

"A check in this amount went missing. As soon as you filled in your name, the bank would have called the police. You would be part of the crime then."

Dana's phone rings again. The caller ID can be seen by everyone. *Weedeater.*

Boyd looks at his watch. "If you prefer, we can continue this questioning tomorrow."

"Not again, haven't I been cooperative? I've given you all the information, everything I know."

"Who is weedeater?"

Dana stares a hole into Boyd's eyes. "J.W. Collins."

"Why is he trying to reach you?"

"He's bringing in marijuana today from Mexico with some bulls to the Rocking H. He wants me to accept delivery."

Dana's text goes off. *FedEx is trying to make delivery, where is your car?*

There is silence in the room.

"Dana, we have enough evidence to arrest you now, even if it is circumstantial. Do you realize how much trouble you're in?"

"Not really, I didn't kill him. I am innocent. Go ahead, ask my sister. I came right out. Of course, I didn't have any blood on me. We were going out to dinner. She even asked me why my face was red. It was red from Ron hitting me that afternoon. I'm telling the truth. I'll take a lie detector test. Give me one now."

"Is there anything anyone else who might want Ron Robinson dead? Think hard Dana. Your very life and freedom depends on it."

"He was on the phone when I walked in the bathroom. His office door was ajar. I'm sure he was expecting someone. Aren't there cameras outside at the dealership? You can look at those and see I left soon."

"If the camera got that angle, you'll be in the clear." Boyd answers, knowing full well that there are no cameras on the premises."

"It is an older building, and Ruby has shared with the detectives Ron didn't want to spend the money on that expense.

Boyd sets a new bottle of water on Dana's table. "Do you need a break?"

"Yes."

"Please leave your belongings here. Officer Pam, can you assist? Detective Martin will meet you outside the door. He will assist you, so you can take a break also."

The ladies leave, and Boyd asks Eddie if he has any thoughts or questions.

Eddie answers. "This is quite the windfall of information. I am waiting till you tell me your thoughts on the 'weedeater' call."

Boyd is contemplating as Eddie departs down the hall.

When Eddie returns he tells Boyd he has an idea. He and Boyd converse in the hall.

"Perhaps, with her cooperation," Eddie begins, "we can set up a sting operation. She is already planning on receiving Jack's delivery. Consider this, sir. Let Dana text J.W. that she is in police custody being interviewed about Ron's death. He'll have to sit on that weed. Maybe we can nab him with all that product ready to sell."

"That's an angle worth considering, Eddie."

Chapter 63

Penelope returns home more frustrated than ever. Terrance agrees to complete the adoption papers for Tito. She is going to confide in her mother tonight and share her story about Tito and the plan to adopt when she returns to Guatemala. She wants Eddie's support too but something deep in her soul tells her she is losing him. She greets her Mu, and Flo at the door, "Did anyone call for me?"

"Is you expecting someone Miss Penny? Perhaps an invitation to the policeman ball?"

"As a matter of fact, I saw him today. It was quite by accident."

"I hope you told him you missed him."

"No, not exactly."

Maebelle overhears. "You saw Eddie?"

"Yes, I bumped into him in the 3 B building."

"Was Boyd with him?"

"I didn't see him."

"I'll call and see if they are free for supper."

"You will not, Mum, I can't have it."

Maebelle looks up from her glasses. "I beg your pardon, Pen, but I buy the groceries in this house. If you do not want to attend, you can eat in your bedroom. My word, I have never known you to be with such rabid behavior."

"Rabid? I've heard it all now."

"Well, I have seen it all. If you are uninterested, you can at least display some descent manners. You have been brought up better than this Penny."

"Uninterested? I am in love with him!"

Everyone is silent. The air is still. No one is blinking an eye.

"If you love him, my dear child, then start acting like it. Communicate with him. What are you afraid of?"

Penny starts crying. "Mumsy, I left a little boy I plan to adopt in Guatemala at the orphanage. He doesn't have any parents. I want to be his parent." She has blurted it all out.

"Can't Eddie be his parent too? Why must everything you do be such a secret? If this little boy brings you so much happiness, then he will bring happiness to those who love you as well. For a person who states they want a partnership, you sure think singularly."

Penny hangs her head. "I know. I'm scared to ask him how he feels about a package deal."

"Dear Penny, I am willing to listen to any problem you might have. Are you needing money for this adoption?"

"No Mum. I instructed Terry to draw up the papers. I have the finances. I visited Terry today and he's taking care of the legal papers, so I can bring the boy to Florida."

"I still don't understand why you wouldn't want Eddie and Boyd to come to dinner."

"I do want Eddie to come, and Boyd too. I'm just afraid it is too much too soon."

"No, you're afraid of too much commitment Penelope."

"You only call me Penelope when you are irritated."

Mae tries to point out the obvious, "When I look at Eddie, I see a strong frame to lean on, Pen."

Always wanting to kid, Flo says "His trusses ain't bad either."

"Yes, Flo, we know you are his biggest fan." Mae giggles because she agrees wholeheartedly.

Flo looks at them both. "If we is, I mean are having guests for dinner, I need to be getting busy."

"Well, Penny?"

"I'm all in."

Maebelle asks Penny to hand her the phone and her address book and immediately dials Boyd's phone.

Boyd and Eddie have decided to release Dana for the evening. They give a stern warning to Dana about sharing their investigation with others. Boyd tells Dana if she wants to clear herself that she will text J.W. Collins and alert him that she is being questioned by the police and can't talk. The police will take it from there. The detectives will return her to the hostel house in a few minutes.

Dana is silent as she leaves the car. She doesn't look back as she enters the hostel house.

Boyd's cell rings and it is Maebelle Merriwether. Boyd shows it to Eddie and then answers.

"Hello, Ms. Maebelle."

"Good afternoon, Detective Price. I heard you and Eddie are in town. I'd like to invite you to dinner for being so kind to me while I was injured."

"That's not necessary at all, Ms. Maebelle. How is your therapy going?"

"Today, my soft cast was removed from my foot. I certainly don't miss it at all."

Boyd laughs. "I imagine truer words have never been spoken. Regarding dinner, I promised Eddie a cupcake as tomorrow is his birthday. We have been busy today and haven't discussed if we need to stay overnight. May I talk it over with Eddie and call you right back?"

"A birthday you say? This most certainly calls for a celebration. We could surprise him!"

"I feel an obligation Ms. Mae, to be up front about your invitation given the relationship between Penelope and Eddie. It's only fair, don't you think?"

"Yes, of course, Boyd. May I hear from you in a few minutes?"

"I promise. Please give me five minutes to discuss it with Eddie."

Boyd starts the car and turns towards Eddie. "We have been invited to the Merriwether estate for dinner." Boyd waits for a response from Eddie who seems dumbfounded.

"Well, birthday boy, the ball is in your court."

"Yeah, I just don't know what sport I'm playing. If we are playing soccer, I feel I am getting kicked. If it's football, I'm feeling sidelined. In baseball, I am striking out."

"Okay, so you're not getting around the bases like you'd hoped, but I believe you are still in the game. As your volunteer coach, I think I need to put you back in." Boyd laughs again. "That used to be a verse from one of my favorite songs. And … I feel I must mention, good food is hard to turn down. Perhaps, spending the night, we can flush out J.W. Collins and wrap up this investigation for good."

"Is the invitation for this evening or tomorrow?"

"The invitation is for tonight. Do you have another buffet to go to that I am unaware of?" Boyd always enjoys sparring.

"There's always the girl at subway," Eddie reminds him.

"Subway or Merriwether? The scales have a heavy list, partner."

"Penny was very apologetic today when I saw her in the hallway, so I guess I can take another swing at the ball."

"Alright partner, while I call Ms. Maebelle, will you call us in a reservation at the bed and breakfast place we stayed before? We can get a quick shower. I'd like to call Dolly and check in and then go to the Merriwether's."

Boyd reaches Miss Flo on the second ring.

"Miss Flo, I know it's rude, but what's for supper? I need to know if I should eat a snack before I get there."

Flo answers quickly. 'If you snack, I'll smack you Mr. Boyd."

"I mean it. We 'gonna have country fried steak with my famous mashed potatoes."

"What makes 'em famous?"

"It's a little potato and a lot of butter." Flo is on cloud nine fixing supper for company.

"May I bring the dessert? It's Mr. Eddie's birthday tomorrow and I promised him a cupcake, and ... I got to warn you, feeding him, uh, I mean *filling* him up is a challenge!"

"Yes sir, oh, I'm up for the challenge. And I'll be proud as punch to make him a birthday dessert. It will be my pleasure."

"Miss Flo, what time shall we arrive?"

"About six or whenever, Mr. Boyd, and bring your appetites. I'll go tell Mae now."

"I'm looking forward to it. No pressure Flo, but you need to know I'm married to a great cook."

"Yes um, that is why you is always happy." Flo laughs and says goodbye.

Boyd has a hell of a grin on his face. Eddie is on the phone giving his credit card to the Inn manager and hasn't paid much attention to the laughs that Boyd and Flo are sharing.

Boyd asks Eddie if he is hungry for round steak and mashed potatoes.

"Since it is my birthday, sir, you probably need to eat less, saving more for me. It's the right thing to do."

"Right thing? You'll be so moon struck to be with Penelope, you won't even see the meat platter being passed."

"You're just hoping, sir."

They reach the Inn and as Boyd is parking, he receives an email from the department.

"Go ahead Eddie inside. I'll tend to this email."

"Alright, sir." Eddie grabs his overnight bag from the back seat, and heads for the entrance of the Inn with a renewed spring in his step.

Boyd opens the email and studies the contents. The information he reads is startling. It's a report that he has anticipated from the phone company. Despite a court order, it has taken weeks to receive the details. Hopefully, the data will provide some valuable information.

Boyd quickly dials Dolly.

"You're not coming home tonight, are you?" Dolly does not pick up the phone saying hello.

"No ma'am, but I am calling to tell you how much I love you. Are you feeling okay today?"

"Eating for three and loving every minute of it. Didn't you tell me it will give you more of me to love?"

"I did, and I do, love you more every day, D."

"Good answer."

"Tell mother I'm dining at Maebelle Merriwether's tonight. This is the mother of the lady that Eddie is trying to impress."

"And *is* he impressing her? Looking at him would make Helen Keller see again. Pure eye candy."

"Wow, I'm jealous."

"Awe, I'm sorry."

"He has that dark skin and all that Spanish sex appeal.'

"I'm getting more jealous now."

Dolly starts laughing, "Well, get home as early as you can tomorrow. I miss you and love you."

Boyd exits the car, grabs his bag from his side of the car and heads on in to join Eddie. He exchanges pleasantries with the receptionist who directs him to the same room the guys occupied before.

The television is on and Boyd glances at the news. ***The election is ten days away, and recent surveys indicate it is a dead heat between the candidates. In the last seven weeks, J.W. Collins has lost considerable support and Daniel Black is narrowing Jack Collins' lead. It is rumored that the Hispanic vote might be a determining factor in this year's election.***

Eddie emerges from the shower and tells Boyd the shower is available.

Boyd is reviewing his email again and doesn't say anything back to Eddie. Finally, he looks up and notices Eddie has vacated the bathroom. It doesn't take the pair long and they are ready to leave for dinner. Boyd has the keys, and Eddie follows him out, locking the door behind.

"Sir, we do not have a hostess gift. Should we stop by the store and get a bunch of flowers or a bottle of wine?"

"Good suggestion, my mind is somewhere else. I'll stop, and you can rush in. I vote for flowers. It's too late to visit a florist so the grocery store will have to do."

"I won't tell Dolly, sir."

Amused, Boyd answers that it is okay. 'She believes grocery stores promote flowers in the home so she's down with the whole concept."

"Down with-it, sir?"

Boyd shakes his head sideways. "Age difference, it's an old saying."

The Publix supermarket is a short distance away, so the guys arrive quickly. Eddie enters the store while Boyd circles the parking lot, looking for an empty parking space.

Boyd travels around the west end, heading south, making a big loop around all the parked cars that belong to people that are shopping inside the store. He pauses to let a car approaching from the highway pull in front of him. He notices several Hispanics having an animated discussion with a man standing outside his truck. He pulls on around, driving past them. In his rear view he can see one burly man doing a lot of the talking, raising his hands in the air. Boyd sees Eddie coming out and stops to pick him up.

"Partner, there is a bit of suspicious activity over in the parking lot. We'd better take a closer look."

Moving back around again, Eddie realizes what Boyd is referring to and looks intently as they get closer.

"You're right Sir, it's trouble and that is J.W. Collins with them. Hurry over there."

"On it," Boyd grabs his radio. "Dispatch 1729, all available deputies, requesting 10-94 for signal 57 Publix shopping center, east parking lot. Possible drug deal going bad."

Boyd screeches his car to a halt boxing in the vehicle bearing a Louisiana license plate. A large Hispanic man has a knife drawn, pointed at J.W.'s neck. Eddie flings open his car door, pulls out his revolver with his right hand, with his badge showing in his left hand.

Eddie hears one of the guys say, "Matalo Cortale el cuello."

Eddie shouts, "If you cut him with that knife, I'll shoot to kill. Put your hands up in the air. Levante tus manos en el aire." He repeats in English shouting, "Throw down your weapon, now. Tira tu arma ahora!"

The guy doesn't want to listen, and he lunges his hand that is holding the knife to stab J.W.

Eddie shoots his gun twice knocking the guy down. Eddie rushes to him and puts his foot against the knife blade and his hand that is still clutching it and kicks the knife out several feet.

Both doors of the police car are open as Boyd has the other two Hispanics held at gunpoint. They are both shouting, "No hablo ingles."

J.W. steps back, unbalanced and clutches his throat. Eddie tells J.W. "Deputy, get your handcuffs out and subdue this prisoner." Several police cars have pulled up now and the officers get out with guns drawn.

Boyd shouts out, "We are Special Investigations, someone call for an ambulance. Eddie, ask the other Hispanic men if they have any guns or weapons. J.W. is pulling the big guy up from the asphalt and the guy spits and curses on him, shouting at him in Spanish.

Eddie realizes that the guy is not in danger of losing his life and tells him to put his hands behind his back, "Andale, Andale!"

The big guy is bleeding, grimacing in pain, but follows Eddie's instructions. Eddie has fired two shots. One bullet has grazed his shoulder, and the other bullet caught his thigh.

Boyd asks two deputies to place the unarmed men in separate patrol cars, taking them to jail.

The injured Hispanic man is helped onto a stretcher and is attended by the emergency medical personnel.

"You saved my life man," J.W. is talking to Eddie.

"That might be true," Eddie responds. Eddie stoops down to pick up his badge that he dropped when he fired his gun with both hands. He clips it back on his belt. He turns to Jack, "Are these guys friends of yours?"

"Never seen them before in my life."

"Is that a fact?" Eddie presses him.

"Never." J.W. is insistent.

"Why was the one trying to kill you?"

J.W. cannot think quickly enough. "Uh, guess they were mad, uh, that I took their parking space."

A couple of other deputies are listening to Eddie and J.W.'s conversation.

Boyd steps closer to them, "Mr. Collins, I saw the three of you talking for a few minutes."

"Are you guys tailing me?"

Boyd doesn't answer, realizing a news crew has arrived on the scene. He looks at the camera man, "Sir please step away." He turns to the deputies and asks them to cordon off an area.

Boyd waits a few seconds, then moves closer to J.W. "Deputy Collins, someone does not pull a knife on you because you took their parking spot. In fact, this isn't the main parking lot at all. It's more of a meeting spot. Would you care to revise your story here or be taken into custody?"

"I'd like to call my lawyer."

"Eddie, please read him his rights."

Boyd turns to one of the deputies, pulls out his badge, and tells him that J.W.'s truck needs to be impounded.

"Yes sir," the deputy answers quickly. "I know who you guys are."

The sheriff arrives on the scene, and Boyd walks over to him. They remain in conversation for several minutes.

The sheriff shakes Boyd's hand and reaches for Eddie's hand too.

"Sheriff, we're turning this over to you, as we are late for a dinner engagement." Boyd looks at his watch.

Boyd and Eddie get in their car, and Boyd uses his cell to call the Merriwether's.

Flo answers on the second ring.

"Hello, this is Boyd Price. I'm sorry we have been delayed, and I apologize."

"Oh, hey, we been watching you on the news. We got everything on hold waiting on you guys. You is, um, are coming, aren't you?" Flo is matter of fact.

"We are," Boyd answers enthusiastically! "We're starving."

"Well, you guys have missed happy hour, but we is all happy seeing J.W. Collins put in a patrol car on the news. I'll put the food on the table and tell Ms. Mae you is coming right on. I suppose you'll be here in a minute."

"Yes ma'am. We're on our way."

Boyd hangs up and looks over to Eddie. "It's never a dull moment in High Springs."

"Agreed sir. This has been a big day, a long chain of events."

Chapter 63

Pulling in the driveway, Boyd is almost whispering, "This place looks beautiful. Someone has been working hard."

"Yes sir, some cooler weather, some rain and lots of tender loving care has made this estate breathtakingly grand and gorgeous."

"Just as I thought I was making headway in Dolly's greenhouse, I am faced with the fact I am a nobody when it comes to this level of landscaping." Boyd is still taking it all in. "We're here, finally, and I for one am hungry."

Eddie asks Boyd if he can wait a second. "I'd like to check on the guy I wounded and call the hospital."

"Of course, I know how you must feel and I admire you for having a high regard for human life."

"Thank you, sir."

"Eddie, I haven't had the opportunity to let you know about my latest email from the state attorney's office. We'll talk after dinner. Go ahead with your call. I'll wait at the door for you."

Stepping inside the door the two are greeted by Flo, who is all sass and smiles. "Miss Maebelle has a surprise for you. Wait here a second."

Around the corner, comes a slight shoe shuffle and Maebelle appears walking on her own, with the help of a cane.

"Getting stronger every day. How are my favorite investigators?" Maebelle is smiling from ear to ear.

The guys are astounded. Boyd embraces her first, "Your determination has paid off for you. We're so happy for you."

Penny is standing close to Mae and offers that "Mum wanted ya'll to be the first to see her walk on her own."

Eddie walks around and kisses Penny's cheek. "Hey, we apologize for being late, and appreciate you holding up dinner for us."

Maebelle points to the table. "Let's hear all about J.W. Collins. The news crew captured his picture getting in the squad car."

Boyd answers, "He will probably bail out in a few hours, but it is enough to scare him a bit. He's lucky Eddie is quick on his feet; no doubt saving his life from one bad hombre. Show us the wash sink, so we can wash our hands, and we'll join you."

They are all seated, and Penny is pouring iced tea into everyone's glasses.

Flo emerges from the kitchen, "Hope family style is okay, boys." She is carrying two bowls; one a sumptuous salad and the other bowl is filled with hot homemade biscuits.

"Yes ma'am," Eddie answers.

"Family style is best, although Eddie's portions might need to be monitored," Boyd teases.

Flo is quick to respond. "Mr. Eddie, you eat all you want."

"Thank you, Miss Flo, you have my heart."

"And I deserve it, Mr. Eddie. I do not get enough appreciation in this household," and she laughs.

"Oh Flo, you do, go on," Mae chimes in.

Flo returns to the kitchen and brings out a platter of country fried steak, surrounded by a ring of sautéed onions and grilled jalapeños.

"Ya'll start passing. I'm going to get the mashed potatoes and fresh green beans. We also have some organic beets from Miss Harriet's garden."

"Who is Miss Harriet?" Eddie winks at Flo.

"She is one of the ladies in Mae's bridge club, Mr. Eddie."

"Mister? It's just Eddie, Miss Flo." Eddie surveys the table. "Don't tell me this is all the food you prepared for two starving policemen." He winks at Flo again. "I'm just kidding you. It will be enough if Boyd cuts back at bit."

Everyone laughs, especially Flo.

Penny has taken her seat next to Eddie but appears a tad quiet.

Eddie reaches for her hand and leans over and kisses her cheek. "I just can't help myself. I hope you don't think me assuming."

Penny smiles and squeezes his hand. "You're here now, safe. That's what matters the most."

"Yes, safe." Mae repeats it.

Boyd takes the opportunity to thank Mae again for the dinner invitation. You know, I am missing my wife's cooking. Being here is a welcomed treat for sure."

"I'm glad to have you both. Flo is excited to be cooking a big meal. She thinks Penny and I eat like birds."

Flo comes from the kitchen with another plate and sets it down. "I declare I am ready to eat too."

Boyd jumps up and pulls Flo's seat out for her.

"Why, Mr. Boyd, thank you."

"Yes ma'am, my pleasure."

Boyd takes his place and Maebelle asks everyone to join hands.

Quickly, Boyd looks at Maebelle, "Would you permit me to say the prayer?"

"Of course," Maebelle smiles.

Boyd begins. "Our Father, we give thanks tonight for Your abundant blessings. We gather in friendship and love, believing You will continue to guide us, knowing we owe our safety to You. We pray for healing for the one injured tonight, as well as others suffering. In all things, we give thanks, Amen."

Everyone in unison, repeats, "Amen."

"Watching the news, I was afraid you men weren't going to be able to come tonight. Didn't I see J.W. Collins being put in a patrol car? It's unbelievable. Perhaps everyone in High Springs saw it on the news. I just feel he is a scoundrel of the highest order, certainly he is not worthy of being our sheriff." Maebelle sounds serious.

Boyd holds the plate of steak next to Maebelle so that she can help herself to some of the meat. Boyd brings it back to his other side and hands it off to Eddie.

"Has everyone had all the steak they want?" Eddie asks with a huge grin on his face.

Everyone stops in their movements, then quickly realize that Eddie is kidding.

"Okay," Eddie says, "you all were warned."

"Oh, Mr. Eddie, It is a pleasure to cook for you. There is no bigger compliment to a cook than to see people enjoy their food."

"Yes, ma'am." Eddie has a full plate and looks over at Penny's small serving.

She returns his gaze with a smile, "I ate a big lunch and a late one at that."

"Is that true Miss Flo? Or is she covering up one of those eating disorders?" Eddie asks.

"Am I being questioned about my eating habits? Now that is assuming," Penny is answering for Flo.

"When I take you to meet my family to eat dinner, it will be an insult to have such a small serving." Eddie is still trying to kid her.

"*When* I go to your family, I will keep your advice in mind, Eduardo." Penny's words seem blunt and Eddie senses she is once again guarded.

"Yes ma'am. Everything is so tasty, Flo. I'm enjoying this home cooked meal."

Boyd reiterates that he too is appreciative and is loving a good Southern specialty.

Mae offers her synopsis on the election next week and gives the detectives her feeling about how the election is going and how the bridge club ladies have impacted the campaign. "It will all be worth it, when our candidate is elected," Mae states emphatically.

Everyone has finished their meal, and Flo starts clearing the plates.

"I'll help Flo," and Penelope grabs Eddie's plate as a well as her own plate and exits the dining room into the kitchen.

"I can help too," Eddie quickly adds.

"You are the birthday boy, oh no you don't," Flo exclaims. "We'll be right back with something special for you."

Eddie looks at Boyd. 'This might be a cake. I'm sure hoping."

Penny brings out dessert plates and it is followed by the biggest chocolate cake Eddie has ever seem. Everyone begins singing Happy Birthday. Eddie's is surprised, more like shocked.

Flo sets the cake down in his face. The top of the cake has the numbers three and nine on top. They are lit candles that resemble sparklers. The song finishes with everyone saying, "Make a wish, make a wish!"

Eddie takes a deep breath, and quickly extinguishes the candles. "Wow, this is a wall of chocolate. Wow!"

Eight layers, six different fillings, I hope you like it," Flo joyfully adds.

Eddie stands up, walks around to Flo and kisses her on the cheek. "Thank you, I'm very honored." He hugs Flo and moves over to Penny and grabs her and kisses her too. Quickly, he circles the table, giving Ms. Maebelle a smack also, eventually looking over at Boyd.

Abruptly, Boyd says, "I'll pass on the smooch train, birthday boy."

Everyone laughs, and Eddie returns to his seat.

Penny begins to cut and serve the cake. The cake is over the top. Eddie is trying to figure out all the fillings; chocolate mousse, almond crème, cherry ganache, chocolate chip, and white chocolate cream cheese. He gives up guessing and Flo tells him the last one; salted caramel crunch.

Eddie is so animated, "This must have taken you all day."

"Well, I had help. Penny wanted extraordinary, and I think it is."

"Absolutely. I am stunned. I hope ya'll are ready to enjoy it with me."

There is little conversation as the cake is passed and everyone dives in to the decadent dessert.

"I am rendered speechless," Eddie states as he rubs his stomach. "No more, I will bust for sure. Thank you so much. I've never dined where I was treated so special." Eddie puts his arm around Penny and kisses the top of her hair, and whispers, "Thank you."

"You are welcome, Eddie. Happy Birthday."

"And I am happy, sharing it with you."

Maebelle clears her throat. "It is a special evening. I truly enjoyed it. Before you leave Boyd, I have a gift for you to take home for the babies." Boyd looks surprised. "If you could be so good to pull out my chair and help me to the living room, I'll get it for you."

"My pleasure." Boyd helps her up and out and lets Ms. Maebelle lean on him as they walk slowly into the formal living room.

"Let me help with the dishes, and I'll be right out in a few," Penny tells Eddie.

"I'll be fine. I need to make a call, so don't rush." Eddie stands offering to remove some plates.

"Nonsense," Penny says. "You can help on another occasion."

Eddie strolls to the outside porch and retrieves his phone from his pocket and makes a telephone call. Engrossed in his conversation, Eddie's back is to Penny as she quietly waits for him to finish.

"I know," Eddie is talking. "I'm excited to see you too. It will be special, I promise." He pauses. "I know, the last time we were together, I left early. We'll pick up where we left off. We have so much to talk about." He is silent and is listening. "I've missed you too. I love you. Goodnight."

Penny is ashen and cannot believe her ears. She is backing out of the room, when Eddie turns around.

"There you are, and walks toward her, embracing her tightly. He kisses her neck, but Penny freezes. Feeling her tense, Eddie looks into her eyes. "Thank you again."

"Oh, you're most welcome. Anything we can do for a police officer to demonstrate appreciation. It's the least we can do to thank you."

Eddie is caught off guard. *Penny is a switch plate. On, off. On, off. And right now, she is turned off. What the devil is going on?*

"Eddie, I've been thinking," Penny begins, I'll be leaving soon for Guatemala."

"What?"

"Yes, Mum's recovery is truly remarkable. This was a good farewell dinner. Perhaps, we can write to one another."

Eddie is blind-sided, and it shows. His pride will not let him probe. He thinks he is on chocolate overload.

Boyd appears, "Partner, are you ready? We need to be heading out."

Eddie answers, "Ready, sir." Eddie takes her hand and drops it softly. "Goodbye, Penn. Safe travels." He leans over and kisses her cheek.

The guys leave, and Eddie doesn't look back to see the giant tear puddling in Penny's eye and falling down her cheek. She stands motionless, as the stillness overtakes her. She is a statue in repose.

On the way back to their bed and breakfast, Eddie is also still and unusually quiet.

Boyd reads him well. "Something is wrong. Can I help?"

"Sir, I'm sick."

"Too much cake?"

"No, I am sure something happened, and I am clueless about what that something is. I don't know, I just don't know, but love shouldn't be this hard. I'm perplexed. It's like she is plucking petals from a flower. She loves me, she loves me not. Maybe she is bi-polar. Of course, I am joking. It's not just my ego that is shattered. I feel knocked down to the core."

Boyd is careful to listen. When he is sure Eddie has finished talking, Boyd tells Eddie, "If it's meant to be, she will be your girl. I have faith that she is, Eddie. Give her the space she apparently is seeking and give her a chance to get her balance."

Eddie is wearing his heart on his sleeve. "I hope we're not playing a game. Maybe I need to buy a couple of vowels. I'm lost, sir." He jumps from joking to being serious.

"I see it man, and I hate it for you. Let's get some sleep. I hope the situation will be better tomorrow." No more words are spoken as they enter their room for the evening.

Chapter 64

Eddie cannot wrap his head around *WHAT* happened. He is, however, resigned. He has already eaten breakfast when Boyd enters the dining room in the morning. Boyd takes a banana and fixes himself a large coffee to go.

"Are we checking out?" Eddie inquires.

“Perhaps, but duty calls right now. Let’s go. Today, we will bring in another witness. I was notified about it late yesterday afternoon. J.W. Collins is scheduled to bail out, and if we have any luck, our next interviewee will run into him at the detention room.”

“Who, Dana?”

“No, Sandy Collins.”

“J.W.’s wife?”

“Yes. Those phone records have finally been obtained by a court order. An abnormal amount of cellular calls at odd times are listed going to her from Ron Robinson.”

“Whew. This is getting uglier and more twisted.”

“We will phone her and ask her to come in. If J.W. is being processed, it might be interesting to see the two collide. The space is getting too small for him to hide. You know, scientists did studies years ago with rats. They kept closing in their space day after day. Finally, they started noticing that the rats were beginning to gnaw on each other till one of the rats ate the other.”

“Is that a fact?”

“Yes Eddie, it’s true.”

“That is some analogy sir, and all you ate for breakfast is a banana.”

Boyd enters the detention area and asks for the center view room with the see-through glass. Eddie takes a seat. Boyd makes the call.

"Mrs. Collins?" A long pause with no voice follows; only shallow breaths. Finally, "This is she."

"Boyd Price, ma'am, with Special Investigations.

"Yes, I just spoke with the department, and told the sergeant that I am coming down now to pick up Jack."

"Yes, ma'am. Please stop to see me when you get here. Ask for Detectives Price and Martin. We have a few questions we'd like to go over with you. Thank you, ma'am. We'll expect you soon."

Eddie is reading the report. *The only report left, and it has to be this bombshell.*

"Could you call the lab, Eddie, and check on J.W.'s truck? It's possible that report is finished."

There's a knock on the door. Boyd waves the deputy in, recognizing him from the parking lot incident yesterday.

"Lt. Price, may I speak freely?"

"Yes sir. Please be seated," Boyd replies.

"Yesterday, I drove Deputy Collin's truck in to the maintenance yard. I worked a while in the canine unit and I need to say, uh, report that Deputy Collins truck had a strong marijuana smell in it. There were brown packages wrapped in twine laying on the floor board. I turned it in with a complete inventory sheet."

"Thank you. I know it is difficult to report on a fellow officer."

"Sir, I don't believe this was a recreational amount. Regretfully, I'd have to say, this was a commercial amount. Deputy Collins might be playing dirty, sir."

"Thank you again for doing your job. Sometimes we must make tough decisions. You've done the right thing."

"Yes sir," and the deputy turns to leave, closing the door behind him.

"I'm going to pull a worksheet for Collins to see if he was working when these phone calls were made. Sir, some calls are over an hour long."

"I know. It has been my belief all along that J.W. Collins did not possess the moxie to be an enforcer. He was probably a puppet and was too blind to see what was really happening. According to Dana, he wasn't aware of her percentage for the sales she was making. She could have told him anything. He was being used like all the people in Ron Robinson's life. When Mrs. Collins comes in, I intend on pressing her hard on some very tough personal questions."

Detectives Price and Martin are startled to see Sandra Jane Collins standing before them. Obviously broken, Sandy looks as though she has died in her shoes. Intending to hammer her down into submission, Boyd knows immediately he is dealing with a woman suffering from physical and emotional pain. She is impoverished. He stands to greet her or catch her from falling, whichever comes first.

"Mrs. Collins, I'm Lieutenant Price and this is Detective Martin. Please have a seat. May I offer you some water?"

"Yes, please, will my husband be coming in?"

"No ma'am, I believe he will remain in custody until you bond him out."

Sandy Collins is adrift, staring at her slightly trembling hands. Eddie hands her a bottled water, and she drinks most of it in a few seconds. Have you taken any medications Mrs. Collins recently that would prevent you from engaging in this interview?" Boyd is concerned.

"Yes, I have been unable to sleep for weeks now, and I am taking Xanax."

"I see. Would you like to have your attorney with you?"

"I understand what you are asking. There is no need to involve anyone else."

Boyd has seen this depth of misery before and recognizes the ashen face that gnawing regret gives you. He thinks she is ready to unload the weight of the world that sits on her shoulders.

"Mrs. Collins, we called you here in hopes of closing our investigation of the Ron Robinson murder. I will be recording our conversation now." Boyd is looking into an empty shell.

"We know from phone records that you and Ron had extensive conversations several times a week, even several times a day. Many calls were made after hours when your husband was working. Will you tell us what happened? We need to hear the truth, ma'am."

Her neck vein appears corded and in a shaking voice, she whispers, "I don't even know how this affair started. I've questioned myself many times; how this happened. I do not know what possessed me. To be sure, I do know Ron Robinson was a terrible man. He preyed on the emotional vulnerabilities of people. At first, his flirtatious comments were appreciated to someone like me whose husband rarely makes a comment about my appearance. He lured me with fancy talk, because he knew I am weak and foolish. His phone calls were frequent, and always flirtatious. He hooked Jack on the idea of becoming sheriff, funding the bulk of the campaign, all the while he was helping himself to me when I was left alone."

"We were doing okay, financially, or so I thought." She hesitates. "Later, I learned Ron was buying and selling marijuana and Jack was in the thick of it. The money we were spending on some of Jack's toys was from Ron's scheming and pursuit of more money. He used Jack. He used me. "His dirty hands are on everything."

Sandy begins to shake but continues to unload her guilt. "I told him that, and then he laughed at me. Deriding Jack was a specialty of Ron's. I hated him for that. Everything about Ron was threatening and unpromising. At first, I was flattered, then I became forced to continue and then he threatened to leave Jack, us, in debt. Ron told me Jack would not only lose the election but… his…. retirement also. He'd see to it."

Sandy's dialogue stalls, and some of her words become inaudible. She struggles for more words, but the depth of her misery is evident.

She takes a deep breath and begins talking once again.

"Ron was drunk the afternoon he called me to come to the dealership right away. He told me on the phone he was telling Jack all about us. He had this insane idea that I wanted a permanent relationship with him. He told me that after the election, Jack would be too busy for me. I walked in the office about five-thirty, and he was in that chair of his, sitting on his throne. The first thing he said to me was, 'I knew you'd come right away. You're so easily led'."

"My blood was boiling inside, and I decided it was my turn to ridicule him."

And laugh I did, wildly, at the notion I wanted a life with him. He stood up and reached across his desk and knocked me to the floor. I lay there, with a broken lamp, and items that fell off his desk with his broad swipe. I was stunned for a few seconds. On the floor, I heard his sardonic laughing. Amid the broken glass, and papers, a gun had fallen too. I picked it up, picked myself up, and took dead aim and fired. He fell back in his chair. I didn't look back. I don't even know how I drove home. In fact, I was sitting in my car in the garage with the motor running when Jack got home that night. He shouted at me that I could have killed myself from carbon monoxide. I did die that night. Jack doesn't realize it. Yes, I feel dead. He tells me I am too tired from the months of campaigning."

"Every day I want to tell him how I ruined our lives, but he tells me I need to rest. Truthfully, after Ron died, Jack changed too. Perhaps, the loss of his biggest supporter affected him more than I can realize." Sandy looks toward the door.

"I won't be able to face him. I can't. Will you help me?"

Her voice fades and she slumps in her chair.

Eddie hurries to prop her up. He looks at Boyd. "I think she needs medical attention. She is cold."

Boyd picks up his phone and dials for an ambulance.

Eddie suggests she drink some water. She is unresponsive to his words. Boyd turns off his recorder and tells Eddie he is going outside to meet the medics.

"Please continue to sit beside her so she doesn't injure herself."

Chapter 65

The ambulance departs for the hospital and is closely followed by a deputy in his patrol car who will remain at the hospital with Sandy Collins for the evening.

Returning to their desks, Boyd and Eddie are silent for a couple of minutes.

"An hour ago, I thought J.W. killed Ron, because he had strong motive," Boyd says in a slow measured tone. But I don't recall the report stating that Ron's office was in disarray when the body was discovered. Sandy said she rushed out."

Boyd and Eddie continue to deliberate the ordeal that has unfolded.

"We need to visit J.W. Collins and tell him about his wife. Are you ready Eddie?"

"Yes sir."

Boyd makes a call to the sheriff and asks if he can meet with him in his office and explain the circumstances and latest events.

The holding area for detainees bonding out is in the west wing of the sheriff's department. Boyd and Eddie approach the sheriff's office and he waves them in.

"You boys have been busy today," the sheriff gets up from his desk chair and shakes Boyd's hand, and then Eddie's.

"Busy and bewildered. Sheriff, has J.W. decided to cooperate?"

"On the contrary. He has lawyered up and keeps repeating his innocence on an hourly basis."

"Is he able to bond out?"

"Yes, he called a bail bondsman, and it's going to be almost an hour before the paperwork is completed. Of course, his truck is impounded, but he is expecting Sandy to pick him up."

"Sandy won't be coming." Boyd pauses. "She is on her way to the hospital. In her languid state, Detective Martin and I thought it best to call for an ambulance. I believe her cave of despair finally collapsed on top of her. In an interview about an hour ago, Sandy confessed to killing Ron Robinson."

"What did you say?" The sheriff is shocked. "Unbelievable! I've known Sandy Collins for years. I will swear she is incapable of killing anyone. Why?"

"She and Ron were intimately involved. I believe Sandy realized her grave mistake and tried to end their relationship. Her humiliation got the best of her and she snapped. The details of her story do not indicate pre-meditation, but rather lashing out in retaliation. The attorneys will sort this all out. Unfortunately, the Sandy you know is indistinguishable now. We interviewed a devastated woman, at the edge of complete despair. Before our very eyes, her spirit and soul vanished under the guilt of what she said she had done."

"I am speechless," the sheriff is unable to grasp what he is hearing.

"We recorded the interview. Now we need to talk to J.W. and convince him to tell us the truth. For her sake, I hope he cooperates and admits to his own involvement in this twisted triad of wrongdoing."

"What office do you want to use? There is an office in the holding compound that you can use to talk to him. It's available now."

"That will be fine." Boyd sighs and looks Eddie's way. "Long day, partner."

"Yes sir, it is."

"I'll get us a drink, and some crackers, sir, and meet you in a minute," Eddie volunteers.

"Thanks."

J.W. strolls in the office escorted by a deputy. Entering the room, he is agitated seeing the investigators waiting.

"Well, if it's not the two blind mice. You guys are skipping up the wrong trail."

"J.W., we are recording this. This is our last time we will be asking for your cooperation. Your campaign is virtually over with last night's news cast. Your wife came in voluntarily to speak to us."

"I wouldn't believe anything she said. She's so tired from this election. Where is she?"

"Fortunately, she is on her way to the hospital. We thought it best to seek medical attention for her." Boyd briefly pauses. "J.W., she confessed about the affair, and the shooting. She is a shattered person, trying to handle the burden of what she thinks she did."

Boyd abruptly stops talking and looks in his bloodshot eyes and stares. When he is sure he has J.W.'s attention, he continues.

"If you let her continue to think she killed someone, then be prepared for her to spend many years in prison. Both of you will be incarcerated at the same time."

Eddie displays no emotion on his face. *Did I hear 'continue to think she killed someone'?*

Collins' eyes close and his head tilts back. His eyes roll back and when he opens them, he breathes out heavily, eventually straightening up. "It's over." Staring back at Boyd, "I hope you're satisfied."

"I get no satisfaction; none.... at all... from learning a fellow officer breaks the law and forgets his oath."

J.W. looks so pained. "I saw Sandy leaving the dealership in a race against time. Couldn't imagine why she was there at that time. I walked into the office and Ron was alive. He lived long enough to gloat to the wrong person."

He shakes his head side to side. "For God's sake, she was my wife! He was my partner, my friend. I finished him for us both." J.W. continues to let out bursts of heavy breathing.

"She didn't kill him. I fired the shot that ended his life. Ron Robinson didn't deserve to breathe any more. It's that simple." J.W. pauses, and in a shallow voice he speaks. "Will I be able to go see her tonight?"

"I can understand your need to see her." Boyd answers in a sympathetic tone. "You can be assured she will be getting the rest and medical attention she needs. The sheriff is outside the door and you will remain in custody for the night. The state attorney will be outlining the charges against you in the hours ahead."

Boyd takes a few steps to the door and knocks. The sheriff enters, and Jack stands up.

"I'm ready." J.W. Collins is exasperated.

The door closes. Eddie reaches for Boyd's hand to shake it. "Sir, good work. How did you know?"

"Eddie, I guessed. I had a gut feeling, and I remembered Robinson's office setting. Everything was in place according to the report. Sandy said items were knocked off his desk and then she hurried out. Also, Ron was found in his chair."

"Very good sir, well done."

"For us both Eddie. I'm glad our work is finished here."

"Yes, sir."

The paperwork is complete, and Boyd and Eddie say goodbye to the sheriff. Boyd drives to the Inn to pick up their belongings. It is after one-thirty when they begin their trip home.

Eddie breaks the silence. "Sir, I believe I missed lunch today. I can make do with a hot dog from one of the snatch and grab it stores, if you can get out of your Mario Andretti role long enough to stop."

Boyd looks at the speedometer. Laughing, "Gee, I hadn't realized."

"Sir, we took that curve like it was a hairpin on the Daytona track."

"Okay. I'll pull over when you tell me."

"I'm good, anywhere, really. We're just a few miles from the interstate. How does *WaWa* store sound to you?"

"You got it."

Getting a sandwich, Boyd points to a table to let Eddie know he'll be seated there. Eddie's hands are full; sandwich, chips, side bowl of soup, and large drink. He places it all down on his side of the table.

"It's a good thing you keep your own expense log," as Boyd notices his 'get by on a snack' has turned into a meal. "Don't you have a family birthday dinner tonight?"

"Yes, but that's four hours away. I can only guess what you are doing tonight sir." Eddie begins to tease.

Boyd's demeanor changes, and he smiles. I'm sending my mother to her home after I give her a giant hug for watching over Dolly. "Then, I am going to smother my wife with attention all night long and hope you don't call me telling me you're hungry."

"Wouldn't dream of it sir."

"Penny for your thoughts? I couldn't resist!" Boyd laughs as he says it.

"I'll give it a few days. Let her miss me, I hope."

"I bet she will too." Boyd reassures Eddie.

"Do you know what's next for us, sir?"

"Some time off, four days to be exact. You'll be emailed some reports to fill out. Me too. State attorney wants two separate final reports."

Driving east down the highway, Eddie asks Boyd how soon before they move into their new house.

"The contractor told me eight to twelve months, but I'm thinking he is ahead of schedule. I promised him a bonus if he gets us in our home before the babies arrive."

"Is that what you're calling them? The babies?"

"It does sound funny. Dolly keeps a journal, and I suspect she has some names written down. Because she is older, she was afraid to get too far ahead in planning until she was further along, and out of danger of miscarriage."

"That sounds cautious and smart. I grew up with three sisters. They are beautiful and loving souls who would do anything for me, including marrying me off to any one of their best friends. It's been a couple of weeks since I have talked to them. We were beginning our investigation. I enlisted their help when Penny visited me at the beach. I talked to my mother last night. She said she will be cooking all day for my birthday dinner. I hoped to bring Penny and introduce her to my family. Once again, she shut me down. Something is bothering her about Guatemala. I can't help her if she doesn't confide in me. However, she does tell Terrance, you know good ole Terry."

"I hear your stinger out, partner. Let it rest. More information will be forthcoming. I have a feeling the situation will work out the way it's meant to be."

"I'm available to help out at your new house. I'm a pretty good painter." Eddie volunteers.

Boyd chuckles. "The house has been painted. How are you at landscaping?"

"Do you have a plan? Or do you mean you need a young back to haul plants around?" Eddie is teasing him.

"I've drawn out a picture, so to speak. I wanted to surprise D when I take her the first time. That's what I call her, D. When the babies are here, she'll need all the help she can get. That's why I want to complete everything I can."

"What time do you want me there tomorrow?"

"Ordinarily I would begin around seven, but tomorrow morning, I don't want to leave so early because I have been out of town a lot. So, I'll do more smothering and then load my tools."

"Okay, let me write down the address. As for me, I will be suffering from smothering of mi familia, so I will get there as quickly as I can."

"Thanks, Eddie. I really appreciate you helping me."

"I'm down with it, isn't that one of your sayings?"

"Yes," Boyd begins to chuckle.

Chapter 66

Boyd's mind is on Dolly as he pulls away from the substation dropping off Eddie. *Stop by the store and pick up a big box of chocolates.* Boyd reaches for his phone and calls Dolly.

"Mom? Hey, I'm on my way home and wanted to stop at the store. Do we need anything?"

"Hey son, Dolly is resting in her room. I know her mood will turn around as soon as she hears you are on your way home."

"I should be there in twenty. Thanks, Mom. I know you'll be anxious to get home as soon as you can."

"Okay Boyd, I can take a hint."

"Mom, you'll have to excuse me. I just want some alone time with her."

"And you deserve it son."

Boyd decides to be cute and ring the bell. On the third ring, Dolly opens the door, and Boyd grabs her up and hugs her tightly, as he walks in.

Dolly catches her breath as Boyd blurts out, “You have really blossomed!”

“Well, thank you Magnum P.I.! Here we go, you are commenting on my weight. I guess we’re headed for divorce,” and she is smiling.

Boyd pulls her to him. “There’ll be no divorce,” Boyd is smiling too.

“In fact, I bring peace offering, Chief Thunder has brought chocolates! Once again, proving to you, that you are beautiful!” He reaches to rub her belly.

Looking embarrassed, Dolly exclaims, “Bo! Your mother is still here, you know.”

“Not tonight D.” And he begins kissing her on her neck, finding her lips, ending it softly, “I love you D.”

“Me three,” enjoying his romantic return.

“Where’s Mother?” Dolly is looking around.

“Oh, she had an urgent errand. I guess she left. You are stuck with me.” Something catches his eye on the left. “Whoa, is that a suitcase I see packed?” Boyd cannot believe his eyes.

“Yes, I’m ready. The doctor told me to get ready. They are coming early.”

“Lordy, we don’t have names picked out yet, or do we?”

Dolly laughs. “Maybe tonight, we can decide on two names.”

"Yes, Eddie already mentioned that I am referring to them as the babies too often."

"How is Eddie doing in the romance department?"

"He's frustrated."

"I guess he is used to girls falling at his feet, and this is different. Am I right?"

"So right. Too bad everyone cannot be as lucky as us."

"Puh…leeze, I was happy single, me and the Captain, drinking dinner together."

Boyd knows she is kidding with him. "Yeah, I'm glad that old goat sailed to another port. You 'gotta admit, dinner with me is a lot more interesting."

"I admit to nothing, except that my feet are big, and they hurt."

"See there, let's go in the bedroom and I'll rub your feet. Captain Morgan never did that for you, now did he?"

"You win, always. I'll take you up on that foot massage."

"You got it. Let me get my bag out of the Tahoe and I'll be right back."

Dolly is waiting on the side of the bed when Boyd returns.

Boyd leans over to kiss her again. "I have missed you so much. Have you missed me too?"

"Absolutely, especially my coffee boy. Love your mother, but most days, she serves me hot tea. Oh, she has a lot of excuses, like she bought a new flavor, she forgot I liked coffee, she thought I would enjoy juice… I'm on to her, just don't want to complain. I don't mean to judge. Who am I kidding? Of course, I do."

Boyd cannot keep from grinning. "Admittedly, I might have mentioned to mother about holding down your coffee intake. Are you feeling good? Have you been to the flower shop? I can hire you an extra person for you to work there if you need them."

"I know you can and will if I don't watch you. One job at a time please. Back to my feet, please."

"Your skin smells so good. Why I am stuck down here on your feet?"

"Oh, I thought that it was your idea, my bad."

"It is, how 'bout your back? Some lotion and a rub?"

"You'll be my superman if you rub my back!"

He scores! Boyd begins rubbing her back, and when he gets to the small of her back, he maneuvers his hand differently. You know I used to have an old girlfriend who showed me this."

Dolly turns around facing him, and her eyes are filled with tears. Before she can speak, Boyd senses she is emotional. "Baby, I am teasing you."

"I know Bo, I'm so happy and lucky to be your wife. Everything makes me cry these days."

"Baby," and he plants small kisses on her eyelids, "I'll get supper for us. Would you like pizza?"

"I know there is something in the fridge you can eat. I'm eating chocolate."

"Then it's pizza. I'll call it in. Three pieces of chocolate now. None later. I'll be your dessert."

"Okay. You talked me in to it."

Boyd reaches for his phone and calls for a medium pizza and two garden salads, then hangs up.

"D, I'd like to name our boy after Eddie, my partner. Is that okay?"

Dolly is surprised. "I am fine with that. I just assumed you wanted him to have your name. I do like the name Jacob."

"It's not necessary to name him after me. Any thoughts on our baby girl?"

"Do you like Janelle? It is part of your mom's name and part of my mom's name. Janet and Ellie."

"I love that D." Bo gives her a kiss and gets up and gets out his wallet for the pizza. He reaches into his bag to remove his soiled clothes and remembers the gift Maebelle Merriwether gave him.

"Here, I almost forgot. Our first baby gift from Maebelle Merriwether. She received a card about the …babies, uh, I mean," and then he slowly says, "Jacob Eddie and Janelle. Janelle what?"

"Janelle Rose. It has a nice sound to it. Don't you think?"

"Yes, baby, anyway, here is our first gift. Mother told her we were expecting two."

"The box looks like a tie box, a bit odd for a baby gift," and Dolly begins to open it. Inside there are two exquisite silver spoons. Dolly turns them over, feeling the weight. *Made in England.* Underneath the spoons, laying on the bottom of the box, are two one thousand-dollar savings bonds.

"Gracious, she thinks a lot of you, Bo."

"I'm overwhelmed, to say the least. All I can tell you is she is one special lady. I'm sure you'll meet one day."

Bo offers his hand to pull her up off the bed, and he just holds her. "It's great to be home," and kisses her neck. "Go to the table and I'll get everything we need."

"Now wait a minute. I may be a blimp, but I can still move around in my own kitchen. And speaking of kitchens, the new one is fabulous. I think you are spending too much money on this house."

Boyd is getting two plates and the utensils. "What would you like to drink?"

"I'd like a glass of wine, but I'll settle for iced tea."

"That's what I'll have too."

"I don't mind you drinking a beer, Bo."

"And I don't mind drinking tea."

"You are incorrigible!"

"This word incorrigible, does it mean strong, handsome and romantic?"

"No, it does not. Ask Siri."

"Yes, it's good to be home with my spit fire."

They are eating, and laughing, and Boyd asks Dolly if she has everything she needs. Did mother help you get the furniture for the twins' room?"

"Yes, we just need to call the store and let them know the delivery date. I'm worried you'll be gone on this investigation when I have to go the hospital."

"I won't be gone. Eddie and I wrapped up the case. It is all up to the state attorney's office now. All Eddie and I have to do is finish up our paperwork."

"This is wonderful news! I admit I am feeling a little overwhelmed and more emotional than normal. We will need a little extra help. I'm sure of it."

"And my everything shall have it. D, you look beautiful in that dress. You are glowing!"

"Yes, I bought this at the La Petite Elephant." Dolly waits for his comeback.

Boyd does not know **what** to say. He only smiles, and they finish their meal.

"I suppose you'll want to take your bath. I'll draw it for you, baby."

"You suppose wrong. The doctor said no more baths. Just showers."

"Well, let's shower together. I want to be close to you. I told Eddie I was going to smother you with attention. I need to hold you."

"Yes, I want that too."

Eddie showers and dresses quickly to join his family in celebrating his birthday. His birthday wish is that Penelope would have been able to join him, but she didn't give him a chance to ask her. It is true, he thinks, that absence makes the heart grow fonder. With the investigation over, he doesn't know when he will see her. *She's got to want to want to be with me.*

Eddie is greeted at the door by his sisters, all hugging him. Edilia looks around and is puzzled he has not brought a girlfriend.

"Ah, my brother is single again?"

"Somewhat," Eddie answers dryly.

Eddie's mother comes from the kitchen. "Eduardo, Feliz Cumpleaños! I saw your picture on television. I am so proud of you, son. You make us so happy. Now, where is this special girl that Edilia says is the one?" She looks around him.

"Mother, she is special, but she was unable to come. I will bring her another day. Just as well that she doesn't see what a pig I can be eating all my favorite dishes. You just try to fill me up," teasing with his dear mother.

"Oh, son, you ask the impossible."

Eddie smiles and is happy to share a special time with his family. Their love never fails him.

Chapter 67

Penny makes up her mind to leave. She purchases her ticket; now to tell her mother goodbye. Penny waits till they are all seated at the dining room table.

"Flo, the roast is superb, and I will miss your cooking when I depart."

Maebelle immediately senses something is amiss. "Penny, what is troubling you? You know I am getting better each day."

Penny grabs her hand and rubs the top of it. "I know Mum, you are the strongest woman I know. You have made such progress. That's why I know I can leave, because you are doing so well."

Flo jumps in, "Leave? Us? And Eddie too?"

Penny swallows hard. “Well, not forever. I need to go and settle the adoption and finish out the year with the orphanage. Maybe Eddie will have sown all his wild oats by then and be ready to date only one person.”

Mae is astounded. “Has he revealed he is dating others? I find this unbelievable dear Penny. Do you have proof of his indiscretions?”

“Well no, I don’t have an eight by ten picture, but there is nothing wrong with my hearing. I overheard him speaking to someone on the phone, looking forward to being with them, and he told them he loved them. I don’t need a ton of bricks dumped on my head to understand what I heard, now do I?”

Maebelle gasps and sets her fork down on her plate.

With watering eyes, she quietly asks Penny when she will be leaving.

“Tomorrow,” Penny answers. “I know it’s a surprise, but you guys are busy with the election in two days and you won’t even miss me. I can’t vote anyway,” trying to make the situation and talk at the table lighter.

“Oh, this is bad, really bad.” Flo says.

“My mind is made up, and this is for best way, I am sure of it. So,… Sunday I will take my rental car back and depart shortly after.” Turning to Maebelle, “I’ve had the best visit Mumsy. I will be in touch more often. I’m going to send pictures of Tito immediately.”

“Are you sure about this?”

"Of Tito? Absolutely. Of leaving? Of course, it is hard, but I am planning on returning so Tito can have an American life and stability."

"Very well," and Maebelle sounds weak in her speech.

Flo is moving food around on her plate without purpose and remains quiet.

"Oh, c'mon now, you didn't think I would be here indefinitely, did you?" Penny shakes her head sideways. "You two can invite Eddie over again after I leave. You'll have to excuse me now, I'm not hungry anymore."

Maebelle and Flo remain seated, exchanging glances.

"Are you alright Mae?"

"Yes, I'll be alright. It's just that I pride myself on being a good judge of character. I truly thought that Eddie was the perfect fit for my Penny."

"Yes um, I still do."

Chapter 68

"Here is your coffee D, giving her a smooch. "Are we going to the Sunday dinner today, or can I beg off to finish some landscaping? Eddie is coming over to give me a hand."

"Oh, we postponed it because I told them you were out of town. I might have mentioned I'm not driving anymore." Dolly looks up to the heavens. "Lord, it's just a small misrepresentation."

"What would my everything like for breakfast? Your wish is my command, as long as it is eggs and bacon."

"Well, darn, that sounds 'kinda limited. Your mother makes a lot of different culinary delights."

"I believe you told me once that I should call my mother when I mentioned she made good soup. Do you want to phone her?"

Dolly begins to laugh and steps into Bo's chest and puts her arms around him. "I did miss you so much and I'm glad my everything is home today."

Placing his hand against her cheek, he gently answers, "But not for the whole day. I wish it was so. Listen, do you mind if I ask Eddie to spend the night.? Are you up for a guest?"

"Of course, that will be nice. I'll take some steaks out of the freezer, so ya'll can grill them."

"Good idea. Now to the breakfast. Bacon and eggs, it is."

"While I'm enjoying my second cup of java, I'm going to phone Rita. I need some sisterly advice on last minute items to buy before the babies arrive."

"Babies? Don't you mean Jacob Eddie and Janelle Rose?"

Dolly rubs her tummy, "Bo, it won't be long now."

"I know baby, I'm getting excited."

Dolly sits at the table, phoning Rita. "Good morning sis."

"Well, good morning! You're sounding chipper."

"I am. Bo is home and I love it. By the way, how is my favorite niece handling her last month of pregnancy?"

"To be honest, I am worried about her low weight gain." Rita answers. "She went to the doctor and he says that Rene is doing fine."

"Guess you are glad the family dinner is postponed. Your favorite sister, Denise, I kid, I kid, is still complaining. She said postponing it interferes with items she needs to advise us about. Apparently, she is making big changes in the farm operations."

"What changes? Did she say?"

"No, but I think it involves cash flow and the reason we haven't received our quarterly dividend from the trust."

"What do you think is the reason? I know the farm went up on the price of leather leaf that we use at the flower shop. Juan told me there was a shortage, and that many plants are damaged from the hurricane winds. I won't hold my breath that she will notify me of anything in advance. Hey Rita, want to come over and go to the new house? Bo and Eddie, his partner, are working on the grounds. He said Eddie might be spending the night with us."

"Well, sounds like everything is moving along ahead of schedule."

"Yes, the house is almost ready. We received an occupancy permission from the power company."

"Gracious, do ya'll need help moving?"

"Bo already hired a company to do that. Except for personal stuff, the moving of furniture will probably begin soon."

"Are ya'll going out to eat tonight with Eddie, is that the name you said?"

"No, I'm taking out steaks, and putting some potatoes in the oven. Hey, why don't you and Roan come too? Bo would love to see his favorite brother in law."

"I'm sure Roan will love to come. Let me bring the salad."

"Okay, thanks for offering. Bo is giving me the look that breakfast is ready."

"Okay, I'll let you hang up."

The phone rings as soon as Dolly hangs up. She panics and looks at Bo. "Absolutely not, no, you just can't leave again."

Bo leans over to kiss her on the cheek. "I'm not leaving. Breathe easy Mrs. Price."

The call is from Eddie, who tells Boyd that he is on the property. "Boss man, you know, the early bird gets the worm. I guess I just have the advantage of youth on my side."

Boyd is stupefied. "You're already there?"

"Yes, I have been raking about an hour."

"Good lord, I'll finish breakfast and be right over." Bo laughs when he gets off the phone."

"I doubt I have ever had the energy he does. I'm getting older than I realized," shaking his head in disbelief.

"Do I need to trade you in for a younger model?" Dolly teases him.

"Too late, I'm in for the long haul."

"Well, you better haul yourself over there. Go on, I'll get the dishes."

Boyd stands up, wipes his face with his napkin and nibbles Dolly's neck. I'll call you later. We're going to grab a sandwich for lunch from Subway unless you want me to come home."

"I'll be fine, really, just fine." Dolly takes both of their plates to the sink as Boyd grabs his keys and wallet.

"Love you D," and holds her in a tight hug.

With her head against his chest, she murmurs, "Me three."

It is a tearful goodbye when Penelope drives away from the Merriwether estate. It might be another two months before she returns. Maebelle is fearful she might not return at all realizing whatever happened to the romance between Penny and Eddie is out of her hands. She watches Penny drive away and turns to Flo for a big hug. Both are consoling each other walking back inside the home.

Penny doesn't look back for fear she will not have the fortitude to return to Guatemala. By morning she will see Tito again and explain to him her long absence and her plans for them both.

In her dreams tonight, she will also think about Eddie, and try to forget about her longing for him.

In the terminal lounge, Penny calls her mother one last time before boarding.

"Hey Flo, just wanted to say goodbye before I board. Thank you again for all your assistance with Mumsy. We are so lucky to have you in our family."

"Yes um, and cause I'm family, I know I have the right to tell you to get on back here."

Obviously, Penny's grin cannot be seen to Flo. None the less, Penny answers her back. "I know you like being in my business, Miss Flo, but sometimes life's journey takes a different road than you expected."

"Yes um, the road you are driving on is a dead-end street. You need to do a quick U turn and get back here."

Maebelle takes the phone. "Penny dear, be safe now, and I hope everything works out. If you need financial assistance, please call me. These legal dilemmas require money, I am sure of it." Her voice becomes emotional. "I love you and want you to be happy."

"I am happy Mumsy, and I love you too. I don't tell you enough, but I do. I know you'll be occupied with the election party on Tuesday and will be surrounded by all your bridge ladies. Ya'll have a great time and I'll be in touch, soon, I promise. Bye for now."

Mae couldn't get her goodbye in quick enough before she hears the line go dead. She hangs up the phone, looking at Flo who is about to burst into tears.

"She'll be okay, Flo. We'll be okay too." Maebelle gives her a faint smile. "I'm glad we'll be busy tomorrow preparing for the election party. It will keep our minds off Penelope. "Let's eat a light supper tonight Flo."

"Yes um," and Flo exits to the kitchen.

Chapter 69

The day seems so very long to Dolly. Reading a baby magazine, she dozes in her recliner and does not hear Janet come in through the back door. The smell of tea brewing in the kitchen arouses her from her nap.

"Hello, I'm back," Janet almost whispers entering the living room. "What can I do to help get dinner ready for tonight?"

Dolly gets up slowly from the chair. "There's not too much to do. I thought I'd make some Hasselback potatoes. Rita and Roan are coming, and she is bringing a salad. Bo and Eddie are going to grill the steaks. Roan will probably supervise the grilling."

Janet smiles. "Feeling alright honey? You look a little tired."

"I don't have a reason to feel tired, but I admit my back and legs are beginning to ache every day."

"What did you eat for lunch today? I was trying to give you and Bo some privacy, so I stayed home and caught up on a few of my chores."

"And that is quite alright. I ate some fruit and cottage cheese. This afternoon I ate some cheese."

"This cheese?" and Janet reaches for the plate next to the recliner. None of it has been touched.

"Oh, well, I guess I didn't eat it. Explains why I am hungry now, but I don't want to spoil my dinner."

"How about a glass of iced tea Dolly?"

"Sounds good," as Dolly follows Janet, stopping by to sit at the table.

Janet hands her the tea and sets another down for herself. "I'll get the potatoes, so we can work on them here."

"Okay, we can use that blue ceramic roasting pan. You remember where I keep it, don't you?"

In short time, the dynamic duo finish the potatoes. Janet peels and Dolly makes vertical slices in the potatoes without cutting all the way through. Together, they add butter and garlic between the slices. They hear the door open and look that way. Beaming, Dolly gets up to embrace Boyd.

"Baby, I'm so dirty and sweaty." He kisses her forehead. Boyd glances at his mother. "Hi Mother." Their hug is interrupted by the doorbell.

"That's Eddie. He's going to need the shower. Could you show him the guest bath D?"

"Of course," as Dolly ambles toward the door. "Welcome Eddie."

"Mrs. Price, I apologize for coming to your door like this. I'm pretty dirty."

"Eddie, please call me Dolly. Let me show you to the bathroom." Eddie follows with his satchel in hand. "Everything you need should be here. Take your time, and thank you so much, Eddie, for helping out Bo today."

"Yes ma'am."

Returning to the kitchen, Janet puts the potatoes in the oven.

"Thank you, Mother, you're such a big help. I remember cooking with my Mom. She was a good cook. I miss her. It has been a year and a half year since she died. I wonder if she can see us down here, the struggles my sisters and I are having. I wonder if her Sunday dinners concept brings her joy or if she is disappointed in our behavior. Janet, you've witnessed the shark frenzy in our family, maybe even overlooked is a better word. I get worried that as hostility becomes a way of life, it all becomes the norm. I want our children to romp and play with cousins like I did when I was a kid. I'm ready to give up my inheritance in exchange for less stress. I firmly believe I cannot fix the Denise's problems. I too, am a willing participant in the arguments we have. I think she is drinking her dinners. As one who used to enjoy that, I never realized how unhappy that can make someone. Of course, I have Bo to thank for showering me with his love. Every day I should be on my knees, thanking God for sending him to me."

Bo is coming up behind her. Kissing her neck, he asks, "Why all the melancholy talk, D?" He is grinning as he says, "You must be pregnant! The devil made me say it," still smiling. Still behind her, his arms reach around her large abdomen and he places both of his hands on her. "My beautiful D. You're going to be the best mommy, I just know it."

Dolly turns around and kisses his chest. "See what I mean Janet?"

Janet is taking the conversations all in. "You two are quite a pair!"

There's a hard knock on the door and Roan and Rita open it.

Roan shouts out, "Get dressed, you've got company!"

Bo leaves Dolly's side and turns to shake Roan's hand.

"Hey, Bro, we just left our house. There's a news report just coming on about your investigation," Roan declares.

"Really?" Bo steps forward to turn the television on.

Breaking News ......WSTP has just learned that the sheriff's campaign is officially over for J.W. Collins in High Springs. The grand jury has indicted him on several charges, including homicide of a prominent citizen and business person, Ron Robinson, obstructing an active investigation, trafficking in cannabis with intent to sell, and misuse of sheriff's department funds. He is currently being held without bond. The six-month investigation conducted by the state attorney's office included the Special Investigations Bureau from Volusia County. More news to follow as additional information becomes available.

With all eyes glued on the television, no one notices that Eddie is out of the bathroom and watching the news story with them.

"Unbelievable," Roan looks at Bo and then over at Eddie. "Hi, I'm Roan," extending his hand.

"Eddie Martin, sir."

"Roan, this is my new ace partner. Turning to Eddie, "Meet my full-of-it brother-n-law, and Dolly's sister, Rita."

"So, this is the case you guys have been working on when you've been traveling out of town?" Roan asks.

"Just following the bread crumbs to and where they lead," Bo interjects. "Can't deny or confirm, Roan. C'mon, let me get you guys a beer on the back porch."

Rita looks at Dolly and Janet and says, "I'll stay here till the testosterone level comes down a bit out there."

"Would you like a glass of wine, Rita?" Janet asks.

"Thank you, Janet," and looks over at Dolly. "Sister, is that the first thing you're going to do after delivering? Have a glass of wine?"

Dolly laughs, "Probably not the first, but on the top five list." Dolly picks up her glass of tea and drinks some. "So tasty!"

Dolly reaches in the refrigerator and gets a jar of salsa out. Janet retrieves a platter and opens a bag of chips. Dolly sighs, "This will have to do. I make no apologies for not being gourmet tonight. C'mon, let's join the guys."

The guys are enjoying a joke about the day's activities. Boyd puts his arm around Dolly and kisses the top of her head. "You okay?"

"I'm good. Why are you drinking iced tea?"

Looking embarrassed, "Just because I know you can't, so I'm good too," and he kisses her head again.

"Please enjoy a beer, Bo. You worked hard all day."

"It's okay, D. I'm having what I want. Don't fret!"

"Okay, the steaks are on the counter getting to room temperature and the potatoes are the in the oven."

Roan asks, "When is the move?"

Bo looks at Eddie, then Roan. "Whenever you two are available! Seriously, I hired two guys to move us. I think they will start tomorrow."

"Are you kidding, Bo?" Dolly is surprised.

"No ma'am, I don't see why we can't start tomorrow. I'm off for four days."

"And he knows I'm off too," Eddie is quick to respond. "I guess that was planned sir. Am I right?"

"Absolutely. It's strictly volunteer, and I volunteered you."

Roan laughs. "I am good at pointing my finger where to put things, but I'm pretty clumsy when it comes to furniture."

"You're off the hook Bro. We are leaving most of the furniture here. Dolly's going to take a few special items."

"I can't believe this. Have you called the furniture company?"

"Called them Saturday. They start tomorrow too."

Still in disbelief, "Are we spending the night there tomorrow?"

"Maybe Mrs. Price, unless you are spending the night in the hospital."

"Well, I'm not feeling it just yet."

"This is exciting news," Rita joins in the conversation. "I can't wait to see it."

Janet hears the phone and says, "I'll get it. Enjoy your guests, D."

"Thank you, Mother."

Turning to Eddie, Rita asks, "Did Bo work you hard today?"

"It was the other way around," Bo retorts. "He was working almost two hours before I got there."

"Wow, and I can't even find a kid to rake a leaf these days!" Rita responds.

"Let's cook these steaks," Bo is anxious to eat.

Janet brings the phone to Dolly, "I'm sorry dear, it's Juan."

"Juan from the fernery?"

"I believe so."

Rita and Roan are visibly surprised. Something must be wrong at Blu Diamond Farms, for their most trusted employee to phone at night. *Most likely, Denise must be up to something again. Definitely, this is a bad sign.*

"Hey there, Juan? This is Dolly. It's good to hear from you."

"Si, I miss seeing you come get the ferns. My Maria and I are waiting for the big day."

"Oh, Juan thank you. Muchas gracias."

"Si, Miss Dolly," Juan speaks slowly. "I have check here and I cannot get my money from the bank. I always go to same bank, same day, same time. They do not want to take it."

Dolly looks alarmed. "Are you sure? Are you talking about your paycheck?"

"Si. Miss Dolly. I tried to reach Miss Denise, but no answer. My Maria and I go to store and get food, pay bills, and my Maria send a little bit of money back to her madre in Mexico."

"Okay, Juan, you are not to worry. I will have my husband bring you money now. Are you there at home?"

"Si, we came back a little while ago."

"Stay there. Mr. Boyd and Mr. Roan will come now. Goodbye." Dolly hangs up the phone.

"Can you please Bo? Juan is so proud, and I think it is difficult for him to call me."

Rita is shaking her head sideways, unable to understand the conversation.

Roan stands up, "Do we know how much money he needs?"

"Darn, I didn't think to ask! I guess I was just caught off guard." At that moment, Dolly drops her glass, and it breaks on the brick pavers, and glass jumps everywhere.

Immediately, Bo looks down and says, "Don't move Dolly. There's a big hunk of glass in your ankle."

Everyone looks down at her foot. Janet rushes to the kitchen for some dishcloths. Eddie grabs a chair and puts it behind Dolly, so she can sit. She does so without questioning. Eddie springs into action, getting on his knees.

"I got this sir." He takes one towel from Janet, places the towel over the edge of the glass and pulls it from the foot. Instantly, he presses another towel against the gash, continuing to fold the towel, thickening it, all the while applying pressure. Eddie tells Janet he'll need another towel to apply pressure so the cut starts to clot. He holds the towel and looks up, "You're okay."

Reassuring Dolly, Boyd tells her, "Yes, you'll be fine. It's alright D. We probably need a couple of stitches though."

"Are you sure?"

"I believe so. It looks that way to me."

Dolly looks around. "Well, I guess we're in a fix, and my timing could not be worse."

Boyd asks Roan, "Can you and Rita go to Juan? I have some cash in the safe in the utility room. Ya'll can take care of that problem. Eddie and I will take D to the hospital. Mother can...."

"Cook the steaks?" Janet interjects. "Not likely. How 'bout I put everything in the kitchen on hold until everyone gets back?"

Boyd agrees. "Let me get Roan and Rita on their way." They follow him to the utility room where Boyd gets a cash box off the shelf. "I don't know how much you'll need, but here's eight hundred."

"We'll find out what's going on and report back," Roan answers him and stuffs the money into his jeans pocket.

Boyd returns to the porch. "Mother, can you tie two of my socks together so I can tie them around Dolly's ankle to keep pressure on it when Eddie takes his hands off?"

"I'll be right back." Janet reacts quickly.

"I have my doubts that Dolly can walk on that foot without losing more blood."

Boyd takes the socks and ties them around the towels. The towels, once blue, have now turned deep maroon. The porch floor is also stained with blood.

Dolly remains quiet, looking away from her injury.

"Mother, could you offer some support while D stands up?"

"Slowly Dolly," Bo tells her, "and then lean on me. Please keep your foot up off the floor."

Boyd begins his walk through the house with Dolly at his side to the front door.

"Eddie, please grab the keys and blanket off the couch and meet me at my Tahoe. I'll take her on the right side, so she can scoot back on the seat. Mother, can you grab a pillow out of the bedroom and bring it, so we can elevate her foot?"

Eddie opens the back door. Bo tells Dolly to pull herself up with the help of the top of the front seat, and scoot back as much as she can. "Eddie, can you jump in the back seat and put your hands under her arms and help pull her back? This way she has the whole seat to stretch out."

In a soft voice, Dolly says, "That's a lot of blood I'm losing."

"I know but we're going to be there quickly." Boyd closes the door, starts the Tahoe and pulls forward over the grass onto the road.

Eddie pulls out his phone and calls the local medical center.

Eddie explains the situation to the facility, telling Boyd, "You can pull up in the emergency lane when we get there. They are coming out with a stretcher." Eddie looks back to Dolly, "Hang in there. We'll be there before you know it."

Dolly's voice is fading as she says, "Thank you."

Boyd turns his emergency lights on as he travels down the road. Pulling into the emergency area, he sees a team coming out with a stretcher. He shoves the Tahoe into park, and hustles around to the passenger back seat. Reaching in, he puts his arms under her and pulls her out still laying down. The stretcher is there to make the transition.

"We're here, D. Stay strong."

Boyd can barely hear her answer. "I will."

She's on the stretcher and into a room where the curtain is pulled in front of Boyd. Boyd pulls it back. "I'm her husband."

"How far along is your wife?" one of the attendees ask.

"The babies can come any time."

"Did you say babies? Two babies?"

"Yes."

"Who is her doctor?" the attending physician wants to know.

"Dr. Nicholas Reed," Boyd answers as he is looking at the towels being removed from her foot.

"Do you know your wife's blood type?"

"No, I do not."

Dolly answers softly. "It's O."

"For the most part, it looks like a clean cut. It'll require stitches, and maybe an artery that needs to be sutured. If you'll excuse us, we'll get her fixed up."

A nurse takes Dolly's hand, "Don't worry now, Mama, you're in the right place."

Boyd kisses her softly, "I'll be right outside the curtain. I love you. Everything is going to be alright."

With eyes still closed, Boyd hears, "Me three."

Boyd steps back and feels Eddie's hand on his shoulder. Eddie reassures Boyd she will be just fine.

"I know. I know. It was just a freak accident."

"Yes, it was. But everything is going to be okay. I think there was a little artery that keeps bleeding out. Let's be patient and wait. Let's step over here."

An aide carrying a cup goes into the room. Another aide carrying a tray of supplies pulls the curtain and then closes it back.

"Sir, I'd like to say a prayer," Eddie says.

"Yes, of course." With heads bowed, Eddie prays to the Great Physician.

"Thank you," Boyd whispers with his head still bowed.

An hour has elapsed and Rita and Roan walk into the emergency area. Boyd stands and gives them both a hug.

"We're waiting. They are stitching her up," and he glances at his watch. He walks towards the curtain and suddenly it is peeled back. The nurse says, "Whoops!"

Boyd leans over Dolly and kisses her ear and Dolly smiles. The doctor is wrapping her leg in gauze and finishes it with some tape.

"I'm Dr. White," and he looks at Bo. There was an artery that was cut. Her ankle is stitched, about ten or twelve stitches. It should heal quickly. You need to keep it dry and elevated, but she can walk on it. We just don't want it to swell a lot tonight. Lab reports indicate her blood count is low but not threatening. We contacted the obstetrician and he has all the reports. We're going to release her now. Her doctor said for you to call him if she has pain she can't tolerate or any fever that may arise. We gave her orange juice, because she is a little queasy."

"I'm hungry, I think." Dolly is quick to explain, and "I'm ready to leave." She looks at the doctor. "Thank you, Doctor. You're a man of few words and I like that."

Boyd reaches to shake his hand. "Thank you, Dr. White."

"The nurse has papers for you to sign and then you're good to go. Take care of yourself, Mrs. Price."

An aide pushing a wheelchair appears. Boyd reaches for Dolly's hand. He moves her legs over gently to one side of the bed. "Lean on me."

He helps her in the chair and the aide unlocks the brake. They are walking out, and Boyd points to the emergency lane where he is parked.

Dolly asks Rita, "Juan okay?"

"Everything is fine, we'll talk later. Let's get you home."

"I think they'll be more leg room if Dolly sits up front Sir," Eddie suggests.

"Probably," and Boyd opens the door. "Try not to put much weight on it D."

"I'm good, I'm fine, now."

Boyd waves to Roan leaving the parking lot. Roan follows close behind him.

The ride home is quiet, and the drive home seems shorter in time.

"You okay D?" Boyd reaches to hold Dolly's hand.

"Yes, I'm trying not to be a baby." She turns to Eddie seated in the back. "Thank you for your assistance."

"I see why Bo holds you in such high esteem. We just left poor Janet to attend to everything."

Bo turns into the driveway. Turning to Dolly, "We're home safe and sound. Give me a second to help you."

"I'm not an invalid. I'm sure I can walk on my own."

Bo looks at Eddie. "Find a mate less stubborn than mine, Eddie. You won't get as many grey hairs."

Dolly opens her car door and sets both feet down on the pavement. "See there?"

"I see," and Bo holds on to her as they walk toward the front door.

Janet opens the door. "Good, ya'll are home. I hope it wasn't too bad for you sweetie."

"It stings a bit. I'll be fine."

"Ya'll go on to the porch, I've picked up the broken glass."

"Thank you. I'm starved. How 'bout you guys?"

Rita and Roan have joined them on the porch. The big blood stain on the pavers does not go unnoticed by the group as they converse.

Bo looks around and announces, "Let's get these steaks cooked. How does everyone want their meat cooked?"

In unison, everyone says out loud. "Well done."

Dolly starts laughing. "I never thought I'd see the day."

Roan and Eddie volunteer to help and they step outside to start the grilling.

"I'm sorry, I tried to get it all up, but it will require some treatment," Janet is offering her explanation.

"It's okay, really." Dolly is embarrassed that she uttered the comeback in light of the bloody stain on the porch.

Rita reaches around Dolly's shoulders. "Let's get you seated at the table while Janet and I put the rest of dinner on the table."

In a few minutes everyone is seated. Boyd leads them in grace.

"Looks yummy," Dolly announces, "and I am starving. I had a light lunch."

"Me too," Eddie states.

After what I witnessed, "I'd hate to see what you'd refer to as a heavy lunch," Bo laughingly shares.

Everyone's spirits have picked up.

Roan begins telling them all, "The fernery has taken a hit. Rita and I were surprised when we drove in. We didn't think it wise to probe Juan until we get more facts. But it's obvious, production is down, and the farm isn't the same."

"Thank you, Roan, for going over there." Bo answers quickly.

"I put your money on the table there," Roan points to the small table at the front door. I asked Juan for his check. It's with the money Bo."

"Thanks."

"What needs to be done at the new house?" Rita inquires.

"There's not much. Just filling the kitchen cabinets. Like I mentioned, the guys I hired are moving furniture tomorrow."

"Why don't Roan and I come over with boxes and load up these kitchen wares in the morning. We can take Dolly a chair and you can sit and tell us where you want things put away."

"Sounds like a plan," Bo answers, and Dolly nods her head in agreement.

"Well, despite the emergency, dinner was delicious," Dolly glances at everyone.

Janet quickly breaks in, "No one is leaving until we have dessert. I made some peach cobbler."

"I'll help serve," Rita jumps up and starts clearing the dinner plates.

"I'm going to pass," Dolly says. "I'm just going to relax in the recliner."

Dolly gets up, followed by Bo who helps her to the chair. Bo and Dolly study her foot.

In a soft, concerned voice, "That's pretty swollen baby."

"I see it is, and it is starting to throb," she whispers. "Let's just get through dinner and say goodnight to our guests and I'll retire early. You'll help Eddie feel welcome and see that he has everything he needs in the guest room, won't you?"

"Of course. I'll bring you a glass of water, baby."

All the guys bring their dishes to the kitchen to aid Janet and Rita in the cleanup. Dolly says good night early and retires to her bedroom. The events of the day are catching up with her, and she feels uneasy and especially tired. Bo finds her on the bed taping a bathroom trash bag over her foot and up her leg.

"May I ask what you're doing?"

"I'm going to get a quick shower. I'll sit on the shower bench. Don't worry."

"Oh, I'm not worried, because I'm going to help you."

They both enter the shower and Bo turns on the water. He shampoos her hair and washes her back, offering small kisses on her neck. In no time at all, Bo tells her it is time for her to get off her foot and dry off. He turns the shower off and steps out with her. He wraps a towel around her and pulls her to him. "I love you baby. I hope you rest easy tonight."

"We both should. I think we're both tired."

Chapter 70

The phone rings early as Flo prepares Maebelle's morning tea.

"Hello, Flo, it's Penny."

"Well, good morning. I'll get your mother. Here she comes down the hall now." and Flo hands Maebelle the phone.

"Good morning dear. You arrived safely I take it."

"Yes, and I'm all settled in. Everyone was excited to see me back and asking how you are doing. There is so much power in prayer, Mumsy. I think I hugged Tito for an hour, although I believe he was squirming to get out of my arms and play with his friend."

Maebelle laughs quietly. "I miss you. The election is tomorrow, however Mr. Collins is in the jail, charged with killing Mr. Robinson."

Penny gasps.

"Yes, it's true. The investigation is concluded. It's been all over the news. Mr. Collins faces many charges."

"All this happened in two days?"

"Yes, our little community can finally come together now with new leadership, I'm hoping. Public faith is at stake here."

"And the bridge club can get back to playing some serious cards." Penny is teasing her Mum.

"Well, I don't know how serious we'll get because we are all getting older. But we have a lovely reception planned for Daniel Black tomorrow evening. I wish you could be here."

"I know. Okay, I just wanted to say hello and tell you I love you."

"It's always music to my ears. Goodbye Penny dear."

Maebelle places the phone down and looks at Flo. "She didn't ask, Flo. She won't either. She is such a prideful girl. She wouldn't want us knowing how much she cares for Eddie."

"Yes 'um, you is so right, Mae."

"Well, after breakfast, we will start on the cookies and bars for the party." Mae sighs, "Time will tell, Flo."

Chapter 71

Bo and Eddie are having coffee on the porch when the phone rings. Bo doesn't want it to wake Dolly up. He answers it before the second ring.

"I thought you were out of town." Denise speaks tersely, in her raspy voice. "That's the reason Dolly gave for postponing the Sunday dinner." *It's Dolly's sister. It's like fireworks for breakfast.*

"Good morning to you, too, how are you?" Bo has his own agenda.

"I wanted to discuss some important changes with my sisters. They are seldom available to communicate with me, unless of course, they are expecting their checks."

"Oh, I am unaware Dolly or Rita even need the money, but I understand Juan is needing his money."

"Are you trying to make a point?" Denise is unafraid to be confronted.

"I already made it. Juan needs his check to pay his bills and feed his family."

"Well, don't concern yourself with our family business. Is Dolly awake?" Denise sounds demanding.

"No, she is not awake. And I only concern myself with Juan's check, when my wife asks me to cover your payroll check with our cash. I don't know what kind of bookkeeping problems you are having, but I can give you the names of some accountants."

"Try to get it worked out. Dolly doesn't need the extra stress. I'll tell her you phoned, Denise. Say hello to your family. Sorry I missed all of the rewarding family time. It's been a great talk." Bo hangs up promptly before any more irritating conversation can occur.

Bo looks over at Eddie, "Another cup?"

"Sure. I take it that is the other sister."

"The one and only. A few months ago, we all waved our truce flags, and the entire family was trying to get along, but then her son, Bingham, got married, and this large burr found a home in her butt. Come on in the kitchen. We'll make breakfast."

Bo grabs some bacon and sausage out of the fridge. He hands Eddie a frying pan. "I'll start the grits, or we can have some of those left-over potatoes grilled up."

Eddie seizes the opportunity, "Let's have both."

"Good idea." Bo looks in the refrigerator. "Alright, here's an onion. Let's chop up some for the potatoes."

Bo reaches in the freezer for a loaf of King's Hawaiian Bread.

"Ever had any of this Eddie? I mean, with French toast made from it? It is killer. Dolly got me hooked on this stuff."

"Sir, all this time I haven't really appreciated you. I didn't know you had this interest in being a chef. I just figured you for a regular old saint.

"Leave off the old, partner, and learn from me grasshopper." Boyd grins. "When I'm not working, I like a bigger breakfast."

Eddie drains the bacon and puts the grease into a crock on top of the stove. He begins frying the sausage as Boyd reaches for another frying pan. Boyd grabs eggs out of the refrigerator.

In a bowl, he breaks eggs, adds brown sugar, half and half, some cinnamon and whisks it all with a fork. He cuts some bread slices at an angle and puts in a slice to soak up the egg and milk mixture. In a few seconds, he turns it over.

"Okay, I need that oil spray. Here we go, into the pan," talking to his bread. Boyd lifts the bread slice out and places it in the pan and adds another slice in the bowl. Boyd looks around the kitchen.

"Man, we rock. Hope the ladies are hungry."

The French toast is looking especially tasty. Apparently, Bo has been paying close attention as to how his wife makes French toast.

Eddie remarks, "You look like a short order cook."

Bo is amused and comments, "I have two good cooks for role models."

Janet is completely dressed when she enters the kitchen.

"Good morning, Mother. I thought you might be sleeping in."

"Are you kidding? With the noise and chatter of you guys having Boy Scout weekend? Is there any coffee for us women folk?"

"Absolutely," Eddie grabs a cup and fills it. "Here, Mrs. Price."

"Thank you, Eddie, there are so few princes left in the world."

"Yes ma'am," and Eddie beams at the compliment.

Sipping coffee, Janet asks, "Is Dolly up?"

"I'm going to check on her now. I'm sure I better enter the queen's room with coffee. Just a sec!" Boyd goes to the porch and pinches an orchid bloom off of one of the plants. He pours a cup and puts her special turbinado sugar and cream in it and puts the orchid bloom on the side of the cup. "I'm always needing gold stars!" Eddie and Janet are laughing when he departs.

"Good morning beautiful," Bo enters the bedroom.

Dolly opens her eyes and smiles at her cup.

Bo pulls the pillow up, so she can sit up, and straightens her covers. "Here you go, before two heads appear!" He leans down and kisses her. "Let me look at your foot to be sure you still have one."

"Not funny," she says, between sips. "Instead of police work, maybe you can go to clown school. We can get you a clown car."

With a playful grin, Boyd explains. "Right now, I'm working on my culinary skills…and your breakfast is ready, so a detour to another career is years off."

Dolly looks at the clock beside her. It is seven forty-five.

"I think you slept pretty good, baby. How are you feeling?"

"I'm good, just worried about showering."

"Before I leave, I'll help you."

"Leave? I thought we were all going to the new house today."

"Oh yeah, we are. Just didn't know you were going *with* me."

"Well, I am. Plan on it."

"Yes ma'am. I can tell you are better," Bo sits on the edge of the bed. "Sorry to spoil your coffee time, but Denise phoned. Your warrior, that's me, put up my big shield and thwarted her spears."

Dolly looks at Bo and laughs. "All this, this behavior, is due to your sleepover? Gosh, you should invite Eddie over again."

Bo is laughing now. "You always get one up on me. I can't compete with your sparring."

"Don't try. I've had years of practice, but I still adore you," batting her eyelashes at him.

Dolly tosses the bedspread off, gets up and goes to the bathroom to put on her robe. With a slight brush to her hair, she goes down the hall to the dining room.

"Good morning everyone."

"How did you sleep dear?" Janet is concerned.

"I did okay. I am surprised I wasn't in lots of pain. But the pain was mild, 'sorta of like a bruise would be. I'm good, really." Dolly turns to Eddie. "There's not usually this much drama in the household, and I accused Bo of having too much fun since you have arrived. It's like a sleepover, as if he was thirteen."

Eddie laughs, "That's some analogy. We sort of entertain each other."

"I know, and Bo takes my ribbing in stride, thank goodness."

. "Shall I fix you a plate D?" Bo asks sweetly.

"Heavens no, I can do it. Then I'm getting a shower and we're going to the new house. I'm excited."

"Well, finish your breakfast so I can clean up the kitchen," Bo pleads.

"Kudos to the chef extraordinaire for the French toast. It is delicious," as Dolly forks the last piece.

Bo bows in appreciation, and in dramatic fashion to make everyone smile.

Chapter 72

The new property is twenty minutes away from downtown Pierson. Passing by the Rooster Restaurant, Dolly recalls the night Bo rescued her from a drinking pattern with her old friend Captain Morgan. He had a way of talking to her and showing her how love and forgiveness make the strongest bonds. She glances at him driving and reaches for his hand. "I am so lucky to be your wife."

Bo has a huge grin on his face. "I hope you love what Eddie and I have done."

They turn into the drive and Bo slows the Tahoe. The brick entry says it all: Price Place, 22 Gardenia Lane.

Down the curving road, standard gardenia trees are on either side. They are quite the focal point, with an underlying bed of white Impatiens plants. In between the trees are white side fences where white drift roses have spread their delicate blooms.

"I can't wait till the gardenias start blooming, Bo, this is so beautiful! Thank you."

"You're welcome. I've had these gardenias ordered for a long time. I insisted on matching pairs. In the world of standards, nurserymen think you're evil to ask for matched trees in heights."

"I know. But they are superb."

He motors on to the entrance of the circle drive to let Dolly take it all in, the fruition of Eddie's and his hard work.

The landscaping is incredible. A big wrought iron flower basket is set on the right of the brick steps, filled with all sorts of white flowering plants, and variegated vines and cascading ivy.

Dolly is brought to tears. Bo reaches over and wipes her cheek with his hand. She takes his hand and brings it to her lips. "You, you…" and she is still emotional. "You spoil me!"

"C, mon, let's go inside," Boyd opens his door and rushes to the passenger side to take Dolly's hand.

Eddie opens the front door. "The guys have brought a load already, Bo."

"Well, that's good. Nothing's broke I hope."

"The builder has done a phenomenal job, Bo. I couldn't be more pleased and appreciative." Dolly spies an arrangement of white blooms on the kitchen countertop. She eyes a card in the six white garden roses, so fragrant. She smells the roses and reads the card.

Six will do what twelve will do. Never forgetting what you mean to me, or the importance of your wisdom. Love, Bo

She hugs him and nuzzles his chest.

"I almost didn't get them here to surprise you. Eddie had to pick them up for me. I wasn't thinking you'd come with me." He kisses the top of her head.

Rita and Roan arrive and get right to work as Dolly directs the placement of items for the kitchen. Dolly is in her happy place. Being a guest in Boyd's home the second night, and in the mix of all the family, Eddie's desire for what Boyd has tugs at his heart. This is what he is searching for; a love so deep, commitment so strong, and a family so supportive. He believes that having these will overcome any problem you could ever encounter.

In his heart of hearts, he knows Penelope Merriwether is that one special person he needs and desires. He will call her tomorrow.

Eddie dials the Merriwether estate. "Good morning, Miss Flo."

"She is not here."

"Ms. Merriwether is gone?"

"Yes um, she is here, Miss Penny gone."

"Gone where?"

"Gwatta-who-careth? That country. She said she's coming back, but I have some doubts."

"May I speak with Maebelle?"

"Yes um, I'll go tell her it's you."

In turmoil, Eddie waits.

Maebelle answers the phone. "It's one of my favorite investigators. Oh, I have missed your smile and charm. You probably know, Pen has departed. She left Sunday. We heard from her late yesterday."

"Why? For the life of me, I don't understand."

"I'm afraid her butterfly behavior is always hard to understand. Short of you going to get her, I don't know when she will be back. It's vague, I'm sorry Eddie, truly sorry, that you and my Penny are not together."

"I love that I have your blessing, Ms. Maebelle. I assure you, I'm not giving up. Goodbye for now."

"God bless you, Eddie."

Boyd senses that Eddie has not received the good news he wants. Eddie confides in Boyd that Penny has left for Guatemala.

"What are you going to do about it?" Bo sounds so serious.

"I told Ms. Maebelle that I wasn't giving up."

"Aren't you?"

"No, what can I do?"

"Go ask Dolly for some advice. I need to check on something in my office, and our work schedule."

When Bo returns a few minutes later, he sits beside Dolly in a matching chair and listens.

"Eddie, I know you love her, but do you feel a solid connection?" Dolly is trying to be compassionate.

"Yes, I do, I just can't figure out what turned her away. I was exercising patience, and giving her space," Eddie sounds frustrated.

"Often, women need persistence and pursuit. My last thought is that a take charge woman always needs a take charge man." Dolly looks at Boyd.

Eddie looks over at Boyd too. "All I can say is I want what you two have."

Immediately, in her witty commentary Dolly responds, "Well, I wouldn't go that far…."

Boyd stands and reaches in his back pocket. "This is exactly what I thought she'd say. Here, take this. You're cleared for another four days." Boyd hands him an envelope.

Eddie is obviously puzzled and opens it;
Delta airlines, round trip ticket to Guatemala. "Sir?"

"Now, get home and get packed. See you when you get back, and Eddie?"

"Yes sir?"

"Thank you for helping to make my grounds beautiful."

Eddie smiles, "My pleasure, sir."

Eddie is leaving as Rita, Roan, and Janet arrive with more boxes.

Chapter 73

Nothing ventured, nothing gained. Truer words were never spoken. Eddie is on the flight. His mind races with questions. He'll go directly to the orphanage. No, he'll get a hotel first. No, he'll call. No, he'll go to the orphanage. It's a full circle of crazy, never ending thoughts.

Finding a hotel downtown, he registers, finds his room and takes a shower. He changes clothes and grabs his badge. Out of habit, he clips it on his belt and takes his light weight jacket with him.

He stops off at the hotel bar, orders a beer and a shot of tequila. Liquid courage is needed. The tequila goes down the hatch without hesitation. The beer chaser is cold, and welcoming. He asks the waiter if he can call a taxi for him and inquires about the orphanage.

"Si, market today, so the taxi may take up to forty minutes." The waiter politely answers.

Thirty minutes to rehearse his talking points. One more stop, he thinks.

Out of the bar and down the street, Eddie walks into a jeweler's shop. A pleasant woman greets him, dressed in black with a triple strand of pearls around her neck.

"What may I show you today? she asks. "My name is Madeline."

"I like that. Your question, that is. You may show me a nice ring."

"I am thinking an emerald with a few diamonds, but I'm not sure I can afford what I want."

"We have some limited Colombian emerald and diamond rings. All are exquisite. Please come with me to the vault."

"The vault?" Eddie is surprised.

"Yes, the owner of our shop is from Columbia and personally designed these rings. They are for the truly discerning customer."

There is a small table with a velvet pad on it. Madeline points to the chairs. "Please be seated." A security guard seated nearby, looking at computer screens, acknowledges him.

Madeline returns with a tray and sits down opposite from Eddie.

"I assume this is for a very special someone. Asking for an emerald shows your impeccable taste."

Eddie almost laughs. "I don't know about my taste, but this lady has the most brilliant jade green eyes. I want something different but if I can't afford what I see, I'll go another route."

The back door opens, and a well-dressed gentleman greets the guard and Madeline in Spanish.

The gentleman gazes at Eddie. In a thick Spanish accent, "It's a beautiful day to be in love, si? My name is Raul and it is my pleasure and honor to show you my designs." Madeline steps away and nods in appreciation that he is taking over the potential sale.

Looking at the tray, he continues, "Si, emeralds from Columbia are rich in color, each in the traditional emerald square cut, all set in platinum."

"What pleases you?" He removes the rings and places them on the pad. "Only you, know the worth of the special someone you are giving this to."

Eddie is impressed, more like blown away by the beauty of the rings.

"Each one is unique," and Raul explains the designs, different shanks and gallery parts of the settings. "Here," handing a jeweler's loop to Eddie. "We offer quality and I am proud to offer you a loop to see the exquisite workmanship. This is not the case with other pieces in the front showroom. But for emeralds, they are my pride. Only the best will do."

Raul has done all the talking because Eddie does not know what to say.

Speaking in Spanish, Eddie tells him he finds beauty in all of them. He will be proud to give any one of them to the girl he wants to ask to marry him.

"A native here?"

"No, I live in Florida and the lady is a volunteer at St. Mary's Orphanage."

"Si, the nuns do great work with the kids there."

Finally, Eddie chooses one and asks the price.

"The price you ask? It's in the ring. On the inside circle those series of numbers are the price."

"This is interesting. I was expecting a round of negotiations," Eddie states.

"I see you are an officer of the law. My brother is the police chief here. I have much respect for the ones that keep our streets safe."

"Although great to hear, I don't live here, Raul."

"Yes, I believe you mentioned that. I am prepared to offer this to you for seven thousand."

Eddie swallows hard. "The ring is truly beautiful, and the truth is she would probably be satisfied with a simple wedding band. But I accept your offer for the one I love."

"Bueno, let's shake hands."

Eddie pulls out his credit card and places it on the table. Raul places the other rings back in the tray and ask the security guard to notify Madeline. Raul writes something on a small piece of paper, and hands the card and paper to Madeline.

In a few minutes, Madeline reappears with the credit card slip. Eddie looks at the invoice. "I'm sorry, this is incorrect. We agreed on seven thousand."

Raul looks over the paper and smiles. "There's always reward for honesty. It is a pleasure to do business with you. Good Luck. Call me for something special for your ten-year anniversary."

Eddie shakes his hand again and slips the small box in his jacket inside pocket and the receipt in his wallet.

Briskly, he walks back to the hotel, and asks if the taxi to St. Mary's orphanage has arrived to pick him up.

"It's right outside, I'll show you," the attendant replies.

Eddie leaves the hotel with hope in his heart for the one he loves. In short time, he arrives, and the taxi driver asks if he would like for him to wait.

"No, thank you."

He opens the door. Kids are running everywhere. Two are playing chase when he hears one child shouting, "Tito, wait for me, Tito," he shouts.

Eddie reels around to see who is being called Tito.

A nun approaches Eddie. "May the Lord's blessing be upon you today."

Eddie smiles, "And with you, sister. I am looking for Penelope Merriwether. I am from America."

"Miss Penny has walked downtown to the market. It might be two hours before she returns, or maybe less. You are welcome to leave a note for Miss Merriwether in her room."

"Okay," and Eddie feels the presence of children staring at him.

"That will be fine. If I may trouble you for some paper, please."

"Of course. When you are finished, I will show you where her room is, and you can place the note there."

"Thank you."

Eddie ponders what he wants to say. He writes down his thoughts and folds the paper in half and places his card in it.

"This way," and the nun walks softly down the hall and points to the room. 'It is alright to put it on her desk." She is barely audible.

The room is stark. One bed, with a simple blanket sitting atop neatly folded. There is an open closet with several outfits. He recalls the bright jade green blouse and skirt he thinks is so becoming on her. A simple lamp is on one corner of the desk, a couple of books, and a large envelope marked Banks, Baum and Button in black bold letters. *Terrance Button, there's no escaping him.*

Eddie closes the door behind him and follows the nun out to the large open foyer. It seems the kids have multiplied.

"How many residents do you have here?"

"Forty of God's children, all special in different ways."

"Yes, ma'am." Eddie glances around and sees Tito again and Eddie smiles at him. Tito does not smile back.

"May I trouble you for a cab?"

"Of course. I'll call for you."

Eddie is reluctant to leave but he has little choice. He will return to the hotel and wait. *NO, he'll wait here. He'll speak with her here in the orphanage where she is comfortable. He'll walk the grounds, find a hill to sit on, and he'll look at the beautiful landscape and practice the perfect words he wants to say.*

"Sister, please cancel the taxi."

Penelope returns from downtown with treats for Tito and his friend Hector. They are rarely seen without each other. She looks for them on the playground, and in the snack room without success. Penny eyes a cardboard fort that has all the markings of Tito. It is his usual hide and seek game. She tries to sneak up on them, but there's an opening where two eyes are peering out that she can see.

"Opee, come hide with us so the police can't find you."

"Police? Are you two in trouble again?"

"No, not us," Tito is matter of fact. "You are in trouble. The policeman is here for you."

"What? What policeman?"

"Now, Tito, you mustn't tell stories. You and Hector come out. I brought you candy."

"I do not tell a story. Go ask Sister Theresa."

Penny does not know what to make of it. She drops off her purchases in the lunch room, and heads down the hall. Sister Theresa stops right in front of her door. "Did you get to see the gentleman before he left?"

"Who?" *I pray nothing is wrong with Mumsy.*

"I do not recall him giving his name. He left you a note. I showed him your room."

She sees the paper immediately on her desk and opens it.

One must have sunshine in their life or they are not living. You are my sunshine. I'm here to reclaim you and Tito and begin our life together. Eddie

Penny is shocked. *Unforeseen, without warning, he has come for me. Why me? A life together? Is it possible the three of us can be a family? He has come a long way to tell me this. I am overwhelmed with hope.*

Penny reaches in her hobo bag and gets her phone. She breathes out and breathes in. It's ringing but she only hears her own breathing.

This is Detective Edward Martin, Volusia County Special Investigations Bureau. Please leave a detailed message.

Penny finally finds her voice, "Um, uh, I'm stunned. Eddie, I'm speechless. I don't know what to say. I am so fearful that I'm not the one."

"Would I have traveled 1200 miles to tell you how much I love you, if my future wasn't with you?"

"Eddie is that you?"

"Yes, I'm here."

"I know, I got your note."

"I'm here, waiting to hear you love me too."

"I do."

"Louder. Please."

"What? It sounds like you're here in my room."

"Not quite, but close enough to hear you. At your door, wanting you to say it again."

Penny slowly walks towards her door opening. Peeking around into the hallway, Eddie is there. He opens his arms wide, "I want you to say it louder."

Penny rushes to him and places her lips on his. He kisses her deeply and, on her neck, keeping his arms tight and holding her. "I love you Penny. I don't understand why you turned away from me."

"I, ..I… I heard you tell someone else you loved them."

He loosens his grip and looks into her eyes. "Impossible," he answers so confidently.

"On your birthday, you were on the phone, and I heard you."

Eddie has a distant look on his face, "My birthday?" He is searching his mind for answers.

"I heard you. You said you loved them and you'd see them the next night. That it had been awhile since you'd seen them."

"My sweet Penny, what you heard that night… I must have been talking to my mother. I was going to a family dinner the next night."

Embarrassed, but still seeking the truth, "Why didn't you invite me?"

"I was going to, but you turned away from me. Hell, I've been giving you space, so you could be sure." He pulls her to him. "Oh my God, we have wasted so much time. And why couldn't you tell me about your desire to adopt Tito? I love kids. I saw him today. He is a beautiful child. Oh Penny, I love you, and want you in my life forever."

"Eddie, I do love you, so much."

"This is what I needed to hear." He kisses her forehead. He bends down on one knee, reaches in his jacket pocket and pulls out the tiny box. "I want you to be my wife, to have my name, have my children, and love me. I will be devoted to you." He opens the box where she can see it. "Will you marry me?"

Penny looks at the ring, and her eyes flood. "Yes, my love. This is so beautiful. I would have been happy with a simple band."

"The first time I saw you, you had that brilliant jade color to your eyes. I melted. This ring reminds me of that first day when I got weak in the knees."

"Eddie, you are so kind and generous. Green is my color and I will love wearing this beautiful emerald with so much pride."

Eddie stands up and takes her hand, and they sit on the edge of the bed. "Penny, let's talk about Tito. Can we adopt him together? Or have you already completed the legal paperwork?"

"The sisters are going to talk to him tomorrow, and then they will release him, and we will able to leave."

"Are you sure, Eddie, you want an instant family?"

"If he is special to you, then he will be to me as well. I promise I will be a good role model."

Eddie pulls her to him. He places his hand at the back of her neck and pushes her lips into his. He kisses her passionately. "We will be happy, I promise you. I will work hard for us. You do not have to live like this. I will provide for you, Penny. You won't need to worry," as he looks around her barren room.

Penny looks around. "Oh Eddie, I live like this because I want to be accepted. Living simple like the nuns is not hard here. It is a necessary choice. I still have all of my allowances for years that I've never touched. Terry put it in a blind trust long ago. I don't even know how much money is there. Mumsy is always asking me if I need money. If she only knew." Penny giggles and Eddie laughs in surprise. "But go ahead and work hard. I want lots of kids. I was an only child, so I'm hoping to get started right away." Eddie squeezes her and holds her. He takes both of his hands up to her face and kisses her again. "Any chance you want to start now?"

Penny laughs. "You couldn't resist, could you? We're going to have a fun marriage, aren't we?"

"I can't wait to start our life together." Eddie whispers in her ear.

"Let's have dinner. Tell me what you want to do."

"Where are you staying?"

Eddie tells her the name of his hotel.

"Let me start the wheel turning and announce my departure. I'll call you tomorrow at the hotel."

"If that's your wish, that's what we'll do. Should I buy you a ticket to fly home with me? Tito will need one too."

"Don't do anything until I can call you. Be patient."

"Okay, I'll leave with longing in my heart. I'll wait to hear from you. Good night love."

He hugs and kisses her and walks to the front of the orphanage.

He politely asks if the sister will phone him a taxi. "Gracias, I'll wait outside."

Chapter 74

The long day of moving is coming to an end.

"Alright, that's enough," Boyd is clearly irritated. "Don't look so surprised. I keep seeing you push boxes and lifting items around. All you're supposed to be doing is supervising." He lightens his harsh words by giving her a hug.

"It's exciting seeing everything coming together," Dolly smiles. "I can't wait to bring the babies home to their new rooms. Of course, it will be a while before they will be by themselves."

"The babies?"

"Whoops, I mean Jacob and Janelle. When are we going to share the name with mother?"

"Whenever you want!"

"Let's do it tonight! Are we spending the night here tonight?"

"We can, and christen our new bed, I mean bedroom."

"You meant bed, I know you."

"Well, you're the one that said let's do it!"

"You know you've been so relaxed lately, Bo. It's so nice having you home. And that was really nice of you to give Eddie that ticket."

"I hope he finds the answer he is looking for. He's a good guy D, and a great partner. Did Denise ever call you back?"

"I don't know. I never looked at my phone. Did she volunteer anything about Juan?"

"Not to me. I believe her words were that I didn't need to concern myself with family business."

"You should have told her you are family."

"You can rest easy I have handled your sister correctly."

The election party and reception are hosted beautifully by the High Springs Ladies Bridge Club.

Ms. Maebelle Merriwether is so proud of her friends. It is a symphony of joyful cooperation. The new sheriff arrives, and Daniel Black is superbly gracious thanking the good citizens. He reflects on his own actions, reminding folks we're all human and we all make mistakes. It is a subtle reference to J.W. Collins.

Sheriff Black asks people to pray for those who are affected by the long campaign. "We need to heal, and the best way is to heal is to get busy, so let's get to work."

So many old acquaintances acknowledge Maebelle, remembering past parties she's hosted. Mrs. Black asks if she can call on her for advice in planning some future events.

"Of course, I will be delighted to assist you and Mrs. Black, a pleasure, indeed."

Chapter 75

Eddie hates leaving Penny, but he knows she has obligations.

He is going to stop in to the jewelry store and thank Raul. After all, it's just money and Penny is worth every dollar he spent on the ring. He'll have breakfast first. Hopefully, Penny will call before lunch.

It's almost eleven when she calls. "Good morning, sweetheart."

"It's not a good morning. Something has happened," and Penny is emotional. Eddie senses she is crying.

"I'll be right there." Eddie hails a taxi and climbs in.

Looking at Eddie in the back seat, the driver notices Eddie's police badge, and asks, "Why don't you have police car? Where is your car?"

"What? I need to go to St. Mary's Orphanage. Please drive quickly."

The driver shakes his head. "You real cop?"

"What?"

"Real cop. You have no uniform."

"Si, Yes, Yes, I'm a real cop, please drive now," as if repeating words make a difference.

"Just see your badge, but you have no car. You wreck it?"

Eddie is annoyed beyond all patience.

In Spanish, he tells the driver to move down the road immediately or he will see to it he is charged with obstructing police business and aiding the robber in a getaway.
"You'll be in jail just as soon as I make the call. Vámanos!"

The driver steps on the gas. Eddie falls back on the seat, nearly giving him whiplash.

The driver starts beeping his horn and vehicles pull over like they are in an ambulance. Around curves, going up and down hills, Eddie is so close to the edges of cliffs, he can count ants on the rocks. "Jesus, Joseph, and Mary," he mutters as he recalls his Catholic upbringing.

Screeching to a stop outside St. Mary's, the driver says. "It's free. Go catch the filthy robber!"

Eddie gets his jacket off the seat. "Si. Amen," as he steps out of the car. Walking inside, Eddie doesn't know what to expect. Penny emerges from an office and waves for him to come.

"Eddie, this is the headmistress of St. Mary's, Sister Donavan. Sister Donavan speaks both English and Spanish."

"Eddie extends his hand. "Buenos Dias, it is a pleasure to meet you."

"And you are Miss Penelope's fiancé. Congratulations. May God bless your union."

"Thank you, Sister."

"Please be seated," Sister Donavan points to the chair beside Penny.

"While Miss Penny was in America with her mother aiding in her recovery, Tito formed a strong bond with another little boy here, Hector. When we first received Tito, he was timid, frail, as you say despondent. But now they are inseparable. Two of the sisters spoke with Tito yesterday. Even though he loves Miss Opee, as he calls her, he doesn't want to leave. He thinks of Hector as his brother. More to the point, he says he won't give up his brother to gain a mother and father. As I mentioned, they have a bond. We feel at St. Mary's that breaking such a bond, separating them, will set them both back emotionally and probably physically. Can you understand?"

Eddie takes Penny's hand in his. "We are able and can adopt both." Eddie looks to Penny and tears fall down her cheek. He squeezes her hand. "We are young and strong. They will be reared in a Christian home."

"Mr. Martin, your compassion is evident. I can see why Penelope has fallen in love, but I am getting to my second point. We have application from another couple who recently lost their three children in a terrible accident. They long for children again. They have taken the boys on several field trips, speak several languages, and the father is a noted attorney. He also serves on the board of directors here at St. Mary's." She pauses, looking empathetic.

"I am sorry, truly sorry. I am afraid if you bring discord, or retribution, that actions such as these will be unsettling to the boys."

A concerned Eddie murmurs, "I see." He looks at Penny. "Are you alright?"

With tears, she nods yes, then nods sideways indicating no.

Eddie squeezes her hand and leans into her. In a tender voice, "I know you are heartbroken and your plans are interrupted. Whatever you want to do, I will try my best." Penny continues to nod, and teardrops continue to fall.

"You can love him from afar Penny, and you can continue to invest in his future, and he can come visit us in our home. We will still make the effort to have him in our lives. This is a new beginning for him, just like you were trying to give him." He wipes her cheek with the side of his hand and pulls a handkerchief out of his jacket and wipes more. He kisses the top of her head. "I believe he wants you to be happy, much like he and Hector. Show him you are happy and want the best for him. Show him you love him so much, that you can let him go to be happy."

Penny breaks down and openly sobs. "I know, I know," she cries out loud. "I know it is selfish to want him when he is being offered so much."

"Tito and Hector are lucky. They'll have a double load of love from his new parents and from us." Eddie stands up and pulls Penny up in his arms. "I know it's hard, let it all out."

Sister Donavan stands too, with glassy eyes. "Thank you, Penelope Merriwether, for your contributions to the orphanage. Please keep in touch. Would you like to say goodbye to Tito? Sister Theresa will go get him."

"Yes, give me a minute to freshen my face. I do not want him to see me crying. He will be sad and may think my Mum has died. He prayed for Mum every day. He has such a tender heart and precious soul." Eddie puts his arm around her waist. Penny nuzzles in his chest, "I love you, Eddie, for trying." He kisses her hair. "I love you too."

"C'mon, I will walk you to the ladies' restroom." Eddie turns to Sister Donavan. "Thank you."

"I wish it could be different for you. You will make wonderful, loving parents," Eddie smiles. Penny leans on him and they walk back to the front entry where she enters the bathroom.

Eddie waits outside the door for his beloved Penny. He ponders everything that has transpired. He is resolved that the situation is out of their realm to repair.

Penny emerges composed and Eddie takes her hand. Tito sees her and runs to her. Penny bends down to be on Tito's level and opens her arms wide.

"Did you hear Opee? Hector and I are going to be real life brothers."

"Yes, I did. I'm so excited for you. I'm so happy." Tito studies her face and looks over at Eddie.

"The policeman is your friend?"

"Yes. I love him like I love you," Penny hugs him so tight. "I will always love you. Do you know that?"

"Yes Opee. Did I tell you that Hector and I are learning football?"

"I'm leaving again Tito, but I will write to you and I expect you to write me back. Will you?"

"Yes. Si. I will write English to you like you want. You'll see."

"Okay. Penny kisses his little head and hugs him. Hector comes to the window. "Tito, Tito, it's our turn."

"Okay, bye," and Tito runs away. Eddie walks towards her and gathers her up. Penny holds him tight.

Eddie calls for a taxi. Penny goes to pack her suitcase. She asks Sister Theresa for a large shopping bag.

"I'll hurry, Eddie."

"Take your time."

The taxi arrives. Eddie says, "It may be a few minutes," speaking to the driver.

Quicker than expected, Penny finds Eddie and he takes Penny's suitcase from her. "Do you have everything?"

"Yes." With tears in her eyes, she turns back for a final glance. She grabs Eddie's hand. "I'm ready to start a new life with you and start our family."

Eddie pulls her chin up to his lips. "I'm ready too. We're going to be great together. You'll see."

In the taxi, Eddie takes her hand. "Are you hungry? You've had an emotional day."

"Yes. We can eat at your hotel if that is okay with you. I'd like to shop a little in the morning to grab a few gifts, mostly for Mumsy and Flo and Henry."

He admired my hat last time, and I told him I would bring him one. Can we leave tomorrow around lunch?"

"I'll get you a ticket. We should be home tomorrow late afternoon." Penny breathes heavily and leans into his shoulder.

Chapter 76

Dolly and Bo spend the night in their big new house. She welcomes Bo's romantic advances and tells him, "I think you have missed me more than you are willing to admit."

"C'mon, baby, let's get a shower. No one is here, and I can walk around in our new bedroom with no one spending the night."

"You mean parade, don't you?"

"Do I? Parade?" and he begins to laugh. "I'll bribe you by washing your back."

"It's a deal because I love the attention. I hope we still have time for us as we embark on our parenting."

"Mrs. Price, I am always going to want to love you, nibble on you and be in your lady bits. You are the only one for me."

"Bo, my life has been a dream since I married you."

He is smiling as he soaps up his cloth and washes her back. "Tired? You put a lot of effort in today."

"Yes, tired, and feeling a little uncomfortable." Boyd leans in to kiss her neck and drops the cloth. Instinctively, Dolly bends over to the shower floor to get it.

"I'll get it, don't strain."

A funny look comes over her face, "Bo. It's time. My water just broke."

"Now?"

"Yes, now. I'll get dressed, and you just might want to get dressed too," teasing him.

"Right. Right away." Bo dries her back off. "Where are your clothes?"

"I'll just put on these, reaching for her pants, and goes to her closet for a fresh blouse. She turns, and Bo is already dressed. His polo shirt is wet where he failed to dry off.

"You're wet!" Dolly exclaims.

"It'll dry." He grabs his phone, his keys, his wallet, his badge, and is leaving the room.

"Want to take me? I am the one delivering, you know."

Bo comes back. "Of course. Where's your suitcase?"

"Rita put it in the foyer closet."

"Right. Ready?"

"Yes," and Dolly laughs out loud. Bo takes her hand. "My shoes. I need shoes."

"Shoes are kept in a closet. The topsiders."

"Stay."

"Bo, I'm not a dog you command. Relax. We have time to leave like normal sane people."

"Right."

Bo opens the Tahoe and pulls out of the garage almost forgetting to open the door. "We'll be there in twenty to thirty minutes. "I'll call the doctor. Siri, call Doctor Reed."

Calling Dr. Reed, mobile.

"Doctor, Dolly Price here. Boyd is having the babies. My water is broken. Broke. Her water broke."

Dr. Reed chuckles. "Okay, I'll be right there."

Dolly is admitted into the Deland General Hospital. Dr. Reed greets Bo in the delivery room. "Good thing you called, as I was planning a fishing trip tomorrow. "You ready?"

"Yes sir." He is holding Dolly's hand. "Love you D."

"Alright, we're going to take her and get an ultrasound, check the positions of the babies, put an IV in, and hopefully deliver without complications. We'll be back in a few minutes. The nurse will come and get you."

Bo leans over and kisses Dolly's lips. "See you in a little while. Love you three."

Bo calls his mother, Rita, and Roan. They will be here as soon as they can.

Chapter 77

Eddie places Penny's suitcase on the floor and embraces her. "Let's go have a glass of wine and relax Pen'. We can talk and have dinner. I know you are deeply saddened. Me too."

"Penny looks into Eddies eyes, "I'm fine, and dinner sounds good. You made me feel so special, taking care of me today. I'll always remember this day you supported me." Eddie kisses her cheek softly.

At dinner Penny begins to laugh a little and suggests to Eddie that they can play a joke on Mumsy. You know Brits aren't noted for their sense of humor," and she laughs again having made the statement.

"When are we getting married, Mr. Martin?"

"Well, Mrs. Martin, it's whenever you tell me."

Penny looks at her ring. "So shocked. So beautiful."

"So are you. As I told Raul, my new best friend jeweler, I melted the first time I saw your beautiful green eyes."

Penny blushes. They dine and talk and laugh. Eddie holds her hand across the table. They share a chocolate cream puff and hot chocolate drink. Eddie pays the bill and they take the elevator and go up to the room. Penny showers while Eddie calls for a ticket and makes plans to check out.

"I'm done. The shower felt so good. A hot shower is what I needed." A towel is wrapped around her. Eddie embraces her putting his hands under her wet hair and kissing her deeply.

"My turn, I'll be out in a few."

Penny puts on a white tee and slips in the bed.

When Eddie comes from the bathroom, he thinks she looks like an angel sleeping in the middle of the bed. His mind runs the full gamut of emotions Penny has endured. He'll let her sleep. He takes the side chair just staring at the woman who is going to be his wife. His heart is full.

In the morning Penny awakes from someone knocking on the hotel door. "Room Service," she hears. She looks around, and Eddie is dressed opening the door. Penny pulls up the covers around her while the hotel employee sets down a tray. Eddie thanks him and hands him some money.

"Good morning angel."

Penny smiles. "I don't know about that, but I will take some of that coffee." She raises out of the bed and gives him a kiss. "Good morning, I slept very well."

"You did. I could barely hear you breathe."

"I think I was spent. The adoption was a big plan that fell apart before my very eyes. "What are we having for breakfast?"

"I called down to the hotel café, and I ordered an assortment. What would you like? Boyd always accuses me of over eating. We kid about my appetite all the time."

"You really admire him, don't you?"

"In so many ways. Before I arrived here in Guatemala, I spent some time with him and Dolly, his wife. Penny, I want what they have, I mean their relationship, and when you meet them, you'll understand why. They have commitment, respect, and so much love for each other.

"My parents were like that."

"And we will be also. I can't wait for you to meet my sisters and my parents."

"I'm looking forward to it. Do you have a big family? Will we have a big wedding? You realize my Mumsy will pull out all the stops for the wedding, don't you? She'll say," and Penny lays on a thick British accent. "It must be an English 'Godden' Penny dear."

Eddie is amused. "Did I hear English garden with Spanish flair?"

"I'm afraid not. You are stuck with English bone China, silver, and English linens. It will be impossible to fight with the queen mother. If she knew we were engaged, she would have called England for silkworms to be shipped immediately," and Penny laughs out loud causing Eddie to laugh with her.

Penny eats some fruit and a pita pocket with scrambled eggs and vegetables. "I'll be ready in a couple of minutes."

"I have three sisters, and I know that 'couple of minutes' means thirty." While she is in the bathroom Eddie packs his suitcase and puts it on the floor beside the door. He keeps thinking about his bride with *all* her belongings fitting into a suitcase the size of his.

"I'm ready," Penny emerges with her auburn hair tied up and wearing a teal cotton dress.

"My favorite color on you," Eddie compliments her once more. "I'll take the luggage down. We have about two hours before we need to be leaving for the airport. Is that enough time for you?"

"Yes, we can walk downtown."

They stroll down the business district and Penny sees a scarf in a window. "I'll be right back."

Eddie waits outside and the taxi driver he rode with yesterday pulls alongside him standing on the sidewalk.

He yells out of his window. "You catch the outlaw yesterday?"

"What?" Immediately, he recognizes the crazy taxi driver from yesterday.

"Si, yes. He's in jail." shaking his head and wondering why he is actually having a conversation with this guy.

"Need a ride?"

"No, no thank you," remembering his wild ride in the old Mercury Marquis.

"Well, when you make your report, you tell them Alberto Gomez helped you catch the filthy criminals." Alberto beats his chest. "I am law abiding citizen," and he drives off.

Penny pays for the scarf, and eyes a beautiful lace edged linen handkerchief for her Mumsy.

She will have it monogrammed for her when she gets home. Penny forgot this place was considered the lace district where artisans bring their home-made fabric items to sell in small boutiques. Penny is paying when she sees a mannequin with the most beautiful dress hanging on it. She is drawn to its intricacy.

"Senora, your change, por favor."

Walking away to get a closer look, Penny tells the clerk, "un momento," The clerk takes the change to her.

"Ah, you like? This is one of Carmelita's designs, all bobbin lace."

"Explain, please." Penny tells the clerk.

"On wooden bobbins, intricate pattern is drawn, with net background. Then the threads are pulled leaving the pattern on top. I not explain as good as Carmelita. Her mother worked in English textiles."

"It is truly beautiful. Is this size correct?"

"Si."

"How many Quetzals?"

"Thirteen thousand. I call, she may take ten thousand."

"Por favor."

The clerk makes the call. With a lot of whispering, she smiles and nods her head yes. Penny continues to shop, finding an apron for Flo and a hat for Mr. Henry.

Penny is delighted. Mumsy will love the dress. Her purchases are bagged, and she is out the door.

"I'm ready," as she puts her arm around Eddie.

"Good. We'll head for the airport after we get our luggage."

"Home." Penny says it out loud. "Home, where we'll start our lives and our family."

Chapter 78

Dolly's family is with Boyd in the waiting room. Janet comes through the door to join them.

"Didn't you want to be in the delivery room with her?" Rita asks.

"Dr. Reed explained to me that with twins, often one is a vaginal birth and sometimes they need to do a c-section on the second baby. He requires more medical personnel, two nurses, two pediatricians, and an anesthesiologist. The ultrasound revealed the girl is turned so the doctor wants to go ahead and take Dolly to the operating room and be prepared for any complications. So, I am here, but okay with it. I don't want to be in the way."

A nurse appears, "Mr. Price?"

Boyd answers her immediately. "I'm here. Is everything alright?"

"You have a baby boy. Seven and one-half pounds, 22 inches."

"And my baby girl?"

"Dr. Reed is trying to turn the baby around in the birth canal. The doctor wants you to come now. You're not to worry."

Boyd turns around, and smiles, "One down, one to go. I'll be back."

Thirty minutes go by and finally Bo appears in the waiting room. "We have two beautiful babies. Jacob Eddie and Janelle Rose, named after you, Mother, and Miss Ellie."

"I was meaning to talk to you about some of my old horse's names," Roan smiles.

Boyd grins, "Yeah, I bet you were."

Janet is tearful. "I had no idea. Oh, son, I'm thrilled."

Re-entering, the nurse asks, "Mr. Price? Congratulations, Mrs. Price is asking for you. You can go back."

"Alright, alright," turning and beaming to everybody. Boyd is excited.

Boyd rushes to Dolly's bedside. "Wow!" He kisses Dolly. Both babies are laying on her chest all wrapped up.

"We did it!" Boyd announces.

"We?" Dolly is tired but manages to get it out. "**We** weren't the ones pushing and pushing."

"I stand corrected. Can I pick one up?"

Dolly laughs, "Yes, get used to it."

"Oh, I will," Boyd kisses the little fellow and just stares at him and smiles. "Hello, Mr. Jake." He walks over and peers down to catch a glimpse of Little Miss Janelle. "Hey there, Princess. Just wait till you see how your mommy decorated your new room. It's made for a princess." Boyd sits down in the rocker beside Dolly.

"You feeling okay?"

"Yes, just tired."

"Rita and Roan are here and Mother also. Are you ready for visitors?"

"Of course!"

The nurse volunteers to go get the other family members. "Is there anything you need, Mrs. Price?"

"Thank you, no. I just drank some apple juice."

The room fills with all the family. Boyd hands over Jacob to Janet. Rita picks up Janelle, and Boyd joins Dolly's side, holding her hand up to his lips. "I am bursting with happiness D."

Chapter 79

Eddie locates his terminal parking stub and gets his bearings. He looks at Penny in adoration and asks, "Are you happy?"

"Yes, very. What's the first thing we need to do?"

"Tell our families, set a date, find a place to live."

"Mother is playing bridge today until about four o'clock. We could surprise her during or afterwards."

"For sure, it will be one or the other," Eddie is looking forward to it. "We can make it if we don't stop to eat lunch. I admit it will be a personal sacrifice, but I'll manage."

The High Springs Ladies Bridge Club is especially chatty today. Ms. Maebelle thanks everyone for their contributions to the after-election party.

"I apologize I left a little early," Betty Jo says. "I have a new friend that I am trying to help. She's my daughter's age. In fact, she's the one I sold my old car to. She's experienced more than her share of life stumbles, made some bad choices, and was in trouble with the police, but she is trying to turn her life around. I really think we can help each other. Since my daughter's death, I have hidden my sorrow in a bar glass. Please pray for me that I can be the influence she needs and that my friend can bring some happiness back in my home."

"Bless you," Maebelle says. The other ladies clap, and all give Betty encouraging words.

"I hope I don't disappoint ya'll more than I already have." Betty answers their applause.

"Well, we are all human and we all make mistakes. Learning from them is the key, lest we all be judged," Maebelle continues to uplift. "Fresh starts and cleaning a slate appeal to every person as you can imagine."

Ruby adds to the conversation, "Real friends keep supporting you and continue to pick you up when they see you need it. I treasure my friendships with all of you." Ruby is getting a bit emotional. "You might have noticed, I do not feel the need to wear red all the time. I feel like I have my own identity now."

"Of course, Ruby, you have been through so much," Elsa Jane sympathizes. Maxine and Adeline nod their heads in agreement.

Maebelle asks Julia to collect the quarters, and Harriet grabs the two decks and the score cards. Quickly, Flo clears the dessert dishes as Harriet deals the cards.

Tommie starts the bidding at two hearts. Maebelle, her table partner, answers her by bidding four hearts, taking her to game. The contract is set, and Tommie begins by going to the board with a low spade. Julia also plays a low spade. The board plays the ace, and Ruby trumps it with a heart. It is a grand play, totally unanticipated. Tommie looks at Ruby, dumbfounded the cards are that unbalanced. Turning to Ruby, Tommie declares, "That is *playing dirty*, my friend."

Ruby laughs out laugh. "I learned from the best, Maebelle Merriwether."

Maebelle clears her throat, and sips her tea, not once but twice. "I would like to remind my friends that talking during the bridge game should be at a minimum."

All the ladies laugh.

"When all of you ladies leave today, I'd like for you to take some of the leftovers home from the reception last night," Maebelle adds.

Coming in the back door, Eddie holds his finger up to his lips, and gives Flo the sign to be quiet. Holding Penny's hand, he pulls her in the door and shows Flo Penny's engagement ring. They both nod their heads yes. Flo's eyes light up in surprise but understands what they are doing and refrains from yelling in excitement.

Flo strolls through to the club to where the ladies are seated, "Sorry, there won't be any leftovers ladies."

Maebelle is in utter shock that Flo could say such a thing. "Florence Williams! What has gotten into you?"

"Your son in law is here eating them all up."

"I declare, have you gone mad? You know I have no such thing! Furthermore, Penelope is in Guatemala." She is irritated and looking around at all the ladies who are absolutely speechless.

"Yes 'um, I'm crazy, and so is Miss Penny, she is crazy in love."

"Mumsy, I'm home," Penny calls to her as she and Eddie walk into the living room. "I'm home for good this time. I'd like to introduce my fiancé to your closest friends. This is Detective Edward Martin."

Maebelle drops the deck she is shuffling, and cards fly everywhere. "Of all the dirty tricks," she says. She is smiling all the time. "Come here, you two." Eddie kisses Ms. Maebelle on the forehead and Penny kisses her cheek. Maebelle looks at everybody. "I couldn't be happier," and Maebelle Merriwether is beaming from ear to ear.

While the ladies say goodbye, Eddie receives a text from Boyd.

The stork delivered! And we have babies. You better come and meet your namesake, Jacob Eddie Price. Everyone is doing great, and we hope you are too.

Eddie texts back. *OMG, Congratulations, partner. I'll be there tomorrow. I am better than great!*

In the hospital room, Roan's phone beeps. He receives a text from Rhett. "*Dad, Blu Diamond Farms is on fire! Come quick!*"